Annie M. Barnes

Life of David Livingstone

The heroic Christian Missionary and Arican explorer

Annie M. Barnes

Life of David Livingstone
The heroic Christian Missionary and Arican explorer

ISBN/EAN: 9783337194291

Printed in Europe, USA, Canada, Australia, Japan

Cover: Foto ©Raphael Reischuk / pixelio.de

More available books at **www.hansebooks.com**

LIFE

OF

DAVID LIVINGSTONE,

The Heroic Christian Missionary and African Explorer.

INCLUDING AN AUTHENTIC AND SOMEWHAT EXTENDED ACCOUNT OF HIS
MORE IMPORTANT TRAVELS, MISSIONARY LABORS, AND DISCOVER-
IES; TOGETHER WITH THE MOST COMPLETE PROCURABLE
INFORMATION TOUCHING HIS LAST ILLNESS AND
DEATH, AND A FULL DESCRIPTION OF THE
OBSEQUIES AT WESTMINSTER ABBEY.

BY ANNIE MARIA BARNES.

("COUSIN ANNIE.")

Diligently Revised, Edited, and Illustrated.

NASHVILLE, TENN.:
PUBLISHING HOUSE OF THE M. E. CHURCH, SOUTH.
SUNDAY-SCHOOL DEPARTMENT.
J. D. BARBEE, AGENT.
1888.

TO
My True and Tried Friend,

MR. WILLIAM A. HAYGOOD,

OF ATLANTA, GA.,

In Grateful Remembrance.

AUTHORITIES CONSULTED.

Blaikie's "Personal Life of David Livingstone."

Roberts's " Life and Explorations of David Livingstone."

McGilchrist's " Life of the Great African Traveler, Dr. Livingstone."

Day's "African Adventure and Adventurers."

Extracts from Livingstone's " Missionary Travels and Researches in South Africa."

(6)

CONTENTS.

CHAPTER I.

PAGE

Parentage—Early Years—His Life as a Factory Boy—The Awakening of Noble Impulses—His Filial Devotion—His "Bred-in-the-bone" Perseverance—Nature's Instructions—Geological Researches—Locked Out—His Patient Submission to His Father's Will 11- 26

CHAPTER II.

His Home Life—The Tender Regard Shown His Sisters—His Keen Sense of the Humorous—A Laughable Episode—The Spiritual Change that Came to Him—He Enters the University as a Medical Student—His Determination to Become a Missionary........ 27- 36

CHAPTER III.

A Question that Vexed the World—The Sources of the Nile—The Bruce, Speke, and Baker Expeditions—England Triumphant —The Spirit that Moved Livingstone... 37- 42

CHAPTER IV.

Livingstone's Arrival at Cape Town—The Popular Theory Concerning Africa—The Trip Across the Country to Kuruman—He Hears of a Wonderful Lake—A Journey Farther Into the Interior—His reception by the Bechuanas—The First Sowing of the Good Seed—Meets with Bubi—A Shocking Occurrence—Poor Sekomi's Troublesome Heart—The Visit to the Bakaa—His First Sermon—Discovers an Iron Manufacturing People—An Amusing Predicament—The Return to Kuruman..................... 43- 58

CHAPTER V.

The Bakatla Welcome Livingstone's Return with Great Demonstrations—His Lion Adventure—He Becomes a Hero—His Marriage to Mary Moffat—Their Home at Mabotsa—They Leave Mabotsa for Chonuane—The Great Chief, Sechele—The Removal to Kolobeng—"Did Your Fathers Know?"—Sechele's Conversion—The Maliciousness of the Boers—Livingstone's Brave Deed—He Establishes a Claim Upon the Bakwains—An Enthusiastic Bellman—The Missionary's Earnest Work Begins to be Rewarded.. 59- 77

CHAPTER VI.

An African Village—The Government of the Bechuana Tribes—Sechele Erects a Church and School-house "To the Honor of God"—Mrs. Livingstone's Noble Labors—The Cheerful Life of the Brave Missionary and His Wife—A Trying Period—Livingstone's Enduring Patience and Unshaken Trust—The African Method of Procuring Meat—The Hostile Attitude of the Boers Grows More Threatening—Sechele's Noble Reply..................... 78- 86

CHAPTER VII.

Livingstone Starts in Search of Lake Ngami—The Kalahari Desert —Sekomi's Treacherous Behavior—The Bushmen and Baklahari—Livingstone's Hospitable Reception—Crossing the Desert—The Scarcity of Water—Sufferings and Hardships—The Deception of the Mirage—Reaching the Zouga—New Hopes and Desires—Livingstone's Absorbing Dream—The Wonderful Lake and the Country Surrounding It—The Return to Kolobeng.. 87-106

(7)

CONTENTS.

8

CHAPTER VIII.

PAGE

How the News of the Discovery of the Ngami and Zouga was Received in England—The Endeavor to Reach the Great Chief, Sebituane—Second Attempt—Mrs. Livingstone and Her Children of the Party—Failure of the Undertaking—Return to Kolobeng—Dastardly Raid of the Boers—Third and Successful Attempt to Reach Sebituane—Incidents by the Way—Sebituane's Death.. 107–123

CHAPTER IX.

Mamochisane Succeeds Sebituane—Her Graciousness to Livingstone—Livingstone and Oswell Make a Short Journey of Exploration—Discovery of the Zambesi—The Charming River Country—The Abundance of Animal Life—Livingstone's Tender Heart—A Pathetic Scene 124–137

CHAPTER X.

A Horrifying Incident — Livingstone Heart-sick Because of the Slave-trade—His Determination to Find a Remedy—A Gigantic Undertaking—He Sends His Family to England—His Touching Letters to Them—The Proposed March from "Sea to Sea" —Another Attack by the Boers upon Sechele—The Indignant Chief's Intended Visit to the Queen....................................... 138–150

CHAPTER XI.

The Departure from Kuruman—Heavy Rains—The Flooded Districts—Terrible Sufferings of the Party—Livingstone's Courage and Trust—Arrival at Linyanti—The Young Chief Sekeletu—Incidents of the Sojourn at Linyanti—The Mission-work Among the Makololo—Sekeletu's Dangerous Rival................... 151–165

CHAPTER XII.

The Start in Search of a Healthy Locality—The Demonstrative Reception by the People—Livingstone Frustrates Mpepe's Wicked Design—Mpepe's Death—Up the Zambesi—A Pathetic Incident—The Valley of the Barotse—Heathenism in its Most Revolting Aspect—The Barotse Dance of Welcome—Livingstone Visits Katonga—Pushes Farther up the River—Continued Discouragement—The Return to Linyanti........................... 166–178

CHAPTER XIII.

Livingstone Again Labors Among the Makololo—His Letter to His Children—The Start from Linyanti for the Coast—Arrival at Sesheke—Incidents—The Journey up the Zambesi—Glimpses of African Natural History—Manenko, the Amazon Chieftainess—Two Native Belles—Approaching the Stronghold of the Slave Traffic 179–201

CHAPTER XIV.

Questionable Hospitality—At the Village of Nyamoana—A Cordial Reception—The Balonda Court of State—Gallantry of Livingstone—Proposed Journey to Shinte's Town—Arrival of Manenko—The Start for Kabompo—Marching Through the Rain —Incidents of the Way 202–216

CHAPTER XV.

The Charming Situation of Kabompo—An Ideal Native Village—The Blot that Obscured the Smiling Fairness of the Scene—The Reception at the Kotla—The Private Interview with Shinte—Manenko Again Heard From—The Impressions Created by the Magic Lantern—Shinte's Water-drawer—Sambanze is given More than a Curtain Lecture—Livingstone is Shocked by a Proposal of Shinte's — Preparations to Leave Kabompo—The Chief Gives Eloquent Proof of His Friendship 217–230

CHAPTER XVI.

A Country of Luxuriant Forests—Further Signs of Idolatry—A
Potent Question — The "Great Lord Katema"—Livingstone
Renders an Important Service—Katema's Gratitude—The Hos-
pitality of His People—The Good Mozinkwa and His Wife—An
Amateur Snuff Manufacturer—The Story of the Cross—A Wind
from the North—Crossing the Great Water-shed of the North
and South Rivers — Inhospitable Tribes — An Extraordinary
"Pikeman"—The Steadfast Devotion of the Makololo.............. 231-245

CHAPTER XVII.

Desperate Straits—The Hostile Chiboque — Livingstone's Calm-
ness and Courage Save the Party—Seized with Fever — The
Men Threaten Mutiny—A Decisive Moment — Livingstone's
Nerve—The Hearts of the Makololo Fail Them—A Gloomy
Sunday—Light Through the Clouds—"Children of Jesus"—
Nearing the Portuguese Settlements—Across the Quango—Hos-
pitality of the People—In Sight of the Sea—Rest at Last.......... 246-258

CHAPTER XVIII.

The Mystery Cleared—Livingstone's Dangerous Illness and His
Recovery—He Calls Upon the Bishop—The Makololo Make a
Fine Impression—Free Passages to England are Offered Liv-
ingstone—The Heroic Stand for Duty—He Takes His Men on
Shipboard—Their Wonder at the Strange Sights—The Depart-
ure from Loanda—Generosity of the Merchants—The Return
Through the Portuguese Settlements—Incidents of the Way—
Pitsane's Little Ruse—At Katema's Town—Shinte's—Home
Again 259-273

CHAPTER XIX.

The Departure for the East Coast—Sekeletu's Proof of His Devotion—The Grave of the Chief Sekote—The Great Victoria Falls
—The Country of the Batoka—A Degraded Tribe—The Gospel
of Peace—Dangers and Difficulties—At the Junction of the Loangwa and the Zambesi—Hostility of the Tribes—A Perilous
Position—The Revengeful Chief, Mpende—In Answer to Prayer. 274-294

CHAPTER XX.

Gradually Increasing Signs of Civilization—Sand-filled Rivers—
At Monina's Village—Death of Poor Monahin—Worn Down
with Fatigue—A Civilized Breakfast—At Tete—Generosity and
Hospitality of Major Sicard—Illness—Arrival at Kilimane—
Greeted with Sad Intelligence—Insanity and Death of Sekwebu
—The Departure for Home—Arrival in England—Enthusiastic
Reception—Livingstone's Extreme Modesty — The Quiet So-
journ at Newstead Abbey—Literary Labors 295-308

CHAPTER XXI.

Return to Africa—The Reception at Cape Town—The "Ma-Rob-
ert"—Object of the Second Expedition—Discovery of the True
Mouth of the Zambesi—The Sail Up the River—Arrival at Tete
—The Kebrebasa Rapids—Unsatisfactory Conduct of the "Ma-
Robert"—Exploration of the Shire—Discovery of Lakes Shirwa
and Nyassa—Steps Toward the Establishment of a Mission
Station—Unexpected News of the Arrival of a Little Stranger. 309-330

CHAPTER XXII.

Going Home with the Makololo—A Second Look at the Victoria
Falls—Painful News—Arrival at Sesheke—Sekeletu's Terrible
Condition—Livingstone Effects a Cure—Painful Forebodings in
Regard to the Makololo—The Return to the Tete—Devotion of
Livingstone's Men—Dr. Kirke Meets with a Loss—The New
Steamer "Pioneer"—Arrival of Bishop McKenzie and Assist-

PAGE

ants—To the Mouth of the Rovuma—Up the Shire—At Chibisa's Town—Liberation of the Slaves—An Errand of Peace Turned Into One of War—The New Mission—Arrival of Mrs. Livingstone, Miss McKenzie, and Others—Disastrous Ending of the Little Mission—Illness and Death of Mrs. Livingstone—Second Exploration of the Rovuma—Again up the Shire—An Appalling State of Affairs—The Curse of the Slave-trade............................ 331–350

CHAPTER XXIII.

Livingstone Again in England—Death of His Mother—"Fear God and Work Hard"—His Impressions in Regard to the Nile Sources—The Return to Africa—The Start for the Interior—Bad Conduct of the Men—The World Loses Sight of Him—Reported Death—Fears and Doubts—Mr. Young Goes in Search of His Safety—Letters—The Dispatches from Bangweolo—Another Period of Silence and Suspense—Stanley to the Rescue.. 351–368

CHAPTER XXIV.

Sore Straits—Loss of the Medicine-chest—Across the Chimbwe and Chambeze—Lake Tanganyika—Moero—At Cazembe's—Atrocious Cruelties—Missionary Labors—The Start in Search of Lake Bangweolo—Desertion of the Men—Return from the Lake—On the Road to Ujiji—Distressing Illness—Across Lake Tanganyika—Arrival at Ujiji—Disappointments—Another Wearisome Tramp—Ujiji Again—Livingstone is Found by Stanley.... 369–390

CHAPTER XXV.

Stanley's Description of Livingstone—Examination of Northern End of Lake Tanganyika—The Departure from Ujiji—The Separation at Unyanyembe—News of the Finding of Livingstone—Later Reports of His Death—Reports Confirmed—The Last Tramp—Illness—Last Hours—Death.................................... 391–413

CHAPTER XXVI.

Devotion of Livingstone's Men—The Body Borne to the Coast—Arrival in England—Universal Sorrow—Obsequies at Westminster Abbey—Inscription Upon the Tomb 414–423

ILLUSTRATIONS.

David Livingstone.. 2
On the Bosom of the Mystic Nile...................................... 36
Rude Methods of Agriculture as Practiced by Bubi's People.......... 50
The Terror of Bamangwato.. 52
Livingstone's Rescue from the Lion..................................... 62
An African Village... 79
Some Inhabitants of the Zouga Jungles.................................. 102
The Wily Bird in His Native Bush.. 114
A Disastrous Elephant Hunt.. 127
The King of the African Forests... 130
A Bevy of Linyanti Belles.. 159
Tribal War-dance... 176
Spoonbill and Companion Birds... 193
One of Shinte's Subjects... 220
A Forest Prowler... 234
Victoria Falls, Zambesi River... 278
On the Zambesi Delta.. 314
Tree-dwellers in Africa.. 320
A Missionary Station in Africa... 342
Baobab-tree and Native Hut... 347
Henry M. Stanley.. 368
Chumah and Susi... 387
Stanley Meeting Livingstone.. 390
Livingstone Carried through the Swamps.................................. 400
Livingstone's Last Journey... 404
Livingstone Carried Into the Hut to Die................................. 405

LIFE OF DAVID LIVINGSTONE.

CHAPTER I.

PARENTAGE — EARLY YEARS—HIS LIFE AS A FACTORY BOY—THE
AWAKENING OF NOBLE IMPULSES—HIS FILIAL DEVOTION—HIS
"BRED-IN-THE-BONE" PERSEVERANCE—NATURE'S INSTRUCTIONS
—GEOLOGICAL RESEARCHES—LOCKED OUT—HIS PATIENT SUB-
MISSION TO HIS FATHER'S WILL.

THE story of no other life can be read with greater profit by the youth of to-day, nor can any other convey to
them a stronger or a more beautiful lesson of courage, faith,
and self-denial, than that of David Livingstone, the intrepid Christian missionary and explorer. From its earliest childhood to its sad and pathetic close, that life bears
eloquent testimony of what determined will, untiring effort,
and a pure and steadfast devotion to an ennobling purpose
can accomplish. Whether as factory boy, or as the resolute young medical student plodding the eighteen miles each
day to and from his university, or as the courageous and
devoted missionary in the very heart of savage Africa, every
incident of Livingstone's striking career affords instructive
and elevating study.

To "Bonnie Scotland" is due the honor of having given
to the world four of its most famous African travelers and
explorers—Mungo Park, Moffat, Bruce, and David Livingstone. Of all these names, each of which has justly won

(11)

its measure of renown, that of David Livingstone stands deservedly at the head.

It was at Blantyre, Lanarkshire, Scotland, a town devoted almost entirely to the cotton factory interests, that David Livingstone was born, March 19th, 1813. His parents were humble but pious and worthy people, who early sought to instill into the minds of their children those higher principles of truth and integrity that should be their guide through life. Of his father many contradictory accounts are given. Some speak of him as an exceedingly stern, hard man; others again as a lenient and kindly one. It is probable that, like so many of his rugged race, he combined in his character both kindliness and rigor. There are various little incidents that go to prove that he was the possessor of many admirable qualities, though so rigid and unyielding on most points. That his children feared him, there can be no doubt; that they also loved and revered him, the after testimony of his famous son bears eloquent witness. When crowned with honors, and when, with the admiration and applause of the whole civilized world directed toward him, he was hastening from the interior of Africa on his first return to England, he declared that he anticipated no greater pleasure than that of sitting by his father's humble fireside and relating to him the many incidents of his travels and explorations. What was the applause of a world, the praise of the highest and mightiest—even the commendation of his Queen—to that aged parent's honest pride and child-like delight in his recitals? But alas! it was not to be. Ere he had yet come in sight of his native shores, the news of his father's death was borne to him. He was so overcome that for days he took little note of what was going on around him. Afterward, when speaking of his loss and of his father's excellence, he declared: "I honor and revere his memory." Again he says: "He deserves my lasting gratitude and homage for presenting me from infancy with a continuously consistent, pious example—such as that the ideal of which is so beautifully and truthfully portrayed in Burns's 'Cotter's Saturday Night.'" Those familiar with this homely yet strong and beautiful picture of the aged and pious cotter can well appreciate the son's loving and tender tribute.

Of his mother there are no conflicting accounts—only the one testimony unwavering throughout: gentle, patient, brave, and tender—such a mother as imprints in letters of gold upon the minds and hearts of her children life's best and noblest lessons; such a mother as causes her influence to be felt from generation to generation. There is strength as well as beauty in the saying of the old Jewish rabbi: "God could not be everywhere, and therefore he made mothers." A mother in the truest sense was the mother of David Livingstone. Though possessed of but little education, she was nevertheless a woman singularly sweet and refined in her manner, quiet and gentle in all that she did. Her loving and kindly nature was in distinct contrast with her husband's sterner, more rugged disposition. In every thing she was a worthy and noble helpmeet to him; to her children a mother whom they might indeed "rise up and call blessed." Her own beautifully consistent Christian example had much to do with keeping alive in their hearts a reverence for sacred things—such a reverence as grows into the character, molding it and building it into a strong and fearless structure, against which the fierce waves of infidel creeds may in after years dash in vain. Beyond a doubt, this sweet and gracious example was oftener productive of good results than were her husband's sterner methods.

Like nearly all the Highlanders, Dr. Livingstone's ancestors were Roman Catholics; but when the Protestant religion was sweeping all else before it in Scotland, the sturdy old chief of the clan was converted to it, and became one of the most uncompromising of the believers.

Dr. Livingstone was always proud of his ancestry—proud in a justly commendable way; for though none of them had ever been rich in this world's goods, or highly distinguished as far as worldly honors go, they had been something better and nobler still—honest, fearless men, with not a stain upon a single name through a long line. How much grander such a record than mere titles, rank, or emblazoned escutcheons! What nobler title can there be than that of "honest gentleman?" what mightier ensign than that of "Truth" indelibly stamped upon one's life-banner?

There was a tradition in the Livingstone family of one of the ancestors, a poor but sturdy and honest old Highlander, who, when he lay upon his death-bed, called his children around him and thus exhorted them: "Now, in my life-time I have searched most carefully through all the traditions I could find of our family, and I never could discover that there was a single dishonest man among our forefathers. If, therefore, any of you, or any of your children, should take to dishonest ways, it will not be because it runs in our blood. It does not belong to you. I leave this precept with you: 'Be honest!'" What a record to stand from generation to generation, unaltered! "Not a dishonest man among us." Ah! truly "a good name is rather to be chosen than great riches, and loving favor than silver and gold."

In the preface to his "Missionary Travels and Researches in Southern Africa," Dr. Livingstone gives a brief sketch of his early life, together with some information in regard to his more immediate ancestry. Throughout it bears the stamp of that modest diffidence so noticeable at all times when he speaks of himself or of things directly concerning himself. No man ever lived and attained to the heights of eminence reached by David Livingstone, and withal preserved a sincerer and more entire forgetfulness of his own identity. It was this singularly sweet modesty of demeanor, this entire putting away of self, that made him more admired and beloved than all the intrepid endurance that carried him through the heart of a savage country, or the bold courage that made him the hero of a hundred hair-breadth escapes. Speaking of his ancestors, in the preface to which we have alluded, Dr. Livingstone remarks: "One great-grandfather fell at the battle of Culloden, fighting for the old line of kings, and one grandfather was a small farmer in Ulva, where my father was born. It was one of that cluster of the Hebrides spoken of by Sir Walter Scott:

> And Ulva dark, and Colonsay,
> And all the group of islets gay
> That guard famed Staffa round."

Dr. Livingstone was very fond of the traditions and the legends of his forefathers, which had come down through line after line as an inheritance to be sacredly treasured

and transmitted from father to son. His paternal grandfather, in particular, was a great reciter of these wonderful
stories.   Not only did he regale his youthful audience with
the fascinating accounts of the deeds and the exploits of
their own ancestors, but he was familiar with all those tra-
ditionary legends that afterward gave the great Sir Walter
Scott so much material for his famous " Tales of a Grandfather."

"As a boy," says Dr. Livingstone years later, when speaking of his grandfather's favorite practice, "I remember
listening with delight, for his memory was stored with a
never-ending stock of stories, many of which were wonder-
fully like those I have since heard while sitting by the African evening fires."

To this grandfather Livingstone was especially attached.
He was a rugged old Scot, with but few of the faults and
many of the virtues of his race.   He was noted above all
traits for his unswerving honesty, thus nobly bearing out the
stainless reputation of his family.   He was the grandfather
alluded to as "a small farmer in Ulva."   For many years
he quietly labored as a tiller of the soil; but as his family increased he found the income from his few acres
altogether insufficient for even their most pressing needs.
This led him to dispose of his farm, and to remove to the
Blantyre Cotton Works, where he hoped to obtain employment not only for himself, but also for his sons that were
large enough to work.

The Blantyre Cotton Works were at Blantyre, a small
manufacturing town on the river Clyde, nine miles above
Glasgow.   The worthy old Scot was not long in procuring
a position, and that, too, one of trust from the very first.

So much for the good name borne by his family, the herald of which had preceded him. He entered as messenger the service of the Messrs. Monteith & Co., proprietors of the factory. A part of his duty was to convey large sums of money to and from Glasgow. Not once did he fail in the trust. Indeed, so unflinching was his integrity, so rare his faithfulness, that he won not only the confidence but the highest esteem of his employers. When too old to longer continue in the discharge of his duties, they showed their appreciation of their trusty servant by retiring him on a pension.

Soon after removing to Blantyre he had also succeeded, as he had hoped, in getting positions in the factory for his sons as well as for himself—positions which they filled with honor and trust, following the example so nobly set by the father. They remained in the employ of the Messrs. Monteith until the war with France broke out, when they all, with the exception of Dr. Livingstone's father, entered the army. The latter, having married in the meantime, now settled down as a grocery merchant, doing business in a small way.

David's tribute to his father at this period of his life was that he was "too honest ever to grow rich." Here we also have a glimpse of the real kindliness of heart that was surely his, since he was never known to turn away a fellow-creature in distress, but, on the other hand, would respond to the appeal, though to his own hurt. It was this constant trust of people, "whose necessities were greater than their ability or desire to pay," that added more and more each year to his own financial embarrassment; for, as has been said, he was only doing business on a limited scale. This pressure finally drove him to the necessity of putting his children out to work, even at tender ages.

It was thus that David entered the mills as piecer when only ten years old. It was hard work for so young a child, the long confinement proving more wearisome than any thing else. He had to work steadily from six in the morning until eight at night, with only a short intermission for dinner.

How many lads thus circumstanced would have surrendered themselves unreservedly to the drudgery of their position, hopeless and careless as to any thing for the future save a life of just such unremitting toil as this! But not so David Livingstone. While not despising his humble surroundings, nor yet rebellious against the hardness of his lot, there was nevertheless born within him—from the moment his hands knew daily toil the pure purpose to raise himself step by step to higher and broader levels, and to make of his life in the end that which would be an honor to God, a satisfaction to himself, and a blessing to his fellowmen.

Thus within the heart of the obscure factory boy, toiling over his spindles in the mills at Blantyre, were planted the first seed of that steadfast and ennobling resolve that gave to the world its greatest Christian missionary and most successful explorer.

He was no dreamer, be it understood—no loiterer, who spent "hours by the way," though that way were but the loom above which he bent, building castles for the future out of the gorgeous fabrics of fancy, or rearing them of such material as speculation gives. It was no dream that had taken such full possession of him, but a pure and steadfast desire. Believing in God with all his heart and soul, as well as in the power and efficacy of prayer, he also believed it possible to bring about the accomplishment he so ardently desired through the very strength and earnestness of his petitions. God was with him – though invisible, yet supreme—and God would hear his prayers.

Thus, boy as he was, he threw the whole force of his rugged nature into this one belief, and clung to it — never faltering, never doubting that in his own good time, and out of the abundance of his mighty compassion, God would send the fulfillment. Until then he could wait; and better still, he could *work*, though the work was of the lowliest kind. Ah! show me the soul that has taken unto itself so mighty and so clean a purpose—that upon its most enduring foundations and within the firmest fortresses of its defenses has built such a hope, such a faith— and I will whisper of a God that never yet let such a trust go unrequited. "According to thy faith so shall it be." Thus spoke the Master, and as steadfast as heaven itself is the prom se these words contain.

One incident of this period of Livingstone's life is especially noticeable and most commendable, as it shows us more plainly than perhaps any thing else could have done the faithful and sturdy heart that beat underneath the coarse jacket, as well as gives us a strong and forcible illustration of those filial traits of character that formed so close a part of himself. The first half-crown he ever earned he laid proudly and fondly in his mother's lap, beseeching her that she would at once expend it in something exclusively for herself, since, he assured her, nothing would give him greater happiness than to see her do this.

What education Livingstone had previous to his entering the mills had been acquired at irregular intervals at the
village school. This only gave him an intense longing for
more knowledge, and with a portion of the small earnings he
received at the factory he began attending a night-school,
which was kept up in part by the proprietors of the mills.
Not content with this, he purchased a Latin grammar: this
he managed to study at odd snatches as he walked back
and forth in front of his work.

David had always been a plodding and persevering
lad. Indeed, his habit of sticking determinately to a purpose was proverbial in the household. His perseverance is
described by one of his biographers as of the kind that is
"bred in the bone," and consequently formed an integral
part of his organization. When an object of attainment
came in view, there was no flagging of the invincible will
until victory had crowned his endeavors. So it was with
the determined youth who took upon himself the mas-
tery of the Latin language in the odd snatches between his
work; so, in turn, with the resolute young student whose
scanty means did not deter him from the undertaking of a
medical course, finished at last only through the most indomitable effort; so with the man whose steady purpose would
acknowledge no defeat, all the while drawing nearer and
nearer its realization—the Christianizing and the opening
up to commerce of a whole savage continent. This was a
work that no one man—nay, nor a thousand men—could
hope to accomplish in a life-time, yet he set about it with
a resoluteness "bred in the bone," like that sturdy perseverance of his, and nurtured in a heart that, first assured of
God's blessing, never felt discomfiture. Even with all his

courage and will, he recognized that this was to be the work not of one but of many a life-time; yet with a faith that knew no faltering, and an unswerving reliance upon that higher Power which guided and directed him, he went hopefully on to the accomplishment of the part he felt to be his. And such a part!

Could the century but give us another David Livingstone, little need would there be for the thousand men, "preachers and prophets in a heathen land;" for, a very host in himself, how the glorious work would speed on to its fulfillment! O! to think of it—a whole race conquered and engirdled by the chains of Christian brotherhood! two hundred million swarthy faces upturned to catch the glory of Christ's love! two hundred million once savage tongues repeating o'er and o'er the name of the King who has come, is gone, and is to come again in the infinite power and splendor of his majesty! Could the earth afford a grander or a more soul-enkindling picture? God send us the Livingstone; but failing this, send us the men—yes, and the women too—and speed the glorious day when the heathen shall cry unto thee as one man, and when from "the rivers to the ends of the earth" all the nations shall give thee praise!

As a proof of that remarkable perseverance so fittingly described as "bred in the bone," David, when nine years old, received from his Sunday-school teacher a copy of the New Testament for repeating the one hundred and nineteenth Psalm on two successive evenings, with only five errors, and these of the most trivial kind. Never was a book more cherished than that one, and never was one more industriously studied. That he found it as "bread to his soul" and as "a lamp to his feet," many incidents of his

after life proved. With him as with Daniel Webster, from
the time that as a child at his mother's knee he had first
learned "to lisp verses from the sacred writings," to the
close of his long and useful career, they were his "daily
study and vigilant contemplation."

Livingstone was an insatiate reader, devouring almost
every book that came in his way. I say "almost every
book" advisedly, for there was one exception. He would
never read novels, declaring that they were perhaps not so
hurtful, but profitless, since they showed him nothing of
"death how to die, nor of life how to live." His great
fondness was for books of a scientific character; next, histories and works of travel. Much of his reading during
the years at the factory was done, as his Latin had been
studied, between the intervals of his work. As these intervals could not at best be more than a moment in length,
we can form some idea as to the full extent of his opportunities.

When about sixteen years of age, Livingstone was pro-
moted from a piecer to a spinner. The advancement not
only raised his wages, but also slightly increased the intervals between his work—those golden moments of opportunity, the value of which he so well knew. Although mere
fractions of time, that would seem useless to the idler and
the dreamer, Livingstone regarded them as precious pearls
to be slipped swiftly yet carefully and deftly along the
string, with good to the slipper at every touch. After all,
these intervals were but snatches, for the machinery of the
cotton-mills of those days did not have the reliability and
the many self-acting properties that the new mills of to-day
have. Much that the looms now do for themselves the spin-

ners of that time had to do for the looms. Hence, there was not then any thing like the opportunity there is now for the looking away of eyes or the keeping away of hands. But, in spite of these many obstacles, Livingstone managed to catch sentence after sentence as he passed and repassed in front of the book so ingeniously fixed upon a portion of his spinning-jenny.

At six o'clock in the morning Livingstone was in his place at the mill; at twelve there was a short intermission for dinner; at eight the great bell clanged, and the day's work was over. With just time to change his clothes and to eat his supper, by half-past eight he was in his seat at the night-school. Here he remained until ten, then returned home to read and study up to twelve—often to a later hour —when his mother, fearing for his health, would literally snatch the book away from him and run him off to bed. None but a most rugged and hardy constitution could have held out against such wear and tear, and this Livingstone fortunately had. It stood him in good turn now—it upheld him again and again amidst the hardships and sufferings of the savage desert.

In this manner—during the hours of the night at home, and in the intervals of his work at the factory—Livingstone read many of the works of the classics, even Virgil and Horace. Often afterward he used to say he had a better understanding of them at eighteen than he had at forty-eight.

In his search for knowledge Livingstone did not confine himself to the reading of books: no one ever should. In time Nature became his teacher: her vast store-houses were his class-rooms; her manifold works were his classics.

From these he learned, as he never could have learned from books or men, lessons sweet and fresh and pure, bearing the imprint of the Great Teacher's own master-mind. From the golden heart of the lily, in the glowing color of the wild-rose, in the imperial bending of the blades of the tall grasses, in the form and motion of the clouds, in the rhythmic flow of the brook or river, in the burst of melody from the bird's throat, in the distillation of the dew-drop, there spoke to him voices as with countless tongues; and each proclaimed eloquently the lesson it had been sent to teach. Who would not learn of such instructors? Who would not stop to catch the music of a language as old as the stars and as clear and beautiful as the blue vault that shuts them from our view in the day-dawn? Hear this great teacher, you who would have clean hands, and fresh faces, and laughing voices, and healthy minds, and pure hearts: "I am Nature. Come and learn of me, and through me of my God."

In the company of his two brothers, John and Charles—at such times as he could spare from his other studies and researches—Livingstone used to go roaming over the hills in search of plant specimens. Then he took to studying the fishes, their haunts and their habits; next, the birds and the various reptiles. Not satisfied with this, he went farther still, and began digging into the earth in search of certain fossil remains he had heard were numerous in that part of the country. In their rambles one day the brothers came to a quarry that had been worked for awhile and then abandoned. With exclamations of delight, David began examining the many curious specimens of fossil shells strewed about—specimens which the workmen had from

time to time excavated from the yielding walls of limestone. Soon he picked up a large fragment of the limestone that had been detached some time, and was of the
hardness of rock. Firmly imbedded in the center was a
large and beautiful shell, perfect in outline. It struck David's attention at once. " How did this shell come into the
rock?" he asked of the old quarryman who was at that
moment looking in upon them. "Why," returned the man,
" when God made the rock he put the shell in it, of course."
Yes, "of course." It all *sounded* plausible enough, but
would it bear the test of careful inquiry? The quarryman,
at least, had never given the matter a thought before. To
him a rock was a rock, and a shell a shell, and one was as
likely to be in a place as the other. It never occurred to
him that the proper home of the shell was in the sea, and
not here imbedded in this limestone cliff; but it did occur
to Livingstone, and with this thought many more came
crowding into his mind. Best of all, he did not let it end
with his thoughts, Plausible as had been the old man's
theory, Livingstone knew it would not do. Something within him told him that. But *why* wouldn't it do? This is
what he resolved to discover; and he did discover it.

Thus the finding of the fossil shell in the depths of the
old quarry led Livingstone to the study of geology—a study
that stood him well years after in the heart of wonderful
Africa, and helped him on in the many valuable discoveries and researches which without such aid he would doubtless never have made.

An incident that occurred during this period of ram-
bling over the Scottish hills will forcibly illustrate a striking point in Livingstone's character. It was a rigid old

Scotch custom of his father's to lock the door at night-fall, by which time every child, large and small, was expected to be within the house. Each one knew this rule only too well, and none as yet had dared to infringe it. One afternoon David had been out on a ramble alone. Absorbed in his quest for some particular plant-specimen, he did not notice the flight of time: thus at the going down of the sun he was some distance from his father's house. With alarm he found that he could hardly hope to reach home, even with his best efforts, before the closing of the door. Nevertheless, hoping against hope, he set off at his most rapid pace. It was as he had feared. On arriving at home he found the door fast barred. He did not call or make a noise or outcry of any kind. Having knowledge of his father's firm adherence to this rule of closing the door, he prepared himself to make the best of the present occasion. Drawing a piece of bread from his pocket, he sat upon the steps, ready to be content with that instead of the meal he had expected, as well as to spend the night there in uncomplaining submission. But it was not so to be. The ever-watchful mother soon found him, opened the door for him, bade him enter, and cried over him, as such mothers will do, especially when they choose to look upon the object of their tears as badly treated. Ever after that, even when he had grown to man's estate, David Livingstone was in time for the closing of the door.

CHAPTER II.

HIS HOME LIFE—THE TENDER REGARD SHOWN HIS SISTERS—HIS
KEEN SENSE OF THE HUMOROUS—A LAUGHABLE EPISODE—THE
SPIRITUAL CHANGE THAT CAME TO HIM—HE ENTERS THE UNI-
VERSITY AS A MEDICAL STUDENT—HIS DETERMINATION TO BE-
COME A MISSIONARY.

IN spite of the generally austere rule of the father, it
would have been impossible to find a happier or more
contented family than that of the Livingstones. Consideration and kindliness for others ruled their every impulse;
love spoke in their every act. Contention and strife, such
as mar the peace and pleasantness of the fairest homes, came
not near their abode. Harsh words and bitter speeches, fret-
fulness and peevish complainings, were unknown there.

Though he was unyielding in the enforcement of those
principles which he deemed just and beneficial to the growing body and mind, Neil Livingstone, the father, was not
the man to look frowningly upon the sports and innocent
amusements of childhood. Harmless recreations, cheery
pastimes, even the more noisy games, were not prohibited.
Often around the broad fireplace in the evenings the father
himself took part in these plays. But the central figure of
all this happy sport—the one governing spirit, up to whom
all the others came in time to look, and to depend upon for
the choicest bits of the evening's enjoyment—was David.
He was never too tired, never too much occupied with his
own pursuits and pleasures to refuse them the share he
could contribute to their happiness.

It is no wonder, then, that he was the favorite of that

happy home, even where all the other brothers and sisters were so well beloved.   But *he* was their idol, the one upon whom the combined treasures of their deepest affection were unstintingly poured.   Without David no home even-ing would have seemed like itself, no enjoyment complete. To his sisters he was the gentlest and most courteous of brothers.   Evening after evening they would watch for his coming, and greet his approach with the happiest of faces. It used to be a custom of his on Saturday evenings—the only evenings of the week-days when he was free from his school duties—to tell them of such things as he thought would not only amuse but instruct them.   In this manner he had a school of his own at home—a school in which the lessons taught carried with them something more than the knowledge one is apt to glean from books alone.   In the after years his sisters often spoke of the feelings of rare de-light with which they looked forward to these Saturday evenings at home.   Kind were the thoughts he gave to oth-ers, and in return kind their thoughts to him.

> The heart is a garden—our thoughts the flowers
>   That spring into fruitful life:
> Have a care that in sowing there fall no seed
>   From the weed of cruel strife.
>
> O loving words are not hard to say,
>   If the heart be loving too!
> And the kinder the thoughts you give to others
>   The kinder their thoughts to you.

As solid and matter-of-fact as was Dr. Livingstone's char-acter in most respects, he had a keen sense of humor and a faculty for the ready enjoyment of many of the lighter things of life.   An amusing situation, a ludicrous blending of the seemly and unseemly, struck him irresistibly.

While out fishing with his brother Charles one day, he caught a large salmon that weighed several pounds. It seems that they had not gone prepared for fishing; and having no bag or receptacle of any kind in which to place the fish, they were for some time at a loss as to what they should do with it. Finally a happy thought struck David.

"I tell you what, Charles," he said, with a merry twinkle of the eye: "we shall have to make a fish-bag of one leg of your trousers. There is plenty of room for both the leg and the salmon," with a suggestive glance in the direction of a somewhat baggy and spacious half of the boy's pantaloons.

They proceeded to make a fish-bag of Charles's trousers leg. Charles himself offered no remonstrance, but seemed greatly to enjoy the novel operation. The fish was at once hoisted and dropped into place, neither the trousers nor the leg that inhabited that portion of them offering any resistance, since there was indeed, as Livingstone had declared, plenty of room for both, with a surplus besides. A leather string was next tied around the garment at the boy's ankle, so as to prevent the fish from slipping out. In this manner they went through the village, where the unnatural and apparently swollen condition of Charles's leg attracted considerable attention, as well as called forth a great deal of commiseration, from the feminine portion of the town especially. Many good women ran after them, their faces filled with pity, and all crying, "Poor lad! poor lad! what *could* have happened to him?" Each had a remedy of her own to suggest, warranted to bring the swelling down in the least number of days, and each was clamorous that he should pay attention to her, and promise to give her remedy the first trial. It was with difficulty that they got through the village. The remembrance of this adventure furnished the brothers with amusement for months afterward.

If David Livingstone was the idol of his sisters, he was the hero of his brothers as well. They looked up to him in every thing, relied steadfastly upon his opinions, and were never happier than when following him on his rambles. He was never cross nor harsh to them, nor did he ever seek to impress them with a sense of his own superior attainments and abilities, but was always gentle, patient, and considerate. If they asked a foolish question, he took time to consider the best answer to give them, without appearing to see how very foolish the question was. He never once willingly hurt their feelings. At their most ludicrous blunders, if made in good faith, he would refrain from laughing; and in every way he encouraged them to talk of themselves, and to express such ideas and opinions as they might have. Between the brothers there was always the utmost good comradeship.

When he was nineteen years of age, a great spiritual change came over David Livingstone. He had always been an earnest and a believing lad. From his infancy he had been taught to revere the name of God. He would no more have forgotten to say his prayers morning and evening than he would have neglected to bathe his face or to take his place at meals. From his mother he had imbibed the most sacred regard for holy things, from his father an unswerving fidelity to the higher principles of integrity and truth. He read his Bible daily; he went to a house of worship regularly each Sabbath; he made every effort to live up to God's commandments. But with all this there had been something lacking—an experience and a knowledge that far surpassed any thing of which he had as yet formed an idea. What was it? The living closer to God each day that passed; the constant realization of his presence in the heart; the ready doing of his will—not through fear, nor yet from a sense of duty, but through love—which is his children's certain assurance of their full acceptance with him. In time all this came to David Livingstone; and as the light grew stronger and more beautiful day by day, so did those desires and aspirations that had first come to the little "piecer" boy, bending over his tasks at the mill, now begin to shape themselves into firmer and clearer mold. Then he had merely longed to reach some higher and nobler plane of action. Nothing definite had fixed itself within his mind. Just what he was to be had occupied no positive place in his thoughts, only as it was held by the pure purpose to make of his life something ennobling to himself and of benefit to his fellow-men. But he saw it all more plainly now. The light had come, and with it the end of all doubt and perplexity, and the beginning of a faith and love that pointed out the way as clearly as though the noonday sun shone upon it. What *could* be more ennobling to himself, or bring greater blessings to mankind, than the earnest and thoroughly consecrated life of a missionary? Nothing; nor could there be " a grander place for man to die than where he died for man." In such hope and in such desire God would surely uphold him.

He was now earning good wages at the factory, or what were considered good wages at that time. His resolution in regard to his future career thus formed, Livingstone determined to devote a part of the proceeds of his labor to the taking of a medical course at the university in Glasgow. He well knew the benefit that such knowledge would be to him and to others in the life he had mapped out. To be able to administer to the ills of body as well as of mind was to carry to poor stricken humanity a dual blessing. Thus he worked during the summer, saving every penny that he could from his earnings in order to take the medical course during the winter. Often it seemed to the brave toiler that, with all his economy and self-denial, he must abandon his desires. The fees were not only heavy in comparison to his light purse, but there were other expenses upon which he had not calculated. But in the face of all obstacles he determinately pushed ahead, asking help from no one, and receiving none, save once from a brother, who, knowing of his straits, insisted on loaning him a small amount.

That this life of hardy toil and persistent application was neither irksome nor distasteful to him, his own words show: "Looking back now at that life of toil, I cannot but feel thankful that it formed such a material part of my early education; and were it possible I should like to begin life over again in the same lowly style, and to pass through the same lowly training." Brave and telling words these to come from a man who had known every up and down of life, from the lowest to the highest. How keen the sting of their reproach should be to those useless and effortless existences that are not only a burden to themselves but a millstone about the necks of others!

In order to attend the lectures at the university, Livingstone had, through the first course, to walk to Glasgow and back each day, a total of eighteen miles. Though it was wintery weather, and often of the severest kind, and though his shoes were not always of the best, nor his attire of the warmest, no word of complaint ever passed his lips. He was only too glad of the opportunity to take his place in the class-room. What were bodily pains and discomforts, even the pangs of hunger and cold, in comparison to this precious privilege? It was noticeable that, no matter what might go amiss with him—whether on the road or at the university—no shadow of his own troubles or perplexities did he ever allow to fall upon his happy family circle. As in the old days at the mill, his home-coming was now joyously hailed.

At length the sublime patience, the indomitable courage, the resolute will of Livingstone had their reward: the course was finished, and the long-desired diploma his. Another point of his many-sided and thoroughly strong and fearless nature came to light with the taking of this diploma. While undergoing an examination, the result of which was to prove his fitness to receive this badge of a work faithfully done, Livingstone dared to differ in opinion with the examining board in regard to a certain subject that was under discussion. This finally led to quite an extended argument, in which Livingstone acquitted himself triumphantly. The board was angry and resentful, of course; but its members could not deny him his diploma, as they doubtless would have liked to do. In afterward speaking of this encounter to a friend, Livingstone somewhat dryly remarked: "Perhaps it would have been the wiser plan, after all, not to have had any opinions of my own." A "perhaps" it merely was with Livingstone, since those who knew him well knew that he was not the one to allow his convictions and opinions to be swayed and controlled by those of other people. When an idea came to him, or a new thought presented itself, he was always fearless in giving expression to it. Never could his opinions and beliefs be purchased at any price. He was ever himself—bold, steadfast, and unflinching in a stand he had once taken from a conviction of right.

3

Now that his medical course was completed, Livingstone felt that the time had come to put into active effort the purpose he had all along kept resolutely before him. His first thought was of the mission-fields in China. A few brave spirits were already there, and the work had begun. However, before he could carry his designs into execution the outbreak of the Opium War with China took place, and he was compelled to abandon all hope in that direction, at least for awhile.

Africa next presented itself. It is true that up to this time it had been a country almost unknown; but so much the better, thought Livingstone; so much greater the need of a fearless, determined spirit to go and find out what was to be found, and to do his share of what was to be done. Though the London Missionary Society—the one great society of its kind at that day—had as yet contributed but little toward the sending of missionaries to the Dark Continent, one was there the fame of whose wonderful discoveries and labors was beginning to reach the ears of the Christian world. This was the Rev. Robert Moffat, who many years before had fearlessly set sail for that savage and hostile land.

Livingstone now offered himself to the London Missionary Society for work in Africa. His application was at once accepted; yet, that he might be the better prepared for what was before him, he was not at once assigned to a field, but instead sent to a missionary training establishment at Chipping Ongar, in Essex, which was presided over by the Rev. Mr. Cecil. Here he was subjected to all kinds of hard labor, such as grinding corn, sawing boards, felling trees, chopping wood, ditching, gardening—in fact, he was required to do any and every thing that was calculated to fit him for the rough life before him. Here he also prac-

ticed feats of walking, usually testing his powers of endurance
to the utmost.   Once he walked to and from London in one
day, a distance of fifty miles in all.   He was completely exhausted, of course—especially as he had taken little, if any,
food on the way; but who can doubt that it prepared him
just that much more for the terrible marches endured with
such courage and fortitude under the blistering sun and
through the scorching sands of Africa?

ON THE BOSOM OF THE MYSTIC NILE.

(36)

CHAPTER III.

FOR four thousand years the same question had vexed and perplexed the whole civilized world: "Where is the source of the Nile?" Age after age men had stood upon its banks and watched its placid current, or again from afar the swollen and angry cataract of its annual overflow—still the same baffling inquiry, "Whence doth it come?" Persians, Greeks, Egyptians, even the Hindoo from the sacred shades of his temples beside the Ganges, had attempted to solve the mystery, and each in turn had failed. The noble façades of the palaces, the imperial shafts of the obelisks, the costly domes of the temples looking down in stately grandeur upon the Nile, had alike crumbled and fallen into dust; cities had arisen, flourished, and were swept away; generation had succeeded generation—still onward rolled the mighty river, as though it would go on forever. But whence *did* it come? What *were* the causes governing the mystery of its annual overflow? As regularly as he looked for the coming of the sun in the morning did the old Egyptian, at the right season, watch for the rising of the Nile; and as little as he knew about the laws governing the one, still less did he know of the causes controlling the other. The mystery had from year to year puzzled the great and wise Menes himself. In order to solve it, if possible, he finally sent an

(37)

army of men into the almost impenetrable wilderness. But few of them ever came back, those who did come having no light to give. Next Cambyses, the sturdy and dauntless warrior, who had failed in little else, undertook the search with a thousand men. Not one of these ever returned to bear witness of the fate of the expedition. Even Alexander the Great, in .the midst of his. many conquests, stopped to give more than a thought to the possibility of making this one, which after all might in many respects prove the greatest of his achievements. Unlike Menes and Cambyses, he went himself with his army. The renown was too tempting to be shared by his men alone. But he bent his course in an eastward direction, and went into India: there he came upon the Indus pouring from its mountain sources, and he clapped his hands and shouted aloud, for he believed that he had found the head-waters of the magic river. But afterward he discovered his mistake, and we may well imagine how very crest-fallen he must have felt. Years later the mighty Julius Cæsar was heard to remark " that there might, after all, be more glory in the discovery of the source of the Nile than in the winning of many battles.'' He too made preparation to go in search of the baffling sources of the mysterious river; but luckily for him, as well as for his splendid soldiers, the enterprise was abandoned.

Thus the mystery, and the doubt, and the perplexity, and the search went on; and from nation to nation, from generation to generation, from father to son, was the same question handed down: "Whence cometh it?"

On the fourth day of November, 1770, James Bruce, a Scotchman, stood in the middle of a small spring in the mountain fastnesses of Central Africa, and, with much excitement and great hilarity of spirits, drank to the health of the King (George III.) from a cup of cocoa-nut shell. These noisy demonstrations arose from the fact that Bruce believed he had found the true source of the Nile, and had at last settled the vexed question of centuries. He was mistaken, in the main, as he himself discovered. Still there was honor in the find, since what he had come upon, though not really the head-waters of the Nile proper, was the source of its most important tributary, the Blue Nile.

In olden times the Egyptian, along with the problem that still remained unsolved in his mind, had a belief that the source of so wonderful a river could lie in no other place than in the great basin of some mighty lake. But *where* was this lake? In what portion of the yet undiscovered country did it lie? A whisper, that it had been seen and bathed in by a party of hunters, once came floating up the river even as high as the old city of Alexandria, where the mystic waters joined those of the blue Mediterranean; yet just where the whisper first started, or by whom it had been borne along, no one seemed to know. Centuries afterward (in the year 1858), an English explorer, Captain Speke, returned to his country from a series of extraordinary adventures and discoveries in the African wildernesses, declaring that the mystery of the Nile source was a mystery no longer, for he had found it in a lake to which he had given the name " Victoria Nyanza " in honor of his Queen. "If that be true, then, Speke," said the President of the Royal Geographical Society, to whom he had made his discovery known, " we must send you back for further investigation, and to establish the claim." And send him back they did, but not alone. This time he was accompanied by one Captain Grant, who was also an Englishman. After many adventures and great perils, these brave explorers finally returned, each steadfastly declaring that in the broad and magnificent basin of the Victoria Nyanza the Nile did indeed have its source. How all England rejoiced! At last the mystery of ages had been cleared up, and by one of her sons!

But was the problem fully solved? Had Speke indeed found the real source of the Nile? No, not quite. While at Lake Victoria Nyanza, Speke and Grant had heard from the natives of another lake which, while not near so large, was equally as interesting and beautiful. They had at once set out for the point indicated, but failing to procure a proper guide, and many things pressing their speedy return to England, they gave up the search, believing that they had been misinformed. However, before leaving the country they confided what knowledge they had gained in regard to the lake to one of their countrymen, Mr. Samuel Baker—afterward the great Sir Samuel Baker—who was at that time with his wife in the heart of Africa.

Baker renewed the search for the lake, his wife bravely sharing in every hardship and danger. At last, one morning, when he was least expecting it, Baker came upon the lake. He found it a wonderful and beautiful body of water, as the natives had declared it to be, but he found it something better still—the other and last remaining source of the Nile. Baker named the new-found lake "Albert," in honor of the good and gentle Prince Consort.

And so it was all cleared up at last, and there was no cause for further mystery. The magic river, as might have been supposed from its volume and from the nature of its annual rise and overflow, had more than one source—it had two; really three, looked at in one light. And all of these sources had been discovered by Englishmen. No wonder the old mother-country felt proud and jubilant! In the midst of the spring whence the Blue Nile issues at Geesh, Bruce had stood drinking King George's health—the first white man that ever gazed upon its surface; eighty-eight years later, Captain Speke had found the waters of the White Nile, or Nile proper, flowing from the basin of the Victoria Nyanza; and now Baker—the last, but by no means least, of the great trio—had come upon the remaining source of the magic river in the bosom of the Albert Nyanza.

Even before Speke had found the first source of the White Nile, the call to go to this same wonderful country had come to David Livingstone. It may be that amidst all his noble resolutions and self-sacrificing purposes he was not unmindful of the many allurements and attractions of this strange, wild land. Perhaps it might be his lot, too, to make wonderful discoveries, and to come upon queer people, and to see strange sights, the description of which would prove of interest and be the source of great instruction to his countrymen. Perhaps, also, it might be given him to settle certain vexed questions in regard to the geography of the "Dark Continent," and to clear up many perplexities concerning its climate, productions, etc. While admitting that such hopes and such aspirations were doubtless his, we, on the other hand, feel assured that something nobler and higher still led David Livingstone into the African jungles. His was to be a mission to the ignorant, the unhappy, and the dying. Though he did go to see and to learn, in order to give to the scientific world much useful information of which it stood in need, yet he was to be himself a teacher—the bearer of "glad tidings." The many phases of this wild and picturesque country he was to open up to the curious eyes of the outside world, yet to the sight of its own savage inhabitants he was to lay bare something grander and more beautiful still—the glorious truths of that Book of all books, the Bible. More, he was to tell them of that Saviour who had died for them, and through whom they were to have an everlasting inheritance in their Father's house of many mansions.

O that there could be found more with Livingstone's zeal, and Livingstone's faith, and Livingstone's vigor! O that others of those who, merely through curiosity, or the love of adventure or of the world's praise, are led into the heart of that savage country, could but go there, carrying with them even a small portion of that spirit which prompted Livingstone to his other and higher mission!

CHAPTER IV.

LIVINGSTONE'S ARRIVAL AT CAPE TOWN—THE POPULAR THEORY
CONCERNING AFRICA—THE TRIP ACROSS THE COUNTRY TO KURU-
MAN—HE HEARS OF A WONDERFUL LAKE—A JOURNEY FAR-
THER INTO THE INTERIOR—HIS RECEPTION BY THE BECHUANAS
—THE FIRST SOWING OF THE GOOD SEED—MEETS WITH BUBI—A
SHOCKING OCCURRENCE—POOR SEKOMI'S TROUBLESOME HEART
—THE VISIT TO THE BAKAA—HIS FIRST SERMON—DISCOVERS AN
IRON MANUFACTURING PEOPLE—AN AMUSING PREDICAMENT—
THE RETURN TO KURUMAN.

AFTER an uneventful voyage of three months' dura-
tion, Livingstone landed at Cape Town, in Southern
Africa. This was in March, 1840, when he was twenty-
seven years old. Previous to his departure for Africa
but little was known of the country. Neither Speke nor
Grant nor Baker had penetrated it. In spite of the information which Bruce, Mungo Park, and others had given of
their travels, the whole country still remained to the greater
portion of the outside world a dark and abandoned corner
of the earth, a continent of heathenism in which they had
no part or parcel. All sorts of terrible theories were held
concerning it. There were ghouls and dwarfs, giants and
genii, and every imaginable kind of horrible monster, that
were constantly prowling about and preying upon the more
peaceful portion of the inhabitants. The whole face of the
country was regarded as an arid and almost barren waste,
where human life could hardly exist, and then only through
the most miraculous interventions and by the most desper-

(43)

ate shifts. Deadly serpents crawled on every side, wild beasts destroyed hundreds of poor unfortunates, while the rays of the sun scorched and blistered every thing that they touched. Even the more intelligent and better read believed to some extent in these wild stories. One rather ambitious Cambridge student had recently gone so far as to write a prize poem in which he made the Sahara the scene of the battle of Armageddon. And the people had actually applauded him for it! No wonder the public mind was so fanciful and unsettled on the subject, since the very geographies themselves were silent, the whole country lying on their maps a perfect blank, with the exception of the Sahara.

It is no wonder, then, that many of young Livingstone's friends dreaded to see him depart for this savage country. It would be little less than a miracle if he ever came back alive—thus they thought and declared. It was especially trying to his mother; still, noble woman that she was, she would have been the last one to deter him from his purpose. The brave missionary himself had no misgivings. God was with him, and thus protected he would be as safe in the heart of that savage country as in his own peaceful home. This implicit trust in the Almighty arm was one of the foundation-stones of David Livingstone's character.

Remaining at Cape Town but a short while, Livingstone went by ship to Algoa Bay, whence he set out across the country for Kuruman, the mission-station of Mr. Moffat. On this his first African journey occurred an incident that showed the stuff of which our future traveler was made. As he was crossing the Orange River, his team of oxen became unruly and ran the wagon aground in one of the shallow places. To add further to the trouble, the brutes themselves got more and more out of order; or, as Livingstone himself described it, "some of them with their heads where their tails ought to have been, and others again with their tails stuck through the yokes where their necks ought to have been." Every moment it appeared as if they would overturn the wagon into the river. However, in a little while Livingstone, with a few dexterous movements, succeeded in getting the oxen into place again, and the wagon up the bank and out of danger.

Notwithstanding the many drawbacks, they found traveling very pleasant, in the main. To Livingstone, especially, it was a novel and varied experience. He liked it, he said, because there was "so much freedom in the African manners." At night they pitched their tents wherever it might please them; made their fire, swung the kettle over it, and then went out in search of game for their supper.

The scenery along the route was exceedingly fine. Beautiful trees bent their luxuriant growths above them; humming-birds and tiny insects of every description, with flashing wings, flew in and out among the mimosas and the low-growing acacias; the stately palms dipped their long, graceful fronds in lovely undulations as the breezes swept over them; the wild flowers were numerous and of the most brilliant colors, while the dense jungle-grass, fresh and cool and inviting, stretched away on every side. It is true that the sun was often unbearably hot overhead, that every now and then a hissing serpent presented itself in their path, and more than one wild beast threatened them with its terrible roar: still these were considered but slight discomforts in the face of so much that was pleasing.

The distance across the country to Kuruman was one thousand miles. The fatigue of such a journey by ox-team was necessarily great; but not once did Livingstone really tire. There was too much to keep his interest alive and to constantly put a spur upon his energies, even if they had flagged.

On this journey he at first endeavored to master the language of the natives. Each of the tribes, he well knew, had a peculiar dialect of its own, but the majority of them were similar in most features. He knew the difficulties that would impede his way until he had learned to address the people in their own familiar speech. In his efforts in this direction he was much assisted by one of the guides, a native of Bechuana, who had often been to the mission-station at Kuruman and had, besides, spent much time at Cape Town.

Before starting upon this journey across the country, Livingstone had heard many wonderful stories of a large and beautiful clear-water lake in the country of the Bakoba, which every one seemed desirous to see. The vegetation along its margin and the majestic sweep of the hills that shut it in on every side were described as something well worth a journey of hundreds of miles to see, to say nothing of the lake itself. Livingstone's curiosity was aroused, his scientific ardor enkindled anew, and he determined to make a visit to this wonderful lake just as soon as he could. Though he had come on one great and pressing mission, still there was another, he thought, to which he might occasionally give his attention without in any way hindering the advancement of the more important one. With something of this in his mind, even from the moment of his quitting Cape Town, he had busied himself as he went along making a collection of plants. Into these botanical researches he entered with much of his old love and eagerness, and soon had many rare and wonderful specimens, which he afterward forwarded to the Royal Geographical Society at London.

Livingstone arrived at Kuruman on the 31st day of July, 1841. He remained there several months, gleaning all the information he could from Mr. Moffat and his fellow-laborers in regard to the country he was to penetrate still farther, and of the people among whom he was going to labor. He also endeavored to familiarize himself with the workings of the mission-station, and to gain as much knowledge as was possible of the language of the Bechuana tribes, among whom it was likely his first work would lie. It was also at Kuruman that Livingstone first met the lovely woman who was to bring so much gladness into his life, and to make for him happy places of even the desert wastes. This was Mary, eldest daughter of the Rev. Mr. Moffat, whom he married in 1844.

On his sailing from England, Livingstone's directions from the Missionary Society had been to proceed to Kuruman, and there await further instructions. However, after remaining some time and no advices coming, he determined to make a journey of exploration farther into the interior in order to glean what information he could from his own observations. On this journey he was accompanied by a brother missionary and two native teachers. Thus, while studying the country and its different phases, the customs and peculiarities of its people, he did not neglect that higher and nobler mission upon which he had come. As he went along, seeing and hearing, he would preach and teach, and strive by every means in his power to bring to a few darkened minds a knowledge of that precious Saviour of whom he had come so far to tell them.

He went first among one of the Bechuana tribes, north of

Kuruman.   Here he found the people in a terrible condition of fear and suffering.   On one side they were harassed by the Dutch slave-traders—or the Boers, as they were more commonly known, and of whom we shall hear more after awhile—and on the other by a dreaded native enemy, Mosilikatze by name, who had encamped upon their borders, every moment threatening to march in and destroy them. The Bechuanas were not disposed to give Livingstone and his companions a friendly welcome, for the Boers and others of their class had circulated all kinds of absurd stories in regard to the missionary and his intentions.   They had tried to make these benighted people believe that Livingstone was a great conqueror, who had come to put every tribe into subjection to his rule.   All this the Boers told because they hated Livingstone, knowing that his noble work would more plainly show up the wickedness of their traffic in slaves.   Should he succeed in enlightening the poor ignorant creatures whom the Boers used as tools to make war upon their own race—so as to capture in these battles the slaves whom the wicked Dutch traders afterward took to the coast to sell to the captains of vessels touching there—they well knew it would put an end to their shameless but exceedingly profitable business.

Regardless of all the Boers had told concerning him, Livingstone soon convinced the deluded natives that his errand to them was one of peace and good-will alone.   It did not take him long to do this, either, as has been intimated; for his kindly manner, his simple and fearless methods—above all, his honest dealings—won directly upon the confidence of chiefs and people.

During this journey some good seed were sown, though no direct result, as he could at that time see, came of his preaching and teaching. Still, for the little gained, Livingstone took heart and thanked God. He believed from the first that it was to be a work of time—one, too, requiring the utmost patience. It would take years for the light to penetrate, even with a feeble ray, the thick darkness in which these people had so long dwelt. But eventually it would come; the flickering beam would gradually grow into the broad and steady blaze. Until that time, he could only wait and work and pray, believing that God, in his own good season, would send the reward.

On the 10th of February, 1842, Livingstone left Kuruman for a second journey into the interior of the Bechuana country. The first person that specially engaged his interest on this visit was Bubi, chief of a tribe of Bakwains, a branch of the Bechuanas. Livingstone left a native teacher with Bubi, hoping and praying that amidst the great gloom one steady light would arise and shine. If he could but lead Bubi out of the darkness, then might others of the people follow.

Bubi was a good chief, and the only thing he lacked to make him a truly great chief was the religion of Christ in his heart. His thorough honesty, and that of his people, was fully demonstrated by their never having touched Livingstone's possessions or meddled with them in any way. This was remarkable, especially as the wagon containing his outfit and that of his companions had stood for a long while unguarded in the principal street of the village, where men, women, and children had free access to it.

Among other things, Livingstone showed Bubi's people how to dig a canal, whereby the water of the river was led into their gardens, thus greatly improving the vegetation.

Alas for Livingstone's hopeful expectations in regard to

4

RUDE METHODS OF AGRICULTURE AS PRACTICED BY BUBI'S PEOPLE.

the conversion of Bubi! The native teacher he left behind soon sickened and died, while poor Bubi himself was burned to death in an explosion of gunpowder with which one of his sorcerers was experimenting. The ignorant creature had seen the flash of the powder when the guns of Livingstone's party were discharged, and, believing they had previously bewitched it, thought he would burn the enchantment out of it. This fool-hardy experiment cost his own life and that of poor Bubi, who was curiously looking on.

Advancing farther into the interior, Livingstone next crossed a portion of the great Kalahari desert. During this march the men were often pressed for food, and Livingstone speaks of the keen delight with which he once sat down to a supper of rhinoceros meat, with porridge made of Indian meal thickly mixed with the gravy. Passing out of the desert, the travelers shortly came to the village of Sekomi, a chief of the Bamangwato. Livingstone thus speaks of these people: "Their conceptions of the Deity are of the most vague and contradictory nature, and the name of God conveys no more to their understanding than that of superiority. Hence they do not hesitate to apply the name to their chiefs. I was every day shocked by being addressed by that title myself, and though it as often furnished me with a text from which to tell them of the only true God and Jesus Christ whom he has sent, yet it deeply pained me, and I never felt so fully convinced of the lamentable deterioration of our species. It is indeed a mournful truth that man has become as the beasts that perish."

He found this place constantly threatened by one great terror—lions. During the night their awful cries could be heard on every side, while in the day-time they were so bold as to show themselves all about the village. Almost on the very eve of Livingstone's arrival a shocking occurrence took place, which made a deep and lasting impression upon him. A woman was actually devoured in her garden by one of these beasts, and within but a few steps of her hut, where were her children and some of her relatives. The cries of the orphan children were heart-rending to hear. During the whole of the night and day following her death the hills and the valleys around echoed and reëchoed with their bitter wails. The effect upon Livingstone was painful and startling. He says: "I frequently thought, as I listened to the loud sobs, painfully indicative of the sorrows

THE TERROR OF BAMANGWATO.

(52)

of those who have no hope, that if some of our churches could have heard their sad wailing, it would have awakened the firm resolution to do more for the heathen than they have yet done."

Though Livingstone at first found Sekomi very stubborn and bitterly opposed to the new religion, which taught among other things the forgiveness of enemies, some precious seed of the brave missionary's planting finally began to stir with a pulse of life. A conception of his darkened condition, faint though it was at first, gradually dawned upon Sekomi. As the voice of conscience grew louder he became more alarmed and distressed. One day, as Livingstone sat beside him reading from the New Testament, and explaining the passages as he went along, in such language as Sekomi could best understand, the chief suddenly sprung to his feet and broke forth: "O this wicked heart of mine! It sometimes makes me angry at every one, and gives me terrible thoughts, and drives me to want to do terrible things! Give me medicine to change it; quick, my friend! O give me medicine, good medicine-man, to change my heart!"

Livingstone lifted up the Testament, and began to tell him how through the teachings of that precious Book alone his heart could be changed, when poor Sekomi cried out again: "No; give me medicine, medicine to *drink!* Give me *medicine*, that my sick heart may be cured! I want no book, good medicine-man! What could I do with a book? I could neither eat nor drink it. O give me medicine, quick, lest my heart die!" He had seen Livingstone, in his office as physician, administering medicine to the sick and suffering, thereby making them well and strong again: thus, poor ignorant savage, the idea had fastened itself within his mind that the sick in spirit must be cured in the

same way.　It was a long while ere Livingstone could make
the difference plain to him, or show him with any degree of
clearness the manner in which the Great Physician is to
cure the sin-sick soul.

The tribe next visited by Livingstone was the Bakaa.
They were terribly afraid when they heard of his coming,
for shortly before that they had murdered a trader and his
whole company, and their guilty consciences made them see
in Livingstone an avenger sent by the Great Spirit.　This
belief was all the more strengthened when they learned that
he carried fire-arms, and could bring down a great beast at
many yards distant.　With the exception of the chief and
two of his attendants, every man, woman, and child forsook
the village on Livingstone's approach.　They were watching him from a distance, and as soon as they saw him partake
of a bowl of porridge with the chief, as a token of his friendly intentions, and afterward lie down and go to sleep, their
fears were allayed, and in a little while they all returned
to the village.

As he had convinced the Bakwains, so did Livingstone
finally convince the Bakaa that his mission was one of mercy and peace alone.　He found them lamentably ignorant
and superstitious.　They had never even heard the name of
God; or if they had, it was but to apply it to some great
chief, living at a distance, who might be expected to come
at any time and make war against them.　Their conception
of a Supreme Being was of a Great Spirit whose chariot
was the clouds, and whose voice when angry spoke in thunder, and when pleased his smile was the splendor of the
noonday sun.　The Great Spirit made his rewards in proportion to the number of scalps taken in open battle, and
his punishments in accordance with the weak inaction of a

cringing and cowardly spirit. They had no knowledge, no idea of a life hereafter, save their belief that the Great Spirit might take some of the more valiant of them to ride with him in his mighty cloud-chariot, and even to enter the brilliant arch that led to his principal abode, which was represented to them by the rainbow.

Livingstone remained for some time among this tribe, endeavoring to enlighten them as to the power of that " precious blood that cleanseth from all sin." Here he for the first time addressed the people in their own language—for he had previously used interpreters—and after the manner of a discourse. This patient sowing was not without its reward, and Livingstone says of himself at this time: " I bless God daily that he has bestowed upon one so worthless the distinguished privilege and honor of being the first messenger of mercy who has ever trod these regions."

Leaving the Bakaa, Livingstone began his return to Kuruman. On this journey he again heard of the wonderful lake, beyond which there was said to be a country abounding in ivory, gold, precious stones, and other valuable and beautiful things. At one time he was actually within a few days' journey of the lake, but not knowing it passed on. However, it remained for him to discover this lake in 1849, as we shall presently see.

Livingstone had now been in Africa two years. In that time he had traveled over quite two thousand miles of country, and seen sights to make his heart both sad and glad. In many respects he had found things quite as dark and forbidding as they had been pictured, while on the other hand there was much to encourage him. Though the whole country abounded in dangers, and the traveler's life was often in peril, still it was far from being the arid and desolate waste which the popular fancy had painted it. True, there were the burning sands, the blistering rays of the sun, the hissing of deadly serpents, and the roaring of ferocious wild beasts; but there were tall, beautiful trees;· bright, waving flowers; luxuriant grasses; broad, fertile valleys; and cool, deep lakes. The people, too, were ignorant and superstitious, and to some extent cruel and blood-thirsty; and there is no question that Livingstone's life might soon have paid the forfeit of his coming but for his manner of dealing with them. He was brave, open, and kind—letting them see from the first that he was their friend, and never once deceiving them. Thus they came to look upon him with trust, and to believe fully that he would do whatever he promised to do. Besides, they soon began to regard his mission as one of benefit to themselves. They did not quite understand it as yet, with the exception of the few he had led into the clear light, but they felt that in some way he meant to do them good; and believing this, they let him go and come among them unmolested. His medical skill and knowledge helped him greatly, for he was often enabled thereby to soothe their pains and administer healingly to the ills of their bodies. Because of this, in time Livingstone's name grew to be a power in that savage land. The poor, afflicted creatures, hearing of the wonderful skill of this "great medicine-man," as he was now called, came to him from hundreds of miles. No wonder they felt impelled to consider him gratefully, and to reverence even the sound of his name, for he never turned away one without first doing all he could to allay his sufferings.

One peculiarity of these people struck Livingstone, and touched a deep chord in his heart. Often he was called upon to remove tumors, cancers, and to perform other painful operations. These poor untutored savages endured the most terrible sufferings without a cry, often without so much as a change of face. Even the women were brave in this respect, scarcely giving a grunt or a moan. The men would say: "A man like me never cries. It is only children that cry out under pain." The women would say: " We are not men, but we know how not to cry." " Yet," adds Livingstone, " when the Spirit of God began to work on their hearts, they would cry out most piteously. Sometimes in church, while I was preaching, they would endeavor to screen themselves from my eyes by hiding under the forms, or by covering their heads with their karosses, as a remedy against their convictions. Often, when they found that that would not do, they would rush out of the church, crying with all their might, as if the hand of death were behind them." Surely in these signs the missionary had much to cheer and encourage him, for well he knew that the hearts thus forcibly worked upon by the power of the Spirit could not be far from complete surrender.

With all that he was doing for both the bodies and the souls of men, Livingstone had yet the time to make many botanical and geographical researches. During these two years he had discovered no less than thirty-two edible roots and forty-three fruits that grew without cultivation— a number of them in the desert, where the outside world had long believed no manner of vegetation could exist.

Livingstone reached Kuruman on his return in June, 1842. No directions had yet come from the Society; so he set out on another journey of exploration, as well as of missionary labor. This time he passed into the country of the Bakatla. Here he found the soil quite fertile, and the people more inclined to follow agriculture as a pursuit than any others he had yet come upon. Among other things, he was astonished at beholding an iron manufactory in their midst.   He at once expressed a desire to pass through it, and make a note of their manner of working it.   Greatly to his amusement, however, he was informed that he could not do so unless he should first prove that he was a bachelor.   No married man, they told him, was allowed to go through, for fear of his bewitching the iron.   A sad reflection this, surely, upon the fairer sex; so thought the gallant Doctor, and so he unburdened himself to those around him.   But it was a just precaution, they assured him; and not altogether unnecessary, since a man subjected to a woman's wiles was himself liable to practice those wiles in turn.   Livingstone soon convinced them of the justness of his claim to enter, and was much interested, as well as surprised, by what he saw. When he asked the chief if he would like to have him come and live among his people for awhile and teach them, he jumped up and clapped his hands, and exclaimed: "O! I shall dance if you do! I shall hop, and I shall skip! If you will do what you say, I will collect all my people to hoe for you a garden, and you will get more sweet reed and corn than myself." This was a magnificent offer, when viewed from a savage point of view, since the chief's share of any thing was apt to be as much as that of all the others together. This was doubtless because he had so many wives to feed. But Livingstone could make no definite promise, for he was at that time undecided as to his plans. However, on reaching Kuruman, and finding that a message had at last come—a message that allowed him much freedom of action —he prepared to return to his new-found friends, the Bakatla, in the valley of the Mabotsa.

CHAPTER V.

THE BAKATLA WELCOME LIVINGSTONE'S RETURN WITH GREAT
   DEMONSTRATION—HIS LION ADVENTURE—HE BECOMES A HERO
   —HIS MARRIAGE TO MARY MOFFAT—THEIR HOME AT MABOT-
   SA—THEY LEAVE MABOTSA FOR CHONUANE—THE GREAT CHIEF,
   SECHELE—THE REMOVAL TO KOLOBENG—"DID YOUR FATHERS
   KNOW?"—SECHELE'S CONVERSION—THE MALICIOUSNESS OF THE
   BOERS—LIVINGSTONE'S BRAVE DEED—HE ESTABLISHES A CLAIM
   UPON THE BAKWAINS—AN ENTHUSIASTIC BELLMAN—THE MIS-
   SIONARY'S EARNEST WORK BEGINS TO BE REWARDED.

THE Bakatla were delighted at Livingstone's return,
and prepared to welcome him with great demonstration. Soon after this, an event occurred which came
near putting an end to the life of our brave missionary.
Although of a higher degree of intelligence and industry
than the majority of their dusky brethren, the Bakatla
were great cowards. They were scarcely ever known to go
into a fight of their own accord, and when on the hunt they
were oftener the pursued than the pursuing. Between the
period of Livingstone's first and second visits a number of
lions had established themselves about the village, badly
frightening its inhabitants. Livingstone tried to organize
an attacking party to go in search of the beasts, and drive
them away. But despite his offer to put himself at their
head, he could only induce some ten or twelve natives to
follow him. They soon came in sight of the lions, on a
small hill thickly set about with trees. At Livingstone's
command the party formed a circle round the trees, gradu-

ally closing in until within easy range of the lions. Selecting a monster beast, that was lying upon a rock as though asleep, Livingstone brought his rifle to his shoulder, and prepared to aim.   Before he could fire, one of the natives—the village school-master, to whom Livingstone had taught the use of fire-arms—raised his own gun and discharged it quickly.   The ball, instead of striking the lion, only flattened itself against the rock whereon the huge brute lay.   He sprung up, lashing his tail furiously, and savagely biting at the spot that had been hit.   Then he dashed forward and broke unhurt through the circle of panic-stricken natives, who were scattering in every direction.   The other lions, through the fear of the natives, were also allowed to escape.   Much disgusted at the cowardly behavior of the Bakatla, Livingstone called upon them to rally and pursue the beasts.   He could do nothing with them, however; and fearing to fire, lest he should hit some of the running men, he prepared to return to the village.   On his way back he came upon a fourth lion, also sitting upon a rock, but instead of being asleep he was staring at the party with angry and threatening eyes.   Livingstone stopped, took careful aim, and fired the contents of both barrels of his gun into the brute.   The lion staggered, and for a moment seemed about to fall.   Seeing this, the natives started to run toward him, clapping their hands and shouting, " He is shot! He is dead!   Hurrah!   hurrah!   hurrah!"   But Livingstone knew better than they did.   Though badly wounded, the animal was far from being dead, and was likely to become infuriated.   Livingstone's coolness and promptness at this critical moment saved more than one life, beyond doubt. "Stop!" he cried out warningly to the rushing natives. "Don't go near him until I have had another shot.   He is not dead; do not so deceive yourselves." While he was ramming the bullets down into his gun, with his back to the rock on which the lion stood, Livingstone heard a shout. Glancing around quickly, he saw the huge brute crouched for a spring upon him. Before he could move out of the way the monster body came flying through the air. One of the paws struck Livingstone's shoulder with crushing force, and the next moment he and the lion went down together. As the great paw held Livingstone's shoulder, the animal gave a horrible growl and shook it as a cat would shake a mouse, or a terrier-dog a rat. In this act the bone was splintered, and the flesh, from the neck down to the elbow, terribly lacerated with the sharp claws. Almost fainting outright, Livingstone nevertheless retained some degree of consciousness. He soon felt himself fast sinking into a stupor that took away all fear, and allowed no sense of horror even as he glanced up into the infuriated brute's blazing eyes. In speaking of it further, Livingstone said it was doubtless such a sensation as patients have when, partly under the influence of chloroform, they see the operation that is taking place without feeling the sharp incisions of the knife. "I have since thought," Livingstone would add when relating the occurrence, "that this peculiar state was probably produced in all animals killed by the carnivora; and if so, it is a merciful provision by our benevolent Creator for lessening the pain of death."

While Livingstone thus lay in the clutches of the lion, Mebalwe, the school-master—who was really something of a brave man after all—leveled his gun, took aim this time more carefully, and fired; but his rifle, which was only a flint one, missed fire in both barrels. However, the flashes served to divert the attention of the lion, and to di-

LIVINGSTONE'S RESCUE FROM THE LION.

(62)

rect his rage into another channel. With a growl as horrible as the first, he left Livingstone and sprung upon Mebalwe, biting into his thigh; whereupon a nephew of the school-master, gaining courage from the dreadful situation of his uncle, drew near and tried to fasten his spear into the brute's shoulder. His attention again diverted, the lion now turned to spring with increased fury upon his new assailant; but before he could do so, the bullet Livingstone had fired took fatal effect, and with a startling cry of baffled rage and hate, that made the rocks far and near resound, the monster beast fell dead.

That evening the Bakatla made a huge bonfire of the carcass, about which they danced in great glee, declaring the slain king of the jungles the largest they had ever set their eyes upon. After that Livingstone was looked up to as second only to the chief.

It was a long time before Livingstone's arm and shoulder healed. They always caused him some pain and much discomfort. On his first return to England he had the greater portion of the splintered bone removed, and a false joint inserted. It was by this false joint that the body of the brave missionary was afterward identified when brought from the heart of Africa.

Intelligence of Livingstone's great lion adventure spread all over the world. In his own country it made quite a hero of him. He was inclined to look somewhat lightly upon it, save as he recognized in it a miraculous escape through God's help. To be exalted for such a thing as this was far from the desire or tastes of a man of Livingstone's temperament. Whenever the subject was alluded to in his presence, by any of his enthusiastic countrymen, he would turn it off with some jesting remark. When they tried to honor him because of it, he gave them to understand that he considered this adventure as the very least of his achievements.   He had done many braver and better and grander things: still for them there was no word of praise. The same world that had taken little note of the daring missionary who had tramped thousands of miles through burning sands and under a blazing sun, enduring all manner of suffering, to carry the glad tidings of eternal life to dying souls, was now going wild over the hunter who had come safely through a thrilling lion adventure.   Such is the standard by which the world ever gauges true courage.

To a young lady who once put the unexpected question, " What were your thoughts, Doctor, when the lion had you in his grasp?" he replied, with a dry humor bordering upon the grotesque, " I was wondering what part of me he would eat first."

Livingstone remained at Mabotsa about three years in all.   It was to this place he first carried his wife after their marriage in 1844.   The home into which the proud and happy husband introduced his young wife, though in the heart of a savage country, was not without many attractions, even comforts.   It was all the work of his own hands, and that made him the prouder of it.   He had put in place every stick, every stone of the house; even the mud of the chimney he had mixed and daubed together, though his wounded arm had barely healed by this time.   Still he cheerfully went on with the work, happy in the contemplation of the joy and comfort that modest little home would afford.   When finished the house was indeed a goodly one, notwithstanding the somewhat uncouth style of its architecture.   Within, every thing was as fresh and sweet and clean as the heart of love could devise, or the willing and diligent hand prepare from the rude materials to be found in that savage land. Without, the garden was a perfect picture of loveliness. There was even a little summer-house, built of plaited straw and stiff reeds ingeniously woven together. Taking all this into consideration, it is not surprising that Livingstone felt loath to quit his pleasant home, as he was afterward forced to do through a misunderstanding with one of the missionaries.

Livingstone and his faithful wife had done good work at Mabotsa. In addition to their own dwelling, a school-house and church had been erected; and many darkened souls were brought to the light through their united and courageous labors. Mabotsa never flourished again as it had done when the Livingstones resided there.

The chief to whom Livingstone next attached himself was Sechele, head of one branch of the Bakwains, as Bubi was of the other—the tribe having been divided some years previous through a disagreement in regard to the chieftainship. They were not divided on any other point, however, and kept up very friendly relations. Sechele's village was only about five days' journey from the mission station of Mabotsa, and Livingstone had once or twice visited Sechele during the period spent with the Bakatla. Having on one of these occasions been so fortunate as to heal a child of the chief's that the medicine-men of the tribe had given up to die, Livingstone had established a claim upon Sechele of which he seemed never to be unmindful. Ever since that time he had been persistent in urging Livingstone to come and take up his abode among his people for a short while, if no longer. From the moment that Livingstone met Sechele he felt strangely drawn toward him. He was of unusual intelligence, reading men and things with an ac-

5

curacy remarkable in one of his race. Livingstone felt that if he could convert Sechele to the truths of the gospel, he would have in him a valuable helper in the work of Christianizing his people.

So it was with many cheerful and hopeful anticipations that Livingstone left Mabotsa in 1846, and took up his abode with Sechele at the village of Chonuane. Sechele had descended from a long line of chiefs, each of whom had in some way distinguished himself from the common run of his people. Sechele's father and grandfather had been great travelers, the latter being also the first savage to tell his people of a race of white men altogether different in habits and appearance from theirs.

Livingstone did not much like the situation of Sechele's village at Chonuane. There was not a sufficient supply of either water or pasturage. However, he determined to remain there for a year or so, at least. Again with his own hands the brave missionary erected his dwelling-place and laid out his little patches of garden; but this time he did not make so pretentious a building, for he did not know but that he might move away at any moment. As he had feared, a drought soon came; the vegetation dried up, and people and cattle suffered greatly for water. He now advised Sechele to remove to some spot near a running body of water—a creek or river—from which canals might be dug to irrigate the land, thus giving the vegetation as much moisture as possible. This would likewise provide an assured supply of water for cattle and people, unless a drought of unusual severity should come and dry up the stream itself; but Livingstone believed that if the stream was full and deep such a catastrophe would not occur for some years. Sechele looked upon Livingstone's suggestion as a wise one, and determined to act upon it at once. The place selected for the planting of the new village was about forty miles away, in a beautiful spot near the banks of the Kolobeng River, from which the station afterward took its name. They were still in the country of the Bechuana, and only about two hundred and fifty miles from Kuruman. On one side of them, though some distance away, was the great Kalahari desert, and on the other the Transvaal, the stronghold of the Boers. Livingstone was so well pleased with the new situation that he determined to settle here permanently, making it the base of his operations in the country surrounding. So for the third time he began the building of a home-nest for his little family. A family it was now, indeed, since a wee stranger had recently come to dwell with them—Robert Moffat Livingstone by name.

At Chonuane, besides the drought, the missionaries—for we must include Mrs. Livingstone along with her husband, since she labored side by side with him—had suffered much for the want of absolute necessities. They had to use parched corn for coffee, and sometimes the pounded roots of a certain tree in place of meal, the bare handful of corn being too precious to convert into bread. But all these discomforts they bore without a murmur—the delicate wife as well as the stronger husband, which proved how worthy she was to be his helpmeet.

As he had hoped, Livingstone found Sechele ready and willing to hear the many truths of which he had come to tell him, and to receive instruction in other things. He accomplished the remarkable feat of learning the alphabet in a single day. He was proud of the praise he received, and redoubled his efforts. When Livingstone came to tell him of the great white throne on which God sat, and of

God himself, before whose shining face the earth and heavens shall flee away and roll together like a burning scroll,
Sechele trembled with fear and terror.   He sprung to his
feet, and walked about restlessly; he wrung his hands, and
looked up imploringly toward the sullen horizon, then angry with the signs of approaching tempest.   Finally, coming back to where Livingstone sat, he threw himself, the
picture of miserable despair, on the ground at the missionary's feet.   "You startle me!" he cried; "you frighten me
out of what senses I have!   You make my bones to shake and
my knees to tremble till there is no more strength left in me!
My arm shakes so I could not draw the arrow!   My head
swims in such a way I could not see how to follow the buffalo!   O! alas is me!   I am undone!   Whither shall I fly?
What shall I do?   Everywhere I look I see the eyes of that
great and angry God fixed upon me!   O white man!" raising his head suddenly with a passionate gesture, and looking at Livingstone with eyes that burned like fire, "why
didn't you come sooner to tell me of this?   Why have you
let me go on all these years without bringing to me a knowledge of these terrible things?"   Dropping his head again,
he raised it after a moment and faced Livingstone, with the
unexpected question: "White man, did your fathers know
this that you have just told me?   Did *they* know of this
angry and frowning God who so punishes all those who do
not try to please him?"   On Livingstone's replying in the
affirmative, he broke forth more piteously than ever: "Then
why didn't your fathers come to tell my fathers?   They
knew all this, yet they let my fathers die in darkness and
ignorance!   They let them go and face this terrible God
without telling them where they were going!"

    What a fearful cry to ring in Christian ears!   What an

accusation to sink into Christian hearts! No wonder the good missionary, as he heard it—even with all he had done—felt sad and reflective. "My fathers died in darkness and ignorance, and your fathers did not come to tell them of that God before whom they went unprepared." Alas! poor heathen, dying in darkness and despair, while just across one ocean were the white men—brothers they called themselves—who knew all these things, yet they came not to tell you! O reader, shall any of these things be said of us years hence? Shall that dreadful cry ring in our ears also, "You knew all this, yet you did not come to tell us?" Shall the bitter memories of neglected opportunities some day make our hearts sick with remorse? O let us pray not so, and work that it be not so; for there is a work for all, even for the smallest. There is a cry from over the seas: "We know not these things; will you come and tell us?" Who of us will heed it? Who of us, on the other hand, will carelessly pass it by? It is not for all of us to go, but it is for all of us to send—our dollars, our dimes, our mites, every one that we can. Who of us will enter into the work

So bravely, so kindly, so well,
Angels will hasten the story to tell?

Gradually light began to penetrate the darkened chambers of poor Sechele's soul. He saw himself a sinner, shut out from the wonderful heaven of which the good missionary had told him, yet not without hope as it had seemed to him at the first. There was still a chance, if he would only arise and take it. Livingstone had told him that this mighty God from his Great White Throne had declared, "He that cometh unto me, believing, I will in no wise cast out." O the preciousness of such a promise! How could any one disregard it? Nearer and nearer Sechele drew to

Jesus, yet with all his earnest faith and humble trust he could not quite forget his savage nature. He wanted all the people to accept this new religion, and to begin to prepare themselves to enter that wondrous abode of the good of which he had heard such beautiful stories. But many of them showed so little concern that he lost patience with them; and one day he astonished Livingstone by breaking forth with much passion · ' They are a stuoborn and an elephant-headed set! They will take nothing unless it is beaten into them. Let me get my good whip of rhinoceros hide, and I will soon have them down on their knees in a body, and begging for mercy at the top of their big, bellowing voices!" It was some time before Livingstone could convince him that this was not the way to make Christians.

The greatest difficulty in the way of Sechele's full acceptance of the Christian religion—as it had been with so many other chiefs—was the putting away of all his wives but one. "Why," he said, "how am I to choose between so many charming women? Then, besides, there will be no end to a bad time; for when they know what I am about they will cry out and wring their hands, each one entreating me to take her. And finally when I do make a choice of one, all the others will think me an ungallant man; and no woman yet has had that to say of Sechele. Further than this," he went on, still more distressed, " you do not know the fuss it will cause me with the different women's relatives. They will each want to go to fight with me; and I shall not know what to do, there are so many of them." On Livingstone's promising to see him safely out of the difficulty, Sechele sent all the women away, with the exception of one whom he confessed to Livingstone he had admired more than any of the others. By Sechele's orders these ex-wives were conveyed in great state to their former homes, having first been well provided for by the chief; so that the sting of their rejection was effectually soothed.

In a little while Sechele, earnest and believing, presented himself for baptism. When the intelligence of what he had done was carried through the village, there was a great outcry from the people. They even came in a body to the chief, entreating him not to forsake the religion of his fathers, as it would surely bring upon the whole tribe the anger of the Great Spirit, and they would all be destroyed. When Livingstone came to administer baptism to Sechele, they stood around him howling and screaming at such a rate that it was with the greatest difficulty he could compose himself for observing the rite in the impressive manner required. Rising from his knees, Sechele looked around upon his people, his eyes streaming with tears, while in a voice of passionate entreaty he thus addressed them: "O you really know not what you do! You are as willful and naughty as headstrong children who are bent on having their way, even to their own hurt. O! I entreat you, be willful and disobedient no longer, but come and let this good man," pointing to Livingstone, "tell you of that which I have found most precious unto my soul. O my brethren, if you would but hear! Am I to be the only one of my people to accept the promises of that great God on the big White Throne? and the only one to go to see him in his heaven? O my children, hearken to the voice of this good man while you may! Hear my own feeble voice, and unbend those stiff necks of yours! O come and be saved while yet there is time!" But they only turned away and began to mock him behind his back, for they were afraid to do so openly

In proof of his earnestness Sechele begged Livingstone to have family prayer in his hut, in addition to the services in the public hall. To these prayer-meetings Sechele invited such of his people as cared to come. As might be supposed, only two or three of them responded; yet it gladdened both Sechele's and Livingstone's hearts to find these two or three in time gradually coming to the light. Sechele himself now undertook to conduct family prayer, and Livingstone was much impressed by the simple beauty and force of some of his petitions. "If he had had the advantages of a thorough education, he would have been a most remarkable man," Dr. Livingstone was heard to say of him again and again. Sechele also began to read his Bible daily, under Livingstone's instructions. His favorite writer was Isaiah, and he used to exclaim, with kindling eyes: "He was a fine man, that Isaiah! He knew how to talk!" But in spite of Sechele's steadfast example and Livingstone's faithful preaching, with the exception of two or three of Sechele's stanchest followers—the same that had first come to the meeting—the people of the tribe remained obdurate. Worse than this, they grew sullen and fault-finding. The unusually severe drought Livingstone had thought possible, but not probable—at least for some time—coming on at this period, they charged it all to the missionary's presence among them; and but for Sechele's fine governing abilities, as well as Livingstone's fearless bearing, there might now have been serious trouble. In the face of this unlooked-for calamity, they were threatened by the aggressive attitude of the Boers. These people, besides circulating malicious reports concerning Livingstone, were now verging upon what seemed an open declaration of war. When Livingstone had first attached himself to Sechele the Boers had, as was their usual mean way of doing, made a great noise about it, and tried to incite other tribes to war against Sechele; for they were too cowardly to undertake it themselves without help. They told the natives that Sechele was one of Livingstone's allies, and was to aid him in his conquest of the country, in return for which Sechele was to be made a great governor when Livingstone set up his autocratic reign throughout Africa. Among other presents Livingstone had given Sechele a large iron pot: this the Boers tried to magnify into an enormous cannon, which they told the poor credulous savages Livingstone and Sechele kept loaded and ready for instant use.

To show how ignorant and superstitious these Boers were themselves, they became greatly frightened when the English Government erected a large telescope on top of an observatory at Cape Town. They said to Livingstone: "What right did your people have to set up that great glass to spy us out and to see what we were doing, even here behind the Cashan Mountains?" The Boers, however, dared not make war openly against Livingstone, not only because of their great cowardice, but for fear of the trouble it would bring them into with England; yet they did every thing in their power to keep the natives stirred up against him. They even tried it with Sechele's people, which was most unfortunate for Livingstone at this time. But for Sechele's watchful eye and wise, firm rule, much mischief would have been wrought in the already rebellious camp at Kolobeng. The blessed rain came after awhile, and the savages grew ashamed of their hostile attitude toward Livingstone. Besides, something happened just at this time that rendered them forever afterward his stanch friends and admirers.

One afternoon news came to the village that a party of

Bechuanas, traveling to Sechele's town on a friendly visit, had been attacked by a black rhinoceros, one of the most savage and dangerous of all the African wild beasts. The furious animal had dashed at the wagon containing the party, and driven one of his horns into the bowels of the driver, inflicting a frightful wound. Thereupon every Bechuana had taken to his heels and left the poor driver to his fate. The rhinoceros, however, instead of staying and finishing the man, took after the fugitives; but being a heavy beast, and the men swift of foot, they were soon beyond his reach. When they arrived at Sechele's camp they were panting and out of breath, for they had run nearly every step of the eight miles. When Livingstone heard the story he deemed it not only his professional but his Christian duty to go to the succor of the wounded driver. Sechele was horror-stricken when he learned of the missionary's intention. It was then nearly night, and the ride was sixteen miles, there and back. "No, no!" said Sechele vehemently; "you must not think of such a thing, my friend, even for a minute. It would be certain death, and we cannot afford to lose you." Discovering that Livingstone could not be dissuaded from his purpose, Sechele's next endeavor was to persuade some of his people to accompany the missionary. But not a man would volunteer, for the Bechuanas had brought too horrible a story—of how the woods between the village and the spot where the driver lay were infested with black rhinoceroses. They declared that they had counted at least twenty. Finding that Livingstone would go, Sechele let his great love for his friend overcome his own fear, and offered himself to accompany Livingstone. Livingstone would not assent to this, and convinced Sechele that, in view of the discontented and rebellious condition of his people, it might be neither safe nor wise for both of them to leave the village at the same time. At length, mounting his horse, Livingstone set off alone. The whole camp followed him to the outskirts of the village, every head adorned with an enormous cow-tail, in order to give him good luck, they said.

When Livingstone reached the end of his journey he found the poor man dead, and beyond all need of help. But there was one thing he felt that he could do for him: he could take the body back with him, and give it decent burial. This he forthwith proceeded to do.

It was long past midnight when Livingstone reached the village on his return, still he found the whole camp up and awaiting him. When they comprehended what he had done, the savages went nearly wild over him, and wanted to take him in a triumphal procession around the village. Livingstone at last dissuaded them from this intention, but he could not prevent the bonfires which they built all about the village, and around which they leaped and danced till morning, singing chants in his praise.

After that, Livingstone had it all his own way with these savage natures; and there was no longer any trouble in getting them to come and hear him preach. Previous to that time Sechele had resorted to various stratagems to draw his people to church. He even hired a bellman, and instructed him to use all the methods and tricks of which he was master to get the people to the preaching. This bellman was not only an enthusiast in every work he undertook—going at nothing half-way, but with a headlong rush that threatened to annihilate all things before him—but he was a great curiosity in himself. He stood over six feet in his bare feet, was gaunt in frame, and had an immense nose, a terrible pair of eyes, and a voice that could be heard from one end of the village to the other. He had a platform built near the center of the camp: on this he used to mount, a full half-hour before the beginning of the services, and yell out at the top of his stentorian voice: "Hi! you woman over there! I see you! You are not making ready to come to church; nor you man either!" Then, as though addressing a visible emissary: "Say, you fellow there, knock that woman down who is not coming to church! And that man, trip him up! Give him a kick where he lies! That is it! Let none escape! Knock them down! Run over them! Trample on them! Beat them, I say! See! see! that woman is trying to put on her pot and slip out at the door to run to the woods! That is right, get after her! Trip her up, catch her, and maul her till she bellows like a rhinoceros calf!" Most of those who caught these terrible words ran at once to the place of meeting, for they did not know but that they might be the next ones knocked down and trampled upon by those dreadful emissaries of the bellman and Sechele, who, it seemed, were running about in search of them. But after the rain came, and Livingstone went on his terrible journey alone, there was no further need of the bellman. The people now came of their own accord to hear the brave missionary who had risked his own life to save that of a poor black man, and finding him dead had shown so much feeling as to bring his body back for decent burial.

Soon many applications were made for membership in the Church; but so conscientious was Livingstone, so great his fear that their admiration for him might lead them into a demonstration they did not really feel, he would not take them in until first assured of the genuineness of their convictions and the sincerity of their intentions. " ' Fifty added to the Church ' sounds very fine at home," he wrote to one of his friends at this time; " but if only five of them are genuine, what will it profit in that great day? I have felt more than ever lately that the great object of our exertions ought to be conversion. Nothing will ever induce me to form an impure Church," he concluded; and nothing ever did. What better proof do we need than this that David Livingstone's work was not for praise, nor for show, but *for the Master?* He hated all sham, all false pretense; he loved the truth and thorough sincerity in every thing. He would never administer the Lord's Supper to a single convert unless he had first, for a year at least, tested his earnestness and seen him live the pure, consistent life that marks those who are really Christ's followers. Thus the work he did was *genuine* work. No wonder its influence has stood steadfast, and widened with the years; for he built not upon the sand, but upon the Rock, against which the floods vainly beat.

CHAPTER VI.

AN AFRICAN VILLAGE—THE GOVERNMENT OF THE BECHUANA
TRIBES—SECHELE ERECTS A CHURCH AND SCHOOL-HOUSE "TO
THE HONOR OF GOD"—MRS. LIVINGSTONE'S NOBLE LABORS—THE
CHEERFUL LIFE OF THE BRAVE MISSIONARY AND HIS WIFE—
A TRYING PERIOD—LIVINGSTONE'S ENDURING PATIENCE AND
UNSHAKEN TRUST—THE AFRICAN METHOD OF PROCURING
MEAT—THE HOSTILE ATTITUDE OF THE BOERS GROWS MORE
THREATENING—SECHELE'S NOBLE REPLY.

DOUBTLESS it will interest the reader to learn something of an African village, as well as to gain an insight into the home-life of the missionaries. The government of the Bechuana tribes, of which the Bakwains were one of the principal branches, was somewhat patriarchal in its form. Though the chief was the head of his people, the father was the head of his family, and no one—not even the chief himself—had a right to interfere with his rule in the household over which he presided. Outside, however, the word of the chief was the supreme law by which all were controlled.

The village was generally erected somewhat in the form of a square, with the residence of the chief occupying the most conspicuous portion, usually near the center. Stretching away on either side of the chief's home, in rows of two double were the huts of his wives, those of his near relations, and of the principal men of his tribe. About the huts of the fathers of families were also arranged, somewhat after the same plan, the huts of their children who had married

(78)

AN AFRICAN VILLAGE.

(79)

and set up house for themselves. As a general thing all the huts were built of tough grass, which in that country often grows to the height of ten or twelve feet. They were neatly and ingeniously thatched with coarse straw, and fenced in with high, strong walls made of tiger-grass. When Livingstone came among the Bakwains he taught them to use stone and mortar, as well as boards sawed from the forest; and soon their village showed the effects of this industry.

Secchele's people, not being so savage as the majority of their dusky brethren, had gone partly clad—that is, with a leopard-skin, or covering of other kind—even when Livingstone first made their acquaintance. Now, thanks to both his and Mrs. Livingstone's judicious instructions, they presented quite a respectable appearance.

The new village of Kolobeng was altogether different from the old one at Chonuane. The houses were arranged in a cluster on the side of a gently sloping eminence instead of in the usual partly circular form. While some of the huts were built of straw, the majority, including the chief's residence, were made of stone or wood. Besides teaching the people to saw boards, Livingstone showed them how to make and press brick. He also taught them to make candles out of the fat of various animals, and soap from a plant called salsola, or from ordinary wood ashes. Thus the people came to have lights in their houses, instead of on the ground in front of them, and soap to cleanse with—two luxuries hitherto unknown in South African life. One of the first things Livingstone had sought to instill into their minds was a love for cleanliness. In time this village in South Africa was regarded with no little wonder and curiosity. Eager sight-seers often came from the remotest tribes to catch a glimpse of it, and to find out if the many extraordinary things that had been told of it were in any degree true.

One of the first things Sechele had done after his conversion was to erect a more commodious church and school-house— "to the honor of God," he declared, " who is from henceforth the defender of my town." Over two hundred men were engaged in this work alone, and when completed the buildings were indeed an honor to Him to whose glory they had been set apart, as well as a credit to the noble savage through whose zeal and devotion they had been erected. Mrs. Livingstone was given charge of the school, and in every way she proved herself a worthy and efficient co-laborer with her husband.

The whole village generally arose at six o'clock in the summer and at seven in the winter. After family worship in the huts of those who had professed conversion to the new religion, they had breakfast. When breakfast was over, the men, women, and larger children assembled at the school-house, where Livingstone and the two native teachers assisted Mrs. Livingstone. The school held until eleven o'clock, when it was dismissed in order that the pupils might go to their work—the men to gardening or ditching and building, the women to the preparation of the noonday meal, and the children to such lighter tasks as they could perform.

Mrs. Livingstone did her own domestic work, like the other women, with such help as her husband could give her. Usually he ground the corn for her in the little mill he had improvised, gathered the vegetables, milked the cow, or did any other part of the rough outdoor work he could. When ground, the corn was baked into bread in an oven Living-

6

stone had constructed in the side of an ant-hill; or it was fried into cakes in a covered frying-pan set in the center of the fire-place. In this same pan the meat was afterward prepared. For a churn they used a jar, in which the milk was shaken into butter. The coffee was boiled in another jar. Livingstone had fashioned the jars out of a stiff clay that became very hard after baking in the sun.

Now, all these things may appear as hardships to those whose lot has always been cast in civilized places; but that they were far from being so regarded by either Livingstone or his brave wife we have their own cheerful words of denial. The gentle spirit of the patient and faithful wife had much to do with Livingstone's enjoyment of this mode of life. He says, when speaking of this time: "There is something of the feeling which must have animated Alexander Selkirk on seeing conveniences spring up before him from his own ingenuity; and married life is all the sweeter when so many comforts emanate directly from the thrifty, striving housewife's hands."

After finishing her dinner, and taking only about an hour's rest, Mrs. Livingstone went next to her infant school, which comprised all the smaller children of the village, usually from seventy-five to eighty in number. This school she conducted entirely alone. It must have been a severe tax upon her, for she was not very strong; but if wearied, she never once showed it, either by look or word. She also had a sewing-class for girls, instructing them two evenings of each week. It would be impossible to rightly estimate the good accomplished by this heroic woman, or to put any thing like its real value upon her influence over the women and girls of the camp. Most nobly did she preserve her gracious heritage as a missionary's daughter and a missionary's wife. No wonder that Livingstone felt as if all the light and strength had forever gone out of his life when she died.

Besides the regular Sunday morning and evening services, Livingstone held public exercises at the church or school-house two nights in the week. A great drum-like gong—one of Livingstone's many ingenious improvisations—called the people to these services as soon as supper and the milking of the cows were over.

During the prevalence of the second and severer drought the camp at Kolobeng had suffered greatly, not only from the want of a sufficient supply of water, but also from the lack of proper food. It was a most trying period for Livingstone, for the many deprivations he was forced to see his gentle wife and delicate babies undergo hurt him more than any thing he had yet been called upon to endure. At times it seemed to him as if his calmness would completely desert him. Once the supply of corn gave out, and they had to use bran for meal. It required the united grinding power of three laborers to render this fit for the baking of bread. Even then it was scarcely palatable. At another time there was no meat, and they were obliged to eat locusts, which were far from a pleasant diet. In the neighborhood of the camp there was a species of frog called *matlemetlo*. These frogs were now looked upon as desirable prizes by those who were so fortunate as to secure a number of them. They were enormously large, and the meat—especially that of the hind legs—was really of a quality not to be despised even under more favorable circumstances. During the dry season they hid themselves in great holes which they dug in the ground, and remained there croaking for rain at the top of their coarse voices. These croakings usually served as the death-knell of the frogs, for the natives were thus led to their hiding-places. Taking the cue from the Bakwains, Livingstone began searching for these frogs; and it must have been pitiable to see the great missionary, whose name was now going from continent to continent, crouched over a hole in the earth and digging with eager hands to secure these croakers for the hungry mouths at home.

Previous to the drought the inhabitants of Kolobeng, not-withstanding their unfriendliness toward Livingstone, had been both just and generous in the distribution of the meat of animals killed by the village at large. This was in great part owing to the influence of Sechele. Still, to do them justice, the men had never—even of their own accord —sought to deny Livingstone his portion of the meat taken. The custom followed out in procuring this meat was for a party of hunters to go forth at regular intervals and beat the woods about the camp. When they came upon a herd of antelopes, springboks, zebras, quaggas, etc., they would surround them and drive them toward an inclosure shaped like a V, which stood near one side of the village. At the pointed end of the inclosure there was a huge pit, into which the animals fell one over the other, and were dispatched by the spears of the natives. The meat was then divided out in proportion to the families, Livingstone getting his share equally with the others.

The rain now coming, and Livingstone's gentle yet firm rule being fully established among them, all might have gone on exceedingly well with the Kolobeng camp from this time, and its inhabitants have felt contented and at their ease, but for one threatening evil. This was the Bo-ers, who were daily growing more and more determined in their stand against Livingstone. Of late they had taken a

new turn, and one that had perplexed and alarmed the poor
savages very much. They had assumed a menacing attitude toward the tribes that had for any length of time sheltered Livingstone and given ear to his teachings. They
had even attacked one of the tribes, and carried into captivity the poor creatures who were not killed or not fortunate
enough to escape from the village. Daily their threats
against the Kolobeng camp became more violent. Finally
they sent Sechele a message to the effect that if he did
not leave Livingstone to shift for himself, and return to
the old trading relations with them, they would attack his
village and kill or make captives of all his people. Another thing that Sechele had done greatly excited their anger and enmity: he had recently allowed a party of white
traders to pass through his territory, and furnished them
with guides to some of the more friendly tribes. One of
the principal speculations of the Boers, whereby they added
greatly to their revenues, was in the ivory trade. Thus,
when they heard of the presence of the white traders in the
Bechuana country, they trembled for their future gains; for
they knew well enough that these Englishmen, who were far
more honest than themselves, would allow the natives a fair
price for the ivory which the Boers had heretofore been in
the habit of getting in exchange for worthless trifles.
Should the natives once get an insight into the real value
of ivory, it was not likely that they would ever again allow themselves to be cheated by the Boers. So the Boers
sent Sechele a very threatening message, not only in regard
to Livingstone, but also in regard to the future passing of
the English traders through his country. Sechele now rose
to the full height of his dignity and courage, and proved
himself as earnest and faithful as he seemed. He returned

the Boers this message : " I, Sechele, am an independent chief, controlled alone by God. God put me here, and him I am to obey, not you. Other tribes you may have conquered, but you will never conquer me as long as that God is with me. The English are my friends. They are good to me. They treat me as their equal. I get every thing I want from them. I would not hinder them if I could from going anywhere about my country they choose. As to the one Englishman who is my friend of all others, and to whom I owe so much, I will stand by *him* to the last." Either this manly and confident reply had the effect of intimidating the Boers for awhile, or else the fear of Livingstone himself was the real cause of their taking no immediate action. As long as Livingstone remained in the camp they never came near it; but their hatred of him, and their mean desire to injure him as much as possible, knew no abatement, as we shall presently see.

CHAPTER VII.

LIVINGSTONE STARTS IN SEARCH OF LAKE NGAMI—THE KALA-
HARI DESERT—SEKOMI'S TREACHEROUS BEHAVIOR—THE BUSH-
MEN AND BAKLAHARI—LIVINGSTONE'S HOSPITABLE RECEPTION
—CROSSING THE DESERT—THE SCARCITY OF WATER—SUFFER-
INGS AND HARDSHIPS—THE DECEPTION OF THE MIRAGE—
REACHING THE ZOUGA—NEW HOPES AND DESIRES—LIVING-
STONE'S ABSORBING DREAM—THE WONDERFUL LAKE AND THE
COUNTRY SURROUNDING IT—THE RETURN TO KOLOBENG.

SEEING things moving along so peacefully and smoothly at Kolobeng, Livingstone felt that he might now
safely leave them for awhile in the hands of his faithful
wife, Sechele, and the native teachers, and put into execution a design he had long cherished. This was to make a
journey of exploration into the country farther north, in
order to find, if possible, that wonderful lake of which so
much had been told him. His purpose was strengthened
by the coming to the Kolobeng camp of the Messrs. Murray
and Oswell, two great English travelers and hunters. They
were also on the lookout for all the geographical knowledge
they could gather, Mr. Murray especially. When they
heard of the lake they were eager to visit it, and proposed to
Livingstone that they should start at once. As they would
prove traveling companions not to be disregarded in a country like this, and had proposed to bear all the expenses of
guides, etc., Livingstone thought it an opportunity such as
he might never have again. In the meantime a number of
messengers from Lechulatebe, an influential chief who re-

sided in the lake country, had also appeared at Kolobeng, bearing a request that Livingstone would visit him, and holding out many inducements for him to do so. This, too, was taken into consideration, for one of the principal objects in view was to establish all the friendly relations possible with the chiefs of that section.

Accordingly, at day-break on the morning of June 1st, 1849, Livingstone, after first committing his little family to God's care, and to the trust and protection of the faithful Sechele, set out with his friends on the journey in search of Lake Ngami. Between them and the country they hoped to reach lay the great Kalahari desert, a portion of which Livingstone had once before crossed. But the journey then was nothing like the present journey was to be. Livingstone earnestly prayed to God for guidance and protection.

Strictly speaking, the Kalahari is not really a desert, since it is far from being devoid of vegetation, or even of water. Most of the growth, however, is of a kind that can exist with but little moisture, and often, strange to say, grows the rankest in the driest places. The vegetation is principally of coarse, stiff grasses that grow to the height of many feet, and of various creeping plants, with here and there a clump of trees or a cluster of shrubs. Where water is found it is usually in small pools formed by the rain, or in the beds of long dried-up rivers. That the Kalahari did at one time, as is claimed for it, contain many water-courses is evidenced by the plainly defined channels of these streams, now glistening bare and arid in the blistering rays of the sun.

The animals to be seen are chiefly of a kind that can long endure thirst, such as the antelope species. Yet others sometimes find their way up into the wildernesses of the desert through the dry channels of the streams, and it is not an uncommon sight to see a drove of buffaloes, or even of elephants, feeding upon the rank grasses. Snakes, mostly of the smaller varieties, both poisonous and non-poisonous, abound in great numbers, and one of the principal dangers against which the traveler has to guard is their often deadly bite. However, they generally give a warning hiss, and with proper caution can be very nearly avoided. Insects, too, are abundant and annoying—ants, caterpillars, bugs, beetles, and roaches.

The route chosen by Livingstone's party across the desert had not been passed over in fifty years or more, even by a native. Previous to that time, however, it had been a highway of travel for the various wandering tribes. But owing to the severe droughts that had prevailed since then, it had become such a parched and desolate waste that even the Bushmen, the most thirst-enduring of all the African tribes, dared not cross it. Livingstone nevertheless believed that by a proper formation of plans, and the right preparation before starting out, he and his little party could get across safely. Moreover, he felt that it would be safer and wiser to risk even the terrors of the desert than attempt to pass through a country where dwelt several hostile tribes who had threatened to attack the explorers should they come near. Livingstone's friends not only approved his determination to choose the desert, but they never for a moment doubted that he would carry them safely across.

As has been stated, the party started from the camp at Kolobeng on the morning of the 1st of June, 1849. For the first two days their route lay through a hill-covered country, with beautiful and fertile valleys between. On the third day they entered the territory of Sekomi, of whom we have before heard. It seems that Sechele held some sort of authority over Sekomi, hence there was not the best of feeling on the latter's side, for he was a very proud and willful chief. In order to propitiate him, as well as to win his good offices in behalf of Livingstone's proposed expedition, a fine ox and two cows were sent forward as presents. Sekomi was quite profuse in his greeting of his old friend, Dr. Livingstone; for he really both admired and liked the brave and kindly missionary, who was not afraid to do his duty even amidst the most trying circumstances. Still, when he learned of the Doctor's intention to cross the desert in search of the lake, he endeavored by every means in his power to dissuade him from it. He believed that if Livingstone was lost in the desert he would be blamed for it, because he had not tried to stop him when he passed through his domains. Thus he sought to impress Livingstone, and to make him believe that this was the chief cause of his opposition to the undertaking; but his real motive in trying to keep the missionary from pushing on will appear in the sequel.

"Do not go," he urged Livingstone. "Turn back now, and return to Sechele. You will die; you will surely be lost in that desert! The thirst will kill you, and the sun will dry you up! Then all the white men, your brothers, will blame me, and doubtless make war against me for not trying to save you when I had the chance."

Somehow Sekomi had gotten the idea that Livingstone was a person of great importance in his own country. Therefore, he really had some fear and misgiving in regard to the consequences likely to follow upon Livingstone's death. So he made up his mind to do all he could to oppose the expedition on this ground, knowing it would never do to give the real reason of his opposition.

To Sekomi's entreaties Livingstone only replied with quiet humor that he was a very "hard-headed man," and bent on having his own way; therefore, he could not go back, because his head told him to go on. At this Sekomi expressed a curiosity to feel the Doctor's head. Permission being granted, he thumped first upon the Doctor's head and then upon his own. Again he thumped alternately upon each, and then stopped with a look of perplexity on his face. Suddenly, a light seeming to dawn upon him, he exclaimed: "Yes, your head *is* hard, sure enough; and so is mine—much harder, in fact, than yours! Now, I know what it is that makes me want to do things with all my might sometimes; it is my head!"

Finding that Livingstone was determined to go on in spite of all persuasion, Sekomi finally sent with him two of his men, to increase his escort, as he said, and to prove his friendly interest in the missionary's plans. But alas! the wily Sekomi was far from regarding the expedition in the friendly light he pretended, as it all soon came out. Knowing Livingstone so well, Sekomi feared there might be a chance after all for the party under his guidance to get safely across the desert—which, by the way, was the last thing Sekomi wanted it to do. Not that he was wicked and cruel enough to desire that the Doctor's life or that of any one with him should pay the forfeit, but only that he did not want them to reach the country about the lake. The truth is, Sekomi had long been enjoying a sort of monopoly of the ivory business from that direction, and he feared that if once Dr. Livingstone and his white companions reached the people there they would open their eyes to the real value of the ivory. So, discovering that he could not stop them by fair means, he did not hesitate to use foul means. The men sent along, apparently as friends, were in reality enemies and mischief-makers, who had instructions from Sekomi to stir up against Livingstone and his party such of the various tribes through which they passed as they could. The men began faithfully at the first opportunity to carry out Sekomi's instructions, and there is no telling what trouble might have befallen had not one of them died very suddenly, and the other, looking upon it as a judgment from that God to whom Livingstone constantly prayed, fled back to his people in terror.

Sekomi's traitorous conduct may seem unaccountable when we recall the convictions he had shown under Livingstone's teaching, and the pathetic petitions he had made to have his "sick heart" cured. Doubtless the poor fellow had been very much in earnest at that time, and perhaps even now was trying to be honest in the new life he was professing to lead. But the old nature would crop out every now and then, and, like so many of us, he did not make the right kind of an effort to keep it down. Hence we must not judge his conduct too harshly, remembering that he was but a savage and under the control of his leading passion—avarice.

From Sekomi's country the way lay principally along the bed of an ancient water-course. The sand at the bottom of the track was exceedingly white and beautiful, with tall cliffs on either side covered with brilliant flowers and graceful festoons of creeping plants and vines. The travelers came next to broad, flat heaths, with rich carpetings of grass and thick clusters of a shrub that bore a blossom as delicate and fragrant as the lilac. Here and there, also, the acacia bloomed, while high over all the magnificent cucumber-tree reared aloft its wealth of snowy treasures— a perfect revelation of delight. On the outskirts of the desert, and even some distance into it, they came upon several tribes of the Bushmen and a sort of outcast tribe of the Bechuana known as the Baklahari. This latter tribe had been driven from its home by some of the more powerful and warlike divisions of its own people, who, doubtless acting under instigation from the Boers, had endeavored to capture the poor Baklahari and sell them as slaves. Though they were exceedingly ignorant and superstitious, almost leading the life of the wild beasts about them, Livingstone found both the Bushmen and the Baklahari kind-hearted and trusty.

The principal occupation of the Bushmen was hunting, in which they were assisted by a breed of dogs but little more miserable looking than themselves.

The Baklahari, having in their former home had some knowledge of the tillage of the soil, followed it here to a limited extent, raising melons, potatoes, and such tuberous plants as the sandy and sterile earth would grow. They, like the Bushmen, also engaged in hunting, but not to the same extent. The skins of the animals thus obtained were traded to the tribes farther east for tobacco, knives, pipes, dogs, spears, and such things. The highest condition of wealth known to these Bushmen was the possession of a cow, or even of a small-sized heifer; and happy indeed was he considered who could procure in the hunt skins sufficient to give in exchange for one of these animals! One question they were constantly putting to Livingstone was, " How many cows has your Queen?" On the answer to that depended their estimation of her position and importance.

The Bushmen were the very lowest class known to African society, if that term may with any propriety be used here. They were looked down upon by the more favored tribes as occupying a position not one whit above that of the dogs with which they hunted.

" No one seems to care for the poor Bushman's soul," said Livingstone; " and yet," he continues, " what a wonderful people they are! always merry and laughing, and never telling lies wantonly like the Bechuanas. They have, too, more of the appearance of worship than the Bechuanas."

How Livingstone's heart yearned over these poor outcast people! and how he desired to remain among them long enough to tell them of that loving Saviour in whose eyes all the world is equal! But he had neither the time nor the opportunity; besides, the language of these Bushmen was so strange and difficult it would have taken a year or more to comprehend it so as to make himself understood in the great truths he had to teach. Moreover, their home and their condition were such that he could not have brought his family to live among them. Still he did not altogether give them over. Many plans were formed for their future benefit and enlightenment. God would surely yet open up a way for some gleam of light to be brought to the poor Bushman's darkened soul.

The Bushmen had always been residents of the desert country: it gave them protection from the more powerful and hostile tribes. The great scarcity of water and the sparseness of vegetable life kept away all invaders; for how hostile soever might be their intentions toward the poor Bushmen, they usually thought too much of their own lives to risk them in so inhospitable a region. Besides, the

Bushman's skill in using the bow and poisoned arrow was well known and dreaded.

The Baklahari, in fleeing from their former home, had settled upon the edges of the desert for very much the same reasons as those that had prompted the Bushmen to choose it as their first and only abiding-place. Being assured of the peaceful intentions of the Baklahari, and doubtless having for them a "fellow feeling that made them wondrous kind," the Bushmen had made friends with them from the first, and they were now as one people.

The scarcity of water did not materially bother the Baklahari or the Bushmen; indeed, they had ingeniously provided against this to a certain degree by obtaining a large supply of water when they could, and hiding it in ostrich eggs in the sand. Strange to say, the water kept fresher in this manner than any other. But their real motive in thus concealing it in the sand was to keep it safe in case of a sudden invasion by any of their enemies.

Sometimes a great company of men, women, and children of the Bushmen and Baklahari tribes would go on a long journey to some road-side well or spring, where they would secure enough of the precious fluid to last them until they could make another similar excursion.

Livingstone had no trouble with either the Baklahari or the Bushmen, although he scarce understood a word of the language they spoke, especially of the latter. However, by various signs, and by the help of one of the guides he had with him, he managed to make his meaning for most of the time clear to them. His manner of treating them was to sit down quietly beside them and talk to them in a gentle and friendly way, giving to the men presents of tobacco and to the women beads or strips of gay-colored cloth. In this way ne often procured supplies of water and gained other needed assistance from them which no threatening or bullying could have forced them to give. Thus we see that it paid to be kind even to "a dog of a Bushman," as they were called. They took to Livingstone at once, and were constantly pressing him to partake of their hospitality. Again and again they tried to urge upon him portions of their scanty fare. Livingstone did not wish to wound their feelings by a refusal, but as this fare generally consisted of the uncooked carcass of a rat, a cat, or a jackal, we may well believe that he declined it as gently, yet firmly, as he could. The Bushmen were often seen by Livingstone and his party devouring with the greatest avidity the freshly killed bodies of such doubtful animals as we have mentioned without submitting them to the process of cooking.

After striking the desert, Livingstone and his friends found the journey not only difficult, but laborious and dangerous. Trials calculated to shake the stoutest nerves beset them on every side. The sand was not only heavy and hot to wade through, but the sun beat down upon their heads with such intensity that it seemed as if man and beast must succumb. They soon gave up trying to travel at all except in the early mornings and the first part of the nights. Even with this precaution their sufferings were great, for the supply of water ran low, and they had to go whole days with not more than a spoonful to each man to moisten his parched tongue. Once their water gave out entirely, and they were three days without a drop. It seemed then as if they must surely die. But as hard as it was for the men, it was worse for the poor animals, for they had been without water much longer. Their tortures were fearful to witness, their piteous moans and bellowings terrible to hear. Livingstone's tender heart was stirred to its depths, and if the others had listened to him the poor dumb, suffering creatures would have been put out of their misery on the spot. But had this been done, the men's own chances of getting out of the desert would have been very uncertain.

Late in the afternoon of the third day that they had been without water, when even the guide had almost abandoned hope of finding any, and every one of the little party felt that death could not be far away, they suddenly came upon a small mud-hole which a rhinoceros had made by rolling himself in what was apparently moist earth. The poor oxen rushed toward it frantically; they had to be beaten off. The dogs sprung forward to lap it up; it was necessary to kick them nearly senseless before they could be gotten away. Such scenes were especially harrowing to Livingstone, and he turned away from them sick at heart. Still he knew that these measures were often necessary in the preservation of more valuable life. That mud-hole apparently contained all the water within reach for eight oxen, ten dogs, twenty horses, and twenty-five men—only apparently, though, for the guide recognized the surrounding indications as favorable, and declared that there was plenty of water at hand. This assertion proved to be correct, as more water was presently found—not affording each man and beast the quantity needed, but enough to greatly appease their raging thirst.

Once the travelers were in such straits that only enough water could be procured for the men and horses, the poor oxen having to be sent back a four-days' journey in order to quench their thirst. Several days after this the party were again without water. For two days not a drop had passed the lips of one of the men, while the beasts went

7

twice as long with unslaked thirst. The poor creatures were
lowing piteously; their steps lagged, their tongues lolled
from their mouths, and it was difficult to urge them onward. Three of the men who had been sent forward to
discover water at length returned with the joyful cry of
" Metse! Metse!"—" Water! Water!" In proof of the
good news, they exhibited the mud-stains on their hands
and knees. Even the oxen seemed to understand the magic
word, and to catch the joyful excitement of the moment:
there was no further need to urge them forward—they went
gladly of their own accord, nearly upsetting the lumbering
old cart in their wild haste, and dragging the driver along
with them. A large pool of rain-water had been found,
and hedging it in, as if to give it a cooler and more delightful appearance, were all sorts of lush and rank-grow-
ing grasses. No wonder the famished oxen rushed toward
it with frantic delight! Livingstone thus speaks of the incident: " It does one's heart good to see the thirsty oxen
rush into a pool of delicious rain-water, as this was. In
they dash until the water is deep enough to be nearly level
with their throats; and there they stand, drawing slowly
in the long, refreshing mouthfuls until their formerly col-
lapsed sides distend as if they would burst. So much do
they imbibe that a sudden jerk, when they come out on the
bank, makes some of the water run out of their mouths;
but as they have been days without food too, they very
soon commence to graze, and of grass there was the greatest abundance all around."

The little company pushed bravely on. Though they
suffered much from the scarcity of water, there was no actual want of food. Sometimes, it is true, the supply ran
low; sometimes it was not of the most palatable quality;

but the men had their guns with them, and occasionally brought down an antelope or two, with now and then a gnu or a giraffe, which proved most acceptable. There were also many edible plants, which served to appease hunger until something more substantial could be found Among them were the leroshua, or scarlet cucumber; the mokuri, a bulbous plant somewhat in the shape of a potato; and the water-melon. The leroshua and the mokuri interested Livingstone very much. The former was a rather small plant, with long, narrow leaves, and a stalk about as thick as the stem of a common tobacco-pipe. This plant sprung from a root, the greater part of it being above ground, and in shape not unlike a cucumber, from which resemblance it took its name. The root was about six or seven inches in diameter, and varied in length from ten and twelve to sixteen and eighteen inches. It was covered with a rind-like substance, which on being removed displayed a "mass of cellular tissue filled with a fluid much like that of a young turnip." It also resembled the turnip in flavor, though not so juicy or so tender. The mokuri was a creeping plant, to which was attached a number of roots, some of them as large as a man's head. It had a flavor something like that of a sweet potato, though flatter, and a little bitter. It was not altogether unpalatable. The water-melon was often found in considerable quantities, especially where the earth was inclined to moisture: though not so large or so sweet as the cultivated melon, it was highly refreshing to the thirst-tortured travelers.

On one occasion, while passing over a sandy tract skirted by stunted trees of the acacia variety, Livingstone's curiosity was aroused by seeing several of his men squatted down in different directions, and all industriously digging in the sand. Inquiring into the matter, he learned that they were hunting for a large caterpillar whose habit it was to bury itself in the sand near these trees, and in the leaves of which it found its food. The men already had a number of these furry creatures, which they afterward roasted and ate with great relish as an extra delicacy. They regarded it as a lack of taste in Livingstone and his white friends that caused them to forego the caterpillars.

Late one afternoon, when the travelers had been about three weeks on the way, as they were journeying over one of the sandiest and most trying parts of the whole course, and men and animals alike were tortured with the heat and nearly dead with thirst, Mr. Oswell who was some distance in advance, suddenly threw up his hat and gave a loud shout. Again and again he repeated it, accompanying it with such wild gesticulations as made the natives who were the nearer to him think he was going mad, and rush to Livingstone for protection. Livingstone himself looked with some amazement upon his friend's extraordinary behavior. Directly Mr. Oswell began crying at the top of his voice: "The lake! the lake! Come and see!" Rushing to the eminence he occupied, they all beheld what did seem a most magnificent lake stretching away for miles. The picture was perfect. In the soft rays of the setting sun the water seemed to catch and retain myriads of bright sparkles, which were in turn reflected in every direction. Even the natives and the dogs were deceived, and rushed forward to leap into the water. That it was but a deception, and not a lake, was soon discovered, greatly to the chagrin of the whole party, with the exception of Livingstone and the guides, who knew that the lake could not be so near. What they had seen proved to be a mirage, caused by the sun's rays shining upon a vast salt-lick covered with incrustations of lime. The lake was nearly three hundred miles away. A little farther on they found some water, and, greatly refreshed, continued their journey till some hours in the night. The explorers were often deceived by these mirages—even Livingstone and the guides occasionally, though they never once supposed them to be the lake, but only pools of water.

Near the close of the afternoon of July 4th they came to the banks of a veritable river. Their shouts of joy drew around them crowds of natives, who stared at them curiously, and not without alarm, for they thought them mad, as the natives of the party had previously thought of Mr. Oswell. They were finally reassured, however, and proved to be very friendly, assisting the travelers in every way they could by offering information and supplies. This river was the Zouga, a deep and beautiful stream with a placid yet swiftly moving current. The natives told Livingstone, what he had previously suspected, that the Zouga flowed into Lake Ngami, and all they would have to do in order to reach the lake was to follow the course of the river.

The journey along the banks of the Zouga was delightful. At almost every step the travelers came upon a sight both novel and wonderful. As to the river itself, it may perhaps best be described in Livingstone's own enthusiastic words: "It was glorious! I never saw any thing more grand. It reminded me somewhat of my own lovely Clyde, though many times more beautiful, I must confess." All along the low, level banks grew tall, magnificent trees, many of them covered with fruits of various kinds. The trunks of some of these gigantic monarchs measured from

SOME INHABITANTS OF THE ZOUGA JUNGLES.

(102)

sixty and sixty-five to seventy feet in circumference. On one of them Livingstone found growing a fruit over a foot in length and from three to four inches in diameter. In shape it was not unlike the banana, though it had a more vivid coloring. Another group of trees presented the compact appearance of a mass of granite, and were identical with granite in their hue.

Everywhere grew beautiful wild flowers and lush sweet grasses. The birds sung in the boughs and the butterflies flew hither and thither sipping sweets. Away up among the tallest branches of the trees monkeys sat and chattered to each other, or mischievously threw nuts at the saucy parrots, who screamed back at them, and shook their brilliant plumage defiantly. Altogether it was a picture to ravish the eye, and to delight the heart, making it feel how good is God and how beautiful the world he has made. To the sun-scorched and weary travelers, just from their toilsome march across the desert, it was indeed as a glimpse of paradise.

After traveling two or three days they came upon another large, fine stream that flowed into the river Zouga from the north. Livingstone inquired of the natives whence it came, and he was told, " O from a country full of rivers! so many, in fact, no one can tell their number, and full of large trees." It was then that Livingstone received the first strong confirmation of his belief that Central Africa was far from being the sandy and barren plateau it had hitherto been represented, even by the geographers. As firm as was this belief, still firmer was the decision formed with the coming of this convincing testimony in regard to the " country of rivers "—a decision that governed and directed Livingstone's future course. He would find out just what kind

of a country Central Africa was. If such as the natives
represented it, and as he had himself believed, a land "flowing with rivers," then what a glorious prospect for opening
up, across the very heart of the continent, a grand highway
of commerce and travel! No further need then for it to be
a land unvisited, dreaded, and unknown! No longer any
necessity for its inhabitants to remain shut out from the
light and knowledge of civilized life! When routes of
travel were opened up, difficulties made less difficult and
dangers less dangerous, others besides himself would come
—come with the pure intention to instruct and to benefit. O what a glorious day for this heathen land, when
its people should both know and be known! This dream
so impressed Livingstone that even after he came to the
magnificent lake, for a sight of which he had braved the
terrors of the desert, it failed to awaken in him any thing
like the emotions he had anticipated.

They reached Lake Ngami on the 1st of August, just
two months from the time of beginning the journey. The
lake was all that it had been represented, and more. As
they looked upon its beautiful expanse of waters they could
detect no horizon, so they concluded that it must be many
miles across. It afterward proved to be fully a hundred
miles in circumference and some twenty to twenty-five miles
in width. It was about two thousand feet above the level
of the sea, from which it was distant some eight hundred
miles. The only objection that Livingstone had to it was
that it seemed to be too shallow in many parts for navigable purposes. However, it was a grand sheet of water, and
it was something to have discovered it, and with Messrs.
Oswell and Murray to have been the first white men doubtless that ever gazed upon it.

On their way back home they had more time and more inclination to make observations of the country along the banks of the Zouga. Going up, their minds had been too much filled with thoughts of the wonderful lake, and with impatience to reach it, to make a long stop anywhere else. But now they journeyed more leisurely, and often lingered for days at a time to mingle with the natives. The people took a great fancy to Livingstone, and tried to get him to stay with them altogether. They feasted the party on every good thing they could set before them. At these entertainments they had a way of forming a circle and dancing around with loud songs in praise of the river Zouga, which they thought the noblest and grandest river in the world. They told Livingstone that those who came to look upon the Zouga never cared to go back again. Even the " messenger sent in haste " often became a permanent sojourner.

Livingstone preached in several places as he went along, and the people came in crowds to hear him. Doubtless many precious seed were thus left to spring up by the wayside. He says of the Bakoba, one of the tribes along the Zouga, and among whom he remained a week or more preaching and teaching: "The Bakoba are a fine, frank race of men, and seem to understand the message better than any people to whom I have spoken on divine subjects for the first time." He greatly enjoyed riding on the river in the canoes of the Bakoba, which were quite ingeniously contrived out of the trunks of single trees, nicely finished and gracefully shaped. He enjoyed the fishing, too, with all the relish of a boy on his first holiday in the country. When his friends, Messrs. Oswell and Murray, once tried to joke him about his enthusiasm, he exclaimed, with a twinkle of humor: "O you must remember that I have been long in a parched-up land!" Some of the fish caught in the Zouga weighed nearly a hundred pounds, many of them as much as fifty and sixty. It often took eight or ten men to haul in one of these larger ones.

Livingstone was much struck by the great fecundity of animal life everywhere visible in this wonderful region. The river fairly teemed with fish. They could be seen at any time leaping in the water. They even approached the banks in great shoals. Elephants, zebras, giraffes, water-bucks, hippopotami, and many other large, fine animals were also found in such abundance that it was no trouble to kill several of them on every hunt. The soil was highly productive, yielding all kinds of vegetables and fruits with but little cultivation, often without any at all. Along the shores of the river Livingstone found wild indigo growing in great quantities. The natives raised two kinds of cotton, which they made into cloth for garments of various descriptions, dyeing it with the indigo and with a bark that gave it a tinge of yellow, as copperas would have done. Altogether it was a magnificent and wonderful country; and the more Livingstone saw of it the more he became enamored with it, and the brighter grew his dream in regard to it.

After safely passing through the desert on their return, the party reached Kolobeng in the autumn of 1849, having been absent a little more than five months in all.

CHAPTER VIII.

HOW THE NEWS OF THE DISCOVERY OF THE NGAMI AND ZOUGA
WAS RECEIVED IN ENGLAND—THE ENDEAVOR TO REACH THE
GREAT CHIEF, SEBITUANE—SECOND ATTEMPT—MRS. LIVING-
STONE AND HER CHILDREN OF THE PARTY—FAILURE OF THE
UNDERTAKING—RETURN TO KOLOBENG—DASTARDLY RAID OF
THE BOERS—THIRD AND SUCCESSFUL ATTEMPT TO REACH SE-
BITUANE—INCIDENTS BY THE WAY—SEBITUANE'S DEATH.

THE news of the discovery of the lake, the river, and
the wonderful country adjacent was at once communicated by Livingstone to the Royal Geographical Society
of London. All England was surprised and delighted:
the name of Livingstone was now on every tongue. Even
the Queen expressed her gratification, and awarded the explorer twenty-five guineas.

In the spring of 1850 Livingstone determined to undertake another journey into the lake country, for the purpose
of making further geographical explorations, and to engage
in such mission work as he could. He had for some time
thought of removing from Kolobeng to a field of labor farther north. He knew that he could not always remain
among the Bakwains, since that would not be just to the
other darkened minds awaiting the coming of the light.
Besides, the station at Kolobeng was getting along so well
under the care of Sechele and the native teachers he felt
that he might safely leave it, for a year or two at least.

Previous to his first journey to Lake Ngami, Livingstone
had purposed trying to reach the country of Sebituane, be-

tween whom and Sechele there was the most cordial relations. Sebituane was a mighty chief, with a large following that made him both admired and feared throughout a
vast extent of territory. Thus Livingstone felt that if he
could secure Sebituane for a friend and ally, it would be
productive of great good in his missionary labors and of
much assistance in pushing his geographical researches
through the country. As it was, he had fixed upon Sebituane's head village as the point at which to plant his next
mission station; and he was therefore much disappointed
when the treachery of Lechulatebe prevented him from
reaching the great chief on his first visit to the lake region.

Lechulatebe will be remembered as the chief of the Ba-
tauána, and as the one who had sent messengers to Livingstone previous to his leaving Kolobeng, with the request that
he would visit his domain. From the extreme cordiality and
insistence of the message, the travelers expected handsome
treatment at Lechulatebe's hands. But it seems that he was
a shrewd and covetous negro, whose real design was to secure
some of the presents he had heard Livingstone was in the
habit of bestowing upon the chiefs of the different tribes
through which he passed. When he found out that Livingstone wanted to take up his residence with Sebituane for
awhile, he stoutly opposed it, for several reasons. Chief of
these was that Sebituane was an enemy of his, and much
hated on account of his great power and popularity. Lechulatebe therefore had no idea of letting Livingstone reach
Sebituane, and perhaps furnish him with fire-arms, show
him their use, and teach him the many tricks of battle
which the white men knew. In that event, Sebituane
would become a more formidable enemy than ever. So he
not only refused to let Livingstone have guides and boats,

but sent men to guard the river to prevent the missionary and his party from crossing, in case they attempted to go upon their own responsibility.

Not to be outdone, and with his usual courage and boldness, Livingstone began the construction of a boat or raft out of the great quantities of rotten wood floating in the river. This he did at the imminent risk of his life, for he soon afterward found out that the Zouga was infested with alligators. However, the wood proved to be so rotten, and the other difficulties so insurmountable, that he abandoned his present intention of pushing on to Sebituane; but that he had not abandoned the purpose altogether the sequel will show.

Thus it came about that, on making his arrangements for this second journey into the lake country, Livingstone's determination to reach Sebituane was fixed, and he made up his mind that he would succeed if it lay within human power. On this second trip he was accompanied by his wife and children—the latter now three in number—Sechele, and twenty of his most faithful Bakwains. The party left Kolobeng in April, 1850. It was with many misgivings that Livingstone saw his delicate wife and tender little ones start out on this long and fearful journey across the desert; but he could not bear the idea of leaving them behind, especially as he did not know when he would return to Kolobeng. So, commending them to the keeping of that great and loving Father who takes note of the tiniest bird's flight, Livingstone bravely set forth.

The difficulties in the way on the second journey were many and great. Again and again Livingstone felt that he would be obliged to retrace his steps to Kolobeng. Hearing various reports of the deadly ravages of the tsetse fly,

whose bite is so fatal to oxen, the party had to choose a
route quite different from the one gone over the preceding
year; consequently, they often lost their way, and were in
great straits besides. The sufferings of Mrs. Livingstone
and the children were intense, and Livingstone felt that
he could not bear to witness them. When they struck the
banks of the Zouga, it was at a point where the trees were
so thick that the men had to cut down numbers of them to
let the wagons pass through. The journey at this stage was
therefore both slow and laborious. But at last the shores
of the lake were reached. The intense delight with which
his children hailed the sight of this wonderful sheet of water deeply touched Livingstone. Tears came to his eyes as
he heard their shouts of childish joy. When he took them
upon the lake in a boat, their spirits nearly ran away with
them. They could scarcely get enough of it. "They took
to playing in it as naturally as ducklings," he wrote, "while
as to the paddling, it was the greatest fun they had ever
known." And no wonder, poor little things! This was
the first body of water of any consequence they had ever
seen.

At the lake were found a party of Englishmen who had
been stricken with fever. One of them had already died,
and doubtless others would have died but for the timely
ministrations of Dr. Livingstone and his gentle wife. Just
as the fever had considerably abated among them, and Livingstone, with Sechele's aid, was preparing to enter the
country of Sebituane, two of his children were stricken
with the dread malady, and for days lay at the point of
death. Finding that the whole lake region was exposed to
the scourge, Livingstone decided to return to Kolobeng,
there to remain until the country should be entirely free

from the fever. This he did as soon as the children were able to stand the fatigue of travel.

While staying at the lake Livingstone's friend and fellow-traveler of the year before, Mr. Oswell, had appeared among them. They were rejoiced to see each other again. Oswell had remained at the lake to hunt elephants. His courage in hunting them without dogs excited the wonder and admiration of the natives. But high as was their opinion of Oswell's bravery, it was even higher in regard to Livingstone's. They believed him to be the coolest and most courageous man they had ever seen. They often said to him: " If you were not a missionary, you would be just like Oswell. You would not hunt with dogs either, and you would bring down just as many elephants as he, if not more; neither would you be afraid of any thing."

On Livingstone's return from the lake he found bad news awaiting him. During his absence the Boers had made good their long-standing threats against Sechele, and entering his village had killed a number of his people, and carried away two hundred children into captivity. They had also plundered the chief's and Livingstone's houses, cutting up the latter's few articles of wooden furniture, smashing his stoneware, and tearing his clothes and those of his wife and children into shreds. But worst of all, they had so mutilated his books and manuscripts as to render them utterly worthless. All the literary work of three years, including his journals, was thus ruthlessly destroyed. This was a severe blow to Livingstone; but when he heard the poor women weeping over their dead and bewailing the children carried into captivity, he thought how much worse it might have been for him, and thanked God that he had escaped so lightly.

In the early part of April, 1851, Livingstone started on his third, last, and only successful expedition to meet Sebituane. On this journey he was accompanied by his family and his old friend, Mr. Oswell. Livingstone often speaks with touching gratitude of the generosity and kindness shown by this fellow-countryman of his. A number of Bushmen, employed by Mr. Oswell specially for the purpose, attended them as an advance guard. Their duty was to go ahead of the party, clearing dense places and smoothing rough ones as much as possible, but principally to dig wells and search out pasturage for the cattle. In this way the dreary passage of the desert was greatly alleviated.

Many of the great plains on the route were covered with stretches of grass, though often not having one stunted tree. In these places ostriches were seen in large numbers. Being very shy, they would of course run off at first sight of our travelers. It was therefore extremely difficult to get a close view of them, while a shot at one was well-nigh impossible. The moment the travelers showed themselves the ostrich would flee, and all the game in the neighborhood would take the alarm and run with him. The Bushmen, however, had an ingenious way of getting ahead of the bird that was amusing to the concealed lookers-on. It interested Livingstone very much, and his children were perfectly carried away watching the strange maneuvers. Whitening his legs with a preparation taken along for that purpose, and fastening across his shoulders a feathered saddle made of the plumage of the birds, the Bushman would start off, carrying the stuffed head of an ostrich in one hand and his bow and poisoned arrows in the other. Thus equipped, he presented a striking likeness to the great, stalking bird he was ready to beguile. Cautiously moving along, the "human bird" would make a feint of picking away at the grass, just as the real ostrich was doing. Then he would turn his head to one side, to gain a better idea of the position of the real bird. Next he would shake out his saddle of feathers, with a movement that ought surely to have put the genuine ostrich to the blush—it was so perfect an imitation. Then, circling around slowly for a few moments, he would suddenly start into a brisk walk, which gradually grew faster until he struck off at the ostrich's well-known long, swinging trot. In this manner the wily hunter soon brought himself within shooting distance of the unsuspecting bird; and before the latter could discover the fraud, or realize his danger, whizz! would go the arrow, and the next instant he would be in his death-throes!

Sometimes the male ostrich, which is of a more wary and suspicious nature than the female, would turn and give chase to this strange-looking bird; and the situation would become extremely dangerous for the hunter, unless he kept his wits about him. If he wished to kill the bird, his one object when pursued by him was to keep him from catching the scent; failing in this, the fraud would be exposed. On the other hand, if he wished to preserve his own life when the bird came uncomfortably near, his only safeguard was either to "get to windward," as the hunters say, and let the bird catch the scent, or throw off the saddle of feathers and stand revealed in his proper form. But occasionally his great anxiety to bring down the valuable bird would lead him to neglect the precautions until too late, when a stroke from the powerful wing would almost instantly deprive him of life.

That the Bushmen, in spite of the many drawbacks and

8

THE WILY BIRD IN HIS NATIVE BUSH.

(114)

the patience and perseverance necessary, were very successful in their slaughter of the ostriches, Livingstone had seen
the evidence in the great quantities of feathers sold to passing traders. As the ostriches have only a few feathers on
the wings and tail, he knew it took a large number of the
birds to produce the plumes the Bushmen annually collected. Our travelers found the Bushmen of the utmost
service in the journey across the desert. Indeed, it is questionable if they would have survived the perils, deprivations, and sufferings that beset them, had it not been for
their trusty advance guard, who, among other things, could
discover water when for miles about them seemed to stretch
a burning and sandy waste. Yet, with all the precautions
which the generous and manly Oswell had taken, a calamity that nearly proved fatal to all befell the party when
they were about two-thirds of the distance across the Kalahari. In some way Shobo, their guide, got them widely
separated from their Bushmen guard. They found themselves in one of the driest and most desolate parts of the
desert. For miles and miles there was not a particle of
verdure, not even a scraggy clump of the hardy karoo
bush; no sign of life anywhere; no sound, not so much as
the lonesome cry of a jackal, or the forbidding hiss of a
serpent. What meager tufts of grass they chanced upon
crumbled to powder in their hands, so well had the scorching heat done its work. The burning sun seemed to be
licking up the blood from their veins, and to their eyes the
glare was well-nigh unendurable. Men and animals suffered not only from the heat, but from thirst; for the supply of water had given out—there was not a drop even to
moisten the tongues of the little children, who lay in the
bottom of the wagon, either begging piteously for water or

too weak to do more than lie and gasp, with their blackened tongues protruding from their mouths.

It surely was most distressing to the strong husband and
father to see his delicate wife and babies undergoing such
horrible suffering.   His own throat was parched and burning, his own tongue swollen and blackened; but with prayer
after prayer to God for succor, he toiled on beside the wagon.
The poor beasts, whose piteous bellowings added to the horrors and distress of the scene, staggered from side to side as
though they would fall to the ground.   For four days they
were absolutely without water.   Livingstone says of this
dreadful time: "The thought of our children perishing before our eyes was terrible; it would almost have been a relief to have been reproached with being the entire cause of
the catastrophe, but not one syllable of upbraiding was uttered by their mother, though the tearful eye told the agony
within."

Happily, on the morning of the fifth day the Bushmen
found them; and as they brought a supply of the precious
fluid for the want of which life had come so near being for-
feited, the greater sufferings of the wanderers were allayed.

Finally, after enduring much additional fatigue, and en-
countering many more hardships—though none so dreadful
as that awful time when they had gone four days without
water—they came to the banks of the Mahabe, a river that
flows into the Tamunakle.   As by following the banks of
the latter stream they hoped to reach Sebituane's domains,
it was with joy that they came upon the Mahabe, knowing
that its junction with the Tamunakle could not be very far
away.   But before reaching the banks of the Mahabe they
had made the acquaintance of a visitor whose presence
would in time have a fatal effect.   This was the much-

heard-of and long-dreaded tsetse fly, whose bite is so de-
structive to the life of horse, oxen, and dog.   Upon man
and the wild animals, strange to say, it has no effect; in
fact, it never even offers to molest them.   The tsetse is not
much larger than the common house-fly, though somewhat
different in shape, and considerably so in color.   It resem-
bles the honey-bee, having the same deep-brown coat, with
yellow bars across the under part of the body.   Its peculiar
buzz, very much like that of the bumble-bee, is never forgotten by the traveler who once hears it.

Livingstone did not at first think that his oxen were
much injured, as he could see no signs of the evil effects of
the tsetse bites: he had yet to learn, through dear experience, that these effects come on gradually, rendering it all
the more terrible to the poor brutes who have the deadly
poison in their veins.   It is several days after the animal
is bitten before it shows the first symptoms, which consist of
a watery gleam about the eye and an unpleasant discharge
from the nose.   Then is noticed a constant shivering sensation, or a nervous drawing together of the coat at regular
intervals, principally along the backbone, as though the
animal was suffering from cold.   A swelling next appears
under the jaws; and although the ox, or horse, can go on
grazing as usual, he grows poorer and poorer, as if he did
not receive any nourishment whatever from the food swallowed.   Finally, he becomes so emaciated and weak that he
dies from sheer exhaustion.   It is generally a month from
the time the animal is bitten until death ensues.

Reaching the banks of the Chobe River, which borders
upon Sebituane's domains, our travelers received the pleasing intelligence that Sebituane, hearing of their proposed
visit, was coming to meet them.   He had already traveled

over a hundred miles from his capital city to do honor to
the brave missionary of whose noble labors among the different tribes he had heard so much. When the news of his
approach became known, he was but twenty miles away,
at the village of Manuku, and anxiously awaiting their
arrival.

In a little while the meeting with Sebituane took place.
His greeting was all that they could have wished it, and he
himself all that they had expected, and much more. Almost his first words to them showed the great, warm heart
beating under the leopard-skin cloak. Noticing the condition of Livingstone's cattle, he exclaimed: "Too bad! Too
bad! Your cattle are all bitten by the tsetse, and will surely die! They are nearly dead now, poor things! But
never mind; I have plenty of oxen, and will give you all
you need."

Sebituane was unquestionably a great chief—"the best
specimen of native manhood I ever met," said Livingstone
in speaking of him afterward. All the way they had heard
Sebituane's praises sounded. Even his enemies had given
expression to their admiration for his wonderful powers;
but the highest testimony came from those he had befriended.
"He is invincible; he is never conquered in battle," said
those against whom he had fought. "He is good; he has
a *heart*," gratefully declared those to whom his bounty had
been extended.

In person the great chief was tall and wiry, with a
well-shaped head for one of his race; a kindly, pleasant expression; and fine, intelligent eyes. His bearing was frank
and manly—quite unusual in a savage.

Sebituane had not been born a chief. He was originally
from the country around Kuruman, where his many excel-

lent traits had won for him a following of stanch admirers. Having some trouble with his people on account of his independent ways, he had left his tribe, and with a few sturdy adherents had boldly cut his way through the entire Bechuana country. As he went along so many attached themselves to him that by the time he had entered the territory on the other side of the Kalahari he had twice the number of his own tribe. A desperate struggle ensued between him and Mosilikatse, a renowned Matebele chief, for the possession of all that magnificent stretch of country lying between the Zouga and the Zambesi. In the end Sebituane was triumphant, which was the means of securing to him a stronger following than ever. He was now deemed the greatest chief in all that section, dreaded even by the terrible Mosilikatse, the oppressor of the Bechuanas.

It would seem impossible to believe that a warlike chief such as Sebituane could have so warm a heart, so benevolent a nature; yet so it was. When he went into battle he was but following out the impulses of his savage nature and obeying the mandates of his savage training—since through that nature and that training he had been taught to look upon courage and success in war as the highest marks of distinction, the most admirable attributes of uncivilized royalty. He saw no cruelty, no barbarity in such a course—only praise and renown; for he had not been enlightened as to the gentler and more peaceful teachings of civilized humanity, or the higher and nobler aims of Christianity. What he might have been under more favorable opportunities was shown by the manly traits underlying his whole character. He was gentle and generous, benevolent to the poor, and honest even in his dealings with enemies.

His hospitality and genuine kindness of heart were proverbial throughout the whole river country. Says Livingstone: "He was adored by all with whom he came in contact." The poor of the different tribes were constantly coming to him for assistance. Not once was such an applicant turned away. "When a party of poor men came to his town to sell their hoes or hides," Livingstone further adds, "no matter how ungainly they might be, he soon knew them all. A company of these indigent strangers, sitting far apart from the Makololo around the chief, would be surprised to see him come alone to them, and, sitting down, inquire if they were hungry. On receiving an affirmative reply, he would order an attendant to bring meal, milk, and honey; and mixing these in their sight, in order to remove any suspicious from their minds, he would make them feast upon a lordly dish perhaps for the first time in their lives. Delighted beyond measure with his affability and liberality, they felt their hearts warm toward him, and gave him all the information in their power. As he never allowed a party of strangers, servants included, to go away without giving them a present, his praises were sounded far and wide."

Sebituane was delighted at the confidence which Livingstone had shown by bringing his wife and children. He at once promised him a permanent settlement in his domains, authority to go anywhere he pleased, and an escort for all expeditions he cared to make.

It had been the greatest dream of Sebituane's life to be on intimate and friendly terms with the white men. Unlike the majority of his savage brethren, he had the highest opinion of the superior condition and abilities of the white race, especially of the English. No wonder, then, that he hailed Livingstone's coming among his people with such hearty pleasure, for it gave to his dream a brighter and a more beautiful radiance—the radiance of reality. Livingstone, too, looked upon this meeting with Sebituane as the dawning of a new and auspicious era, both as regarded his missionary labors and his geographical researches. With Sebituane's powerful protection ever about him, he would be enabled to command a wider and more inviting extent of territory than any he had yet known. But alas! it was not to be. In less than two weeks after their meeting the great chief was stricken down with inflammation of the lungs, from which he died in a few days. He lived just long enough to hear Livingstone preach one sermon, the Sunday after his arrival in the country. This was the only proclamation of "glad tidings" poor Sebituane ever heard. On the Sunday afternoon that he died, Livingstone went to see him, carrying his little son Robert. "Come near," said Sebituane as soon as he recognized Livingstone, "and see if I am any longer a man. No, I am not. I feel that I am not. I am undone! Alas! is me; I can no longer even move myself as I might wish." He seemed fully sensible of his dangerous condition, and realized that death might come at any moment; but he was calm and brave through it all.

Taking the hand of the dying chief in his, Livingstone knelt by the couch of skins, and endeavored to speak comforting words—to tell him of the hope there is after death for all who trust. But the pall of darkness that had so long covered poor Sebituane's soul was too heavy to be lifted in a moment. It would have taken months perhaps for him even to have begun to see clearly, and now there were but a few hours. One of the native doctors, who was standing near, catching the word "death," turned upon

Livingstone, demanding: "Why do you speak of death? Sebituane will never die. It is not for such as he to leave this world where he is so much needed. Do not say the word to him again, lest you disturb him." Thus did they believe, these adoring people of his, that their great chief could not be otherwise than immortal—so mighty were his deeds, so matchless his powers.

Noting the ominous expression on the faces around him, and catching many murmurs of disapproval, Livingstone refrained, though sorely against his will, from speaking further to Sebituane in regard to death, "fearing," as he adds, "that if I had persisted the impression would have been produced that by speaking to him of death I wished him to die." For the same reason Livingstone was also afraid to give Sebituane medical attention; for if he failed to cure, he would assuredly be charged with killing the chief. Then the people in the first agony of their loss would doubtless have put him and his family to death. It surely must have been one of the most trying and painful experiences through which Livingstone had ever been called to pass. Had he been alone in the country, he would have faced the situation unflinchingly, and have fearlessly ministered to the needs of Sebituane's body and soul. But there were his gentle wife and helpless little ones to think of, and for their sakes he drew back. So, all that he could do was to offer up a silent yet fervent prayer to God in Sebituane's behalf. While the words were yet rushing from Livingstone's overcharged heart, Sebituane raised himself upon his elbow, and glancing tenderly at Livingstone's little son, said to one of his attendants: "Take Robert to Maunku [one of his wives], and tell her to give him some milk." These words, expressing kindly thought for another, were the last the great chief ever uttered. Surely so brave, so beautiful a soul was not shut out from the light of its Father's mansions, because of the very darkness that had so long shrouded it here.

Thus Sebituane died almost within view of the great spiritual light that was about to dawn upon him. This seemed to distress Livingstone more than any thing else. Constantly before him was the reproach: "I surely did not do all that I could have done for poor Sebituane. There were many opportunities I might have embraced even in that short space of time. O if I had but known that death was so near, would I not have utilized every moment, nay every second, in preparing him for the end?" His lament over Sebituane, when he saw the great chief lying dead before him, was as touching in its overwhelming tenderness and agonized pathos as David's lament for Absalom: " Poor Sebituane, my heart bleeds for thee; and what would I not do for thee now? I will weep for thee to the day of my death! Little didst thou think, when in the visit of the white man thou sawest the long-cherished desire of years accomplished, that the sentence of death had gone forth. Thou thoughtest that thou shouldst procure a weapon from the white man which would shield thee from the attacks of the fierce Matebele; but a more deadly dart than theirs was aimed at thee; and though thou couldst well ward off a dart—none ever better—thou didst not see that of the king of terrors. I will weep for thee, my brother, and I would cast forth my sorrows in despair for thy condition. But I know that thou wilt receive no injustice whither thou art gone. Shall not the Judge of all the earth do right? I leave thee to him. Alas, alas, Sebituane! I might have said more to him. God forgive me, and free me from blood-guiltiness! "

CHAPTER IX.

MAMOCHISANE SUCCEEDS SEBITUANE—HER GRACIOUSNESS TO LIV-
INGSTONE—LIVINGSTONE AND OSWELL MAKE A SHORT JOURNEY
OF EXPLORATION—DISCOVERY OF THE ZAMBESI—THE CHARM-
ING RIVER COUNTRY—THE ABUNDANCE OF ANIMAL LIFE—LIV-
INGSTONE'S TENDER HEART—A PATHETIC SCENE.

SEBITUANE was succeeded in the chieftainship by
his daughter, Mamochisane. She was a very intelligent and kindly disposed young savage, with many of her
father's nobler traits of character, though with little of his
governing ability.

Livingstone received permission from Mamochisane to
visit any part of her domain he desired. She also kindly
proposed to furnish him with an escort at any time. Leaving his wife and children under Mamochisane's protection,
Livingstone, with his friend Mr. Oswell and twenty of the
Makololo men—as Sebituane's people were known—began
a short exploration into the country. They took a north-
easterly direction, and proceeded toward the town of Linyanti, on the Chobe River, about one hundred and thirty
miles distant. Linyanti was the capital city of the Makololo, and was the point from which Sebituane had started
to meet Livingstone. Passing through Linyanti, Livingstone and his companions kept on north-eastwardly, and on
the third day of August came upon a magnificent river,
right in the heart of the continent, and flowing, as they
afterward discovered, "almost from sea to sea." This was
the Zambesi. known by the natives of that section as the

Sesheke. Although it was in the dry season, the breadth
of the river was not less than three hundred yards at any
point—at many places it was more than six hundred yards.
The current was very deep and strong. Livingstone's ex-
clamation on beholding this majestic stream was, "How
glorious! How magnificent! How beautiful!" while Oswell enthusiastically declared, "Not even in India have I
seen so fine a river!" The natives told them that, like the
Nile, the Zambesi had its annual overflows, often rising
twenty to twenty-five feet, and flooding the lands for fifteen
miles on each side of the stream. When Livingstone's party
were crossing, the current, that leaped about in miniature
waves, lifted up their canoes and made them "roll beautifully." Livingstone thought it one of the prettiest sights he
had ever beheld. The scenery along the banks was grand
beyond description. Livingstone feelingly declared that it
was even more beautiful than his own firths of Forth and
Clyde, of which it forcibly reminded him. So deeply did
it impress him that he felt the tears welling as his thoughts
wandered back to his home so far away in "Bonnie Scotland." But he manfully restrained the emotions, and with
a great effort kept back the tears; "for if I had not," he
humorously remarks, "the old man who was conducting us
over might have said, 'What on earth are you blubbering
for? Afraid of the crocodiles, eh?'" With such light
bits of digressive humor as this Livingstone often sought
to hide his deeper feelings.

In writing to his brother Charles about the discovery of
the Zambesi, Livingstone rapturously affirmed that it
was the first *real* river he had ever seen. Again and again
he heard of most wonderful rapids some miles above and of
great water-falls below. Both he and Oswell felt a keen

desire to go on a voyage of discovery in each direction, and would doubtless have done so had not their time been limited. Livingstone's great object in coming to Linyanti and the country surrounding it had been to find a healthy and convenient locality in which to plant a mission station, and he felt that he could undertake no further expedition until that vexed question was satisfactorily settled. On a future visit, however, Livingstone beheld the great Victoria Falls, named by him in honor of his Queen, and which is looked upon by many as his most important geographical discovery.

Livingstone and Oswell found the country around the Zambesi, as it had been about the Zouga, extremely prolific of animal life. The forests abounded with game of every description, and the river with fish of various kinds. All along the banks were the most magnificent trees they had ever seen, among them numbers of the " machabell-tree," that bore quantities of a large yellow fruit, something like the plum in its nature, only much larger, with enormous stones, and very refreshing in quality. The leaves of this tree were exceedingly beautiful and glossy, and the tree itself presented a most charming sight. It was the " favorite food of the elephant," as evidences of a recent visit from these beasts were soon discovered. Indeed, so numerous were the elephants in this region that it was not uncommon to see them in vast droves even in the close neighborhood of the villages. The natives made constant war upon them, a party of hunters often bringing down eight or ten of them on one hunt; but with all this slaughter they did not seem to decrease. To obtain the valuable tusks was of course the hunter's principal object; though the heart of the beast, when cooked after a style peculiar to the native African, was a great delicacy. The Makolo-

A DISASTROUS ELEPHANT HUNT.

(127)

lo enjoyed an extensive trade in ivory, getting in exchange
for it beads, tobacco, pipes, knives, and other similar articles. Buffaloes, elands, water-bucks, koodoos, rhinoceroses,
and many other animals, abounded; but the elephant was
the most coveted reward of the hunter's efforts. Sometimes
these elephant hunts would end most disastrously. The infuriated beasts, maddened by the pain of the spear-wounds,
would charge upon their assailants, trampling them with
their huge feet or tossing the life out of them by one swing
of their mighty trunk.

The lion, that terrible king of beasts, was often seen; but
he did not terrify the natives, as he generally does those unused to meeting him. Livingstone learned from the Makololo many things in regard to the lion he had not known
before. It has been a popular belief that the lion would
always make the first attack upon a man, even if the latter
showed no disposition to molest him. Livingstone, with all
his experience in the country, was of this opinion too; but
the Makololo soon convinced him that the lion rarely attacks a man first. However, this is true only during the
day-time, or on a clear moonlight night. On a dark night
there is much danger, unless the hunter or traveler can be
surrounded by a glare of light. It was also generally supposed that the lion was the master of every other beast of
the forest. The Makololo showed Livingstone many proofs
to the contrary. In the rhinoceros, elephant, and buffalo
the lion had more than his match, and often his equal in
the giraffe—one blow from the small but powerful hoof of
the latter animal being all that was necessary to crush in
the lion's head as though it were an egg-shell. The lion
himself seemed aware of his danger from these animals, and
would never be seen willingly near either of them.

Close to one of the villages where Livingstone and his party stopped there was a beautiful ford, to which the buffaloes went in great herds to drink. Occasionally a lion would go thither. Once Livingstone saw a medium-sized buffalo bull catch an unusually large and strong-looking lion, and kill him outright by one toss of the horns. At the mere sight of an elephant the lion would often turn and flee; though sometimes, doubtless when suffering the pangs of hunger, he would creep upon and devour a young calf that had happened to stray from its mother.

Livingstone gives us this picture of a near acquaintance with the lion: "When a lion is met in the day-time, a circumstance by no means unfrequent to travelers in these parts, if preconceived notions do not lead them to expect something very noble or majestic, they will see merely an animal somewhat larger than the biggest dog they ever saw, and partaking very strongly of the canine features; the face is not much like the usual drawings of a lion, the nose being much prolonged like a dog's; not exactly like such as the painters paint it—though they might learn better at the Zoological Gardens—their ideas of majesty being usually shown by making their lions' faces like old women in night-caps. When encountered in the day-time, the lion stands a second or two, gazing, then turns slowly around, and walks as slowly away for a dozen paces, looking over his shoulder; then he begins to trot, and, when he thinks himself out of sight, bounds off like a greyhound." But when first molested, or angered in any way, the lion will fight to the death, as Livingstone knew only too well from painful experience.

The true king of the African forests was the rhinoceros. Even the elephant feared its approach, and would try to

9

THE KING OF THE AFRICAN FORESTS.

(130)

get beyond its reach. Indeed, every animal seemed to stand in mortal terror of the rhinoceros; and no wonder! With one blow of its sharp horn, or horns—for there were some varieties with two—it had been known to split a tree asunder. The consequence of such a stroke to an animal's body may well be imagined. Livingstone's party witnessed a fearful encounter between an elephant and a rhinoceros, in which the former was completely disemboweled by one thrust of the death-dealing horn.

In the neighborhood of the Zambesi Livingstone saw for the first time a new species of the water-buck, which the natives called *leche.* It was a superb creature, with fine ringed horns " bending outward and inward," quite unlike the gemsbok of more southern Africa, whose beautiful long horns point straight over its back with the regularity and precision of guardsmen's muskets. Unlike the gemsbok, too—whose coat throughout is of an intermingled black and gray—the stomach and chest of the leche, together with a broad patch over the eyes, are nearly all of a pure white, only here and there a fleck of gray shading off into a soft brown. The remainder of the body is of a light brown, except the limbs, which are of a darker hue. The male leche is distinguished from the female by a handsome mane resembling that of the gnu, but thicker, smoother, and finer in every way.

Though he had ample opportunities to go in pursuit of game, and was fond of vigorous exercise, Livingstone engaged in hunting only when the flesh was needed for food. To him it appeared cruel in the extreme to slaughter innocent and defenseless animals for the mere love of the sport. Daily his great, kind heart was pained by the wholesale butchery he saw going on around him. Indeed, one of his biographers remarks that "so overflowing was his well of human kindness he seems to have regretted the death of even the very lion or alligator that was about to make a mouthful of him." With a heart so tender, he could not but be deeply moved and pained by witnessing the incident about to be related.

One evening, after a long and hard day's march, our travelers stopped to arrange their camp for the night at the head of a beautiful grass-covered plain, out of which rose here and there a low, cup-shaped hill. At many places there were pools of crystal water, left by the rain. Besides the tall, rich grass, there was no verdure save at varied intervals a few clumps of the flat-topped and bushy-growing mimosa. The hills, however, were covered with dense clusters of the "idoro" bush, interspersed with patches of the "watch-en-bechen," or "stop-awhile" thorn. At the commencement of this beautiful, park-like plain there was a luxuriant forest of "machabell" and "mamo-sho" trees, the latter very tall and magnificently proportioned, and bearing a fruit like the walnut in appearance, and not unlike it in taste and in the outer hull and inner shell. In the shade of these trees, and near a pool of clear water, the camping-place was prepared. The next morning, as Livingstone stood upon the summit of one of the hills about a half-mile from the camp, making observations through his telescope, he beheld, near the center of the valley, about a mile and a half distant, an unusually large elephant cow with her calf. The calf was rolling in one of the pools of water, which Livingstone could see had been made quite muddy by the plunges of the little animal. The mother was standing by the side of the pool contentedly fanning herself with her long ears, and gazing with maternal pride and pleasure upon her offspring. It was a pretty picture, which Livingstone contemplated with feelings of appreciation. But suddenly he descried some of his men, whom he supposed were at that moment lounging about the camp, cautiously approaching the elephant and calf from the rear. Totally unconscious of danger, the proud and happy mother-elephant continued the flapping of her long ears and watched the demonstrations of her big, noisy baby. Directly, while the men were creeping nearer and nearer, she went into the pool and stood there spouting the water from her great trunk in gentle showers over the body of the calf, who returned the sport by throwing diminutive jets from its own baby trunk over its mother with apparently the greatest enjoyment. As she stood there wagging her tail from side to side, and playing at fireman's hose with her calf, it did Livingstone good to gaze upon the scene. But there were the approaching men, and his heart grew sick as he foresaw the slaughter soon to take place. He knew that he could not save the elephant, even if he were with the men, as the natives were too covetous of the ivory to heed his commands; yet he felt that if he were nearer he might do something to save the poor little calf. He determined to make an effort, though he was at so great a distance. Calling an attendant, Livingstone bade him run as fast as he could and tell the men to spare the calf; but as he gave the message he doubted whether the attendant could reach the spot in time. It was fully a mile and a half the way he had to go; besides, he was an old man, and, like the majority of his race, not much given to fast running unless fleeing from danger. The messenger dispatched, Livingstone once more turned his glass upon the scene at the pool. The men were within fifty or sixty paces of the animal, and he could catch from their movements that they were beginning the pipings and the sarcastic salutation that usually preceded an attack. The piping was accomplished by blowing into reeds or between the fingers of the hands locked together. After piping a few moments, and thoroughly attracting the attention of the animals, the men began their chant, which was something like this: "O chief! O chief! O chief of a great tribe, we have come to kill you! Start not, and gaze at us with thy wide, round eyes, for this which we say is of a truth. We have come to lay you low, you of a mighty following, and we bold men and brave! O chief! O chief! O chief, thou shalt die; but not thou alone, but many more with thee! All those of your race that come within reach of our spears. It must be done. The gods have said it, and we have said it, therefore is there no falling back. O chief! O chief! prepare, then, to die!"

As the sounds of the first shrill piping fell upon their ears, both animals rushed from the pool and turned as if to flee. The calf did get several paces in front of its mother, but, catching sight of the advancing men, returned in great fear. Reaching out her huge proboscis, the mother-elephant drew the trembling calf nearer her side and held it there, to reassure the frightened young creature, as well as to shield it from danger. Next she worked herself around until she stood between the calf and the men, then began to move slowly but steadily away, working the calf along in front of her. Every now and then she would give the timid and frightened little creature a caressing stroke with her trunk, seemingly to bid it keep up its courage. While thus seeking to get beyond the reach of the men, as well as to shield the calf from their darts, she kept looking back to see how they were gaining upon her. Occasionally she would separate herself from the calf and make a movement as if to return and attack the pursuers. Then, apparently thinking better of it, and recalling the danger the calf would be in should she deprive it of the shield of her body, she would hug up nearer to it and endeavor to increase the onward progress. It was pitiful, as well as touching in the extreme, to watch the conflict between her anxiety to protect her offspring and her desire to attack, and put to rout if possible, the on-coming slayers. The men could have charged upon her at once, but such did not seem to be their wish. Doubtless they had intended from the first to get her into a more favorable position, one in which all the advantage would be on their side. They kept within fifty or sixty paces of her, however, and continued their pipings and shoutings. Two or three hundred yards or more from the spot at which they had started her there was the bed of a partially dried river-course that formed here a somewhat steep depression. As she was going down the hitherward bank of the stream they suddenly charged upon her with fierce shouts, driving their spears, to the number of fifteen or more, into her body. The pain seemed for a moment to fairly madden her. Turning, with her sides dripping blood from nearly a score of wounds, she began making every effort of which her waning strength was capable to carry herself beyond the reach of her assailants, apparently for the moment having forgotten her calf. As she fled from it the frightened little creature gave a piteous bellow and sprung into the water. It was at once dispatched by the men. Hearing the cry of the calf, the dam stopped instantly in her wild flight, and wheeling suddenly, came plunging back toward it, shrieking with rage and fury. She at first headed straight for the calf, then, apparently changing her mind, changed her course also, and the next moment was charging full upon the men who were now standing in a cluster watching her movements. Seeing the animal approach with such mad determination, they immediately began scattering in every direction, falling over each other in their haste and terror. They were all so fortunate as to get out of her way except one poor fellow. As he wore a bright scarlet cloth twisted about his shoulders, he seemed to serve as the one particular target upon which the enraged beast had fastened all her attention. Heading straight for him—though he had turned and sought to protect himself behind a clump of scrubby mimosa—she caught her trunk within the gaudy folds of the cloth about his shoulders; then lifting her head high in the air, she lifted the unfortunate man with it, and the next moment, with a terrible shriek of rage, threw him at full length upon the ground—life no doubt becoming extinct on the instant. As she turned to seek a second victim, another shower of spears greeted her. This was too much for her already weakened condition through the previous loss of blood. Leaping into the air with a spasmodic movement, she caught upon her feet, though unsteadily, and staggered from side to side, with the blood spouting in torrents from the fresh wounds she had received. For a moment she reeled thus, like one drunken, then with a wild shriek of mortal pain sunk to a kneeling position. The next instant she fell over on her side, gave two or three convulsive lunges with her huge feet, and was dead.

Livingstone did not witness the conclusion of this unequal and cruel contest. After the first shower of spears and the dispatch of the calf, he had turned away from the revolting spectacle, sick at heart, and made his way back to the camp. The messenger sent by him to save the calf, it is needless to add, did not arrive in time. The sick and pained feeling Livingstone carried back with him to the camp was in no wise relieved, he tells us, even by the knowledge, afterward borne to him, that, as leader of the party, a portion of the ivory was his. Most gladly would he have put aside all selfish interests, and foregone any share of profit, to have looked to the last upon that happy scene as he had first gazed upon it before the cruel hunters had come to overwhelm it in blood and to quench it in death. Truly, " the bravest" are always " the tenderest; the loving, the most daring."

CHAPTER X.

A HORRIFYING INCIDENT—LIVINGSTONE HEART-SICK BECAUSE OF
THE SLAVE-TRADE—HIS DETERMINATION TO FIND A REMEDY—
A GIGANTIC UNDERTAKING—HE SENDS HIS FAMILY TO ENGLAND
—HIS TOUCHING LETTERS TO THEM—THE PROPOSED MARCH
FROM "SEA TO SEA"—ANOTHER ATTACK BY THE BOERS UPON
SECHELE—THE INDIGNANT CHIEF'S INTENDED VISIT TO THE
QUEEN.

WHILE stopping at one of the towns along the
course of the Zambesi, Livingstone met with an
incident that changed the whole current of his after life.
As he and Oswell were the first white men to visit that region, they were called upon by large numbers of natives.
Among these visitors one day was a dandy-like young fellow who came strutting into their presence, and wearing
a gorgeously flowered dressing-gown. Livingstone was
amused by the fellow's airs, yet surprised to find such
goods upon the back of a savage in this remote corner of
the Dark Continent. On making inquiries he was horri-
fied to learn that the goods had been obtained from a tribe
called the Mambari in exchange for some boys, turned over
to them as slaves. Livingstone's horror and indignation
were increased when he found that this man was one of Sebituane's people. Pushing his investigations still farther,
he was amazed and more thoroughly horror-stricken than
ever to learn that only the year before the slave-trade had
been fully organized in Sebituane's domains.

How bitterly did Livingstone now regret the many mis-
haps that had kept him from reaching Sebituane! Above

(138)

all, what a great calamity had been Sebituane's untimely
death! He did not believe the good old chieftain had
known of the existence of this evil in his country; but if
he had, Livingstone felt that he could soon have obtained
from him the help and encouragement needful to combat
it. Livingstone must now battle alone in its overthrow;
and such a battle as it was to be! Even the thought of
it was enough to make the stoutest heart quail. Livingstone, however, gave no sign of drawing back, or of being
dismayed. His abiding faith in God was to him a sure
prophecy of success in the end. He knew that it was not
to be the work of one mortal man, yet he would do as much
as lay within his power. He not only felt this to be his
present duty, but accepted it as his life-work, and took it
up gladly.

Though Livingstone had no knowledge of any natives
selling members of their own families into slavery, many
were the proofs of different tribes having sold the children
of others to the Portuguese traders. And now came to
him the master inspiration of his life—an inspiration that
struck its firm roots into the very depths of his soul, and
grew into a purpose from which not even the thought of
wife and children could turn him. The spiritual as well as
the moral welfare of the whole country depended upon his
success in overcoming the evils of the slave-traffic.

The one consuming desire of the African seemed to be to
possess articles of European manufacture and commerce.
Hence Livingstone believed that if he could open up a
highway of traffic whereby goods might be brought into the
country, and given in legitimate exchange for ivory and
other articles of native production, a vise-like grasp would
be gained upon the dread monster of slavery, and its throt-

tling to the death would be but a matter of time.   This
highway Livingstone believed could be established through
the Zambesi River, if it stretched from sea to sea, as claimed.
But did it lead from sea to sea?   This question he determined to solve by exploring from one side of the continent
to the other.   It was a gigantic undertaking for one man,
but Livingstone determined that he would make the attempt if it cost him his life.   Better die nobly doing a duty,
he thought, than to shrink like a coward from the mere report of danger, and live with the remembrance of obliga-
tions ignobly shirked.   How loudly that voice sounded in
his ears! how thrilling the words, "Greater love than this
hath no man, that he lay down his life for his friends!"
Ah! that was the key-note of Livingstone's whole courageous and unselfish life; and he struck it bravely, and held
to it firmly, and sounded it broadly.   No wonder it awakened all the minor chords of his own heart, and sent sweet,
grand music into the hearts of others.

What was to be done with Livingstone's wife and children?   They could not remain where they were, for Sebituane's death had been followed by ominous signs of revolt
by the people he had so long and so judiciously governed.
There was considerable opposition to Mamochisane, principally because she was a woman and her governing abilities were distrusted.   Besides, some of the old warriors
argued that if hostilities should arise she could not lead
them into battle; or if she had sufficient courage to take
command, she was unskilled in the art of war.   It was a
bad business from beginning to end, they declared, this putting of a woman, and a young woman at that, to rule over
the Makololo; and they could not see why Sebituane had
so ordered it.

There was more or less commotion in various parts of the territory, and Livingstone felt that a serious outbreak might occur at no distant time, especially as a rival claimant to the chieftainship had appeared in the person of Mpepe, a half-brother of Mamochisane. Livingstone's old station at Kolobeng was also unsafe, owing to the near proximity of the Boers on one side and the Caffres on the other. He thought of repairing to Kuruman; but Mr. Moffat and his wife were some distance up the country, and there was no telling when they would return—there was every probability that they would go on a visit to England. Livingstone's own hopes now turned to England as a refuge for his dear ones, but the depleted condition of his purse forbade their going. In this dilemma the generous Oswell came to the rescue, proposing to defray the entire traveling expenses of Mrs. Livingstone and the children to England. At first Livingstone felt that he could not accept so great a favor, even at Oswell's hands; but the latter pressed the offer in such a way that Livingstone could no longer refuse. His acceptance was with tears of joy and gratitude and a pressure of the hand that Oswell could never forget.

It was with a lighter heart than he had carried for many a day—although he should be separated from his dear ones for at least two years—that Livingstone took his family down to Cape Town and saw them safely on board a vessel bound for England. But when he embraced them for what might be the last time, his heart was heavy and sad enough. He promised them and himself that if his journey across the continent was successful he would join them in England at the expiration of two years.

It was on the twenty-third day of April, 1852, that Livingstone stood on the wharf at Cape Town and watched the good ship that was fast bearing from him his dearest earthly treasures. As she passed onward from his sight he bravely wiped away the unbidden tears and turned resolutely to the work before him. He was about to enter upon the longest and most dangerous journey he had ever undertaken. The route he had mapped out extended from Cape Town to the Portuguese settlement of St. Paul de Loanda on the west coast of Africa, and thence right across the continent to Quilimane on the Indian Ocean, and directly at the mouth of the Zambesi River. A glance at the map of Africa will convey to the reader some idea of the magnitude of this undertaking; but a mere comprehension of distance can give little understanding of the intrepidity, the unparalleled determination that planned the enterprise and carried it through. It seems scarcely possible that one man could have done so much, and accomplished even more than he had hoped; yet there is no calculating the possibilities of a single soul that burns, as did Livingstone's, with the love of God and men. He had intimated to his friends that he might accomplish this journey of fully five thousand miles in something like two years. Indeed, it had been a strong hope in his heart that he would rejoin his family in England in two years. Alas! it was nearly five years before he saw them again.

Livingstone remained at Cape Town a few weeks, making preparations for his journey. While there he wrote the following letter to his wife, which gives full proof of the tender love that ruled his heart:

CAPE TOWN, May 5th, 1852.

My Dearest Mary: How I miss you now, and the dear children! My heart yearns incessantly over you. How many thoughts of the past crowd into my mind! I feel as if I would treat you all much more tenderly and lovingly than ever. You have been a great blessing to me. You attended to my comfort in many, many ways. May God bless you for all your kindnesses. I see no face now to be compared to that sunburned one which has so often greeted me with its kind looks. . . . Let us do our duty to our Saviour, and we shall meet again. I wish that time were now. You may read the letters over again that I wrote at Mabotsa—the sweet time you know. As I told you before, I tell you again, they are true, true; there is not a bit of hypocrisy in them. I never show all my feelings; but I can say truly, my dearest, that I loved you when I married you, and the longer I lived with you I loved you the better. . . . Let us do our duty to Christ, and he will bring us through the world with honor and usefulness. He is our refuge and high tower; let us trust in him at all times, and in all circumstances. Love him more and more, and diffuse his love among the children. Take them all around you, and kiss them for me. Tell them I have left them for the love of Jesus, and they must love him too, and avoid sin, for that displeases Jesus. I shall be delighted to hear of you all safe in England.

Your ever most affectionate,   D. LIVINGSTONE.

And here is one to his eldest daughter, who was at that time in her fifth year. How eloquently it speaks of the proud and loving father that he was; and how entirely it refutes the accusation that Livingstone was a somewhat cold and undemonstrative man in his family circle:

CAPE TOWN, May 18, 1852.

My Dear Agnes: This is your own little letter. Mamma will read it to you, and you will hear her just as if I were speaking to you, for the words that I write are those that she will read. I am still at Cape Town. You know that you left me there when you all went into the big ship and sailed away. Well, I shall leave Cape Town soon. Malatsi has gone for the oxen, and then I shall go away back to Sebituane's country, and see Seipone and Meriye, who gave you the beads and fed you with milk and honey. I shall not see you again for a long time, and I am very sorry. I have no Nannie now. I have given you back to Jesus, your friend—your papa who is in heaven. He is above you, but he is always near you. When we ask things from him, that is praying to him: and if you do or say a naughty thing, ask him to pardon you, and bless you, and make you one of his children. Love Jesus much, for he loves you, and he came and died for you. O how good Jesus is! I love him, and shall love him as long as I live. You must love him too, and you must love your brothers and mamma, and never tease them nor be naughty, for Jesus does not like to see naughtiness. Good-by, my dear Nannie.   D. LIVINGSTONE.

Livingstone left Cape Town on the 8th of June, 1852, and arrived at Kuruman early in September. Here he learned that the Boers had again attacked his old friend Sechele, killing many of his people and carrying numbers of women and children into captivity. They had besides destroyed the remaining household goods, clothing, books, and such things as had been spared to Livingstone during the first raid on Kolobeng, and such as he had since been able to collect. As he humorously but pathetically said afterward, "they had saved him the trouble of 'making a will' in case his death should have been near, since there wasn't so much as a pot remaining."

The following letter, which Sechele had sent to Kuruman for Livingstone, by the hand of Masabele—the one wife the chief had retained after his conversion to Christianity—affectingly narrates the disaster that had overtaken the brave Bakwain and his unfortunate people:

Friend of my heart's love, and of all the confidence of my heart, I am Sechele; I am undone by the Boers, who attacked me, though I had no guilt with them. They demanded that I should be in their kingdom, and I refused; they demanded that I should prevent the English and Griquas from passing [northward]. I replied, "These are my friends, and I can prevent no one" [of them]. They came on Saturday, and I besought them not to fight on Sunday, and they assented. They began on Monday morning at twilight, and fired with all their might, and burned the town with fire, and scattered us. They killed sixty of my people, and captured women and children and men. And the mother of Baleliring [a former wife of Sechele] they also took prisoner. They took all the cattle and all the goods of the Bakwains [Bechuanas], and the house of Livingstone they plundered, taking away all his goods. The number of wagons they had was eighty-five, and a cannon; and after they had stolen my own wagon and that of Macabe, then the number of their wagons [counting the cannon as one] was eighty-eight. All the goods of the hunters [certain English gentlemen hunting and exploring in the north] were burned in the town; and of the Boers were killed twenty-eight.

Yes, my beloved friend, now my wife goes to see the children, and Kobus Hae will convey her to you. I am

SECHELE, the son of Mochoasele.

During the attack Masabele had hidden herself in a cleft of rock overlooking the village. She had with her her youngest child, a babe of only a few months. Terrified by the noises of the combat in the village below, the child began to utter piercing cries. Some Boers were immediately seen to turn and approach the spot, as though attracted by the child's screams. Overcome by the thought that their hiding-place was about to be discovered, and scarcely knowing what she did in this dire extremity, Masabele took off her bracelets and gave them to the child to play with. Fortunately this quieted it almost instantly. Both their lives were doubtless saved by this device, as the Boers, unable to locate the place whence the sounds had issued, turned as if mystified and went away.

These tidings from Kolobeng moved Livingstone greatly, especially on Sechele's account. He did not see that he could do any thing, however, in the urgency of the work he had undertaken, but advise Sechele to seek a safer and

10

better-fortified place, nearer the station of Kuruman, and there establish himself, attracting to his new town as strong a following as possible.

As to how Livingstone received the news of the loss of his own property, his letter to his wife will give the clearer insight, as well as furnish a more extended account of the attack on Kolobeng. We give only such parts as bear upon the matters in question:

KURUMAN, 20th Sept., 1852.

My Dearest Mary: Along with this I send you a long letter; this I write in order to give you the latest news. The Boers gutted our house at Kolobeng. They brought four wagons down, and took away sofa, table, bed, all the crockery, your desk (I hope it had nothing in it—have you the letters?), smashed the wooden chairs, took away the iron ones, tore out the leaves of all the books and then scattered them in front of the house, smashed the bottles containing medicines, windows, oven-door, took away the smith-bellows, anvil, all the tools—in fact, every thing worth taking. They went up to Limaue, went to church morning and afternoon, and heard Mebalwe preach. After the second service they told Sechele they had come to fight, because he allowed Englishmen to proceed to the north, though they had repeatedly ordered him not to do so. Sechele replied that he was a man of peace; that he could not molest Englishmen, because they had never done him any harm, and always treated him well. In the morning they commenced firing on the town with swivels, and set fire to it. The heat forced some of the women to flee, the men to huddle together on the small hill in the middle of the town; the smoke prevented them from seeing the Boers, and the cannon killed many poor Bakwains, sixty in all. The Boers then came near to kill and destroy them all, but the Bakwains killed thirty-five and many horses. They fought the whole day, but the Boers could not dislodge them. They stopped firing in the evening, and then the Bakwains retired on account of having no water. The above sixty are not all men; women and children are among the slain. The Boers were six hundred, and they had seven hundred natives with them. All the corn is burned. Parties went out and burned Bangwaketse town, and swept off all the cattle. Sebubi's cattle are all gone. All the Bakhatla cattle gone. Neither Bangwaketse nor Bakhatla fired a shot. All the corn burned of the whole three tribes. Every thing edible is taken from them. How will they live? The Boers told Sechele that the Queen had given off the land to them, and henceforth they were the masters, and had abolished chieftainship altogether. . . . I wait here a little in order to get information when the path is clear. Kind Providence detained me from falling into the very thick of it. God will preserve me still. He has work for me, or he would have allowed me to go on just when the Boers were there.* . . . We shall remove more easily now that we are lightened of our furniture. They have taken away our sofa. I never had a good rest on it. We had only got it ready when we left.† Well, they can't have taken away all the stones. We shall have a seat in spite of them, and that too with a merry heart, that which doeth good like a medicine.

What brave and cheerful words these! and how noble the man who uttered them! "Well, they can't have taken away all the stones. We shall have a seat in spite of them." Sunny indeed must have been the heart that could thus meet disaster! His whole life was an eloquent illustration of the beautiful truth that

> To the sunny soul that is full of hope,
>   And whose beautiful trust ne'er faileth,
> The grass is green and the flowers grow bright,
>   Though the wintry storm prevaileth.

With the sad news of the attack upon Kolobeng had also

---

* Livingstone here alludes to the breaking of his wagon-wheels when he was about half the distance between Cape Town and Kuruman, which accident had detained him on the road a week or ten days, and kept him from reaching Kolobeng at the time first planned. Had he reached it at that time he would have been there when the Boers made their raid, and his life might have paid the forfeit.

† It is presumed from these words that the sofa in question was a home-manufactured one.

come the intelligence that the Boers had renewed their vows of vengeance against Livingstone, and declared that he should never again cross their country alive. These threats did not trouble Livingstone, but they had a serious effect upon the men of his expedition. Every one of them deserted, and there was much delay and difficulty in procuring others; for, in spite of the dire threats by the Boers, Livingstone had determined to push on. Through the friendly aid of one George Heming, a colored trader who was on his way to establish business relations with the Makololo tribes, the necessary force of men at length joined the expedition. But unfortunately, as Livingstone tells us, "they were the worst possible specimens of those who imbibe the vices without the virtues of the Europeans." From this description, and form what afterward occurred, we glean that they were very trifling fellows—more of a drawback than a help. Still, Livingstone was determined to proceed, and he felt that even these natives were better than none.

When the travelers reached a point about forty miles north of Kuruman they came upon Sechele, with a small body of attendants—bound for England, he declared, to lay before the Queen a complaint as to his treatment by the Boers, and to ask that his wrongs be righted. So firm was his belief in the justice-loving nature of the English people that he did not for a moment doubt that their Queen would at once interest herself in his behalf. He knew that the Queen lived somewhere in England; but as to the locality of England itself he was wholly ignorant. Yet, it could not be very far, he thought, since so many of the English people were constantly coming over to his country. If *they* could walk it, he was sure that *he* could walk it too. Anyhow, he was going to make the attempt.

In vain Livingstone tried to reason with Sechele, and to persuade him to go back, telling him of the many impediments that lay in his way, especially of the great ocean that was to be crossed. But all this had no effect upon Sechele; his mind was too firmly made up to be changed even by Livingstone, in whom he had more confidence than in any living person. He argued that " if the great white-winged things "—the ships, as he had heard them called by the natives who had wandered down to the Cape and back —" could take others across, it was very certain they could take him too, since he was no larger and no heavier than the average man!" Finding it useless to persuade him further, Livingstone, with many misgivings, saw the determined chief wend his way toward the Cape.

The sturdy Sechele held doggedly to his course and to his intentions until the Cape was reached. Here several English officers, who were both amused at his determination to seek the Queen and filled with genuine indignation against the Boers on account of their dastardly behavior, took quite an interest in him and kept him at their quarters. They gave him clothes and money, and it is believed finally dissuaded him from his purposed visit to the Queen, promising themselves to right his wrongs in time by completely exterminating the Boers. Some months later Sechele again appeared among his people apparently content with his journey, although it had ended at the Cape.

That Sechele had profited greatly by his visit, though in quite a different manner from what he had expected, was shown by his putting into operation many useful ideas and hints he had obtained while at Cape Town, and all of which proved that he had been a close observer of the modes of civilized life. One of these was the sending of offenders to labor on public roads, which he found to work like a charm.

Acting upon Livingstone's advice, Sechele now looked about him for a suitable point whereon to establish his new village, which he at the same time determined to make the show village of the country. A favorable situation was soon found some miles nearer the mission station of Kuruman. So well did Sechele improve upon the hints and ideas caught at the Cape that his town soon became prosperous, and, as Livingstone had hoped, he was not long in attracting to himself a numerous following.

It will interest our readers to learn that Sechele yet survives, with his good wife Masabele, and is still nobly endeavoring to live up to his Christian profession. His present village is some forty or fifty miles from the old station of Kolobeng, and is surrounded by many modern improvements seldom met with in the heart of so savage a region, and among natives. But when Sechele himself appears, the mystery is all explained. He still preserves a mission station among his people, which is at present upheld by a Hanoverian society. His regard and reverence for the name of Livingstone are unbounded. Most eagerly does he listen to and read all he can glean that relates to the great missionary. At the news of his death he was so deeply affected that he refused to take any food for many days.

It is a wonder to many, especially to the missionaries who labor among his people, how Sechele gained so much knowledge of the Bible. He is also a preacher of great earnestness and power, and regularly takes part with the missionaries in exhorting his people.

CHAPTER XI.

THE DEPARTURE FROM KURUMAN—HEAVY RAINS—THE FLOODED
DISTRICTS — TERRIBLE SUFFERINGS OF THE PARTY — LIVING-
STONE'S COURAGE AND TRUST—ARRIVAL AT LINYANTI—THE
YOUNG CHIEF SEKELETU — INCIDENTS OF THE SOJOURN AT
LINYANTI — THE MISSION - WORK AMONG THE MAKOLOLO —
SEKELETU'S DANGEROUS RIVAL.

IT was in December, 1852, that Livingstone, in company
with George Heming, the colored trader, and the men
they had hired as attendants, started from Kuruman on the
trip of thousands of miles to St. Paul de Loanda. While
not deterred from going by the threats of the Boers, he
thought it " the better part of valor " to give them as wide
a berth as possible. He therefore proceeded toward the
country of Sebituane by a route entirely different from any
he had before taken. His first principal stopping-place was
to be Linyanti, the capital of the Makololo. Here he designed remaining until he could make the further arrangements necessary to the journey.

This time Livingstone's party did not cross the Kalahari,
but only went along its edge. They found traveling much
less laborious and torturing than it had been heretofore;
for a heavy rain had recently fallen, and there was plenty
of water for both men and cattle, as well as grass and·
water-melons in abundance for the oxen. At one point on
his route Livingstone met with an English traveler, a Mr.
Macabe, who told him that, having lost his way and the
supply of forage giving out, his oxen had subsisted upon

the melons alone for twenty-one days.   He had undertaken to cross the desert at its widest part, and had it not been a wet season he would have perished.   As it was, he had a most eventful experience.

Though the heavy fall of rain removed all danger of suffering from thirst, it seriously impeded Livingstone's progress.   Deep and dangerous pools appeared along the line of march, and on drawing near Sebituane's domains Livingstone found that in many places the whole face of the country was flooded.   At one point the wagons had to be abandoned, and it then seemed inevitable that the remainder of the journey must be made on foot.   It was a frightful undertaking.   The travelers were often wet all day, and for nearly one-half of that time they had to wade through water waist deep.   Sometimes they had to swim for their lives.   Again, the marshes over which they passed, besides being covered with water, were filled with thorns and reeds that offered great resistance to their advance.   The thorns tore their clothing, the sharp edges of the reeds cut into their flesh like the keen blades of knives, but still they pushed bravely on.   To add to the distress, most of the men had deserted, and the three who had been left were constantly quarreling among themselves, or stealing the scant supplies that remained.   After contending for nearly a week with these swollen rivers, piercing reeds, and torturing briers, two of the three men died from the exposure. There were now only Livingstone, Heming, and one of the attendants.

A great danger into which they were always running while pushing their way through the overflowed regions was the numerous crocodiles and hippopotami.   Finally, on reaching a comparatively dry spot, our travelers constructed a raft, on which they got over the remaining flooded parts of the country; but on getting into the forests beyond, new trials were encountered.   The heat was intense, the buzzing insects stung them, the dense vines tore their faces or tripped their legs, the thorns cut into their already lacerated flesh. In many places they had to go down on their all-fours and crawl, generally emerging with raw and bleeding knees. Livingstone somewhat alleviated his own sufferings by tearing his handkerchief in half and binding a portion about each knee.   Once, however, even his brave heart failed, and, thinking the hour of death had come, he uttered the first despairing complaint that had ever passed his lips: "O God, have I indeed seen the last of my wife and children? Is this to be the breaking up of all my connections with earth, the leaving of this fair and beautiful world, knowing as yet so little of it?"   Then began a communing with himself as to the nature of the hereafter.   What was it to be?   Where did it lie?   "My soul, whither wilt thou emigrate the first night after leaving this body?   Will an angel soothe thy flutterings? for sadly fluttered wilt thou be on entering upon eternity.   O if Jesus doth but speak one word of peace, how quickly will it establish in thy breast an everlasting calm!   Death is indeed a glorious event to one going to Jesus.   But whither *does* the soul wing its flight?   What *does* it see first?   There is surely something sublime in passing into the second stage of our immortal lives if washed from our sins.   But O to be consigned to ponder over all our sins with memories excited, every scene of our lives held up as in a mirror before our faces, and we looking at them and waiting for the day of judgment!"   Then came stronger and more helpful thoughts—a return of that trust which had been with him and upheld him in hours of trial and danger.   From his lips came words of humble and beseeching prayer—vows of reconsecration to the service of the Master, and entreaty that for the sake of the work that yet lay before him the servant might be spared, all unworthy as he was: "O Jesus, fill me with thy love now! and I beseech thee accept me and use me a little further for thy glory.   I have done nothing for thee yet, and O how I would like to do something!   O do, do, I beseech thee, accept me and my service, and take to thyself all the glory!   O succor now, I entreat thee, for sake of the work yet to be done, thy servant, and give him to see how best to promote the glory of thy kingdom!"

Ah! surely this impassioned prayer was heard—a new charm set about the life upon the preservation of which depended so many precious results—since on the third day of May Livingstone, with his small remnant of bleeding and famished followers, reached the town of Linyanti.   Their condition excited the compassion of the kind-hearted Makololo, and they were immediately given the best of every thing in the place, with kind and sympathetic attendants to alleviate their bodily sufferings as much as possible.

Livingstone found that a change had taken place in the government of the Makololo.   Being distressed by the signs of dissatisfaction on every side, and having really no desire for the position into which she had been thrust, Mamochisane had prevailed upon her younger brother, Sekeletu, to become chief of the tribes.   While he lay in the hut recovering from the afflictive experiences of his journey to Linyanti, Livingstone was much exercised as to the reception Sekeletu would give him.   Any fears that he may have entertained were put to rest on his first meeting with the chief. Sekeletu was very young, only about eighteen years old, and it was difficult to surmise what he would be when he grew older; yet it was plain to see that he was simple and kind-hearted, with the promise of many of his father's noble qualities, though with nothing like his intelligence.

When Sekeletu learned the object of Livingstone's proposed journey to the coast, he declared his intention to provide him with all the necessary equipments and to give him an escort of Makololo men. Livingstone thanked God for putting such generous impulses into the young chief's heart. Had it been otherwise, Livingstone would not have known whither to turn for aid. The many disasters through which he had just passed—the loss of his wagon, oxen, and the various supplies obtained at Kuruman—had left him without means of getting on in his hazardous journey. Sekeletu's generous conduct was therefore like the bright rays of the sun breaking through dark clouds. But if Sekeletu had chosen an opposite course, Livingstone would have pushed onward, even if he had been compelled to go crawling on his hands and knees. Such was the indomitable courage and heroic determination of this man, who had surely been fashioned in Heaven's most kingly mold.

Sekeletu's proposition was that Livingstone and his companions should make the greater part of the journey in canoes by way of the Zambesi and its tributaries. These canoes were to be furnished by the chief, while men, also furnished by him, were to go along the banks, leading oxen—the oxen to be ridden at stages of the journey where the navigation of the streams proved impracticable, and to serve as means of carriage when the rivers had to be left altogether. Sekeletu also informed Livingstone that it was his intention to accompany him on many miles of his journey, especially through the greater part of his own territory, in order to gain in behalf of the expedition the friendliest interest of his people.

Livingstone's independent spirit would not permit him to receive so many benefits from Sekeletu without making some return. He therefore examined his scanty store for something of real value—not a gaudy trifle that would prove of no service whatever. He bestowed upon the chief some powder, wire, flints, percussion-caps, an umbrella, a hat, and three goats and some fowls—the latter purchased from a company of strolling peddlers. The chief was delighted, but he had neither expected nor desired any reward.

While waiting for the required traveling preparations and for his restoration to health and strength, Livingstone engaged in missionary work among the Makololo. He found them a tribe of more than average intelligence— quick in their perceptions, and very easily impressed; but he could at first see little good resulting from his efforts. In the end, however, he began to feel encouraged; and so promising were the evidences given that his old desire to plant a permanent mission station in the Makololo country returned in full force. It caused him to decide at once that should his journey to the coast prove successful he would no longer delay the matter. But the country of the Makololo was at certain seasons very unhealthy, especially that portion around Linyanti. If Livingstone established the station, it would therefore have to be at some other point. When the subject was broached to Sekeletu, he expressed his willingness to remove to a healthier locality. In fact, he was ready to go anywhere and to do any thing if Livingstone would reside among his people. He had grown so much attached to Livingstone that he could not bear the thought of separation from him, even for a year or so. He declared that in Livingstone he had found "a new father;" and his devotion to the noble missionary was touching to see. He would remain near Livingstone as much as was possible, gazing into his face and hanging upon his words as if fearful that he would miss some look or expression meant especially for him. He never failed to hear Livingstone's sermons, and the missionary was hopeful that Sekeletu would soon be brought to a knowledge of the Saviour.

Livingstone had no trouble to get the Makololo to hear him read and explain the Scriptures. Indeed, they came in such crowds that sometimes they could not all get within sound of his voice. He generally preached in their public meeting-place, called a kotla—a great open-sided hut that stood under the trees near the center of the village.

Livingstone was much distressed, and yet often amused at the behavior of some of the women. They usually came in groups and sat on mats spread upon the floor. Occasionally a woman, in making a restless movement, or in getting up to go out, would plant her foot or her elbow upon the dress of another. Instantly the offender would be given a shove, which, if she chanced to be upon her feet, sent her sprawling upon other women. These would pummel the poor unfortunate, and roll her about in a very rough manner, until some of her relatives came to protect her. Then would ensue a most deafening uproar. All this time Livingstone would strive to make himself heard, with what success can be readily imagined.

This skirmishing among the women was only one of the many annoyances to which they subjected Livingstone when he began to preach at Linyanti. They would laugh at the simplest thing that happened. If a child cried, or a sleepy old man gaped, or a sleepier old woman nodded, an outburst of merriment would be heard from one end of the kotla to the other. Sekeletu finally took this matter of indecorum in hand, and before a great while good order was maintained throughout the kotla.

Learning from Livingstone that one of the first requirements of civilized life was that women should go thoroughly clothed, Sekeletu gave orders that every woman of his household should make for herself full clothing out of such material as was at hand. This they all did readily, except the chief's favorite wife, a very tall and very determined young woman. Sekeletu was greatly provoked to see her come into the kotla one day with less clothing than she had formerly worn. Going up to her quietly, he remonstrated against her appearance, and tried to induce her to return to her hut for more clothing. She was very willful, or else maliciously inclined to see how far she could carry things with the chief; for she paid no heed whatever to Sekeletu's gentlemanly remonstrances. This behavior was more than he could stand, for, though generally mild and kindly disposed, he was very quick and determined when thoroughly aroused. Getting out of patience at last, he gave the woman a ringing box upon the ear, and took her by the hand to drag her toward the tent. This caused loud giggling on all sides, which the woman resented with flashing eyes and an expression that boded no good to the women who were triumphing over her.

Livingstone found the Makololo women in general very harmless, with quick sympathies for real suffering and many generous impulses. No one could have nursed him more tenderly than they did through the sufferings caused by the exposures of his journey to Linyanti.

Among the few effects left to Livingstone was a small

A BEVY OF LINYANTI BELLES.

(159)

looking-glass, which he kept hanging from the side of his hut. It was at first an object of great terror to both the men and women, as they believed it to be through Livingstone's witchcraft that their faces could be made to appear in the little shining square of glass; but gradually they grew more assured, until they came to regard it with much fascination, especially the women. They would make daily trips to the mirror, first asking Livingstone's permission, however. When they came, seeing him busily engaged in reading, they did not think that he paid any attention to them; yet he was so greatly amused at some of their expressions and their manner of acting that he could hardly keep from laughing outright.

"My! my! is *that* me?" one of them would say in a disconsolate voice as she beheld her reflection in the mirror. "Well, I never would have believed it! I really thought that I was better-looking than *that!* What a big mouth I have, to be sure! while in my eyes there is really a squint! As to my ears—well, they are indeed, as I have been told, nearly as large as pumpkin-leaves. And my chin, how short it is! And see, O dear! O dear! my head *does* shoot up in the middle as that horrid woman said it did!"

"I would have been pretty, yes, really pretty," another one would sigh forth regretfully, "if it hadn't been for my high cheek-bones. What a pity that I cannot pound them down!"

One morning a man came to look in the glass. Believing the Doctor asleep, he thus broke forth: "People have told me that I was very ugly, but I wouldn't believe them. Who ever does want to believe that they are ugly? or worse yet, to be told of it? But now, alas! alas! I know that I am very ugly indeed; for now that I have seen myself, I can no longer persuade myself that I am even good-looking."

Livingstone remained at Linyanti much longer than he had anticipated. He did not think it safe to venture upon that far more arduous portion of his journey to the sea until he had thoroughly regained strength and buoyancy. In the meantime he employed himself, as we have seen, both in teaching and preaching among the Makololo. He could not bear to be idle even for a time, doubtless believing with Dr. Adam Clarke that "the great secret of real happiness consists in never allowing one's energies to stagnate."

At first the Makololo seemed unwilling to be taught any thing from books—even the alphabet, or how to spell. They expressed a fear that they should be bewitched by the strange-looking volumes. Whenever Livingstone opened one of them all who saw it would stand some distance away, in an attitude plainly suggesting that they were ready to run. This amused Livingstone, and yet he felt sorry for the poor superstitious creatures, and tried to lessen their fears. It was decided that two of the oldest medicine-men should first become Livingstone's pupils, in order, by the exercise of certain "spells," to take away any evil influences that might dwell in the books. The medicine-men themselves were somewhat afraid, but two were found who were willing to go, after they had been allowed to prepare their "spells" and "charms," and to anoint their bodies with something that looked like a compound of rancid butter, tar, and red paint. When the experiment had been made, and the two medicine-men came out safe and sound, there was great rejoicing throughout the village for several days. A dance of congratulation was tendered them, and a mighty feast given in honor of both pupils and teacher.

11

After this the people began to go in slowly, one at a time, to be taught from the books, but not until they had obtained some "charm" from the medicine-men. As long as Livingstone kept the book to himself—especially the Bible —and did not ask them to take hold of it, they seemed to have no fear. Thus it was that they came to hear him preach, and he entered into the work with all his soul and strength, for he was a faithful missionary. He had labored thirteen years among these dusky children of the Dark Continent, and he looked upon it as the grandest work in which a man could engage. Had not the Prince of Peace, the King of all the earth, himself engaged in it? Often did Livingstone say: "God had an only Son, and he was a missionary and a physician. A poor imitator of him I am, or wish to be. In this service I hope to live, in it I wish to die. May God accept my service, and use me for his glory. A great honor it is to be a fellow-worker with God." Again, speaking of his proposed march across the Continent, and of the many things it involved, he says: "It is a great venture. Yet would I venture every thing for Christ. Pity I have so little to give." What a reproach his modesty and devotion are to some of us with our vain boastings and our barren gifts!

The extracts below, taken from Livingstone's journal, and which were written during his sojourn at Linyanti, will give his own impressions of his mission-work among the Makololo:

Banks of the Chobe, Sunday, May 15th.—Preached twice to about sixty people. Very attentive. It is only divine power which can enlighten dark minds like these. The people seem to receive ideas on divine subjects slowly. They listen, but never suppose that the truths must become embodied in actual life.

Sunday, June 15th.—A good and very attentive audience, but immediately after the service I went to see a sick man, and when I returned toward the kotla I found that the chief had retired into a hut to drink beer, as the custom is; about forty men were standing singing to him, or, in other words, begging beer by that means. A minister who had not seen so much pioneer service as I have done would have been shocked to see so little effect produced by an earnest discourse concerning the future judgment; but time must be given to allow the truth to sink into a dark mind, and produce its effect. The earth shall be filled with the knowledge of the glory of the Lord—that is enough. We can afford to work in faith, for Omnipotence is pledged to fulfill the promise. The great mountains become a plain before the Almighty arm. The poor Bushman, the most degraded of all Adam's family, shall see his glory, and the dwellers in the wilderness all bow before him. The obstacles to the coming of the kingdom are mighty, but come it will for all that.

> Then let us pray that come it may,
> As come it will for a' that;
> That man to man, the world o'er,
> Shall brothers be for a' that.

Of his later labors among the Makololo, Livingstone gives these additional pictures:

When I stand up all the women and children draw near, and having ordered silence, I explain the plan of salvation, the goodness of God in sending his Son to die, the confirmation of his mission by miracles, the last judgment or future state, the evil of sin—God's commands respecting it, etc.; always choosing one subject only for an address, and taking care to make it short and plain, and applicable to them. This address is listened to with great attention by most of the audience. A short prayer concludes the service, all kneeling down and remaining so till told to rise.

A quiet audience to-day. The seed is being sown, the least of all seeds now, but it will grow a mighty tree. It is as it were a small stone cut out of a mountain, but it will fill the whole earth. He that believeth shall not make haste. Surely if God can bear with hardened, impenitent sinners for thirty, forty, or fifty years, waiting to be gracious, we may take it for granted that his is the best way. He could destroy his enemies, but he wants to be gracious. To become irritated with their stubbornness and hardness of heart is ungodlike.

While waiting at Linyanti, Livingstone proposed to Sekeletu that they should go in quest of a suitable spot for the intended mission station. Sekeletu at first hesitated to accompany Livingstone, because the route mapped out lay directly through the section where lived his half-brother, Mpepe, who had of late become his most dreaded enemy. When Mamochisane resigned her claim to Sekeletu it greatly angered Mpepe, who thought he had a better right to the chieftainship. Vowing vengeance, he retired to the territory of some of the worst factions of the tribe, where he was now trying to stir up a revolt. He not only threatened Sekeletu's life, but he made two secret attempts against it, both of which happily failed. To add further to Sekeletu's danger, Mpepe was upheld by all the half-caste Portuguese tribes along the river, and by the Portuguese traders. The reason of this was that Mpepe favored the slave-trade, and had declared that should he become chief the traders might have it all their own way. Sekeletu, on the other hand, was strongly opposed to the wicked and inhuman practice—more so than ever since he had heard Livingstone preach so earnestly against it.

Taking into consideration this state of affairs, it is not surprising that Sekeletu felt some trepidation in regard to going with Livingstone. Had open warfare impended, he would have cared little for it, since the better classes of the Makololo—and these formed a mighty following—were on the young chief's side. But he well knew how cruel and treacherous Mpepe could be, and feared some blow in the dark. Yet Sekeletu was a brave young chief, though effeminate in appearance, and it did not take him long to decide that he would go, despite the peril. When Livingstone learned the true state of affairs, he felt some solicitude for the young chief, but determined not to let Sekeletu get out of his sight. How fortunate it was that he should have so decided, the sequel will show.

CHAPTER XII.

THE START IN SEARCH OF A HEALTHY LOCALITY—THE DEMON-
STRATIVE RECEPTION BY THE PEOPLE—LIVINGSTONE FRUS-
TRATES MPEPE'S WICKED DESIGN — MPEPE'S DEATH — UP THE
ZAMBESI—A PATHETIC INCIDENT—THE VALLEY OF THE BA-
ROTSE—HEATHENISM IN ITS MOST REVOLTING ASPECT—THE
BAROTSE DANCE OF WELCOME—LIVINGSTONE VISITS KATONGA
—PUSHES FARTHER UP THE RIVER—CONTINUED DISCOURAGE-
MENT—THE RETURN TO LINYANTI.

ON leaving Linyanti to seek a healthy location for the
proposed mission station, Livingstone was accompanied by Sekeletu and one hundred and sixty of his men.
The chief himself was closely attended by his own mopato,
or body-guard, which consisted of a picked company of
twenty-five or thirty young men of his own age.   Livingstone thus describes the procession as it wound away from
the village toward the river: " It was pleasant to look back
on the long-extended line of our attendants, as it twisted
and bent according to the curves of the foot-path, or in and
out behind the mounds, the ostrich feathers of the men waving in the wind.   Some had the white ends of ox-tails on
their heads, hussar fashion, and others great bunches of
black ostrich feathers, or caps made of lions' manes.   Some
wore red tunics, or various colored prints which the chief
had bought from Fleming [Dr. Livingstone's fellow-trav-
eler]; the common men carried burdens; the gentlemen
walked with a small club of rhinoceros horn in their hands,
and had servants to carry their shields; while the Machaka,

(166)

battle-ax men, carried their own, and were liable at any time to be sent a hundred miles on an errand, and expected to run all the way."

The intention of the party was to march overland along the banks of the Chobe River until they struck the Zambesi at the town of Sesheke, whither Sekeletu had sent orders that thirty-five canoes of the first make should await them. On the journey through the country to Sesheke they had to pass through several villages. At each of these the people ran out in great crowds, and on Sekeletu's approach, surrounded by his fine-looking body-guard, they at once prostrated themselves before him, touching their foreheads to the ground in token of their devotion. An ox was slain and roasted, while great calabashes of beer were handed around.

When they had gone about sixty miles on their journey, they came upon Mpepe and some of his followers. Hearing of Sekeletu's proposed visit, Mpepe had formed a plot against his life. This was, to engage him in a pretended friendly council, then to make a sudden thrust with his battle-ax when Sekeletu least expected it, and cut off his head. The wicked Mpepe would have succeeded in this plot had it not been for Livingstone. Suspecting treachery, in spite of Mpepe's friendly pretensions, Livingstone kept his eyes keenly open, as he had determined he would do, and warded off the blow intended for Sekeletu. Exasperated by this dastardly attempt upon the life of their well-loved chief, the body-guard of Sekeletu seized the treacherous Mpepe, and, carrying him to a grove outside the village, dispatched him with their spears. This had the effect of entirely demoralizing Mpepe's followers, who fled in dismay, fearing that they might share his fate. Mpepe's death put an end to all signs of rebellion.

The travelers struck the Zambesi not at Seshcke, as had been intended, but at a small village some miles above. From this point Sekeletu detailed messengers to the head man of the village of Seshcke, asking him to send up the canoes. While awaiting the arrival of these boats the men engaged in hunting, in order to procure meat to dry for their use on the journey up the river. Although much against his desire, Livingstone took charge of the hunting party. He decided to undertake it rather than trust it to the Makololo. They were poor marksmen, and would only have wasted the powder had they gone alone, and powder was very precious with the party.

The country surrounding the village was flat, diversified here and there by cup-shaped mounds crowned with clusters of trees. Vast herds of elands, zebras, antelopes, and other game were daily seen upon the plains; but as they were very shy, it was difficult to get near enough to kill them with spears—hence Livingstone's guns were of great service. One day the hunters, headed by Livingstone, shot a beautiful cow eland that was standing in the shade of a small tree not far from the river-bank. " It was evident," says Livingstone, " that she had lately had her calf killed by a lion, for there were five long, deep scratches on both sides of her hind quarters, as if she had run to the rescue of her calf, and the lion, leaving it, had attacked herself, but was unable to pull her down. When lying on the ground the milk flowing from her large udder showed that she must have been seeking the shade from the distress its non-removal in the natural manner must have caused her." Tears came to Livingstone's eyes as he saw this innocent and beautiful creature stretched out in her death-struggles. The Makololo, too, seemed touched by the pathetic sight.

One of them, Labeolo by name, said to Livingstone: "Do you think that great man, Mr. Jesus, of whom you have told us, and who is Lord of all the earth, as well as Master of the beasts, will like it when he knows how we have slain this beautiful creature of his who was doing us no harm?" Although the life of the lovely creature had only been taken to sustain their own, Livingstone felt the rebuke deeply. On the other hand, he felt rejoiced at this proof of the good effect his preaching had had upon the Makololo. They evidently had a very clear idea of "the great man, Mr. Jesus," who condemned every act of cruelty.

The canoes having arrived, the party embarked and moved up the broad, beautiful current of the Zambesi. It was a delightful journey, and one that Livingstone enjoyed more than any he had yet taken. At many places the river was more than a mile wide; at others its surface was broken by small islands that arose fairy-like from out the glistening expanse of water, bearing aloft miniature forests of mango and palm. All along the banks were stretches of tall date-palms, with their gracefully curved fronds swaying in the breeze. Every now and then from a cluster of these palms a lofty palmyra shot many feet above the others, its feather-like mass of foliage appearing ready to be detached and sent whirling away by the first ungentle wind that blew over it. There were also many luxuriant vines with brilliant berries, and everywhere wild flowers in prodigal abundance.

In many parts of the Zambesi shallows and rapids made navigation at the dry season extremely difficult, and in some places very dangerous. However, as copious rains had fallen previous to their embarkation, Livingstone's navy had no trouble in getting along until they came to the Falls of Gouva. Here the river narrowed to a width of seventy-five or eighty yards, and they had to disembark and carry the canoes and supplies about a mile overland. While making this detour they stopped part of a day at a small village a half-mile or more from the river. Livingstone heard of a man who, taking advantage of the elevated position of the Gouva Falls, had led the water through a rudely constructed canal into his garden for the purpose of irrigating it. This man, thought Livingstone, must have been very superior to the rest of his race—doubtless had been much of a traveler, and had somewhere during his travels gained the idea of the canal. They were shown the garden, and could see many signs of the rude trench that led to the river. In the garden, although it had been neglected for many generations, they dug up some succulent roots shaped like potatoes. Indeed, the Makololo pronounced them potatoes at first sight. They were quite waxy, and exceedingly bitter to the taste.

One of the most beautiful spots visited was the valley of the Barotse, in which lived a tribe of the same name. They were of the same government as the Makololo, and most cordially received Sekeletu and his party, joyfully hailing him as their chief. This valley, remarkably fertile and covered with vegetable growths in great variety, was about one hundred and twenty-five miles in length and from fifteen to thirty-five in width, with the Zambesi flowing almost directly through the center. As the Zambesi, like the Nile, had its overflows at certain seasons, the valley of the Barotse, being very low ground, was at such times thoroughly inundated. To avoid the destruction of their villages the Barotse had built them on mounds beyond the reach of the rising waters. The idea of raising these mounds, which were necessarily artificial all through, was said to have been conveyed to the Barotse by a former renowned chieftain of theirs, whose son still survived. The name of this chief, as also that of his son, was Santuru; and if report spoke truly, he must have been almost as good and wise as the great chief Sechele. Santuru had taught the Barotse, among other things, the art of planting these mounds thickly with trees, not only to strengthen them, but to afford shade from the fierce rays of the sun. As this valley was entirely free from the ravages of the deadly tsetse fly, the Barotse owned an abundance of cattle. When the heavy rains began— heralds of the approaching floods—the villagers would drive their cattle off to the high ground, where they were safely penned. As food was not plentiful here, they grew very lean and ill-conditioned; and it was amidst great rejoicing of the natives, as well as of the famished brutes themselves, that they were conducted back to their rich pasturage grounds on the subsidence of the floods.

So very fertile was this valley of the Barotse that Livingstone desired to experiment with it in raising wheat and other grains; yet he soon discovered that it was so rich the grain would run entirely to straw. Even the grass grew twelve to fifteen feet high, with stalks as thick as a man's thumb.

While passing through the country of the Barotse, Livingstone was daily shocked and pained by the numberless harrowing sights he was called upon to witness. He was not only greeted by some of the most revolting aspects of the slave-trade, but he also saw heathenism in its lowest and most forbidding form. The utmost cruelty was shown by children to parents, and by parents to children. The old were made to do all the drudgery, while shocking murders were of daily occurrence. It was not uncommon to see an old woman who could hardly stand beaten for something she had failed to do—something doubtless far beyond the poor old creature's strength to do.

One day, as the party were journeying through a forest, a girl not more than fifteen years of age came staggering from behind a tree to meet them, and to beg for something to eat. She was a most pitiable-looking object, being entirely naked and emaciated to a mere skeleton. She had run away to escape the terrible yoke of slavery. Livingstone spoke kindly to her, and sought to detain her, so as to do something for her if possible; but she grew alarmed, thinking it was his intention to return her to her people, who had tried to sell her to the slave-traders. Springing away, she fled deeper into the woods in front of them. Two days later they came upon her body, more than half devoured by a hyena, while that which remained was so horribly mangled they could scarcely recognize it.

At another time the travelers saw a large crowd of slaves bound to each other by a heavy chain that bent them down and cut into their flesh at every step taken. Livingstone turned away sick at heart. He was powerless to prevent such cruelties, but prevailed upon Sekeletu to remain in the Barotse country long enough for him to preach half a dozen times to these poor, ignorant, and sin-cursed people. He had little hope of good results in so short a time, and in the face of so much darkness, wickedness, and superstition; yet he prayed that a portion at least of the precious seed might take root and grow, if only with a feeble shoot. Although all was uphill work, all stony ground, where it seemed that the most vigorous seed could not struggle into life, he did not lose heart altogether; his "wall of trust" was too firmly built to be battered even by the enemy's heaviest fire, and he too courageous a soldier to long harbor thought of defeat. Because of this patient endurance, these mighty, steadfast endeavors, his life grew better, braver, nobler, day by day. Let us take the lesson of this example close to our hearts, and keep it there, remembering always that

Highest aim and true endeavor,
    Earnest work with patient might;
Hoping, trusting, singing ever;
    Battling bravely for the right;
Loving God, all men forgiving,
    Helping weaker feet to stand—
These will make a life worth living,
    Make it noble, make it grand.

The Barotse seemed to care very little for what Livingstone had to tell them. They were noisy, cowardly, cruel, and ungrateful; yet they had some redeeming traits, prominent among which was their hospitality. They received the Makololo and their young chief with much rejoicing and the slaughter of many oxen—this last being the highest proof they could give of the sincerity of their welcome. They also endeavored by every means to show Livingstone how pleased they were to have him in their country.

Livingstone would have liked to plant his mission station somewhere among the Barotse, because he felt that so great were their ignorance and darkness they needed the enlightenment of Christ's gospel more than any tribe he had yet come upon. But alas! owing to the overflow of the river, the valley at certain seasons was extremely unhealthy, and once a year was visited by the dread scourge, fever.

Livingstone staid among the Barotse as long as he could, preaching, praying, and teaching, and left at last trusting God for the result.

The party made detours up the various tributaries of the Zambesi, stopping at the towns, all of which were under Sekeletu's government.   At each town the travelers were received with enthusiastic demonstrations—the young chief especially.   Huge bonfires were built, the most deafening noises were made on all kinds of rude instruments, while the people hallooed and sung at the top of their voices. But the greatest demonstration of all was the dance of welcome, in which the whole village joined, the men shouting themselves hoarse and the women falling down from sheer exhaustion.   On one of these occasions, as Livingstone stood near two young men who were dancing as though their lives depended upon it, he overheard the following conversation.

"This is awfully hard work," said one, "and I can't really see the good of it.   What is the use, now, of dancing one's self nearly stiff just to welcome the chief, when we might take some other way of showing how pleased we are that he has condescended at last to visit us?"

"It is indeed very hard work," agreed the other, "but then it isn't without its profit.   There is, in truth, very great profit in it, as you will soon see.   Why, just to think, man, of the cows the chief will order to be slaughtered, and how we will feast upon them!   So, just remember this now, and kick your legs as high as you can, for the higher you kick the more chance there will be for you to attract the attention of the chief himself; and then who knows but what he will be so gracious as to give you a whole ox all to yourself?"

As this feast of freshly slaughtered meat seemed to be the one great object all the people had in view when they came forth to dance before Sekeletu and his attendants, the young chief, who well knew the long-established custom of his father, did not disappoint them.   He had at hand every means of gratifying them.   Years before his death Sebituane, with that forethought so characteristic of him, had established throughout his territory various cattle stations.   These were kept well filled, and placed in charge of men who thoroughly understood their business.   Thus Sekeletu found no trouble in gratifying the desires of his people in this direction, and at the conclusion of the dance the chief invariably gave the order for a feast of slaughtered oxen to be made ready.

The dance alluded to is thus described by Livingstone: " It consists of the men standing, nearly naked, in a circle, with clubs or small battle-axes in their hands, and each roaring at the loudest pitch of his voice, while they simultaneously lift one leg, stamp heavily twice with it, then lift the other, and give one stamp with that; this is the only movement in common.   The arms and head are thrown about also in every direction; and all this time the roaring is kept up with the utmost possible vigor.   The continued stamping makes a cloud of dust around, and they leave a deep ring in the ground where they have stood.   If the scene were witnessed in a lunatic asylum, it would be nothing out of the way, and quite appropriate, even, as a means of letting off the excessive excitement of the brain; but the gray-headed men joined in the performance with as much zest as others whose youth might be an excuse for making the perspiration stream off their bodies with the exertion. The women stood by clapping their hands; and occasionally one advances into the circle composed of a hundred men, makes a few movements, and then retires."   Sometimes, again, the women joined in with as much spirit and energy as the men, and often had to be borne away limp and nearly lifeless, having fallen through exhaustion.

Another dance engaged in by this people was the tribal

TRIBAL WAR DANCE.

(176)

war dance.   This, however, was only indulged in on hostile occasions, or when the braves were going forth to battle. Then spears and clubs and a most unsightly and ungainly lot of head-gear were used, and all with frightful effect.

Hearing that Katonga—a town of the Barotse some distance above their capital, Naliele—was situated on high ground, Livingstone went in that direction with a part of the Makololo men.   In the meantime Sekeletu, with his more immediate attendants, remained at Naliele to take part in a great feast that was to be given in his honor.

Livingstone's object in going to Katonga was to find the long-sought point for the mission station.   His hopes, however, were again doomed to disappointment.   Though the situation at Katonga was on exceedingly high ground, and the surrounding country was the most beautiful and fertile he had yet seen, it was almost, if not equally, as unhealthy as the valley of the Barotse.

The view from the high ground of Katonga was one of the loveliest upon which Livingstone's eyes had ever rested.   It commanded a stretch of country that lay in a beautiful prairie-like expanse for miles on every side.   In the miniature valleys that nestled between the low, cup-shaped hills thousands of noble animals were grazing—cattle of various kinds—all belonging to the Barotse.   Besides these were vast herds of leches, a kind of antelope, feeding in the utmost security.   Numberless arms of the river here glanced off in different directions, adding yet greater beauty to the scene.   Livingstone was loath to turn his back upon a country so enchanting, but the intelligence gained that this Eden had its serpent in the shape of the annual visits of the deadly fever drove him away discouraged.

As the current of the river at Katonga ran fully five

12

miles an hour, it suggested to Livingstone the increasing rise of the country above.   He therefore determined to extend his journey still farther up the stream.   As Sekeletu had sent runners ahead to tell the people of Livingstone, he was everywhere received with the greatest delight.   From the story the runners spread the natives believed he was a powerful chief who had displayed great condescension in visiting them.   They hailed his approach with exclamations something like these: " Behold! the great chief." " Behold! he of the mighty power and of the strong hand approacheth."   " See! here comes the lord, the great lion. Let us make ready, O people, to receive him."   Livingstone says of this expression, " the lord, the great lion," which in their language was rendered " tau-e-tona: " " It soon came to sound so much like ' saw-a-tone,' or the great sow, that it was all I could do to preserve my gravity whenever I heard it."

Livingstone continued his explorations as far as the junction of the Leeba with the Zambesi.   Not finding the healthy spot for which he looked, he gave up the quest for the time being, and started to rejoin Sekeletu.

On their voyage down the river the Livingstone party unexpectedly came upon the chief at the small town of Ma-Sekeletu, which meant the mother of Sekeletu, and was so named because it was the home of the young chief's mother. Having remained here several days, and being most royally entertained by Sekeletu's mother, the party began their return to Linyanti, which they reached after an absence of nine weeks.

CHAPTER XIII.

LIVINGSTONE AGAIN LABORS AMONG THE MAKOLOLO—HIS LETTER
TO HIS CHILDREN—THE START FROM LINYANTI FOR THE COAST
—ARRIVAL AT SESHEKE — INCIDENTS — THE JOURNEY UP THE
ZAMBESI — GLIMPSES OF AFRICAN NATURAL HISTORY— MANEN-
KO, THE AMAZON CHIEFTAINESS — TWO NATIVE BELLES — AP-
PROACHING THE STRONGHOLD OF THE SLAVE TRAFFIC.

O UR travelers reached Linyanti from their explorations in the river country in September, 1853.   Livingstone did not at once begin his preparations for the long
journey to the coast, as it might be supposed he would have
done, considering his great anxiety to be off.   With all his
ardor he had much discretion and a happy faculty of keeping
cool and patient under the most tantalizing circumstances.
He was still suffering from the effects of his former attack
of fever, and considerably prostrated from the fatigues of
his recent journey up the river.   He therefore determined
to stay in Linyanti until he had recovered his usual health
and spirits.   While thus waiting he engaged in teaching the
Makololo.   At this period he wrote the following tender
and touching letter to his dearly loved little ones so far
away:

SEKELETU'S TOWN, LINYANTI, Oct. 2, 1853.

My Dear Robert, Agnes, Thomas, and Oswell: Here is another little letter for you all. I should like to see you much more than
write to you, and speak with my tongue rather than with my pen;
but we are far from each other—very, very far. Here are Scipone
and Meriye, and others who saw you as the first white children they
ever looked at. Meriye came the other day and brought a round

basket for Nannie. She made it of the leaves of the palmyra. Others put me in mind of you all by calling me Rananee and Rarobert, and there is a little Thomas in the town; and when I think of you I remember, though I am far off, that Jesus, our good and gracious Jesus, is ever near both you and me, and then I pray to him to bless you and make you good. He is ever near. Remember this, if you feel angry or naughty—Jesus is near you, and sees you, and he is good and kind. When he was among men those who heard him speak said, " Never man spake like this man;" and we now say, " Never did man love like him." You see little Zouga is carried on mamma's bosom. You are taken care of by Jesus with as much care as mamma takes of Zouga. He is always watching you and keeping you in safety. It is very bad to sin, to do any naughty things, or to speak angry or naughty words before him.

My dear children, take him as your Guide, your Helper, your Friend and Saviour through life. Whatever you are troubled about, ask him to help you. Our God is good. We thank him that we have such a Saviour and Friend as he is. Now you are little, but you will not always be so; hence you must learn to read and write and work. All clever men can both read and write, and Jesus needs clever men to do his work. Would you not like to work for him among men? Jesus is wishing to send his gospel to all nations, and he needs clever men to do this. Would you like to serve him? Well, you must learn now, and not get tired learning. After some time you will like learning better than playing, but you must play too, in order to make your bodies strong, that you may be able to serve Jesus.

I am glad to learn that you go to the academy. I hope you are learning fast. Don't speak Scotch. It is not so pretty as English. Is the Tau learning to read with mamma? I hope you are all kind to mamma. I saw a poor woman in a chain with many others, up at the Barotse. She had a little child, and both she and the child were very thin. See how kind Jesus was to you! No one can put you in chains unless you become bad. If, however, you learn bad ways, beginning only by saying bad words, or by doing little bad things, Satan will have you in the chains of sin, and you will be hurried on in his bad ways till you are put in the dreadful place

which God hath prepared for him and all who are like him. Pray
to Jesus to deliver you from sin, give you new hearts, and make you
his children. Kiss Zouga, mamma, and each other for me.

 Your ever affectionate father,   D. LIVINGSTONE.

About the middle of October Livingstone began to make
ready for the long and tedious journey before him. Sekeletu gave him all the aid in his power; indeed, he seemed as
anxious for the success of the undertaking as Livingstone
himself. The latter had made clear to the chief the importance of the expedition and the advantage that the opening
up of such a highway of traffic would prove to his people.
But we must do Sekeletu the justice to say that he was actuated as much by love and admiration for Livingstone as
by a desire of benefit from the enterprise.

The most of Sekeletu's people warmly favored the expedition, and he had no trouble in getting men to accompany
Livingstone. Many more presented themselves than it was
necessary to take. Still, despite these promising signs, there
were some croakers, principally old men and women, who
believed that these modern ideas and innovations would
surely bring death and destruction wherever meddled with.
At a *picho*, or conference, held by the head men of the
tribe, preparatory to Livingstone's departure, one of these
old croakers piped out, "Where is this man about to take
these of thy people, O chief?" pointing to the men who had
been detailed to go with Livingstone. "Dost thou know?
Doth any one know? Can he tell himself? Blood! blood!
I smell blood. It is on his garments and theirs! Beware!
beware! beware, O chief!" How long he would have talked
in this strain it was not given him to show, for at this point
the chief indignantly commanded him to leave the assembly, and all present greeted him with grunts of dissatisfaction and hisses and groans of disdain. His words had no

other effect upon any one, except a few old croakers like
himself.

It had been decided that twenty-seven picked men should
accompany Livingstone, all of them young and hardy.
About one-half of them were Barotse men. As these were
acquainted with many of the tribes to the north, it was suggested by Sekeletu to Livingstone that they would be of far
greater value to him on this stage of his journey than the
Makololo, though the Makololo were more desirable in
every other respect. Livingstone preferred that none but
Makololo men should go with him; but, save in one or two
instances, the Barotse proved very clever and trusty, quite
unlike the majority of their race.

The only question propounded to Livingstone by the Makololo that showed any thing like a misgiving in regard to
the expedition was: "In the event of your death, will not
the white people blame us for having allowed you to go
away into an unhealthy and an unknown country of enemies?" Livingstone hastened to reassure them by declaring that there were none of his friends who would think of
blaming them for such a thing; but to make the Makololo
altogether easy on this point, he would leave with their chief
a book, which in case he was lost would explain to his friends
all about the journey. Livingstone instructed Sekeletu to
send this book to Mr. Moffat if he should not return by a
given time. The book alluded to was a volume of journals,
and it was most unfortunate that it should have been lost, as
afterward happened. Sekeletu kept it as Livingstone had
requested. As the specified time passed away, and much
more, and there was no sign of the brave missionary, not a
word from him, the young chief in despair delivered the
book to a trader, requesting him to carry it direct to Mr.

Moffat.   The book never reached its destination, nor could any trace of the trader be found.   Livingstone always deeply regretted the loss of these journals, as in addition to accounts of his travels, missionary labors, and explorations, they contained many valuable descriptions of the habits of numerous wild animals, birds, etc.

Before finally entering upon this perilous journey Livingstone naturally felt apprehensive, but not once did he shrink from the undertaking.   To one of his nature there was no such thing as turning back when once his face had been firmly set in any direction.   He wrote to his brother-in-law, Robert Moffat, at this time: " I shall open up a path into the interior, if I perish in the attempt."   Grand, stirring words these—words that plainly show the mighty determination that moved him, the unconquerable spirit that carried him forward.   Again he asks with telling force, " Can the love of Christ not carry the missionary where the slave-trade carries the trader?"   Ah! truly it could in his case, and it did.   His last prayer on leaving was: " May God in his mercy permit me to do something for the cause of Christ in these dark places of the earth!   But should I fail in this undertaking, O God, be a Father to the fatherless and a husband to the widow, for Jesus' sake."

Although the preparations for this journey had taken Livingstone some little time, they were few in number and simple in details.   The baggage was reduced to as small a compass as possible, and consisted of only such articles as the party were absolutely compelled to have.   Indeed, at the last moment many things were left which it seemed they could not do without; but Livingstone knew that it was almost as bad to start out on such a journey overloaded as it was to go with nothing at all.   The outfit consisted of ten or twelve pounds of biscuit, two or three pounds of tea, twenty pounds of coffee, and about half as much sugar. Besides these provisions, there was a tin canister containing a few pieces of cloth and a small collection of beads, as propitiatory presents for the unfriendly tribes they should meet on the way. In regard to this matter of presents, Livingstone would have liked to go better prepared, but he had no means of his own to enlarge the supply, and he was unwilling to allow Sekeletu to do so. If his slender store should prove insufficient, which he did not doubt, he trusted in a beneficent Providence to show him another way out of the difficulty. A second canister contained a small stock of medicines, a nautical almanac, Thomson's Logarithm Tables, a Bible, and a lined journal. Much has been said in praise of this lined journal. Every page of it was an eloquent witness of Livingstone's patient and painstaking nature. It was truly a wonderful book, being a "strongly bound quarto volume with a lock and key." Nearly every line of the writing within was as neat and clear as though it were lithographed. Occasionally, however, there was a page with the "letters beginning to sprawl," or a blot or two here and there where the unruly pen had refused to carry the ink smoothly. Doubtless these were done at times when, we are told, he "could neither think nor speak, nor tell any one's name, possibly not even his own if it had been asked him; at times when he felt the fiery tongues of the fever lapping up every atom of his vitality. But to go on with the outfit: there was a change or so of clothing for Livingstone, and a suit each for the Makololo men when they should reach civilized life. Their stock of fire-arms and ammunition consisted of three muskets, two rifles, one double-barreled gun, five or six pounds of powder, and about one hundred and fifty pounds of ball and shot. A small gypsy tent, a horse-rug, two blankets for Livingstone's use, a magic lantern, and a sextant and compass, completed the equipments. At the last moment Sekeletu gave Livingstone two or three elephant tusks, which he was obliged to take, or else deeply wound the generous young chief. It was fortunate that he took them, as it afterward proved, for they were the means of providing the starving party with more than one meal.

Surely never before did an expedition of such vast importance start out with so little preparation; but what this little band lacked in the quantity of its appurtenances it made up in the quality of its members. They were all men of pluck and endurance, and were indued with a determination to follow their brave leader wherever he might lead them, even to the death.

The party left Linyanti on the third day of November, 1853. Nearly seven thousand people assembled to see them off, and made the ground fairly tremble with their shouts as the line of brave and sturdy men went filing by. The route was to be first by the Chobe to its junction with the Zambesi, over much of the way Livingstone had previously gone with Sekeletu, to its junction with the Leeba; thence along the latter river until the countries of the Lobale and the Londa were reached, the one on the right bank of the river and the other on the left: at this point they were to leave the canoes and make the rest of the journey on the backs of the oxen which Sekeletu sent along for the purpose. Sekeletu accompanied the expedition as far as Manuku, the town at which Livingstone had first met Sebituane. Here he left them, after a most affecting scene with Livingstone.

The average speed made by the canoes on their way down the Chobe to Sesheke was five miles an hour, the men who were leading the oxen along the bank regulating their progress by that of the boats. But of course neither the party on the water nor that on the land could keep up this rate all the time, nor did they attempt to travel steadily through the day. The general plan was to paddle or march from six to eleven o'clock in the morning, and from four to seven in the afternoon; but sometimes, owing to different controlling circumstances, these hours were varied.

At Sesheke the travelers met with a warm reception from Moriantsane, a brother-in-law of Sebituane, and the head man of that village. Livingstone had met Moriantsane on his previous visit with Sekeletu, as they were returning down the river, and had been greatly impressed with him. In some respects he reminded him of Sebituane, though he had nothing like that great chief's intelligence or tact in managing affairs. Moriantsane supplied them with milk, meal, honey, and other delicacies, and sent messengers up the river to the different villages, with instructions to see that the people had food ready for Livingstone and his attendants.

Livingstone preached to the natives several times while at Sesheke. His favorite place of instruction was under an enormous camel-thorn tree that stood near the bank of the river. He had no trouble in getting together an audience: the moment it was announced that he was going to preach men, women, and children began filing in long lines from their huts, all intent on getting there as soon as possible, and all moving forward in the best order. This was one of the principal things Moriantsane had sought to impress upon his people when he heard of Livingstone's expected return—that they must preserve the utmost quiet and attention throughout his stay, especially when he was instructing them.

Once while Livingstone was preaching, Moriantsane's keen eyes saw two young men who were busily working on a skin instead of listening to the missionary. The indignant old man rose up in the assembly, and hurled his spear straight at the offending young men. Had they not been previously warned, so that they dodged just in time, he would surely have killed one of them. After that the people took care to cease every employment the moment Livingstone began to speak.

While at Sesheke the explorers had a novel encounter with alligators, and one that came near proving fatal to a brave Makololo man. The river was fairly alive with the hideous creatures, and they seemed to grow bolder and more savage as their numbers increased. Many poor women and children, and even men, had been devoured in the presence of their terror-stricken relatives. The children seemed to be the alligators' special object of prey: they were generally caught as they went to the river for water. One afternoon as Livingstone and three or four of his men were crossing the river in a canoe, they were attacked by an alligator of unusual size. A sudden stroke of the huge scaly tail sent one of the men who was not on his guard headforemost into the river. Immediately the monster brute wheeled around, and as the poor man came up caught him by the thigh. Livingstone shut his eyes in horror, for he thought the man's last hour had come, there not being a gun or weapon of any kind in the boat with which to assist him. But the Makololo was not only brave, he had great presence of mind. Even while in the alligator's grasp

188 LIFE OF DAVID LIVINGSTONE.

he had managed to reach a small, square, ragged-edged javelin he wore at his belt. With this he dealt the animal a sudden and tremendous blow behind the shoulder. Writhing with the pain the alligator instantly let go, and began furiously lashing the water all around with his tail. The instant the man felt himself released he made a straight dive, and, coming up out of the water a little distance away, was hauled into the canoe. He was unhurt, save by the alligator's teeth upon his thigh, and this wound was more painful than serious.

Moving on up the Zambesi, our party—thanks to Moriantsane—found a warm welcome from the people of the villages, and also food in abundance. This generally consisted of meats and fruits of various kinds. Many of the fruits were pleasant and refreshing to the taste, and curious and interesting in their formation. One was about the size of an orange and nearly of the same color. Inside it was composed of a number of seeds or pins, something like those of the orange, "imbedded in layers of a pleasant juicy pulp." Livingstone afterward learned that from the seed and rind of this fruit the natives derived a substance not unlike a variety of nux vomica, which in turn was converted into a capital substitute for strychnine. Another fruit, called mabole, was about the size of the date, and when stripped of its seed and dried had much the appearance of the date. In this state it was most palatable, with a flavor of strawberries, strange to say. When thus dried it could be kept a long time, and our travelers found it a serviceable addition to their stock of edibles. Still another of these fruits was the mamosho, which has been already described.

The course of the party up the Zambesi is thus detailed

by Livingstone: "When under way, our usual procedure is this: We get up a little before five in the morning; it is then beginning to dawn. While I am dressing, coffee is made; and having filled my pannikin, the remainder is handed to my companions, who eagerly partake of the refreshing beverage. The servants are busy loading the canoes while the principal men are sipping the coffee; and that being soon over, we embark. The next two hours are the most pleasant part of the day's sail. The men paddle away most vigorously. The Barotse, being a tribe of boatmen, have large, deeply developed chests and shoulders, with indifferent lower extremities. They often engage in loud scolding of each other, in order to relieve the tedium of the work. About eleven we land, and eat any meat which may have remained from the previous evening meal, or a biscuit with honey, and drink water. After an hour's rest we again embark, and I cower under an umbrella. The heat is oppressive, and being weak from the last attack of fever, I cannot land and keep the camp supplied with fresh meat. The men, being quite uncovered in the sun, perspire profusely, and in the afternoon begin to stop, as if waiting for the canoes which have been left behind. Sometimes we reach a sleeping-place two hours before sunset, and, all being troubled with languor, we gladly remain for the night. Coffee again, and a biscuit, or a piece of coarse bread made of maize-meal or that of the native corn, make up the bill of fare for the evening, unless we have been fortunate enough to kill something, when we boil a potful of flesh. This is done by cutting it into long strips and pouring in water until it is covered. When that is boiled dry the meat is considered ready."

Along the river-banks they saw many trees of new and

pleasing varieties. Some of these Livingstone succeeded in
classifying; others puzzled him greatly. Numerous interesting birds, plants, and vines also attracted his notice.
Some of them were new and strange to him, while others
seemed as old friends. Among the birds that he readily
recognized were pigeons, plovers, and turtle-doves. The
low, sad, yet exceedingly sweet plaint of these doves, cud-
dled together in the sweeping branches of the trees, sounded
·very familiar, as did also the clamorous cry of the plovers
wheeling overhead. Soon from among the latter Livingstone detected an alien sound, and one that struck oddly
upon his ear. It was a harsh, metallic-like call that sounded like the tap of a hammer upon a copper kettle. After a
time he discovered that this peculiar cry came from a bird
known among the natives as the setula tsipi, or hammering-
wire—a name that was indeed appropriate. It was of the
plover species, though a little smaller than the average size
of that bird. Livingstone also discovered something else
in regard to the hammering-wire—that it was identical with
the bird so famous for its close friendship with the crocodile
of the Nile. The reader will doubtless recall some of the
stories of how this bird has been known to enter between
the distended jaws of the crocodile, and there feed upon the
many tormenting insects that attach themselves to the inside of the animal's mouth. Because of this friendly aid
the crocodile looks upon the little hammering-wire in the
light of a benefactor, and never willingly molests it in any
way, sometimes lying for hours with widely open jaws, pa-
tiently waiting for the bird to get through and come out.
One of these birds being shot by the party, Livingstone
made a closer examination of it, and found growing from
the top of its wing at the shoulder a sharp spur very much

like that of a cock's, and about the same size. This he readily inferred was given to the bird as a means of defense. He discovered many other beautiful and interesting things in regard to the different birds and their habits, thereby contributing to the useful facts of African natural history.

In some places, principally where the banks were steep, Livingstone came upon several strange birds'-nests. Some of them were hanging from the midst of low brambles, some were pendent from the trailing tangles of vines, while others were in holes in the sand which had been dug out by the birds' sharp bills. Sometimes the mother-birds were on the nests, sometimes the eggs were exposed. Three of the birds that thus built their nests in the sand were the bee-eater (a species of the sand-martin), the king-fisher, and a bird for which Livingstone could get no name, it being in shape somewhat like the pigeon, only its plumage was not quite so brilliant or so glossy. In the nests of the bee-eater were found from four to seven eggs, pure white in color, and about the size of a wren's egg. The eggs of the king-fisher were of the same whiteness, only they were more globular in shape.

Livingstone saw quite a number of white cockatoos. If one of the party chanced to go near the limb on which a cockatoo was sitting, he would at once show fight. Every feather on his body seemed to stand out, while the crest at the top of his head, which can be opened and shut at pleasure, would be thrown forward and backward with a rapid movement, his small eyes all the while sparkling and flashing like diamonds, and his voice ringing out in harsh and defiant screams almost human. And yet he is a very pretty bird when in repose.

Pigeons and canaries were seen in large numbers, the former being vivid green in color, and somewhat larger than our common pigeon. Along the Leeambye valley many canaries were caught and tamed by the natives, and charming little singers they proved to be. Tame pigeons were also seen hopping about the yards of the huts. This great love for birds, Livingstone learned, had been instilled into the people by that clever and intelligent chief, Santuru, who had shown them how to construct their tree-covered mounds. At one of the villages Livingstone was astonished to see a miniature menagerie. In it were various kinds of wild animals and birds, all getting along in perfect harmony.

A queer bird that was often seen, and interested Livingstone particularly, was the snake-bird—so called because it swam about in the water with its whole body submerged, except its head and neck, which it darted from side to side like the movements of the snake.

One great enemy of the birds on land was the boomslang, or tree-snake, which made sad havoc among the smaller birds especially. Attention was generally drawn toward the spot where the boomslang lay waiting to seize its prey by the affrighted chatter and shrill screams of all the birds in that neighborhood. They seemed either unwilling or unable to flee from the impending danger. Doubtless they were paralyzed through fascination. The boomslang's usual mode of procedure was to select a limb of a convenient tree, around which it coiled all but its head and several inches of the upper part of its body: these it held erect, ready to dart out after any bird that came within its reach.

Among the aquatic birds Livingstone noticed flamingoes, herons, snipes, spoonbills, cranes, geese, and others—too

SPOONBILL AND COMPANION BIRDS.

many to name. The whale-headed stork was the most
singular bird of all that he had seen, and strangely attracted him. He first saw two of these birds standing on
a little island-like strip near the bank of the river, and
running their large, broad, ungainly bills in and out of the
tall, rank grasses that grew along the waters' edge, in search
of fish and snakes. These bills were shaped very much
like the body of a whale, from which resemblance they took
their name. At the end a sharp hook came down over the
front part of the bill, turning inward. This hook the bird
used to tear open the carcasses of dead animals, whose
entrails it devours, leaving the other portions untouched.
The rest of the bird's body resembled that of the common
stork, only its legs were longer. Livingstone's men tried
to get nearer to the birds they saw, but they were too quick
for them. They next tried to get a shot at them: this also
the cunning storks circumvented by suddenly wheeling
straight up into the air, and then to the thick branches of
a cluster of trees, where they remained until the enemy were
out of sight. In color the whale-headed stork is brown,
with spots of a darker shade intermingled in some places
with a grayish spot here and there, each feather of the wings
being tipped with gray and white. The following in connection with this curious bird is related of Mr. Pethrick,
the great English traveler: "Having traveled fifteen hundred miles up the Nile, he was hunting one day, and among
other odd creatures which inhabit that region discovered
these singular birds. He was anxious to take some of
them alive, that he might send them to London; but their
long legs carried them through the swamps so rapidly that
he found it impossible to take them. They kept in flocks,
and if fired at flew up from the ground, and, after circling

around for awhile, would light on the tallest trees and remain there until the hunter was gone. Their nests are on the ground near the water, and perhaps surrounded by it, and are of the rudest kind. For two years Mr. Pethrick labored to raise some of these birds by taking the young from the nest, and raising them by hand, or by hatching the eggs under hens, but failed. At length he obtained some very fresh eggs, and having a hen about to set, he took part of her eggs away and put in the eggs of the bird. The hen did not seem to know that she had been imposed upon, and took her seat in good faith. In due time she came off with her brood, and among the number were five with enormous bills which seemed to puzzle her greatly. But she soon found that their conduct was much stranger than their looks; for cluck and scratch as much as she would they paid no attention, but seemed bent upon rushing into the pond which the negro boys had dug and filled with water. The mother-hen was greatly distressed, but they went their own way; and she took the rest of the brood and went hers. The birds were fed on fish, and when the opportunity offered they were shipped to England. Every care was taken on the voyage to keep them in health; but they sadly missed their home and food, and one died, then another, and finally a third. Two, however, survived. A pond was given them in the Zoological Gardens, and fish in abundance supplied, and they soon revived. The scientific name of the bird is *Balæniceps Rex,* which means the whale-headed king."

Livingstone also saw a countless variety of beautiful and brilliant wild-flowers, which gave him opportunity for testing his botanical knowledge. Much of the flora being new to him, it sometimes puzzled him greatly; but he soon had quite a number of rare plants pressed and classed into a collection that did him much credit. Once, while passing a certain point on the river-bank, he came upon one of the most beautiful trees he thought he had ever seen. It was in full bloom, and the fragrance was delicious. It reminded him of his own loved hawthorn-hedges at home, only the flowers of this African tree were as large as great dog-roses, and the haws "the size of boys' marbles."

All along their journey up the Zambesi they found the crocodiles numerous; indeed, at some points they had great difficulty in getting past them. The young ones seemed almost as savage as the old ones, and would bite furiously at the spears of the natives when thrust in among them. The men with Livingstone occasionally hunted for crocodile-eggs, which were a great delicacy when prepared in a certain way.

As long as they were in Sekeletu's territory our party fared well, people and head men vying with each other in showing them attention. The manner of these Makololo people, when bestowing benefits, was so hearty and so polite in every respect that Livingstone could not but mark the contrast between them and the other tribes among whom he had lived—even the friendly Bechuanas, who, it must be said, were as much noted for their avarice as for their peaceableness. If an ox was given by the Makololo, they would say to Livingstone with the greatest simplicity: "Here, father, is a little bread for you." On the other hand, when the Bechuanas presented a goat they would cry with a loud voice and a great flourish: "Behold! behold! an ox!"

On the 27th day of December the party reached the Leeba at its junction with the Zambesi. The desired route was now as near due west as they could possibly make it. As the Leeba seemed to flow from that direction, they passed on up that river. They soon began to meet with cool and somewhat equivocal receptions from the various chiefs, the reason being that they were fast approaching the extreme boundaries of Sekeletu's territory. In a little while they would be out of it entirely: then who could tell what dread evils would lie in their path?

At the village of Manenko they found the people governed by a female chief of the same name. This was in the country of the Balonda, when they were well out of Sekeletu's domains. When they reached Manenko's village the chieftainess was making a visit of state to a neighboring town; but she heard of their arrival before they had been many days in her capital, and sent a very dictatorial message to them to the effect that they must remain there until she chose to come, as she wished to see them. Accompanying the message she sent as a present a basket of manioc-roots, doubtless thinking thereby to conciliate them, and that it would serve as a salve for the rather sharp sting of her imperious command. Livingstone neither cared to remain in the town nor to show himself in the least swayed by the haughty will of the domineering Manenko; so he sent her word that his time was precious, and that after the necessary season of rest he would push on whether she came or not. The people of the village were thunder-struck at Livingstone's boldness, and heard in dismay that he intended to go on in opposition to Manenko's command. They had been so accustomed to obey her without questioning, knowing her imperious nature, that they were terrified to think of the consequences to Livingstone should he persist in disregarding her message. They were literally overwhelmed with surprise at the turn affairs next took. Catching from the drift of Livingstone's reply to her haughty command something of the nature of the man with whom she had to deal, and being also nearly consumed with curiosity in regard to him through the several reports that had reached her, Manenko entirely changed her tactics. Her next communication was in the form of a polite request that the whole party should visit her at the village where she was then, and offering all kinds of inducements to them if they would come. But this Livingstone also declined, for, as he had already spent four days in Manenko's village, he had no more time to waste.

As they were encamped near another village, the chief, Sheakonda, with two of his wives, three of his sons, and a score or more of his people, visited them. All were greatly struck with Livingstone's appearance, and wanted to fall down on their knees to him, thinking him a mighty chief from over the wonderful sea of which they had heard. Their reason for thinking he had come from beyond the sea was that his face was so white and his hair so light and straight that the sea-water had washed the color out of one and the kink out of the other as he came swimming through it. This revealed in part the fearful state of darkness and ignorance in which they dwelt. Livingstone was too noble to take advantage of their superstition and turn it to his own purposes, as many might have been tempted to do under the circumstances; so he explained to them as well as he could that he had not come *through* the water of the sea, but *over* it by means of a great ship—which he tried to describe to them—and that his face had always been white and his hair straight. But he could make nothing clear, and was forced to receive their homage.

Sheakonda and his people were most frightful-looking ob-

jects. When they first approached the camp Livingstone
and his entire party believed that they had come for a hostile attack, and began preparing for it as well as they could ;
but the chief and his companions soon convinced them of
their friendly intentions. They were almost nude, having
only a piece of the skin of some animal bound about the
waist. From head to foot their bodies were tattooed in all
kinds. of hideous devices, their teeth were sharpened off to
points, and their hair dressed straight up from their heads
and made to stand out stiff with rancid animal fat. But in
spite of their hideous looks, they were inclined to be very
friendly, and immediately on reaching the camp greeted Livingstone and his men with assurances of their peaceful intentions. The chief displayed much hospitality, inviting
Livingstone and his head men to the village, and promising
to give them as much manioc-root as they could eat. The
wives of the chief, however, did not seem so generously inclined, and had evidently come to camp with an eye single
to business. Each brought a basket of manioc-roots, which
she signified a desire to exchange for butter or for any
kind of fat the party might have with them. This fat they
were anxious to possess in order to polish up their bodies,
as well as to dress their hair anew. Desiring to be on the
best of terms with them, Livingstone requested his men to
make the exchange, though they could ill spare what little
fat remained from the last animal they had slain. They
had a pound or two of butter, which they had with difficulty obtained at one of the villages through which they had
passed. Livingstone also directed his men to give a portion
of this to the women, who were overjoyed when they saw it.
The moment the elder of the two wives received the butter
she began rubbing herself with it, not waiting to get away

from the camp. The other, however, was more deliberate. She waited until she was some distance away, then stopped and rubbed the butter on her body with as much relish as the other had shown. She seemed to be the chief's favorite wife, and the belle of the village as well. The style she assumed was enough to have put to the blush the most finished drawing-room young lady of to-day. Around her ankles were various iron rings, to which were attached small bits of sheet-iron, with here and there a fragment of brass. These, striking together as she walked, gave forth a tinkling sound, the effect of which she tried to increase by a mincing stride. This amused Livingstone greatly, and he compared it to the jaunty step he had seen some of the dragoons at home affect when off duty and passing the inspection of feminine eyes.

Livingstone found Sheakonda "a fine specimen of the unsophisticated savage." He was struck with awe and much disturbed in his mind when Livingstone read to him a chapter from the New Testament, and explained it to him through an interpreter. He wanted to learn more, and entreated Livingstone to remain longer and teach him. It was one of the sorest trials through which the good missionary had been called to pass to have to refuse him. The only way he could reconcile himself to the refusal which circumstances forced him to make was to form the resolution to return at some future day, should life and strength be spared to him, for the purpose of missionary labor among Sheakonda's people.

On reaching the confluence of the Leeba and the Makonda, one of Livingstone's men picked up a small piece of steel watch-chain. This caused a hope to spring up in Livingstone's heart that some English travelers might be near.

His disappointment was very great, therefore, when he learned that this was the point where the Mambari crossed and recrossed in going to and coming from Masiko on their slave-dealing expeditions, and that the chain was doubtless dropped by one of them.

The Mambari brought Manchester goods, beads, etc., into the valley. Finding it much to their advantage, they worked upon the credulity of the natives by telling them that both the calico and the beads came out of the sea. As the articles were altogether different from any they had ever seen, or even dreamed of, the poor ignorant creatures readily believed the story. But when Livingstone came he told them better. They were overcome with surprise when he explained to them how the cloth was woven and printed. They exclaimed: "How is it possible for *iron* to spin, weave, and print so beautifully? Truly they who make them do that are gods."

On coming into the valley of the Leeba and the Leeambye, Livingstone's heart began to fail him for the first time since he entered upon the journey. He felt that he would soon be brought into contact with the most revolting aspects of the slave traffic, and he knew not how he should be able to endure the sight without rushing to the rescue of the miserable victims.

CHAPTER XIV.

QUESTIONABLE HOSPITALITY—AT THE VILLAGE OF NYAMOANA—
A CORDIAL RECEPTION—THE BALONDA COURT OF STATE—GAL-
LANTRY OF LIVINGSTONE—PROPOSED JOURNEY TO SHINTE'S
TOWN—ARRIVAL OF MANENKO—THE START FOR KABOMPO—
MARCHING THROUGH THE RAIN—INCIDENTS OF THE WAY.

———

THE farther Livingstone and his men went up the river
the more frequent became the cool receptions accorded
them by the chiefs. From some they met with a questionable
sort of hospitality—that is, they would be invited into the
villages and fed, but on preparing to leave they would find
that many of their most valuable things had been stolen.
Sometimes, too, they encountered great danger from warlike tribes; but Livingstone's courage and tact always carried them safely through. Many tribes through which
they passed while ascending the Leeba were governed by
female chiefs. Nearly all of them were quite friendly,
though not inclined to give themselves much trouble to entertain the travelers. Most of them were strong-minded
and determined women, and often showed more tact in the
conduct of both state and family affairs than two-thirds of
the male chiefs Livingstone had met.

On the 6th of January the party entered the village of
the female chief Nyamoana. Livingstone was by no means
favorably impressed when he learned that she was the
mother of Manenko. He was afraid she might possess
some of her daughter's determined qualities, and give him
trouble; but Nyamoana proved agreeable and tractable in

(202)

every way. She was a popular ruler, and her tribe one of the largest and most important. Her power was enhanced because she was the favorite sister of Shinte, the greatest Balonda chief in all that country. His territory extended for hundreds of miles, and the chief himself did not know half his people. Nyamoana's tribe had but recently come to their present locality, having removed thither from one more unhealthy farther down the river; hence their new village was far from being complete. Notwithstanding this fact, Nyamoana prepared to receive the Livingstone party in the grandest style the village could afford. She gave them audience sitting on a raised couch covered with skins. This hastily improvised throne was placed midway of a circle about thirty paces in diameter, which was raised a foot or more above the level of the ground, with a trench extending around it. By the side of Nyamoana sat Samoana, her husband. He wore a short kilt of red and green baize, which hung from his waist two-thirds of the distance to his knees. His hair, as well as that of his wife, was dressed with the most consummate skill of the Balonda hair-dresser's art, being made to stand out stiff with some kind of rank-smelling tallow, and adorned with numerous feathers, principally those of small birds. Samoana held in one hand a spear and in the other a curiously carved broadsword of antique pattern. This sword attracted Livingstone's attention at once. It was about eighteen inches long and three broad, of finely tempered steel and most skillful workmanship. Livingstone wondered how Samoana came into possession of such a weapon in the heart of a savage country, where none of the people were known to be skilled in such arts. Afterward, on questioning the chief in regard to the matter, he could learn nothing. Samoana

either did not know the history of the sword or did not
care to tell it.

Just behind the chief and her husband was a hideous old
woman with a "bad squint in her eye," and an emaciated
form that seemed little more than skin and bone. This was
a witch-doctor, whom every member of the tribe looked up
to with reverence, because of the superior wisdom she was
supposed to possess. Outside the trench surrounding the
raised circle of earth, on which were enthroned the chief and
her husband, sat about two hundred of the people, ranging
in age from the youngest children to old men and women.
The men were armed with spears, bows, and arrows—one
or two having broad-swords similar to Samoana's.

On approaching the assembly, Livingstone and his party
laid down their arms about forty yards distant. The Makololo men then took their places on the outside of the raised
circle, while Livingstone went on to within a few feet of the
couch of skins on which sat Nyamoana and her husband.
Standing erect in front of them, Livingstone threw both
arms upward over his head, let the palms of his hands come
together, and then brought his arms down again to his side.
He next made a movement as though taking some sand
from the earth, and with the same hand rubbed vigorously
once or twice across his chest. This he had previously
learned was the Balonda manner of salutation. Evidently
much pleased that he had so soon become versed in their
court etiquette, the savage pair bade him come still nearer,
and motioned to him to occupy a mat that had been spread
in front of them; but before taking his place upon it, Livingstone made Nyamoana one of his courtliest bows. This
seemed to flatter her very much, for she smiled all over her
ebony face, showing a perfect set of snow-white teeth.

After making his bow to Nyamoana, Livingstone turned and bowed to Samoana, and began to address him. The little savage was distressed at this procedure, and, with one eye on Livingstone and the other on his wife, made violent gestures to signify that he was but a figure-head in the royal show; that to his wife belonged all the honor, and to her Livingstone must address all his remarks. Livingstone then made Nyamoana another bow, and, catching a second gesture from her, at once took his place upon the mat she had pointed out.

On trying to converse with the chieftainess, Livingstone found that, with all his knowledge of the native dialects, he could make little progress either in comprehending her or in making himself understood. He therefore felt under the necessity of calling one of his men, Kolimbota by name, to act as interpreter. Livingstone describes the "palaver" that now ensued as not only roundabout in the extreme, but highly amusing. Hearing Livingstone call one of his men, and thinking this was the manner of conducting state interviews in his country, Nyamoana also called one of her men. Kolimbota then proceeded to repeat to Nyamoana's man what Livingstone said. The man delivered it to Nyamoana's husband, and the latter to Nyamoana— all this in accordance with the directions of Nyamoana who seemed to think that the more roundabout the form of procedure the more fashionable it would be. As may be presumed, it took some time to dispose of even a few sentences. To add to the ludicrousness of the proceeding, Nyamoana, her husband, and her speaking-man delivered their parts in voices raised so high that all in the circle outside could hear every word, which it was doubtless intended they should do. Livingstone was nearly deafened, especially by the shouting of Nyamoana's speaking-man, who had a voice that would have brought a fortune to an auctioneer.

Livingstone frankly avowed the object of his expedition. Nyamoana was greatly interested, and declared her friendliness to the undertaking, assuring him of all the aid she could render. Her next questions were of the country whence Livingstone had come; then of Livingstone himself. Thinking to gain her interest still further, and to establish the utmost confidence and good-will between them, Livingstone called her attention to his hair, then to the whiteness of the skin of his arms and chest in comparison with that of his hands and face, which had been bronzed by the sun. Nyamoana seemed delighted at this assertion in regard to the sun, as well as flattered by a certain suggestion it conveyed. "Then it was the sun, after all," she exclaimed, "that turned my people black! Now, if you were to go like my people," pointing to their nude bodies as she spoke, "you would be as black as they! We are, then, of a common origin, after all." Deeming it no harm to allow her thus to deceive herself, Livingstone silently acquiesced. He next called Nyamoana's attention to his hair, which, being somewhat long and of a light brown color, had excited the admiration of all the savage tribes he had visited. "My! my!" exclaimed Nyamoana in great wonder, "is *that* hair? Why, surely it is not! No! no! it is the mane of a lion, and not hair at all." She would not believe that it was his hair until she had felt of it and pulled it to see if it grew to his head. She thought it was a wig he had made for himself out of lion's hair, as her people sometimes made wigs for themselves out of the fibers of the "ife" which they dyed black and twisted, so as to resemble their stiff and woolly locks.

Nyamoana was charmed with Livingstone and his courtly manner, and at the end of the conference declared that he and his men should have the liberty of her village and the utmost hospitality of her people. Pleased by her cordiality, and wishing to make what return was in his power, Livingstone drew still nearer, for the purpose of showing her his watch and pocket-compass, and to explain their workings. But when she heard the watch tick she became frightened, and nothing could induce her to look at watch or compass. Her husband, however, showed keen interest in both—they were the greatest curiosities he had ever seen, and he did not want Livingstone to put them up again.

Livingstone and his Makololos remained with Nyamoana and her people some five or six days, during which time they were most hospitably entertained and accorded the greatest deference. On expressing his intention of continuing the journey by means of the canoes up the Leeba, Livingstone met with much opposition from Nyamoana. It was of the friendliest sort, however. She told him she did not believe the Leeba was the nearer and better route; that there was another that lay by way of the land, and if he could but find that she was sure it would prove the less difficult and dangerous. With a view to his gaining information about this route, she advised Livingstone to visit her brother, Shinte, the powerful Balonda chief to whom reference has been made. He had been quite a traveler in his youth, and could tell much of the country, as he had doubtless penetrated it to a considerable distance. Another reason Nyamoana had for dissuading Livingstone from taking the river route was that she had heard that there was a large and dangerous cataract and numerous rapids higher up the stream. Before they were aware of it, she suggested, he and his men might be drawn into some of these perilous places and dashed to pieces on the rocks. There was still another reason, and perhaps the most important of all. The majority of the tribes along the river-banks farther up were extremely hostile, and even with all Livingstone's tact it was doubtful if the travelers could go through in safety. Livingstone felt grateful to Nyamoana for her friendly interest, and after consultation with his men determined to visit Shinte, although he had not fully made up his mind to abandon the river route.

While the explorers waited at Nyamoana's town to make the necessary preparations for the land journey to Kabompo, the town where Shinte lived, the Amazon-like Manenko appeared upon the scene, much to Livingstone's chagrin. Her curiosity to see Livingstone had been so great that, notwithstanding her indignation at his refusal to heed her messages, especially the last one, she had determined to follow him up the river. Hearing of him at her mother's town, she had hastened on as fast as her rowers could bring her, fearing that she might again miss him.

Manenko arrived in great state, accompanied by her husband, Sambanza, and a small retinue of attendants, the whole procession headed by a strapping drummer with an enormous drum covered with ox-hide, upon which he beat noisily and incessantly. Nyamoana and her attendants met and welcomed the approaching visitors, and then ensued the loud pounding of a second drum and the rattling of many gourds.

Manenko and her husband ran forward to greet Livingstone after the fashion of their people. When within a few steps they stopped suddenly, fell upon their knees, and dipped their foreheads over as though they would strike them against the ground; then picking up a handful of sand, they rubbed it upon their arms and chest, and once more bowed their heads over, finally rising to their feet while they scattered more sand over themselves, this time in a shower that covered the greater portion of their bodies.

Livingstone was not prepossessed with Manenko's appearance, though he afterward found out that she had a good heart with all her Amazon-like propensities. She was only about twenty years of age, but well-grown, and exceedingly tall for a woman. Her limbs were strong and massive, and her carriage in every way masculine. She had gotten herself up in grand style, in order to make as deep an impression as possible upon Livingstone. Her only covering was a short kilt-like skirt that hung from her waist to within a few inches of her knees. About her body was a profusion of charms and medicines, pendent from every conceivable fastening-place. The exposed portions of her body were thickly smeared with a horrid-smelling compound of rancid butter and red ocher. When Livingstone asked her why she did not go better clothed, she was quite indignant, and pointing to the charms and innumerable little sacks of medicine that dangled from her person, declared that she was so well clothed that no one could possibly outdo her. Finding that Livingstone meant all he said in the kindliest spirit, she admitted that as a chief it was necessary in order to win the proper influence over her people, and to impress them with a sense of her bodily endurance, that she should show her utter indifference to any clothing that protected her body from the weather.

When Manenko heard of the proposed visit to her uncle, Shinte, she declared that it was the very thing, and announced her purpose to go with the party. Livingstone

14

was taken aback at this announcement, and when he
learned that Manenko designed taking charge of the baggage of the party and directing the whole arrangements of
the journey, his chagrin knew no bounds.   But he was
satisfied that it would not do to oppose the will of the
determined Manenko.   It was like putting the hand out
against an impetuous stream of water, and hoping by this
feeble means to stop its onward rush.   However, he had
made up his mind that he would exercise his authority in
regard to the baggage at least; but she gave him such a
tongue-lashing that he was glad to leave her in complete
possession.   His sturdy Makololo were also driven away by
this "black Mrs. Caudle," as Livingstone called her.   But
the most amusing thing of all was that Manenko followed
after Livingstone, and pointing to her attendants, who
meekly stood about waiting upon her pleasure, said with a
most patronizing air as she laid her hand upon his shoulder:
"Now, my little man, you just take it easy and make up
your mind to do as the rest are doing—that is, as I tell
them to do."   These words, and the tone in which she
spoke them, humbled the Doctor's vanity for many a day.
True, he was a small man, but he didn't like to be told of
it by this Amazon, who towered full a head above him;
neither did he like to be patronized in so condescending a
manner.   Still he excused it all on the score of Manenko's
training.   Had she been a civilized feminine ruler, our
fearless and independent Doctor would not have submitted
so tamely.   The first stage was the crossing of a stream
that flowed past Nyamoana's village.   Before Manenko entered the canoe in which she was to cross, her doctor
fastened more "charms" to her body.   He also waved his
arms above her head two or three times, muttering some in-

cantation designed, as Livingstone conjectured, to drive out whatever evil might still be lurking within her. The doctor had with him a queer-looking basket, supposed to contain medicine. This he placed on the ground at his feet. While passing near it one of Livingstone's men called out to another in a loud voice. The doctor turned upon him angrily, looking hurriedly at the basket as if afraid something therein had been greatly disturbed by the noise. As the party were embarking in the canoes, Manenko's drummer began thumping vociferously upon his great, ungainly instrument of ox-hide. The din was so deafening that Livingstone was really thankful when a drizzling rain set in and compelled the musician (!) to desist. This rain proved something more than a drizzle; after awhile it began to come down in a copious shower, to which there seemed to be no diminution. In vain Manenko's doctor and her husband uttered their incantations and made frantic gestures, with the hope of frightening the rain away, as they said. Down it poured steadily, in spite of them.

The party having crossed the stream and marched into the forest, it was thought best by some of the older members to call a halt and take shelter from the rain; but to this proposal Manenko would not listen. On she went at a pace which few of the men could equal. Even Livingstone, on oxback as he was, found it difficult to keep up with her. He was further annoyed by her turning around every now and then to encourage him with a motherly and patronizing air. The Makololo's admiration of the pedestrian powers of Manenko and their astonishment at her pluck and hardihood were unbounded. They frequently exclaimed: "There never was such a woman before! But Manenko is no woman; Manenko is a chief and a soldier."

This pleased her so much that she smiled most benignly upon the admiring Makololo; and from that time forth she was their sworn protector. Livingstone preferred that his men should restrain their enthusiasm, as it seemed but an incentive to Manenko to redouble her efforts. Wet, cold, hungry, and thoroughly exhausted, every one of them was rejoiced when near the close of their first day's march Manenko ordered rest and refreshment.

As they advanced, Livingstone noticed further evidences of a discovery he had made while sojourning at Nyamoana's town—that the Balonda were not only a very superstitious people, but much given to idolatry. They were the first of the African tribes among whom he had noted the latter tendency. Each hut in the towns had its hideous idol rudely carved out of wood, while the distorted image of a human figure of some kind was placed near the entrance to every village. Thus, while continuing the journey to Shinte, the travelers could always tell when they were nearing a village by seeing these blocks of wood set up in some conspicuous place about a quarter of a mile from the town.

The way to Shinte's capital lay through dense forests, and often across swamps formed by the junction of small streams which were in many instances barely passable. For several days the rain continued to fall in torrents, increasing the discomforts and difficulties of the journey. Livingstone was still weak from the fever that had seized him at Linyanti just after the exposures of his march thither. Besides this, for the past three weeks his diet had been most unsatisfying, there being a scarcity of cattle in the Balonda and other tribes of that section. Many whole villages did not own more than half a dozen head. Their principal articles of subsistence were vegetables, fruits, and roots. A long continuance of such fare as this, when he had been used to meat at least once a day, often three times, rendered Livingstone very weak, and it was all that he could do to keep up through the journey. The hardships of the way were still further increased by the fact that they were often sorely pressed for a sufficiency of food of any kind. They found the inhabitants of many of the villages reluctant to grant them even a scanty supply of the commonest food. Such a contrast as they were to the generous and hospitable Makololo! It was but natural that Livingstone should turn with feelings of deep longing to his old friends at Linyanti.

Several times Livingstone would have lost heart but for the indomitable Manenko. She had established herself close by his side from the start, and kept constantly chatting with him in the liveliest manner as they went along. Once, seeing that the brave missionary was about to give way, through weakness superinduced by want of proper nourishment, Manenko herself went off to beg food for him at one of the villages. Although the head man was a subject of her uncle, she only succeeded in getting five small ears of maize. These she roasted for Livingstone after a fashion of her own, and never had any food seemed so good to him. After this brave and generous act, he had a better opinion of the Amazon-like yet warm-hearted Manenko.

Occasionally the wearied and famishing party were refreshed by the mushrooms which the rains had caused to spring up during the night. Some of them were as large as the crown of a man's hat, and snow-white in appearance. Others were of different colors—one variety of a dark blue, quite unlike any Livingstone had ever seen before. Sometimes, too, they found an artificial bee-hive filled with golden honey. Then, indeed, they had a feast; yet they took good care to leave full value in exchange for the store they had abstracted. These artificial hives were formed by stripping the bark whole from a tree, then sewing it up and closing both ends; a hole was next made in it for the bees to pass in and out, after which it was hung up to a tree.

As they drew nearer to Shinte's town the people grew more hospitable, especially when they learned that Manenko was Shinte's niece. Once or twice this hospitality sheltered them from the rain in a very curious fashion. The inhabitants of some of the towns lent them the roofs of their huts. Livingstone tells us that these resembled nothing so much as a Chinaman's hat. They were made of straw, and could be lifted on and off at pleasure. The villagers took them off and brought them to Livingstone and his men at their camping-place, with the polite tender of their use for the night. Livingstone having accepted them with thanks, his men would prop them up on stakes driven into the ground, and they then had a very comfortable shelter from the rain.

Our travelers at times spent the night in the huts within the villages, not always finding people who were obliging enough to remove their roofs and convey them to the place of encampment. As they were stopping at one of these villages an amusing thing happened. We will let Livingstone relate it in his own words: "One night we were all awakened by a terrible shriek from one of Manenko's ladies. She piped out so loud and so long that we all imagined she had been seized by a lion, and my men snatched up their arms, which they always place so as to be ready at a moment's notice, and ran to the rescue; but we found that the alarm had been caused by one of the oxen thrusting his head into her hut and smelling of her; she had put her hand on his cold, wet nose, and thought it was all over with her."

Nyamoana had taken the trouble to send runners forward to notify Shinte of Livingstone's approach, and to suggest that he should receive the missionary cordially, as he was a most wonderful man. When within twenty-five or thirty miles of Kabompo, Livingstone's party were met by messengers from the chief. These brought the assurance of Shinte's most hospitable welcome. At the same time they said to Livingstone that their chief "felt highly honored at the prospect of entertaining three white men in his town at one time." This intelligence made Livingstone's heart beat quicker than it had for many a day, and for the time he forgot his weakness and his fever. Who could the other two white men be? If Europeans like himself, how great would be his joy at once more beholding the faces of fellow-countrymen! This thought was like an invigorating tonic; but he could not believe such good news possible. There was surely some mistake. "Are you sure they are *white* men?" he asked the messengers. "Yes, quite sure," was the reply. "And are they of the same color as I am?" "Yes, of the very same color." "And have they the same hair?" At this question they for the first time observed Livingstone's hair, from which he now removed his cap. They were as much amazed at the sight of it as Nyamoana and her people had been. "Why, is *that* hair?" they asked in astonishment. "It surely is not! It is a wig. It is a wig that you have made of the mane of a lion, only it is softer and straighter than the hair of a lion. What beast *can* it be of whose hair you have made the wig you wear?" On being allowed to examine it, and to pull it to see if it really grew to his head, they exclaimed with more amazement than ever: "Well, well, well! we never saw the like before! This white man," turning to the Makololo attendants, and pointing to Livingstone, "that you have brought hither must be of the same kind that lives in the sea. Where did you get him? Yes, yes, the sea has surely washed all the kink from his hair and made it as the lion's." "And those other white men, whom you say are approaching the town of your chief —have they hair like mine?" repeated Livingstone. "We know not if their hair is as yours," was the answer. "Their messenger never stated. Only this much we do know: they sent our chief word that they were white men, and he is now preparing for their reception and for yours." "And from what direction are they approaching?" "From the west." "Ah!" thought Livingstone, "that is the direction whither white men live. Can it be that they are Europeans from the coast?" His hopes were raised to the highest pitch; but, alas! they were doomed to a crushing disappointment. The other white men expected at Shinte's town, and for whom he had made such great preparations, turned out to be half-caste Portuguese slave-traders—the very last persons with whom Livingstone at that time cared to come in contact. They were the lowest and vilest of their class.

CHAPTER XV.

THE CHARMING SITUATION OF KABOMPO—AN IDEAL NATIVE VIL-
LAGE—THE BLOT THAT OBSCURED THE SMILING FAIRNESS OF
THE SCENE—THE RECEPTION AT THE KOTLA—THE PRIVATE IN-
TERVIEW WITH SHINTE—MANENKO AGAIN HEARD FROM—THE
IMPRESSIONS CREATED BY THE MAGIC LANTERN — SHINTE'S
WATER-DRAWER — SAMBANZA IS GIVEN MORE THAN A CURTAIN
LECTURE—LIVINGSTONE IS SHOCKED BY A PROPOSAL OF SHINTE'S
—PREPARATION TO LEAVE KABOMPO—THE CHIEF GIVES ELO-
QUENT PROOF OF HIS FRIENDSHIP.

K ABOMPO, the capital of the Balonda tribes, stood
in a delightful green valley, with a clear and beautiful stream winding through it.   Beyond, it was shut in
by many verdure-crowned, cup-shaped hills, their outlines
being rendered more easily traceable by the deep blueness
of the sky that closed about them.   The valley reminded
Livingstone of one among his own native hills, where
Mary, the fair Queen of Scots, had witnessed the battle of
Langside; only the Scotch scene was but "a miniature of
the much greater and richer landscape before him."   It
was pathetic to see the brave yet often home-sick man constantly coming upon some charming bit of scenery that recalled his fondly loved home-land so far away.   Every river
that flowed in quiet and lovely meanderings reminded him
of the Clyde; every vale took on the entrancing phases of
one he had known and loved among the hills of Caledonia,
while the mountains were the very same, only lacking the
bonny heather so dear to Scottish eyes.

(217)

The arrangement of Shinte's capital was both neat and picturesque. The village, with its cluster of huts, stood near the upper end of the valley. It was completely embowered by tall, beautiful trees, many of them of the banyan variety. The huts were well and strongly built. They had square walls, the first Livingstone had yet seen in any native African village. The roofs were circular and compactly thatched with straw, so that the inhabitants were comfortably sheltered from the weather. There were numerous broad streets leading through the town, with rows of magnificent trees planted on both sides. Attached to each hut was a patch of ground inclosed with a firm and well-arranged fence of stout poles set upright in the ground an inch or so apart. Between these intervening spaces were run back and forth long wisps of stout grass ingeniously woven together, and worked in much after the fashion of the strands linking the half-panel, half-wire fences of to-day. In these patches of ground were growing tobacco, sugar-cane, bananas, and many kinds of vegetables, which proved that Shinte's people were far from being amateur farmers. The bananas were especially attractive, throwing their tall, graceful shoots, with their long and beautiful leaves, high above the roofs of the huts, while their green-and-golden bunches of delicious fruit, from the ends of which were pendent streamers of vivid scarlet and purple, made glowing flecks of color here and there. Growing outside the fence inclosing the patches, in many instances just where they could throw their shade about the doors of the huts, were immense specimens of the *Ficus indica* family, which the natives held in high veneration.

Livingstone thought that he had never seen a more prepossessing native town, nor one in which the people showed

greater evidence of thrift. But the fair picture was over-
shadowed by the presence of the two half-caste Portuguese
slave-traders, who were even at this early date preparing to
enter upon the horrible business that had brought them
thither. They already had with them a company of slaves,
the greater part women and children, and all of them in
chains. The Makololo could not restrain their indignation at this inhuman spectacle. "They are not men who
treat children so!" they declared. While deeply regretting
the revolting sight that they had been called upon to witness,
Livingstone could not but feel glad of the opportunity that
had afforded them such a lesson. He hoped they would
take it deeper and deeper to heart as time went on, and
feeling thus would steadfastly make up their minds to throw
the full weight of their opposition against the advance of
the slave traffic in their own section.

About eleven o'clock on the morning after their arrival
at Kabompo, Shinte gave Livingstone and his attendants a
grand reception in the kotla. As the intrepid Manenko
had given way beneath the heavy burden she had put upon
herself during the march, and was lying in one of the huts
completely exhausted, Sambanza claimed the honor of presenting Livingstone and his Makololos to Shinte. While
they were getting ready to start from the huts for the kotla,
three volleys of musketry in rapid succession greeted their
ears. Livingstone, inquiring what it meant, learned that
it was the Portuguese slave-traders and a company of
Mambari, who accompanied them, firing a salute in honor
of Shinte. He also learned that it was the custom of these
people to go fully armed all the time, and to fire rounds
complimentary to the chiefs of the various villages where
they stopped. This had the effect of working upon the

ONE OF SHINTE'S SUBJECTS.

royal vanity, as the wily traders knew it would do. With their fire-arms they also took along a drummer and two trumpeters, whose sole object seemed to be to see just how much noise they could make.

The kotla, or place of audience, was about a hundred yards square. At the upper end grew two magnificent specimens of the banyan-tree, the more tender and pliable of their many graceful fronds drooping over in curves of sinuous beauty. Within the shadow cast by one of these trees sat Shinte, on a throne formed of a mound of grass and rushes, covered with a glossy leopard-skin. He had arrayed himself in his grandest style. A flashily checked short jacket covered the upper portion of his body, the lower edge just reaching to the waist. From the waist downward hung a kilt of scarlet baize edged with green. About the neck were fastened numerous strings of shining glass beads, while his limbs, which were all perfectly nude, were bound about with various bands of copper and iron. Around the wrists were an immense pair of copper bracelets, from which dangled numberless little bits of brass and iron. His ankles were inclosed by bands of the same device as those of his arms. On his head there was a massive helmet formed of beads closely woven together, the whole being surmounted by a great cluster of goose-feathers. Near him sat three youths with large sheaves of arrows hung over their shoulders and a bow in their hands. Behind these were about one hundred women, clad in green and red baize—the wives of Shinte. One of them, who Livingstone learned was the chief's principal wife, sat somewhat in front of the others. She was more gaudily dressed than her companions, having, in addition to other articles they had not, a curiously shaped red cap trimmed with beads and feathers, like the helmet worn by her husband. She was of the Matabele or Zulu tribe, and was much honored by Shinte. Livingstone was no little surprised to see these women present at a public reception—all the more so when they sat in honored seats near their royal spouse, and were allowed to do as they pleased all through the various ceremonies. He says: "In the south the women are not allowed to enter the kotla, and, even when invited to come to a religious service there, would not enter until ordered to do so by the chief; but here they expressed approbation by laughing and clapping their hands to different speakers; and Shinte frequently turned around and spoke to them."

When Livingstone and his party entered the kotla, the whole of Manenko's suite saluted Shinte by throwing their hands up over their heads and clapping them loudly together; then apparently taking up a handful of sand, they rubbed their chests vigorously. Sambanza applied to his chest genuine ashes, with which he had taken the precaution to provide himself. Seeing that the space beneath one of these trees was unoccupied, Livingstone made his way toward it, very grateful for the shade it afforded, since the sun was now high in the heavens and shining with great power. What next took place can be best described in Livingstone's own words: "The different sections of the tribe came forward in the same way that we did, the head man of each making obeisance with ashes which he carried with him for the purpose; then came the soldiers, all armed to the teeth, running and shouting toward us, with their swords drawn, and their faces screwed up so as to appear as savage as possible, for the purpose, I thought, of trying whether they could not make us take to our heels. As we did not, they turned round toward Shinte, and sa-

luted him, then retired. When all had come and were
seated, they began the curious capering usually seen in
pichos. A man starts up, and imitates the most approved
attitude observed in actual fight—as throwing one javelin,
receiving another on the shield, springing to one side to
avoid a third, running backward or forward, leaping, etc.
This over, Sambanza and the spokesman of Nyamoana
stalked backward and forward in front of Shinte, and gave
forth, in a loud voice, all they had been able to learn, either
from myself or people, of my past history and connection
with the Makololo; the return of the captives;* the wish to
open up the country to trade; the Bible as a word from
heaven; the white man's desire for the tribes to live in
peace; he ought to have taught the Makololo that first, for
the Balonda never attacked them, yet they had assailed the
Balonda; perhaps he is fibbing, perhaps not; they rather
thought he was; but as the Balonda had good hearts, and
Shinte had never done any harm to any one, he had better
receive the white man well and send him on his way. Sambanza was gayly attired, and, besides a profusion of beads,
had a cloth so long that a boy carried it after him as a train.
During the intervals between the speeches the women behind Shinte burst forth into a sort of plaintive ditty; but
it was impossible for any of us to catch whether it was in
praise of the speaker or themselves. A party of musicians,
consisting of three drummers and four performers on the
piano, went round the kotla several times regaling us with
their music. Their drums are neatly carved from the trunk

---

* It seems that very soon after starting on the journey to the sea
Livingstone persuaded a trader to relinquish his captives and allow
them to return to their homes; not, however, without first reward-
ing him pecuniarily, as we may well believe.

of a tree, the ends covered with the skin of an antelope. The piano, named 'marimba,' consists of two bars of wood placed side by side—here quite straight, but, farther north, bent round so as to resemble half the tire of a carriage-wheel; across these are placed about fifteen wooden keys, each of which is two or three inches broad and fifteen or eighteen inches long; their thickness is regulated according to the deepness of the note required; each of the keys has a calabash beneath it; from the upper part of each a portion is cut off to enable them to embrace the bars and form a hollow sounding-board to the keys, which are of different sizes, according to the note required; and little drum-sticks elicit the music. Rapidity of execution seems much admired among them, and the music is pleasant to the ear. In Angola, the Portuguese use the marimba in their dances. When nine speakers had concluded their orations, Shinte stood up, and so did all the people. He had maintained true African dignity of manner all the while, but my people remarked that he scarcely ever took his eyes off me for a moment. The sun had now become hot; and the scene ended by the Mambari firing off their guns."

There were about a thousand persons present at this reception, which was a fine proof of Shinte's power and standing in the section. Owing to some misarrangement, Livingstone and Shinte were kept apart all through the exercises, so that at the close they had not exchanged a word. Livingstone thought it was in accordance with Kabompo court etiquette, while Shinte kept waiting for the Doctor to make the first advances, it not being in accord with his dignity to make it himself. But it was remarked by others besides Livingstone's own attendants that Shinte scarcely removed his eyes from the missionary.

Soon after the meeting at the kotla Livingstone received from Shinte the summons to a private interview. He found the chief quite frank and straightforward and inclined to be friendly. He was about fifty-five or fifty-six years old, of medium height, and very dignified in bearing. Livingstone met Shinte in that open, fearless manner he had always found the most winning with the African chiefs and people. Shinte was pleased with Livingstone, and heartily approved the plans of the proposed expedition from the moment they were made known to him. At the close of the conference Livingstone asked the chief if he had ever seen a white man before. Shinte hastily replied: "Never. You are the very first white man I have ever seen with a white skin and straight hair. Your clothing, too, is different from any I have ever seen." Thereupon he set to work with great curiosity to examine the various articles of Livingstone's dress.

On receiving the hint "that Shinte's mouth was bitter for want of tasting ox-flesh," Livingstone hastened to present him with an ox, though he could ill spare it. The chief was delighted, for it was a great treat, his people being almost as destitute of cattle as Manenko's. Livingstone thought it too bad that the Balonda, especially those of Shinte's town, should not possess cattle, since they had such capital grazing-ground for them. He also thought it a good opportunity to let fall a hint into Shinte's ear; so he told him of the Makololo and the Barotse and of the immense herds of cattle they possessed. When he had done this, and got Shinte's enthusiasm aroused to the proper pitch, he asked the shrewd old chief if he did not think it would be a first-rate idea for him and his people to trade with the Makololo for cows. Shinte jumped at the suggestion, de-

15

claring it the very thing.   On his return from the coast
Livingstone was greatly pleased to find that Shinte had so
far followed his advice as to get for himself three fine cows,
one of them the sleekest and fattest heifer Livingstone had
yet seen.

When Shinte was proffered the ox by Livingstone, he
was much elated, and declared that he was going to give a
feast right away to his chief wives and principal men.
Alas! he soon found out that there was an opposing force
to consult first.   As he did not consult it, he was violently
taken aback when he came in collision with it unawares.
When Manenko heard that Livingstone had presented an
ox to her uncle, she became so indignant and so angry, because the transaction had taken place without her knowledge or consent, that she almost drove her attendants to
their wits' end by her furious reproaches.   "The white man
belongs to me!" she indignantly declared, "and all he pos-
sesses is mine!   I brought him here and his belongings too,
therefore the ox is mine, and not Shinte's!   What right has
Shinte to it, anyhow?   I will show both him and the white
man that Manenko is not to be fooled with."   Calling several of her men, she made them go at once and bring the
ox to her before Shinte could get it.   When they returned
with it, she ordered it slaughtered immediately.   At first
she said that Shinte should not get one smell of it; but
after awhile, relenting somewhat, she sent him a leg of the
ox.   Just what Shinte thought of this behavior of Manenko's was not known, as he kept his own counsel in regard to
the matter.   Evidently he had long ago learned the folly
of opposing his will to Manenko's.

While at Shinte's town Livingstone gave several exhibitions with his magic lantern.   At first the people were

greatly frightened, and it was only after the second or third exhibition that he could induce them to approach near enough to hear what he had to say in regard to the pictures. He gives this description of one of the first exhibitions: "The first picture exhibited was Abraham about to slaughter his son Isaac; it was shown as large as life, and the uplifted knife was in the act of striking the lad; the Balonda men remarked that the picture was much more like a god than the things of wood and clay they worshiped. I explained that this man was the first of a race to whom God had given the Bible we now held, and that among his children our Saviour appeared. The ladies listened with silent awe; but when I moved the slide, the upright dagger moving toward them, they thought it was to be sheathed in their bodies instead of Isaac's. 'Mother! mother!' all shouted at once, and off they rushed helter-skelter, tumbling pell-mell over each other and over the little idol-huts and tobacco bushes; we could not get one of them back again. Shinte, however, sat bravely through the whole, and afterward examined the instrument with great interest."

In time, when the patient and frank manner of Livingstone had more fully won upon the confidence of the people, especially the women, there was no trouble in getting them to the exhibition. They often came in such crowds that not half of them could get within sound of Livingstone's voice, or catch a glimpse of the pictures. As many of the pictures were upon Bible subjects, Livingstone found them a profitable means of teaching the Balonda sacred truths. Soon the fame of the magic lantern extended for miles outside of the village, and he had at the exhibitions other excited and wonder-struck lookers-on besides Shinte's people.

Livingstone was highly amused while at Kabompo by watching the maneuvers of Shinte's chief water-drawer. She was a large, masculine-looking woman, almost as determined as Manenko. As she passed along the streets she would ring a bell as a signal for every one to keep out of her way. Livingstone was told that it was considered a great offense for any one to come near her while she was going for or returning with the water, as in this way an evil influence would be thrown about it, rendering it unfit for the chief to drink.

Before he had been many days among the Balonda, Livingstone was shocked to find that they were much given to intoxication—a thing almost unknown among the tribes farther south. They brewed a kind of beer that was largely drank among them, even the women imbibing it sometimes to a disgraceful extent. On one occasion poor Sambanza, who had hitherto kept clear of the evil through fear of his sharp-tongued spouse, got so drunk that it was all he could do to steer himself to the royal hut. Manenko saw him coming, and the rapidity with which she "bundled him in," as Livingstone expressively said, betokened a still warmer reception to come.

Livingstone's spirits were considerably raised on learning from Shinte that he had been quite a traveler in his youth, and that he had men who had gone with him on these travels, who "knew all the paths leading to the white men." He told Livingstone that several of these followers —headed by one Intemese, who knew the language of most of the tribes between Kabompo and the coast—were at his service as attendants; also that it was his intention to furnish him and his little company with enough provisions to last them through several stages of their journey.

The following incident occurred a night or two before the departure from Kabompo. It had a harrowing effect upon the sensitive nerves of the brave and kindly man whose tender heart bled as he thought of the woes of some of the miserable beings among whom his lot had been cast. Let Livingstone tell the incident: "One night Shinte sent for for me, though I always stated that I liked my dealings to be above-board. When I came he presented me with a slave girl of about ten years old. He said that he had always been in the habit of presenting his visitors with a child. On my thanking him, and saying that I thought it wrong to take away children from their parents—that I wished him to give up this system altogether, and trade in cattle, ivory, and bees-wax—he urged that she was to be 'a child' to bring me water, and that a great man ought to have 'a child' for that purpose, yet I had none. As I replied that I had four children, and should be very sorry if my chief were to take away my little girl and give her away, and that I would prefer this child to remain and carry water for her own mother, he thought I was dissatisfied with her size, and sent for one a head taller. After many explanations of our abhorrence of slavery, and how displeasing it must be to God to see his children selling one another, and giving each other so much grief, as this child's mother must feel, I declined her also. If I could have taken her into my family for the purpose of instruction, and then returned her as a free woman according to promise I should have made to her parents, I might have done so; but to take her away, and probably never be able to secure her return, would have produced no good effects in the minds of the Balonda. They would not then have seen evidence of our hatred to slavery; and the kind attention of my friends would, as it almost always does in similar cases, have turned the poor thing's head. The difference in position between them and us is as great as between the lowest and the highest in England; and we know the effects of sudden elevation on wiser heads than hers, whose owners have not been born to it.'

At their last interview the chief seemed so much affected by the impending separation that he could only converse in broken sentences. He had become closely attached to Livingstone, and it pained him deeply to see him go. As Livingstone was about to withdraw at the close of the interview, Shinte called him back, and taking from his neck a string of beads, to which was attached a large sea-shell, threw it around Livingstone's neck before the latter had time to surmise his intention or offer any remonstrance. "There now!" cried Shinte, "you *have* a proof of my friendship!" Livingstone afterward discovered that it was indeed a signal mark of the chief's favor and esteem, and the highest honor in Shinte's power to bestow. In fact, in regions farther from the sea it was considered "of as great value as the lord-mayor's badge in London." They had not been many days on their route until Livingstone learned from his men that "for two such shells a slave could be bought; and five of them were looked upon as a handsome price for an elephant's tusk worth ten pounds." Though he had no intention of dealing in elephant tusks, and the mere thought of the purchase of a slave made his blood run cold with horror, Livingstone felt his heart warming more and more toward the manly and generous savage who had given him so magnificent a proof of his friendship.

CHAPTER XVI.

A COUNTRY OF LUXURIANT FORESTS—FURTHER SIGNS OF IDOLATRY
—A POTENT QUESTION—THE "GREAT LORD KATEMA"—LIVING-
STONE RENDERS AN IMPORTANT SERVICE—KATEMA'S GRATITUDE
—THE HOSPITALITY OF HIS PEOPLE—THE GOOD MOZINKWA AND
HIS WIFE—AN AMATEUR SNUFF MANUFACTURER—THE STORY OF
THE CROSS—A WIND FROM THE NORTH—CROSSING THE GREAT
WATER-SHED OF THE NORTH AND SOUTH RIVERS—INHOSPITABLE
TRIBES—AN EXTORTIONATE "PIKEMAN"—THE STEADFAST DE-
VOTION OF THE MAKOLOLO.

LIVINGSTONE left Kabompo on the 24th of January, 1854. His course to Loanda was to be directly
west by north-west. For some distance from Shinte's town
the way lay through deep, luxuriant forests, interspersed
with fertile plains. The party found it difficult to push
their way across some of these plains, as they had been covered with water to the depth of several feet by recent heavy
rains. As long as they traveled in Shinte's territory they
were provided with an abundance of food and given shelter
at night.

Livingstone continued to note evidences of the idolatrous
tendencies of the various tribes. In the forests medicines
and "charms" were fixed to the trees, as propitiatory gifts
to an unseen power of which they seemed to stand in great
dread. Sometimes bundles of twigs were fastened among
the limbs of the trees, to which each passer-by was expected
to make an addition, or else suffer most dreadful consequences through the anger of the invisible spirit.

Livingstone ascertained that white men had been heard of by older members of the tribes, yet no living man could be found who had ever seen one.   The Doctor was therefore a great curiosity to the people, who eagerly examined his hair, his skin, and his clothes.   One day he and his men unexpectedly entered a small village in the depths of a large forest.   It was at noon, and the inhabitants were all enjoying their "siesta."   Livingstone's sudden appearance in their midst so frightened the villagers that fully two-thirds of them fled to the woods.   The women especially were terror-stricken, and one of them went into convulsions as Livingstone approached.   When they saw Intemese, and heard his explanations, their fears were somewhat allayed.

The men sent by Shinte were of great service; indeed, Livingstone could not have gotten along without them—yet they had one trait that annoyed him greatly.   After begging food at the villages they would steal it from him..   Still they were "very clever and good-natured fellows" and most valuable guides, as they knew the country well.

While passing through the country of the Loanda, he overheard one of the inhabitants ask a Makololo man, who had been telling him of the cattle possessed by his people. "if he brought a canoe down by water to the Makololo's country, could he barter it for a cow."   An affirmative answer was quickly given, and seemed to please the Loanda men greatly.   Livingstone made a note of this, and sought to foster the desire among others of the tribe.   He also marked a valuable suggestion conveyed by the Loanda man's question—"a belief in the existence of a water communication between the region in which Livingstone then was and that whence he had started."   How encouraging, after all, the prospect seemed for the opening up of "legitimate com-

mercial intercourse" between the more remote tribes of the
continent, and thus in time entirely crushing out the slave
traffic. The farther Livingstone proceeded the more heart-
rending became the evidences of the inhuman practice.
Nor were the chiefs and people behind the traders in their
acts of inhumanity. Of one chief in particular, Matiamvo
by name, Livingstone learned that "if he fancied any thing
—for, example a watch-chain of silver wire—he would sell
a whole village to buy it. If a slave-trader visited him, he
took possession of all his goods; then, after ten days or a
fortnight, he would send out a party of men to pounce upon
some considerable village, and having killed the head man,
would give the trader all the inhabitants to pay for his
goods." All this made Livingstone very unhappy, and
with all his fervor he prayed for the speedy coming of that
day

When man to man the world o'er
Should brothers be for a' that.

The scenery of the Loanda country was most charming.
Beautiful green meadows, through which trickled thread-
like streams, stretched away for miles. The uplands were
picturesque, and luxuriant in verdure. The abundance of
vegetable food was almost fabulous, though greatly to Livingstone's regret there was little game. The people told
him that at one time there had been a plentifulness of animal life, but that it had either decreased through the ravages of disease, or else the animals had grown shy from
hunting and withdrawn to distant regions. Occasionally
they came upon a lonely, prowling animal, usually of the
leopard or tiger variety; but instead of making signs of attack, it would slink away, as if conscious of its own weakness in the absence of its fellows.

A FOREST PROWLER.

(234)

Several weeks after starting, the expedition came to the town of a chief named Katema. He was very bombastic, and amused Livingstone on their introduction by making a speech that was self-laudatory in the extreme. He began by announcing himself as "the great Moene [Lord] Katema, of whom you have heard." As the Doctor had never heard of him, the self-laudation was all the more notable, as well as amusing. Livingstone and his fellow-travelers were received by this "great Lord Katema," seated on some banyan-boughs raised in imitation of a throne, and covered with skins of various small animals. Behind him sat his wives, as Shinte's had done, while three or four hundred of his people were seated in a semicircle around him. From his pompous demeanor, Livingstone expected an overwhelming reception. He was therefore much surprised when, at the conclusion of Intemese's speech—in which he had made known to the chief Livingstone's "history, doings, and intentions"—Katema placed before him twelve large baskets of meal, half a dozen fowls, and a dozen eggs, saying: "There! give that to the white man and his friends, and tell them to go to the houses my people will show him, and cook and eat, and he will then be much more fit to speak with me at the audience I will give him to-morrow." Of course the party needed no second bidding, but at once went to the huts to prepare the feast which the generous Katema had provided. In their hearts they voted him a capital host for ministering to the inner man instead of detaining them by the long and monotonous ceremonies of a public reception.

At the private interview accorded him, Livingstone was still more amused by a repetition of Katema's bombastic speech—this time with some additions. Rising from his couch, and "looking as if he had fallen asleep tipsy, and dreamed of his greatness," Livingstone tells us, Katema thus delivered himself: "I am the great Moene Katema [Lord Katema], the father of Matiamvo. There is no one in the country equal to Matiamvo and me. I have always lived here, and my fathers before me. There is the house in which my father lived. You found no human skulls near the place where you camped? Well, I have never killed any of the traders, as some have done. They all come to me; they come in trust. I am the great Moene Katema, of whom you have heard." Nevertheless, Livingstone found him possessed of a fine stock of both "humor and good humor." He put trust in him from the first, "for," as he pointedly remarks, "a man who shakes sides with mirth is seldom very difficult to deal with."

The personal appearance of the chief is thus described: "He was a tall man about forty years of age; and his head was ornamented with a helmet of beads and feathers. He had on a once snuff-brown coat, with a broad band of tinsel down the arms, and carried in his hands a large tail made of the caudal extremities of a number of gnus, which had charms to it."

On closer acquaintance Livingstone found his estimate of Katema's character correct; for he was not only "not difficult to deal with," but he was most generously inclined. Livingstone's frank and courageous manner had a good effect upon the chief. He soon intimated his purpose of sending three guides with Livingstone into the country beyond. He also told the explorer of a better route than that by which he had planned to go. It was more northerly, and hence much longer; but Livingstone did not mind this, especially when the chief told him that it would take him

around many of the more dangerous and disagreeable of
the overflowed plains, and out of the direct course of the
slave-traders. Livingstone felt that he would be willing to
take almost any route in preference to that cursed by the
" bitter Nemesis of the slave-trade."

While at Katema's town Livingstone rendered a most
important service to the chief. Unlike the Loanda and Balonda chiefs, Katema had a fine herd of cattle raised from
two he had purchased from the Balabale many years before. They were beautiful animals, almost as white and
fully as graceful as elands. As they had been allowed to
run in a semi-wild state, they were now so shy that they
could scarcely be approached. Katema knew nothing of
obtaining the milk from them. When Livingstone spoke
to him of it he was greatly surprised; he did not see how
such a thing could be possible. Securing one of the least
timid of the cows, Livingstone showed Katema how to extract the milk from the udder. The chief was delighted
when he found that it was quite easy, and that he himself
could do it. Livingstone also showed him how, besides being drank, the milk could be put to the purposes of curding
and churning. Katema's joy increased, and he declared
that there was nothing he would not do for Livingstone in
return. His joy and gratitude, however, did not cause him
to present a cow to Livingstone for meat; perhaps he did
not think of it. Livingstone was forced to kill one of his
own oxen, as the mouths of some of his men were daily
growing more and more " bitter for want of tasting ox-flesh."
The companion of the ox that had been slain seemed incon-
solable at his loss, and went about lowing piteously. For
many days he would take no food, and his cries were distressing. The Makololo, looking pitifully at the poor ani-

mal, said: " Poor fellow! poor fellow! 'Now,' he thinks,
' they will kill me as well as my friend, and I might as well
die of my own accord.' "   Katema and his people, on the
other hand, thought that Livingstone had in some way bewitched the ox, and begged him to give them a charm
against the animal.

Livingstone was much taken with Mozinkwa, the head
man of Katema's village, and his wife—he had but one.
Both of them were above the average run of savage intelligence.   They lived in a little hut to themselves in the
midst of a large and well-tended garden.   Their home
was a picture of neatness, order, and thrift.   The garden
was inclosed by " a living and impenetrable wall of banyan-
trees," and another tree threw its delightful shade about
their door-way.   Mozinkwa and his wife were extensive
cultivators of cotton, which occupied a large field back of
the premises.   In the garden grew many plants " used as
relishes to the insipid porridge of the district "—castor-oil
plants, Indian brignalls, yams, sweet potatoes, beans, and
peas.

Livingstone was much affected by the reverence paid him
by Mozinkwa and his good wife, and was most grateful for
their lavish hospitality.   On parting with them he promised
to bring the wife enough cloth from " the white man's country " to make her a dress.   But, alas! on his return he
found the good woman dead, and the heart-broken Mozinkwa moved away, as he could not bear to remain on the spot
where his faithful companion had died.

Quendende, the father-in-law of Katema, was quite a
character in his way.   His personal appearance is thus described by Livingstone: "A fine old man, with long woolly
hair reaching to the shoulders, parted on either side, and

the back hair gathered into a lump on the nape of the neck." He was a great snuff-taker, and spent much of his time manufacturing the "titillating powder" in a private establishment planned and erected by himself, and which had the pretensions, if not the facilities, of more modern ones.   Here Quendende dried the tobacco-leaves before a fire until they were of the desired crispness, when they were pounded in a mortar and pronounced ready for use. Quendende entertained Livingstone and his whole party at his cluster of huts, and occupied himself in teaching the Makololo to take snuff.

On attempting missionary labor among Katema's people, Livingstone found them ready to listen, but dull of comprehension.   They seemed deeply interested when he told them of the mighty and gracious God who had sent his own Son to earth to die for sinful men, and who had really died in their stead.   Livingstone described the last agony on the cross in such a manner that the people were much moved, and many of them cried out in the excess of feeling.   And all this, he assured them had been done through pure love and pity for the lost souls of men, such as theirs were if they did not accept this gracious Saviour who had come to suffer and die for them.   When he told them of any thing else it did not seem to impress them much; but this story of the Saviour, pierced by thorns and wounded by spears, enduring death for the sins of others, even for those who mocked and spit upon him, always wrought most powerfully upon their feelings.

Livingstone made a deep impression upon Katema and his people.   On parting with them, many ran after him and entreated him not to leave.   His Makololo men had also won the confidence of the people to such an extent that when they were departing the people said to them: "How we wish our children could go back with you to the Makololo country! Here they are all in danger of being sold." Poor creatures! they foresaw only too well the danger that threatened them. On saying good-by to Katema, Livingstone presented him with several small articles, at the same time apologizing for the meager offering. But Katema was delighted and expressed his thanks over and over again. When Livingstone asked what he should bring him from the coast, he smiled broadly while he said: "Any thing from the white people's country will please me greatly, and make me very thankful; but, if you have a mind so to do, you may bring me another coat just like this one," pointing to the old snuff-colored garment he wore, "as it is nearly worn out." Livingstone promised that he would keep the request in mind, and the two parted with mutual expressions of regard and good wishes.

The intrepid little band started from Katema's town on the 20th of February, 1854, in the presence of a vast concourse of regretful people. Before they had proceeded very far Livingstone had a novel experience. For the first time since he had been in Africa he felt a cold wind blowing from the north. Heretofore, in the country of the Bechuana, the Makololo, the Barotse, and other South African people, the cold winds had always blown from the south. This recalled the invigorating breezes of his own bonny highlands, and for a few moments home-sickness threatened to overcome him.

The travelers skirted many flooded plains, a few of which they were compelled to pass through. Luckily, however, the water was not more than knee-deep in any place, and often but ankle-deep. Still, it was sufficient to bring on

many threatening symptoms of sickness More than once
Livingstone received warning premonitions of the coming
on of his old malady, the fever; and but for the liberal
quantities of quinine with which he from time to time dosed
himself, he would doubtless have been stricken down. As
it was, he felt very weak and scarcely able to endure the
hardships of the way; but his resolute courage and intrepid
will forced him forward. His one passionate desire was to
reach the coast, and the "only dread that seemed to possess
him was that he might succumb before accomplishing his
purpose."

On getting over the flooded plains the party came somewhat suddenly upon higher lands. Here, upon an almost
level yet considerably elevated plateau, Livingstone found
the water-shed of the northern and southern streams. The
streams running toward the north fell into the Kasai, or
Loke; and this, in turn, emptied into the great river Congo, since called Livingstone River. The streams on the
south unite to pour into the Zambesi. Passing beyond this
plateau, Livingstone saw some of the deepest and most
beautiful valleys his eyes ever gazed upon. Indeed, their
great fertility was a revelation to him. As each of the
valleys was drained by a running stream, it was not rendered unhealthy by innumerable pools of stagnant water;
nor were the trees impeded in their growth by standing in
these slimy pools, but grew to a great height and with much
luxuriance. Many of them reared their tops to the distance of one hundred and fifty and two hundred feet, with
"sixty and eighty feet of clean, straight trunk ere the
branches were reached." In every direction the earth was
covered with a luxuriant carpet of grasses, bespangled
with gay clusters of nodding wild flowers, whose rich per-

fume filled all the air. The people of this pleasant and
beautiful country were not in accord with it. They at
first refused to give the travelers any food unless they were
compensated by a liberal supply of gunpowder. As Livingstone had not an ounce of this valuable commodity to
spare, the whole party seemed doomed to perish with hunger. But luckily after awhile they came to a village near
the Kasai, ruled over by a chief named Kangenke. He
was not inclined to "play the generous host;" still, in consideration of a small quantity of beads and a yard or two
of cloth, he gave the famishing men food, and sent guides
with them to show the way over the river. As they were
passing over the Kasai one of Kangenke's guides, pointing
to the current, said: "Though you sail along it for months
you will turn without seeing the end of it." As the Kasai
and its tributaries unite to form the Congo, which "falls
into the Atlantic Ocean four degrees north of Loanda,"
whither Livingstone was bound, its course was "long enough
to give these untraveled savages a high notion of its extent."

On crossing the Kasai, they found the tribes on the
farther bank were so inhospitable and avaricious that food
could not be obtained at all save in return for some article
or articles from their now fast-diminishing stores. Neither
was there any game in these woods, not so much as an antelope or a buck; or if there was, they did not chance to
come upon it. The evening after they had crossed the
river one of the guides sent by Kangenke caught a blue
mole and two mice, which he dressed for his supper, much
to the envy of the other and less fortunate and much famished men who looked on. All this began to tell upon Livingstone, who was already run down by the fatigues and

hardships of the journey. In a few days he had become so weak that he could not have held his gun straight, even if there had been any thing to invite his fire. Fever had also set in again, in spite of his liberal doses of quinine.

The following is a revolting picture of the people among whom the explorers now found themselves: " In most cases they were outwardly very repulsive. Never seen without a club or a spear in their hands, the men seemed only to delight in plunder and slaughter, and yet they were utter cowards. Their mouths were full of cursing and bitterness. The execrations they poured on one another were incredible. In very wantonness, when they met they would pelt each other with curses, and then perhaps burst into a fit of laughter. The women, like the men, went about in almost total nudity, and seemed to know no shame. So reckless of human life were the chiefs that a man might be put to death for a single distasteful word." Yet, despite all this, there were redeeming sides to the picture. Sometimes Livingstone was surprised by an unwonted exhibition of tenderness. The head man of one of the villages once showed him the remains of a burned hut in which his favorite child had been consumed. "She perished in it," he said with deep feeling, "and we have all removed from our own huts and built here around her in order to weep over her grave."

Katende, chief of one of the villages near which they passsed, sent a very insulting message to Livingstone, declaring that he must send him either " a man, some tusks, beads, copper rings, or a shell, before he could be allowed to go on through the country." Livingstone sent him one of his shirts, an article he could ill spare, together with the reply that, "if he liked, he might come and take any thing else, in which case he would reach his own chief naked,

and have to account for it by telling him that the chief Katende had taken them." This reference to Livingstone's
chief, and the suggestion of possible future vengeance, so
frightened Katende that he dispatched the party word to
go on, and sent them some meal, manioc-roots, and a pair
of fowls. However, he retained the shirt.

After leaving Katende's town they came to a river with
a wooden bridge. Here a "pikeman" appeared and demanded toll before he would let them over. They offered
him one thing and another, but nothing pleased him except
the copper bracelets of the Makololo. It took three of
these bracelets to pay the toll, and even then the greedy
pikeman was not half satisfied; to the last he looked covet-
ously upon the remaining bracelets.

Their way now lay across a country intersected by flooded
streams, many of which were difficult to cross. Through
more than one of them they had to swim, with their little
possessions in bundles upon their heads. The Makololo
were surprised to see Livingstone swim across in his clothes,
and to do it as well as they could without any. They had
not known before that he could swim at all. From that time
they had a higher opinion of his possibilities, and frequently
showed their contempt for difficulties as long as they had
Livingstone to guide them. They would say: "He swam
the river in his clothes. He can take us through any
thing." Wonderful confidence to have in the powers of
one poor, weak, half-sick man! Yet what a host he was in
himself, when we come to think of it, weakened though he
was by exposure and worn down by disease! But it was
not merely the little episode at the river that had strengthened their faith in Livingstone. They had seen him
tempted and tried; they had seen difficulties heaped in his

way—difficulties sufficient to dishearten any mortal man—
yet he had emerged from them all triumphantly. No
wonder they felt firmly established within their souls the
old rock-built trust of Ruth: "Whither thou goest we will
go, and where thou diest there will we die also." O the
beauty and the grandeur and the strength that lie in a
pure and unflinching devotion to a noble aim! O the possibilities within the scope of him who is girded "in God's
own might!"

> In God's own might
> We gird us for the coming fight,
> And, strong in him whose cause is ours,
> In conflict with unholy powers
> We grasp the weapons he has given—
> The light and truth and love of heaven.

CHAPTER XVII.

DESPERATE STRAITS — THE HOSTILE CHIBOQUE — LIVINGSTONE'S
CALMNESS AND COURAGE SAVE THE PARTY—SEIZED WITH FEVER
—THE MEN THREATEN MUTINY—A DECISIVE MOMENT—LIVING-
STONE'S NERVE — THE HEARTS OF THE MAKOLOLO FAIL THEM —
A GLOOMY SUNDAY—LIGHT THROUGH THE CLOUDS—"CHILDREN
OF JESUS"—NEARING THE PORTUGUESE SETTLEMENTS—ACROSS
THE QUANGO—HOSPITALITY OF THE PEOPLE—IN SIGHT OF THE
SEA—REST AT LAST.

ON reaching the Chiboque country Livingstone and
his men were beset by the most desperate troubles
and dangers they had yet encountered. Their supply of
provisions was exhausted—they had not a pound of any
thing on hand. There was no alternative but to kill one of
the riding oxen. The poor creature had been reduced to
mere skin and bones through the lack of proper nourishment.
As was the custom, a quarter of this ox was sent to the
chief of the nearest village, praying his hospitality. Of
this act he at the time took no further notice than to greed-
ily accept the beef and order the men who had brought it
to go back whence they came. The next day was Sunday.
As Livingstone was on his knees imploring succor from that
Source that had never failed him, a message arrived from
the chief. He now affected contempt for the quarter of beef,
and demanded more valuable presents. Among these were
itemized "a man, a *whole* ox, some powder, or a bundle of
cloth." As Livingstone had none of these last to give, and
would have yielded his own life rather than have given the

(246)

first, he so informed the chief—at the same time adding, with his wonted courage, that he was ready for any thing that the chief might will.

A few hours after the sending of this message a band of the Chiboque arrived. It was plain to see from their make-up that their intentions were not friendly. Livingstone, anticipating trouble, had in the meantime placed his men on the defensive. When the Chiboque saw the bold courage with which the men had prepared for the attack, they lost much of their self-assurance, and began to run hither and thither all out of order, brandishing their swords and axes aimlessly, and making all manner of high-sounding threats. Seeing that they were not going to fight, Livingstone took a seat upon a camp-stool with his double-barreled gun across his knees and quietly awaited events. Finally the Chiboque chief consented to come into the circle with some of his men and take a seat near Livingstone, for the purpose of talking matters over. The chief was still clamorous for a man, an ox, or a gun. After considerable parleying, Livingstone gave him a bunch of beads and a large handkerchief. But, instead of satisfying him, these things only made him greedier for others. Livingstone was determined on giving him no more if he could help it, and equally as determined not to spill blood. It was a trying moment—perhaps the most trying through which he had been called to pass—and required that he should keep that splendid courage of his from wavering a hair's-breadth. At length, gaining something of an insight into the character of the man with whom he had to deal, and noting how ready his little band were to fight, the chief agreed to compromise the matter with an ox. A poor, tired beast, that seemed unable to go much farther, was given to him on his promise to send them something to eat. All that ever came from him was a small basket of meal and a leg of the same ox that Livingstone had given him. But Livingstone was glad to be allowed to go on undisturbed, and did not stop to press his rights.

New dangers and difficulties still arose. They were beset on every side. Hostile bands of natives repeatedly threatened to attack them. For days they were without any food except a few berries and roots found in the forests. The terror of the situation was great indeed when Livingstone was stricken down with the fever, and some of his men, rendered desperate by hunger, strove to excite the others to mutiny. One Sunday, as he lay in his tent so sick that he could barely move his head from side to side, there was a dreadful din on the outside. It was a collision between those of his men who wanted to remain with him and those who seemed determined to desert and go back. He put his weary head through an opening in the tent and commanded silence. Loud, scornful laughs alone greeted him. Feeling that every thing would be lost—the weaker being compelled to succumb to the stronger—if some sort of authority was not exercised at once, he aroused himself to the emergency. It was a fearful strain upon his wasted strength, and called for every atom of will-power there was within him. Springing from his rug, he seized a pistol and darted from the tent. When they caught sight of his determined face the principal conspirators started off on a run. Pointing the pistol at them, he ordered them back. They came meekly, with crest-fallen countenances. He told them that he alone was master, and intended to be to the end of the journey. Then, noting how subdued they were, he began talking kindly to them. He assured them that in every thing he meant well by them; that he would lay down his life for them, if need be. In proof of this he begged them to recall the many times he had said, in answer to the demands of impudent chiefs for a man, that he would die rather than yield one of them up to slavery. He then called on them to witness his own suffering, which was greater than any of theirs. In conclusion he entreated them to have courage and faith, believing that the hardships and dangers they were enduring would soon end, for he had besought the Almighty One in their behalf, and he would hear the prayer. It is almost needless to say that Livingstone's courage and his gentle yet firm remonstrance effectually quelled all mutinous inclinations of his followers.

Day after day the chiefs of the tribes became more exacting in their demands. Almost hourly a fight seemed imminent, and the men of the expedition had to be constantly on the defensive. At last even the hearts of the brave and faithful Makololo failed them, and they began to weep, bemoaning their lot and begging most piteously to be carried back to their pleasant homes. This was torturing to Livingstone—more trying than the threatened mutiny had been. He was sincerely attached to these men. They had followed him unmurmuringly through dangers and trials enough to have dismayed the stoutest hearts; they had obeyed without a question his every command; they had even faced death with him time and again, unflinchingly; but now they were completely broken down in body and spirit; fierce hunger gnawed at their vitals, and they were no longer men, but children. Livingstone's heart bled when he thought of their sufferings, and he asked himself over and over if he had done right in bringing them with him. All his powers of soothing and persuasion utterly failed to revive their drooping spirits, and he went into his tent to pray—to seek aid from that One who alone could help him now. While he was addressing that Ear that never turns away from an earnest, heart-felt petition, his prayer seemed almost miraculously answered. One of his chief men came into his tent, and seeing him upon his knees, fell down beside him, saying: "We will never leave you, father. Do not be disheartened. Wherever you lead we will follow." Nor did this man speak for himself alone. When Livingstone came to the tent-door he was met by the others with the same protestations. "We will never leave you," they said, "never mind where you may take us. We will trust you to the last. We are all your children; we know no one but Sekeletu and you, and we would die for you." They were true to their word ever afterward. Not once did they show the least wish to desert him. A new spirit seemed to have entered into them— a new spirit of love and devotion.

Soon after this episode the party were troubled by a chief who demanded valuable gifts. Livingstone simply answered by defying him; but no hostile demonstrations were made, and the travelers were allowed to pass unmolested. The Makololo men lavishly praised Livingstone's managing ability, and loudly asserted their belief in that higher and mightier Power upon whom he was constantly calling for aid. They said: "We do not fear now. We are your children and Jesus's." How quick had Livingstone's God answered his passionate prayer! Here were the same downcast Makololo of the week before, now buoyant and hopeful, declaring themselves "children of Jesus," and as such fearing no danger, dreading no death!

The love and devotion of Livingstone's men for him were

proved not long after this, when the ox he was riding threw him into the river.   More than twenty of them made a rush for him, and each one afterward regretted that he had not been the fortunate man to bring him to the shore.

On the 24th of March the expedition approached the Portuguese territory.   Livingstone had now to part with Shinte's shell—most reluctantly, as we may suppose—in order to procure guides to lead him to the " white man's country," as the settlements beyond the Quango were called. Here, too, he dismissed the men Shinte and Katema had sent, which was according to the agreement he had entered into with the chiefs.   Only himself and his trusted Makololo were left to finish the journey.   As they drew nearer the Portuguese settlements they found " the conditions and cir-. cumstances of travel growing more and more propitious." Here is one of Livingstone's graphic pictures of this part of their journey: " Every village swarms with children, who turn out to see the white man pass, and run along with strange cries and antics; some run up trees to get a good view; all are agile climbers throughout Loanda.   At friendly villages they have scampered along-side our party for miles at a time.   We usually made a little hedge around our sheds; crowds of women came to the entrance of it, with children on their backs, and long pipes in their mouths, gazing at us for hours.   The men, rather than disturb them, crawled through a hole in the hedge; and it was common to hear a man, in running off, say to them: ' I am going to tell my mamma to come and see the white man's oxen!' "

On the 30th of March, when so weak from repeated attacks of the fever that he had to be led by his faithful Makololo to keep him from falling, Livingstone reached a stretch of high ground overlooking a beautiful and fertile valley through which flowed a broad and glistening river. Here and there grew dense clumps of trees, while clusters of brilliant wild-flowers lent gladness and gayety to all the scene. Far away along the horizon stretched lofty mount-ain-ranges, their majestic fronts crowned with a deep-blue haze. As weak as he was, Livingstone could have shouted aloud for joy on recognizing that noble river as the Quango, and realizing that beyond it lay hospitable territory. But his troubles were not yet over. The Bashinge, a tribe on the side of the river where the party were encamped, made themselves so troublesome that Livingstone feared he would never get past them alive. The chiefs were most violent in their demands; but they might as well have demanded the moon, or any other unattainable thing, so utterly was it out of the power of the broken-down little band to grant the requests made. They were themselves in need of donations, and must have moved to compassion the hearts of any other people in the world. These savages were surely carried beyond themselves by the greed of gain. Nearly every thing the Livingstone party had started with on this journey had been sacrificed. Only Sekeletu's tusks, Livingstone's instruments, and the clothes worn by the men were left. The clothes were in such tatters that they could not even lay claim to the name of apparel. Made desperate by hunger and the tantalizing nearness of friendly succor, the explorers determined to march on through the hostile Bashinge, and attempt the passage of the river, even if they fell by the way.

Arrived at the Quango, a fierce-looking Bashinge chief presented himself with the request for " a man, an ox, or a gun," which had to be paid, he vowed, before they would be permitted to cross the river. It was a desperate moment.

They knew not what to do, for the chief was accompanied by a band of men equally as fierce-looking as himself. Livingstone's heart sunk like lead in his bosom. Surely God had at last deserted them. But no! Even while his worn and haggard face turned toward the unsmiling heavens in the last entreaty of soul-born prayer, the help that had never yet failed them came. Just as they deemed every thing lost, a young half-caste Portuguese sergeant by the name of Cypriano de Abreu made his appearance, and compelled the chief to let Livingstone and his men cross the river. Cypriano himself ferried the party over; and their great joy, when a half-hour later they found themselves on the other side of the river and in friendly territory, can be imagined but not described.

After crossing the Quango, Livingstone and his Makololo entered upon a vast prairie-like expanse covered with a dense growth of grass. In many places this grass was seven or eight feet high, and completely hid the travelers from view as they went onward. Three miles beyond the river they came to a cluster of neat, square houses, in front of which were groups of men dressed in military uniform. This proved to be a Portuguese barracks, over which their new-found friend, Cypriano, had command—it being an offshoot of the larger post farther on. The young sergeant must have had a warm, sympathetic heart, which was greatly touched by their forlorn appearance, for he caused each one to be entertained as bountifully as the place would afford. Livingstone describes the first meal at the Portuguese barracks as "a most sumptuous one," consisting of roasted maize, ground nuts, boiled manioc-roots, with guavas and honey for dessert. Poor fellow! he would have deemed any nourishing edible "sumptuous" after his long fast and his former subsistence upon roots and berries. Livingstone's reference to an act he felt tempted to commit during the progress of the first meal is pathetic: "I suspect I appeared particularly ravenous to the other gentlemen around the table. Had they not been present I might have put something in my pocket to eat by night." They remained with Cypriano three or four days. He not only ransacked his garden to feed them, but slaughtered an ox, which caused the starving Makololo to shout aloud with joy. On parting with the young sergeant he gracefully crowned his other good deeds by presenting them with enough food to last several days.

On the 13th of April, after three days of unusually hard traveling, Livingstone and his men arrived at Cassange, "the farthest inland station of the Portuguese in West Africa." The commandant of the barracks invited Livingstone to supper and to spend the night with him, and gave his men directions to provide well for the Makololo. He supplemented this kindness in the morning by presenting Livingstone with a suit of clothes and pressing him to remain several days, until he was somewhat recruited in health. Livingstone decided to remain, and during his entire stay at Cassange the commandant acted the part of a brother in all things.

The tusks that had been given to Livingstone by Sekeletu were sold at Cassange, and many needful articles bought. The Makololo could scarcely credit it when they learned the true value of the ivory. To them the price seemed fabulous. For instance, one of the tusks purchased two muskets, three small barrels of gunpowder, a lot of beads, and English baize and calico sufficient to furnish clothing for the whole party. With another tusk Livingstone bought

enough calico to pay their way thence to the coast, for as
calico was the current money of the districts he well knew
the need of it. The remaining two tusks were sold for
money, which Livingstone laid aside to buy a horse for Sekeletu.

As the party left Cassange—Livingstone much strengthened by his rest, and the Makololo happy and radiant in
their new clothes—the whole population turned out to see
them off. Even the merchants left their stores and stood
in groups along the way to bid them Godspeed. Livingstone appreciated this exhibition of interest and regard,
and felt the deepest gratitude for the unvarying hospitality
with which he had been treated by every one in Cassange.
"We parted," says he, "with the feeling in my mind that
I should never forget their disinterested kindness. May
God remember them in their day of need."

All was smooth marching now. The dangers and terrors
that had so long menaced their way were left far behind.
All about them were friends, while among their stores was
an abundant supply of articles with which to buy food and
entertainment. As they came nearer to the sea the Makololo began to get frightened; for now a distrust, the seeds
of which had been sown by a party of mischief-making
Mambari some distance back, was finding lodgment in their
hearts—a distrust of Livingstone's real intention in carrying them to the coast. "He is taking you there to sell you
for slaves," the Mambari had whispered in their ears; and
although they did not heed it then, they thought of it now;
and the more they thought of it the more the tiny seeds
swelled into life, until they burst into full-grown plants of
suspicion. They now recalled all the terrible things they
had seen and heard in the Balonda country. Livingstone

observed their strange actions, and from a conversation he chanced to hear learned what ailed them. He called them together and, facing them squarely, said: "I see what you are driving at; and if you suspect me you may return, for I am as ignorant of Loanda as you are; but nothing will happen to you but what happens to myself. We have stood by each other hitherto, and will do so to the last." This manly and straightforward speech was not without its effect upon them. They grew heartily ashamed of their suspicions, and as memory carried them back to the many times Livingstone stood between them and death, or a fate worse than death, they fell upon their knees in front of him and begged his forgiveness.

On first coming in sight of the broad and boundless sea, the Makololo were transfixed with wonder. It was like suddenly beholding a new world—or, rather, the end of the one in which they had all along lived; for they said of it afterward, when describing their feelings on that occasion: "We marched along with our father, believing that what the ancients had always told us was true—that the world has no end; but all at once the world said to us: 'I am finished; there is no more of me.'"

As they drew near the end of their journey grave doubts and fears began to seize Livingstone. How would he be received? What good, after all, would result from this undertaking? Would he find friends here to help him through with the great enterprise he had on foot, and for which he had sacrificed so much? or would it all fall back upon himself? Would there be one ear to listen, one hand to raise itself in unison with his, one heart to catch and retain the fire of his own enthusiasm, one other brain to help him plan toward the success of the end? Ah! surely,

surely it must be. He had heard that out of a population
of twelve thousand souls there was but one genuine English gentleman in Loanda. This was Mr. Gabriel, the
English commissioner for the suppression of the slave-trade.
The very title sounded inviting, but would the gentleman
himself be found equally so? How would he receive the
"friendless, penniless, powerless" man who came entreating
succor not only for himself, but for others? Would he prove
to be a gentleman "possessed of good-nature, or one of those
crusty mortals one would rather not meet at all?" These
were the speculations that revolved through Livingstone's
mind as he toiled down the steep declivity leading to the
city of Loanda. He was indeed a most pitiful-looking object, notwithstanding the care and attention he had received
from the kind-hearted Portuguese during the last few days.
He was greatly emaciated; he had a distressing cough; his
old malady, the fever, was not yet cured; and all these
bodily woes were increased by " dysentery of the most
aggravated character." He had barely entered Mr. Gabriel's porch when "a good omen gladdened him." Beautiful flowers and shrubs of various kinds were blooming in
pots on every side. "Ah! surely," thought Livingstone,
"the man who loves flowers, and who takes the pains to cul-
tivate them, must have a warm and sympathetic heart."
Nor was he mistaken. The welcome afforded the worn and
weary man was all that he could have desired. The first
thing the warm-hearted Mr. Gabriel did was to put Livingstone to bed. " Never," says he, "shall I forget the luxuriant pleasure I enjoyed in feeling myself again on a good
English couch after six months' sleeping on the ground."
He was soon asleep, and the good Mr. Gabriel, coming in
shortly afterward, rejoiced greatly at the soundness of his

17

repose.   At last he had come to the end of his journey, for a time at least—this steadfast " soldier of the cross;" at last all the terrors and dangers of the way were over, and as a child upon its mother's breast he laid him down to his hard-earned rest in the house of his friends.   All the "toils of the way" seemed as nothing, now that he had found sweet repose.   O pilgrim, toiling toward that other and fairer city where there is rest forever, take heart, and remember

> That city to which you are going
>   Will more than your trials repay;
> For all the toils of the road will seem nothing
>   When you get to the end of your way!

CHAPTER XVIII.

THE MYSTERY CLEARED—LIVINGSTONE'S DANGEROUS ILLNESS AND
HIS RECOVERY—HE CALLS UPON THE BISHOP—THE MAKOLOLO
MAKE A FINE IMPRESSION—FREE PASSAGES TO ENGLAND ARE
OFFERED LIVINGSTONE—THE HEROIC STAND FOR DUTY—HE
TAKES HIS MEN ON SHIPBOARD—THEIR WONDER AT THE STRANGE
SIGHTS—THE DEPARTURE FROM LOANDA—GENEROSITY OF THE
MERCHANTS—THE RETURN THROUGH THE PORTUGUESE SETTLE-
MENTS—INCIDENTS OF THE WAY—PITSANE'S LITTLE RUSE—AT
KATEMA'S TOWN—SHINTE'S—HOME AGAIN.

L IVINGSTONE reached Loanda on the 31st day of
May, 1854—just six months and twenty days after
the time he started out. And now, what had been accomplished, what discovered, through this journey? Many,
many things. First of all, he had cleared up the mystery
concerning South Central Africa. He had found it, as he
had hoped, a country watered by numerous streams. He
had also found that instead of being the vast and sandy
desert many had pictured it—even the better informed of
the geographers—it was a fertile and populous region,
where grew all manner of vegetation. Best of all, he
found fully one-half of the streams navigable, or in a condition to be rendered navigable at no very great outlay.
The only drawbacks were the rapids and shoals in some of
the rivers, and the inhospitable and warlike spirit of many
of the tribes along the banks. But what engineering skill
might do for the one, could not the humanizing and civiliz-
ing influence of the great plan of honest and remunerative
commerce he had on foot do for the other?

The hardships and exposures to which Livingstone had been subjected produced a serious effect upon him, as was inevitable.   He lay at the point of death for several weeks during which time he received unremitting care and attention from his new-found friends at Loanda.   But he did not die, although at one time even the physicians thought his case hopeless.   God had too great a need on earth for his faithful servant to call him away from the work he had so grandly begun.   In a month he was up and out.   His first call was upon the bishop of the port.   He took with him his faithful Makololo, all neatly dressed in their cotton stripes.   The Portuguese prelate was greatly impressed by this meeting, and Livingstone went away hoping and believing that the handful of tiny seed he had scattered behind him would eventually spring forth with the beauty and vigor of the mustard-bush, sheltering many in its branches.

Although able to be up again, Livingstone looked so worn, so much run down, that several commanders of English vessels that touched at Loanda, during that time offered him free passages, and tried to induce him to return home at least for awhile, until he had partially recruited his health.   The captain of Her Majesty's ship, the " Forerunner," was particularly urgent in his offer.   But against them all—against the tempting prospect of soon rejoining his dearly beloved ones—he firmly held out.   After all that he had suffered, not one word could have been said against the justness of his going.   But Livingstone had passed his word to Sekeletu that unless hindered by Providence he would bring the Makololo safe to their homes again; and that promise he meant to keep at any cost.   The risks, the dangers of travel—even the fearful ravages of the fever— would again be endured to redeem his pledge to the faithful

Sekeletu. O what a man was this!—a man of whom it might well be said, " Behold in him the noblest work of God!" How many of us, thus tempted, tried, and allured, could turn our backs upon the flowery plains of ease and comfort, and, facing the stony front of toil and suffering, cry with an *honest* ring, " Thou first, O Duty?" When we contemplate the life of this man, and find that the rugged grandeur and devotion of his manhood had never suffered by any contrast nor been impaired by any test, we feel that there is no sacrilege in our reverence for him. In thus honoring the man, we surely honor more the God who made him.

While at Loanda Livingstone took his Makololo on board an English vessel that was lying in the harbor. He said to them as he pointed to the sailors: " These are all my countrymen, sent by our Queen for the purpose of putting down the trade of those who buy and sell black men." The Makololo replied, as they gazed about them with fascination: " Truly, dear father, they are just like you." Every thing they saw on the ship filled them with new wonder. The sailors were very kind to them, giving them a part of their dinner, and showing them all the interesting objects on board. They even asked the captain to let them fire off a cannon for the benefit of the Makololo. His consent was given at once. When the cannon was discharged the Makololo were much startled by the report and the reverberations, but after the smoke had cleared away they clapped their hands and showed their delight like little children. As the smoke from the great gun wreathed about them, Livingstone said: "That is what we put down the slave-trade with." They were much pleased to hear that, and approached the cannon and examined it more closely. But the ship itself excited their wonder and curiosity more than any thing else.   They said to Livingstone: "You told us it was a boat.   Why, it is not a boat at all!   It is a town! And," looking up in astonishment at this moment to where some of the sailors were hanging among the shrouds, "what kind of a town is that where you must climb into it by ropes?"

The Makololo became favorites with the people, especially with the sailors, around Loanda.   They were given steady work to do, and were well paid for it.   Sometimes they helped load or unload vessels; again they collected fire-wood, which they sold to the towns-people.   In this way they accumulated money to buy many articles of use and ornament to take with them to their country.   But the time had now come for the plucky adventurers to turn their backs upon the hospitable shores of Loanda and their faces toward the dangers and privations that lay in the home-ward journey.   The merchants of Loanda so fully ap-proved Livingstone's scheme of opening up the west coast to trade with Central Africa that they promised to aid him to their utmost ability should the undertaking ever as-sume definite shape.   As a proof of their good intention and of their friendly interest in the natives, they provided handsomely for the little expedition about to start upon its return.   They also gave many presents to the Mako-lolo individually.   So many gifts were sent to Sekeletu that for a time the party scarcely knew how to take care of them; but at last they were all stored away for transporta-tion.   Among these presents were a horse, saddle, and bridle, and a colonel's uniform, from the bishop.   The merchants sent several bales of cloth and packages of beads, two don-keys, etc., besides a musket and a liberal supply of ammu-

nition for each of the Makololo.   Mr. Gabriel presented
each with a suit of fine cotton stripes and a red cap, while
the bishop bestowed upon them a nice cotton blanket apiece.
In addition, the merchants gave them orders to a number
of friends along the route for supplies of every kind—one
of these orders being for ten oxen.   Among the trophies
the Makololo carried back to exhibit to their people were
many very fine fowls.

Thus equipped, they bade farewell to Loanda on the 20th
of September, 1854.   The first part of their route lay
through the Portuguese settlements, and over much of the
way they had come.   They were again most kindly entertained by their old friends, the commandant and the sergeant.   They had not gone far when first one and then another of the men were seized with malarial fever.   This ne-
cessitated frequent stoppages, and it was not until the 20th
of December that they reached the village of Pungo Adon-
go, still in the Portuguese settlements.   Here Livingstone
was entertained by Colonel Pries, a wealthy planter; and
here too he learned the sorrowful news that the "Forerunner"—the ship by which he had sent numerous dispatches
and papers to England, including a journal of the march
to Loanda—had gone down at sea with every thing and
nearly every soul on board.   This was the very ship in
which he would have sailed had he yielded to persuasion
and embarked for England.   With characteristic patience
and determination, Livingstone began the task of reproduc-
ing his dispatches while with Colonel Pries.   The undertaking was truly herculean, especially for a man in his
weakened condition; and it is remarkable that he accomplished in a few weeks what it would doubtless have taken
other men months to effect.   Says one of his biographers:

"The labor thus entailed must have been very great, for his ordinary letters covered sheets almost as large as a newspaper, and his maps and dispatches were produced with extraordinary care."

After emerging from the eastern frontier of the Portuguese settlements, Livingstone turned considerably southward of the route over which he had come on the previous journey. He did this in order to avoid many of the hostile tribes encountered before. On this course the tangled vines were so dense that the party had often to stop and cut them away before any progress could be made. Sometimes the bales carried by the donkeys and oxen would be jerked from their backs and thrown to the ground.

The men of the country southward from the Portuguese settlements were great dandies, and seemed to care more for the ornamentation of their bodies and of their belongings than for any thing else. They wore their hair on their shoulders and dripping with oil. Their bodies were also saturated, and their clothes were thickly smeared with the unctuous compound. They went about playing upon all sorts of rudely devised musical instruments, like the love-sick troubadours of old. These instruments were all decorated with strips of gay-colored cloths. Their guns, when they carried any, bore the same style of decoration. The women were not far behind the men in affectation and vanity. Their especial hobby was the raising of dogs for lap pets, and it was no unusual thing to see one belle followed by a dozen of these canine favorites. But this picture lost its attractiveness when it was learned that many of the dogs were fattened for the owners to eat.

At one point on the journey Livingstone came upon some Portuguese traders who were traveling with a gang of slaves.   The situation was such that there was no alternative but to travel awhile in their company.   One of the slave-girls was very ill.   It was all she could do to walk, but her cruel master urged her onward.   Finally she dropped beside the path.   Finding that it did no good to urge her further, now that she had fallen to the earth and seemed unable to rise, the hard-hearted man abandoned her to her fate.   After they had gone some distance, Livingstone and his men made some excuse to return.   Their object was to search for the poor girl, and to remain with her, either until she died or until she was able to go on to some settlement.   Although they returned to the spot and searched diligently, beating all about in the bushes through the whole day, they could not find her.   She had doubtless become frightened at the cruel desertion, made a superhuman effort to rise to her feet, succeeded, wandered off bewildered into the woods, and was either lost or devoured by some wild beast.   This incident served to increase Livingstone's determination to accomplish the great work before him.

Their route led them again through a portion of the dangerous and inhospitable country along the Kasai River.   Many times they were in desperate straits—death stared them in the face; and before they were barely out of the unfriendly region the Makololo had been well-nigh fleeced of every hard-earned article they had brought from the coast.   An occurrence about this time showed the engineering ability of some of Livingstone's men.   Kawawa, one of the chiefs, sent them word that they could not cross the river unless they first gave him a man, an ox, a gun, or a robe.   In order to give more force to his words, he dispatched a body of men to guard the ferry.   That night Pitsane, one of Livingstone's principal Makololo, who during the day had seen where several canoes were hidden under the overhanging bank, swam to them in the darkness, secured one of the largest, and brought it to his companions. The river was then crossed as noiselessly as possible, the men and the merchandise in the boat, and the horse, oxen, and donkeys swimming. After they had all reached the opposite shore, Pitsane returned with the canoe and restored it to its former place without detection. The next morning, when Kawawa's party saw Livingstone's men encamped on the other side of the river, they were very angry and much mystified. At first they could not imagine how the passage of the river had been made, especially as the canoes remained in place; soon, however, the humorous Pitsane appeared and began making the movements of one swimming, and pointing toward the canoes. This provoked the Kawawa men, and they shouted across the river: "You were ugly, bad things to take our canoes without letting us know!"   "O no, not at all," Pitsane returned.   "All's fair in love and war, and we have done you no harm.   We must return your compliment, however, by saying you are very good, and we thank you for the loan of your canoe." The Makololo, especially Pitsane, were much amused and delighted at the trick that had been played upon the surly old Kawawa and his people; but the conscientious Livingstone had taken care to place some beads and cloth, more than twice the amount of the ferriage, in the boat Pitsane had carried back. As Kawawa and his people found the articles soon after, their mortification was lessened.

Soon after leaving the Kasai, Livingstone began to suffer anew from the fever. He was therefore greatly rejoiced when he came in sight of his old friend Katema's town.

Katema and all his people gave the travelers a hearty welcome. .A cow was slain, and an abundance of meal and honey provided. Livingstone had not forgotten Katema's request. He·had brought him the long-coveted coat, and many other things—among them a cloak of red baize, a cotton robe, a quantity of beads, an iron spoon, and a tin pannikin filled with powder. But as great as had been Katema's joy in welcoming them, still greater was Shinte's. Nyamoana was with him, having changed the site of her village nearer to Kabompo in consequence of the death of her husband. One thing, however, was wanting on this occasion, to lend spice and vigor to the proceedings, and that was the presence of the indomitable Manenko. She had intended to be present, but was deterred from coming by a burn on her foot. She sent Sambanza to represent her.

Here Livingstone for the first time witnessed that novel proceeding called *kasendi*, which is the strongest ratification of the ties of friendship known to African custom. On this occasion Pitsane and Sambanza were the parties interested. The ceremony is thus described : " The hands of the parties were joined, and small incisions, sufficient to cause bleeding, made in the hands, on the pits of the stomachs, the right cheeks, and the foreheads. Drops of blood were conveyed from the wounds of each on a stalk of grass and dipped in beer—the one drinking the beer mixed with the other's blood. During the drinking of the beer members of the party beat the ground with clubs, and muttered sentences by way of ratifying the treaty. This ceremony constitutes the parties engaged in it blood-relations, each being bound to warn the other of impending evil, even if it involves the disclosure of an intended attack on the tribe of the other by his own chief. After the ceremony they exchanged presents, Pitsane getting an abundant supply of food, and Sambanza receiving Pitsane's suit of green baize, faced with red."

Shinte insisted that Livingstone's party should remain with him several weeks. This they were glad to do, as they were much worn down. It was not until the 6th of July that they bade the chief good-by and started down the Leeba, some in canoes that Shinte had furnished, and the others leading the horse, oxen, and donkeys along the banks. Twenty days later the Barotse portion of the Makololo were at home. The scene on their entering the village is said to have been indescribable. Livingstone was really glad when it was all over, and they were seated in the kotla ready to give an account of their travels. For months they had been given up as lost, and their return was as from the grave. During their entire absence not one word had been heard from them; and as the time fixed for their return had long since elapsed, it was no wonder that they had been regarded as dead.

Pitsane was the speaker in the kotla. He described with native eloquence every thing that had happened. When he told of the narrow escapes they had had from death, women cried aloud, and men started up with clinched fists, vowing vengeance against the dastardly chiefs. Livingstone at length quieted the troubled waters. At the very beginning of so promising an outlook for the future commercial intercourse between the various tribes, he did not desire that seeds of animosity and revenge should be sown. He drew the people gradually away from the contemplation of these things, and entreated them to join with him in returning thanks to God for his goodness in leading them out of every danger, and to beseech him for help in bringing to complete success the undertaking that now seemed to promise so well. They were heart and soul in the work with Livingstone. As savage and untutored as they were, they seemed to realize with wonderful vividness just what its accomplishment meant to them. When he remonstrated with them for their lavish display of hospitality on this occasion—the village having been ransacked from one end to the other to make a feast for the returned travelers—and expressed to them his regret at his inability, and that of his men, to give them any thing in return, they quickly stopped him. " It does not matter, good father," they declared, looking upon him with reverence and gratitude. " You have opened a path for us, and now we shall have sleep [peace]."

It was only too true that the Makololo had returned to their people almost as poor as when they left them. The many things purchased with their earnings at Loanda had been resigned one by one to satisfy the rapaciousness of the chiefs along the route, until now only the striped clothes, red caps, a few trinkets, and the fowls were left. But this impoverished condition had no adverse effect upon their loyal people; indeed, it seemed to make them more loyal. They said to the returned Makololo: " Though you came back ten times poorer than you have, yet would you have gained by the journey."

Livingstone's men, when dressed in their striped suits and red caps, presented a dashing " appearance " to eyes unused to such splendor of array. They tried to walk as they had seen the soldiers at the Portuguese military barracks walk when on duty, and spoke of themselves as their " father's braves "—meaning Livingstone.

The most joyous demonstrations took place when Livyanti was reached. Sekeletu affectionately threw himself upon Livingstone's neck, and the brave Makololo could hardly loose themselves from the embraces of their families. The wonderful story of their adventures was once more related, and again Livingstone had to play the part of an advocate of peace. Sekeletu was proud of his horse, and of his donkeys, and of every thing that had been brought to him, but prouder than all of his flashing colonel's uniform, which made his eyes dance until they seemed ready to dance out of his head. Nothing would do but he must don the uniform on the spot. On Sunday, when he appeared in this array for the first time in public, so great was the sensation he created that for a long time Livingstone could not divert the attention of the people from Sekeletu to himself in order to go on with his sermon.

For many days the returned Makololo were the "heroes of the hour." Among the first things they asserted to their "stay-at-home brethren" was that they had seen the end of the world. The next moment, however, they were considerably posed with this query: "Then, if you went to the end of the world, you reached Ma-Robert [Mrs. Livingstone]?" Considerably crest-fallen, they were obliged to acknowledge that they had not. "Then, rest assured," was the decisive answer, "you are mistaken. If you did not see Ma-Robert, you have not been to the end of the world after all, but only think you have."

At Linyanti Livingstone found many letters and papers awaiting him. From these he learned that he had long since been given up for dead by the outside world. And no wonder! For two years he had disappeared as completely as though the earth had swallowed him up. For two years there had come no word, no sign to cheer the anxious hearts that awaited tidings from him—hearts that had at last, with one exception, lost all hope. Much of this painful suspense would have been averted had the "Forerunner" not gone down at sea with his letters and dispatches. But doubtless by this time the second batch had reached England, and the anxiety in regard to him was at least partially allayed. Only his faithful wife, as has been intimated, refused to believe him dead. She clung to hope to the last, finding her daily solace and strength in the beautiful and comforting words of the ninety-first Psalm. Ah! surely that God who had always been her husband's refuge would keep him now "under the shadow of his wings." And he had indeed been thus kept, and delivered at last from "the snare of the fowler, and from the noisome pestilence." Livingstone's first act on getting back to Linyanti was to dispatch letters to his faithful and waiting wife. His heart was greatly cheered to find, besides the letters and papers awaiting him at Linyanti, many sadly needed supplies—with them a box from Kuruman, containing among other articles some clothing, medicines, lemons, lemon-juice, quince jam, tea, sugar, and coffee. This gift, which was Mrs. Moffat's, was accompanied by a most affectionate letter, so written that it showed plainly, in almost every line, that she had little hopes of his ever living to read it.

At last the herculean enterprise of marching to the west coast and back had been accomplished. It was no longer a matter for doubt and speculation, but an assured fact. Viewed in whatever direction one might look at it, it was truly a wonderful journey. Had Livingstone succeeded in performing this much with every facility at his command, with every necessary means of transportation at his hand, with a sufficiency of provisions for man and beast secured, then would it have been a most extraordinary feat.   But when we recall the desperate straits to which he was put, the meagerness, often complete barrenness, of all supplies, the fearful odds against which he had to battle, it seems truly amazing that he should ever have succeeded, even in part.   One of the most remarkable points about the whole matter was that he had brought every one of his men back with him.   Not a life had been sacrificed.

But how had Livingstone himself come out of this journey?   Very much the worse for it, so far as bodily ills were concerned.   He was not only worn down to mere skin and bones through the terrible ravages of the malarial fever, but, from having to sleep so much on the damp, wet ground, often in little pools of water, he had contracted rheumatic fever in a most aggravated form.   So severe were the attacks that they had seriously affected his hearing.   Further than this, he had nearly lost the sight of one eye, by having it struck by the branch of a tree as he was riding through the forest.   But in spirit Livingstone was as brave, as cheerful, as determined as ever.   Not for these bodily ills—which would have given many men the excuse to turn their backs forever upon what still lay before— would he renounce the work he had begun, even for a time. He had determinately taken his stand, he had resolutely started in the path—from that time to this he had never swerved either to right or to left, nor did he intend to do it until God's own hand laid him helpless by the way, and placed upon his ardor the seal of eternal inactivity.

Not the least of Livingstone's achievements on this journey to the sea were the many geographical discoveries he had made, an account of each one of which he had found

time to transmit to the Royal Geographical Society.   Nor
was this done in the least slipshod sort of a way—as might
have been excusable amidst the many difficulties under
which he labored—but with the utmost care and exactness.
Indeed, so accurate was he, so painstaking, even in the
midst of the most adverse surroundings, that the Society
was loud in its praise. The unanimous verdict regarding him
was that " no explorer on record had determined his path
with the precision he had accomplished."   As might be
supposed, the Society was not slow in showing its appreciation in a more substantial form.   In May, 1855, a gold
medal was awarded him—the highest honor in the Society's
power to bestow.   This occasion is spoken of as one of
" great interest."   Many distinguished speakers reviewed
the work of the now famous missionary and explorer. All
of them agreed in declaring that " the simplicity of his arrangements gave additional wonder to the results."   The
account of his recent march to the sea was contrasted with
that of one that had just reached them of a Portuguese expedition led by a Col. Monteiro from the east coast into the
interior.   In comparing the two, Lord Ellesmere, one of the
speakers, pointedly remarked: " I advert to it to point out
the contrast between the two.   Col. Monteiro was the
leader of a small army—some twenty Portuguese soldiers,
and a hundred and twenty Caffres.   The contrast is as
great between such military array and the solitary grandeur of the missionary's progress as it is between the actual
achievement of the two—between the rough knowledge obtained by the Portuguese of some three hundred leagues of
new country, and the scientific precision with which the
unarmed and unassisted Englishman has left his mark on
so many important stations of regions hitherto a blank."

18

CHAPTER XIX.

THE DEPARTURE FOR THE EAST COAST—SEKELETU'S PROOF OF
HIS DEVOTION — THE GRAVE OF THE CHIEF SEKOTE—THE
GREAT VICTORIA FALLS—THE COUNTRY OF THE BATOKA—A
DEGRADED TRIBE—THE GOSPEL OF PEACE—DANGERS AND DIF-
FICULTIES—AT THE JUNCTION OF THE LOANGWA AND THE ZAM-
BESI—HOSTILITY OF THE TRIBES—A PERILOUS POSITION—THE
REVENGEFUL CHIEF MPENDE—IN ANSWER TO PRAYER.

A LLOWING himself barely two months' rest at Lin-
yánti, Livingstone made ready to depart on the yet
untried paths to the east coast. The journey to the west
coast had not been altogether as satisfactory as he had
hoped, and grave doubts were beginning to rise in his mind
as to the possibility of soon opening up in this direction the
route of commerce of which he had so long and so fondly
dreamed. As elsewhere stated, the chief obstacles in the way
were the many shoals and rapids in the rivers, and the hostile
bands of natives along the banks. Then, much money would
be needed—a great deal more, he feared, than he had at first
supposed. Who would be found to give this money? Surely, when he had brought them to see things as he now saw
them, his own countrymen would do it. But this might
take a long while, and the need of immediate action was
pressing. It is true that the success of his undertaking
had aroused in many of the natives a desire to establish
trading relations with the distant tribes. Even now a few
of the more intrepid of Sekeletu's men were engaged in or-
ganizing a party to proceed to the Portuguese settlements

with a supply of ivory. In the interim Livingstone determined on trying the east coast. Without doubt the waters of the Zambesi would reveal a more promising outlook. He had no trouble whatever in procuring volunteers to go with him on this second expedition. In fact, many more offered than it would have been either safe or wise to accept. They all said they were anxious to go, so that they could return and relate " strange, fine things," as did their brethren who had been to the west coast. Forty-five or fifty of the more promising of those who presented themselves were selected. They left Linyanti on the third day of November, 1855. Sekeletu, with two hundred additional men as an escort, accompanied them as far as Kalai on the Leambye River. The party were in the best of spirits, being well provided for through the forethought and generosity of Sekeletu.

On this east passage there were many routes opened up to him, but Livingstone, for reasons already made known, chose the one along the Zambesi; although he well knew, from information he had received, that it was the most difficult and dangerous of all. Some of the most hostile tribes in Central Africa lived in the vicinity of this river.

They had not traveled far when a violent storm of thunder, lightning, and rain overtook them. And now occurred an incident which proved, far more than many high-sounding words could have done, the genuineness of Sekeletu's devotion to Livingstone. In some way Livingstone and Sekeletu became separated from the rest of the men. They were soon wet to the skin, and having no extra clothing they were in a lamentable plight. But luckily Sekeletu had his blanket. When night came on they were still lost from the party. Knowing not what else to do, and being overcome with fatigue, they both lay down on Sekeletu's blanket at the foot of a tree. When Livingstone awoke in the night he was lying on one half of the blanket and covered with the other half, while Sekeletu was taking the rain upon the wet ground. This circumstance affected Livingstone deeply. He says in allusion to Sekeletu's noble conduct: "I was much touched by this act of genuine kindness. If such men must perish by the advance of civilization, as certain races of animals do before others, it is a pity. God grant that, ere this time comes, they may receive that gospel that is a solace for the soul in death."

On the island of Kalai, on which is situated the town of Kalai, where Sekeletu and his men afterward took leave of the expedition, they found the grave of Sekote, a Batoka chief who had been conquered by Sebituane. He had retired to this island, where he had died. The grave was in a remote part of the island. It was covered over with human skulls and those of various animals, as was the custom of decorating the graves of chiefs in that country. At the head of the grave were heaped into a mound seventy large elephant tusks, surmounted by the head of a hippopotamus. Around him were buried many of his relatives, including one or two of his wives. Their graves were ornamented with tusks, and with the heads of crocodiles and hippopotami, but with no human skulls, this being alone a chief's distinction.

On the 13th day of November Livingstone, with Sekeletu and a picked band of his men, entered canoes to visit the great falls on the Zambesi. He thought this must indeed be a sight worth seeing, as the natives themselves were so impressed with it. Even Sebituane, in the short while they had been together, had mentioned the falls. One of his questions had been: "Have you smoke that sounds in your country?" On Livingstone's answering in the negative, he continued: "Well, then, when you go to my town, Linyanti, and sail some miles down the river, until you come to another river, and then go up that for a distance, you will there come to the great puffs of smoke that sound so loudly they will fill all your ears with a rush and roar, such as you never heard before." Of course Livingstone knew that he must mean a cataract of some kind; and ever since then his curiosity had been aroused in regard to it. Now, for the last five or six days—in fact, ever since he had been in the country of the Batoka—he had continually heard of the smoke that sounds. He afterward learned that the natives called this wonderful cataract the falls of Mosioatunya—the literal meaning of the word in their language being, "smoke does sound there." Before they had gone far in the canoes, the steadily increasing flow of the tide indicated to Livingstone that they were approaching the great falls. Awhile later they came to a place where the sweep of the waters onward was so rapid that the canoes had to be taken out and carried along the banks. When six miles away, Livingstone saw the tops of the mountains of spray that whirled off their spirit-like forms in whatever direction the wind was blowing. He learned that on a clear day these columns were visible to the naked eye for the distance of twenty miles or more. The rush and roar of the waters can also be heard for fully two miles away, while long before the traveler by land reaches this powerful cataract he is made aware of its proximity by the trembling of the ground beneath his feet—this, of course, being caused by the immense volume and force of the falling waters.

VICTORIA FALLS, ZAMBESI RIVER.

(278)

Livingstone was awed beyond the power of words to describe as he came within full view of this magnificent freak of nature. Even its minor points were far beyond the wildest play of his imagination. The men launched the canoes again some distance above the falls, and gradually and carefully made their way to an island in the center of the stream, the outward edge of which hung directly over the chasm of the falls. Livingstone found that this island divided one portion of the cataract from the other. Creeping to the verge, with feelings of the deepest awe, he peered down into the fearful abyss into which the waters so madly plunged. The stream at this point seemed to be some two thousand yards wide, and leaped downward over the sheer, precipitous face of a wall of rock to a depth which it was impossible to properly estimate at first sight. Later Livingstone learned, through actual measurement, that the stream was something over eighteen hundred yards in width, and that the waters plunged a distance of full three hundred feet. What rendered this phenomenon all the more awe-inspiring was that the fissure into which the waters leaped was not more than eighty or eighty-five feet in width. Thus the force of the waters, being compressed into so small a compass, in their mighty reaction threw upward the vast columns of spray to the height of from two hundred and fifty feet to three hundred feet. At a distance this unbroken mass of seething water presents the appearance of clouds of drifted snow. In a " prolongation of the rocky chasm " at the eastern end of the falls " the tormented river " found an outlet. This prolongation continued for thirty miles or more, and as it was very zigzag in its course, the water was constantly thrown from left to right, and from right back to left again. In consequence of this, it

went roaring and boiling on its way, in many places sending up columns of spray to a considerable height. The
Makololo told Livingstone that at a point farther east the
fissure was deeper than it was at the falls. At this place
the walls sloped so gradually that any one accustomed to
it might go down in a sitting posture. A knowledge of this
fact had once been taken advantage of by a party of the
Batoka when pursued by the Makololo. But they had not
been cautious enough : in attempting to go too fast, they
soon lost control of themselves, and were hurled to pieces
on the rocks below.

The longer Livingstone gazed upon this mighty spectacle of nature the more vividly he realized the majesty and
grandeur of God, and the utter insignificance of his creature, man. All about the falls the scene was remarkably
picturesque and beautiful. Along the river-banks grew
trees of magnificent foliage—among them the baobab, that
mightiest monarch of the African forests; the palmyra, with
its long, graceful, and feathery leaves; the mohonou, in
shape and foliage much like the lovely cedar of Lebanon;
and the tall, willowy motsouri. Here and there the broad
surface of the river was dotted with miniature islands, each
covered with a luxuriant mass of vegetation, amidst which
were many glowing blossoms spangling it like stars. As
the sunlight fell full upon the cloud-like columns of leaping spray it crowned them with all the brilliant colors of
the rainbow. But the grandest sight was at night, when
the falls "shone with a yellow, sulphurous haze, shadowed
by clouds of pitchy blackness, as if belched from the crater
of a burning mountain." It is no wonder that the natives
looked upon this cataract in fear and awe; no wonder that
its grandeur and beauty so impressed them that they des-

ignated it as the abode of their god, Barimo.   That was the
highest tribute they could have paid to its "power and
mystery."

Livingstone at once communicated to the Royal Geographical Society a knowledge of the discovery of these
falls, and forwarded a description of them—at the same
time conveying the intelligence that he had named them
the "Victoria Falls," in honor of his sovereign.   This news
created a great stir throughout the world.   The name of
Livingstone is forever associated with the discovery, and it is
considered by many as his most distinguished achievement.

On the 20th of November Livingstone bade adieu to Sekeletu, and with his attendants moved northward through
the country of the Batoka.   This tribe was very singular
in some things.   It was a rigid custom that at the adoles-
cent period every male and female must knock out the front
teeth.   This caused the lower teeth to grow long and bent.
The upper lip sunk in, while the under, borne outward by
the growing teeth, presented a most unsightly appearance.
When they were asked their reason for this hideous custom
they replied that they observed it to make themselves look
more like the ox.   Those who retained both rows of teeth,
they said, resembled the zebra; and they had no regard for
the zebra, while, like many of the African tribes, they had
the highest veneration for the ox.

In going into the Batoka country Livingstone left the
Zambesi for awhile, but after a considerable detour he returned to it several weeks later at a point farther eastward.
The open plains over which he was now passing, covered
with short, luxuriant grass, made traveling more of a pleasure than a hardship, and the little band pushed onward in
the best of spirits.   It was nothing like going to the west

coast, where there had been great overflowed plains, tangled vines, and fallen trees to obstruct their way.   To add
to the pleasure, the district abounded in vegetable and animal life.   There were all sorts of delicious fruits, which
hung from the trees in tempting nearness, while immense
herds of animals were constantly crossing their path.   It
was no trouble to bring down, at almost any time, a fine
buffalo, an antelope, or an eland.   Flesh-meat was therefore in great abundance, and the Makololo's heart kept as
merry as a song.   They passed by the ruins of many villages, the extent of which showed the great populousness of
the Batoka tribes before so many of them had been exter-
minated in the long and fierce war with Sebituane.   At the
river Dila they came to a spot where Sebituane had lived
for awhile after his conquest of the country.   It was a most
charming place, and the Makololo had never ceased to regret their departure from it.   It was not only beautiful and
fertile, but an exceedingly healthy region.   Sekeletu had
given Livingstone's head man, Sekwebu, instructions to
point it out to Livingstone, as he thought perhaps the latter
might find in it the long looked-for spot at which to plant
the mission station.   Livingstone was entirely pleased with
it, but he could not as yet decide upon any thing definite—
at least not until that other great dream of his life had assumed a more realistic shape.   Livingstone particularly
admired the fine, large trees that grew everywhere about
this favored spot, yielding fruits in rich abundance.   Many
of them were real monsters of the forest.   He noticed a fig-
tree that measured fifty feet in circumference.   The heart
had been burned out, and some one had recently used it as
a lodging-place, for within it were the remains of a bed
and a fire.

Beyond the Dila the expedition met with a tribe that were inclined to be very hostile, especially when they recognized Livingstone's men as Makololos. They had not forgotten the old enmity, nor forgiven the old injuries, and though overcome were not conquered. After their defeat by Sebituane they had retreated to this spot, where they had ever since remained sullen and vindictive. When the explorers came in sight these people brandished their battle-axes and prepared to rush upon them. Nothing but Livingstone's cool courage saved their lives. With the exception of this instance they found the Batoka quite friendly, many of them coming long distances to bring presents of fruit and maize.

At the village of Monze Livingstone was much disgusted at the manner of salutation accorded him by some of the inhabitants. This was by throwing themselves upon the ground and rolling from side to side in the dirt, at the same time slapping their thighs vigorously. All the while they were grinning most horribly, and between the grins shouting out the oral welcome, " Kina Bomba!" As soon as they began these antics Livingstone cried out to them, "Stop! I don't want that!" But misunderstanding him, and misconstruing his words to mean approbation, they tumbled more wildly, slapped themselves more vigorously, and grinned more horribly than ever. In complete disgust Livingstone turned his back upon them, and waited for them to tire themselves out and to get up from the ground. He speaks of this tribe as the most thoroughly degraded of any he had met in Africa. They must indeed have been low in the scale of degradation to excite the loathing of one so tender and warm-hearted. And yet they were kind and peaceable creatures, and welcomed the travelers with the best their humble village would afford. Monze's people wore their hair all gathered up into a mass on top of their heads and woven into a cone, sometimes rising a foot or more in height.

On the 18th of December the explorers reached the Kafue, which was the largest tributary of the Zambesi they had yet seen. Here they found the village of a chief by the name of Semalembue. He treated them handsomely, giving them thirty baskets of meal and maize, and an abundance of ground-nuts. Livingstone remained among this people long enough to preach once or twice. The chief, as well as many of the people, seemed greatly impressed with Livingstone's words, especially the gospel of peace he proclaimed. Semalembue said to him: "Now, if what you tell us be indeed true, then can I both eat and sleep in peace after this, in the hope of the coming of that day when all shall be peace."

While at this place Sekwebu pointed out the direction of a wonderful fountain, some two and a half days' journey distant, which emitted steam at one point and boiling water at another. "There," said he to Livingstone, "had Sebituane been alive he would have brought you to live with him. You would be on the bank of the river; and by taking canoes you would at once sail down to the Zambesi, and visit the white people at the sea."

As long as the travelers were in the domains of the tribes that owed allegiance to Sekeletu, they were most hospitably entertained—with the one exception noted. But they were now fast approaching the confines of this territory, and in consequence grave doubts and fears possessed them. For the last few weeks they had gradually veered around from their long detour, and were now again coming back toward the

Zambesi—although, as the record of their journey states, they had not at any time " departed very far from its channel." Within a " few days of the New-year's-day of 1856 " they became aware that they must be very close to this " king of African rivers." Over their heads flew immense flocks of wild fowls—geese, ducks, herons, spoon-bills, and many others—and by these signs they knew that the feeding-grounds of the feathered tribes could not be far away. They now feasted royally, for Livingstone's gun brought down a number of the fattest of the geese and ducks. A day later they came to the banks of the noble river at a place where it was much broader and more rapid than they had yet seen it, except at the falls.

At first the tribes along the course of the river from the point at which they had struck it were inclined to be very friendly. They were great agriculturists, and at almost every village men, women, and children were seen in the gardens, and all working industriously. As the soil was exceedingly fertile, the crops were luxuriant; but, what was better still, they seemed well tended, and not left to grow up in weeds, as in many other places. These people were known as the Maran, and some of their customs were quite peculiar. Among other things, they pierced the upper lip and inserted into the opening a shell. The head man of the principal village presented Livingstone with a basin of rice, the first he had seen in a long time.

The farther eastward they proceeded the more hostile grew the attitude of the various tribes. At one place they tried to spear one of the Makololo who had gone to bring water, and would doubtless have succeeded in doing so but for Livingstone's timely appearance. The enraged savages now rushed upon the brave missionary. He was at once

surrounded, while one of the band in a "sort of wild mania"
brandished his battle-ax threateningly about Livingstone's
head. All now seemed at an end for the intrepid man.
But not so. Calmly facing his assailant, he looked him
unflinchingly in the eye, and commanded him to put up
his ax. Before that piercing glance the man slunk away
as if caught in some petty act. The Makololo coming up
at this moment, and seeing the danger of their fondly loved
father, made ready to attack the men who surrounded him.
But at a signal from him whom they had never yet dis-
obeyed they restrained themselves—though it was plain to
see that they longed to hurl themselves upon the band, and
that each brave man there was willing to sacrifice his own
life in an attempt to rescue him who had so often stood in
the jaws of danger for them. Had they closed with the
savages, as they started to do in the heat of the moment,
all would indeed have been over—not only for Livingstone,
but for themselves, since the hostile band outnumbered
them five to one. As usual Livingstone's masterly courage
and cool management saved both himself and his men. An
hour later they parted from the people in real friendliness.

Much to Livingstone's alarm he now found his ammunition—that is, the balls and shot—running low. If it should
come to a battle with the natives, it would certainly be bad
for him and his men, unless they could in some way add to
their store. At length he resorted to the expedient of melt-
ing into balls two pewter plates and a piece of zinc he
chanced to have. In addition he exhausted all the hand-
kerchiefs of the party in buying spears for his men. Although danger constantly threatened them, and death often
seemed but a question of a moment, their real troubles did
not begin until they had reached the confluence of the Lo-

angwa and the Zambesi.   Here they seemed to have come
to a climax, their lives more than once hanging by the slen-
derest thread, which the least unguarded movement of theirs,
to right or to left, would have snapped in twain in a twink-
ling.   It was a miracle that they should have escaped—a
still greater source of wonder that not one of them fell by
the hands of savage foe, and that not once was a battle necessary.   What other man than Livingstone could have carried them through with such a record?   On reaching this
point Livingstone seems to have realized to its fullest extent the danger that menaced them; but well he knew
where to go for the strength and help needful to face it.
We find the entry below in his journal, under the date of
January 14th, 1856.   Could that God to whom he poured
forth the whole burden of his heart, of whom he so fervently entreated succor in this hour of need, refuse to hear or
to grant so pure and earnest a prayer?   No wonder this
trusting and intrepid soldier of the cross passed through
every danger unscathed:

"14th January, 1856.—At the confluence of the Loangwa and Zambesi.   Thank God for his great mercies so
far!   How soon I may be called to stand before him, my
righteous Judge, I know not.   All hearts are in his hands,
and merciful and gracious is the Lord our God.   O Jesus,
grant me resignation to thy will, and entire reliance on thy
powerful hand.   On thy word alone I lean.   But wilt thou
permit me to plead for Africa?   The cause is thine.   What
an impulse will be given to the idea that Africa is not open
if I perish now!   See, O Lord, how the heathen rise up
against me, as they did to thy Son!   I commit my way unto
thee.   I trust also in thee that thou wilt direct my steps.
Thou givest wisdom liberally to all who ask thee—give it

to me, my Father. My family is thine. They are in the best hands. O be gracious, and all our sins do thou blot out.

> A guilty, weak, and helpless worm,
> On thy kind arms I fall.

Leave me not, forsake me not. I cast myself and all my cares down at thy feet. Thou knowest all I need, for time and for eternity."

They were now encamped near the village of a chief by the name of Mburuma, and momentarily expecting an attack. For two or three days Livingstone had been trying to get across the river, but the hostile natives not only refused to lend him the necessary canoes, but also to allow him to proceed at all. Livingstone soon learned that the cause of their fierce hostility lay in the fact that at one time, not many years before, this section had been invaded by an Italian slave-dealer, who had at first professed great friendship for them—even marrying the daughter of their chief—but who had at last repaid their trust by carrying off a number of the people into captivity. It is true that they had pursued, overtaken, and slain him, and thus had their revenge; but ever since they had vowed deadly vengeance against every one with a white skin.

The next morning early, January 15th, at a little after sunrise, the natives began to collect about the camp. All of them were fully armed, and it was evident that their intentions were any thing but friendly. Livingstone at once addressed them. He frankly told them the object of his visit to their country, and that he was then on his way to the sea on an errand that would in the end prove of the greatest benefit to them. He next stated the object of his errand. They seemed to be favorably impressed by his words, and began to assume a less hostile attitude, though many of them from time to time cast upon him and his men most threatening and vindictive looks.

Livingstone was still extremely anxious to cross to the other side of the river, but he did not know how to manage it without precipitating an attack. He came fearlessly to the point at last, and asked the natives for the loan of their canoes, at the same time displaying to their view some beads and copper ornaments. He again opened a conversation with them. He assured them that he had not come to make slaves of any of their people, but that his mission was directly opposed to all such horrible practices. He proposed to them that, in proof of his intention to carry none but his own people out of the country, the band of natives should stay and see them cross the river. Whether it was Livingstone's frank manner, or the boldness of his proposition, or the sight of the beads and ornaments, that had the desired effect, it was hard to tell. Perhaps it was all three. After considerable parleying, the majority signified their willingness to receive the trinkets and to allow the strangers passage of the river. They then sent two men after the canoes. While they were gone, and his own men getting ready to embark, Livingstone amused the savages by showing them his watch, pocket-compass, and burning-glass. He was not so sure of these people yet, and did not know at what moment they might get him and his men into a trap, and then make an attack. So he stood with those searching eyes of his fixed upon them to the last, and back to back with his men while they were entering the canoes. Not until the last one was in did he take his place. Even then he kept his eye upon the savages along the bank. As the canoes shot out into the stream Livingstone lifted

19

his hat, thanked the people for their kindness, wished them peace, and then bade them adieu. They seemed charmed with his manners, and stood staring after him in immovable fascination until the boats were safely over, which was doubtless the very thing Livingstone wished them to do.

After crossing the river and proceeding some distance, Livingstone was surprised to come upon the ruins of a village where Europeans, doubtless Portuguese, had once lived. The houses, many of which had not entirely fallen into ruins, were built of wood and stone, and though simply constructed were yet novel objects for this part of the country. Among the ruins they found the remains of a stone church and a broken bell. The bell had the letters I. H. S. and a cross engraved upon it.

Nine days later, on January 23d, they were again stopped by the hostile demonstrations of the people of a chief by the name of Mpende. This chief, having been badly treated by a party of Portuguese traders, had vowed that no white man should ever again cross his country. He was even at this time waging a determined war with the Portuguese along his frontier. The travelers were now in great straits. Their provisions had entirely given out, and several of the oxen, which farther back had been bitten by the deadly tsetse fly, were either dead or in a dying condition. Besides, they were in the territory of one of the most bloodthirsty of all the Zambesi chiefs. But they bravely faced the situation, putting their trust in that God who had never turned a deaf ear to their cries for aid. As they approached Mpende's village, Livingstone—although his mind was weighed down by fears and anxieties—could not help enjoying the extreme beauty of the scene. The village stood in the midst of a green valley, surrounded on all sides by forests of stately trees, some spangled with blossoms and others gemmed with fruits. In the background rose a lofty, conical-shaped hill, about the summit of which the fleecy clouds hung like snow-white curtains. The expedition marched bravely up toward these wooded heights, and near the bank of a little stream that sung its happy way through the smiling valley pitched their tent. They had no sooner done so than a crowd of the natives came rushing out to them, making all manner of hostile demonstrations.

Livingstone and his men were in a sad plight. Their clothes were worn into rags, and they had not a pound of provisions of any kind. Most distressing yet, they had not tasted food for nearly three days—their only means of subsistence being a few roots they had obtained in the forest. One thing that led them to face the dangers of Mpende's village, instead of trying to skirt around it, was that they hoped through some means to procure food. But with all his diplomatic skill, Livingstone failed to make their needs known—or, if he did, there was no promising response from the people, who still circled about the new-comers, uttering horrid cries and brandishing strange-looking weapons. They ceased after awhile, and withdrew to the village evidently to prepare for an attack. In the meantime, the pangs of hunger were growing unbearable. Aware that his men could not fight in this condition, Livingstone was reduced to the necessity of slaughtering one of the oxen that had not shown the worst effects of the tsetse bites. The men were much cheered by their hearty meal. As they sat around the camp-fire, on the alert for an attack at any moment, they said to Livingstone: "You have seen us fight elephants, good father, and thought us very brave, but you do not know yet what we can do with men. Just wait, and

see, and have no fears." Livingstone replied that he hoped
that they might all get away without any fight; that he was
averse to shedding men's blood, even from necessity. That
night he prayed with all the fervor of his trusting heart:
"To thee, O God, we look. And O thou who wast the
Man of sorrows for the sake of poor vile sinners, and didst
not disdain the thief's petition, remember me and thy cause
in Africa! Soul and body, my family, and thy cause, I
commit *all* to thee. Hear, Lord, for Jesus' sake!"

The next morning at sunrise a body of Mpende's people
appeared again. They came nearer the encampment this
time, uttering the same horrid cries, and brandishing some
red substance instead of the strange-looking weapons. They
finally lighted a fire, threw a lot of charms into it, and
then departed, giving vent to a series of cries and screams
more hideous than ever. This they probably did in the belief that it would not only frighten their enemies, but render
them powerless to resist an attack. Livingstone wondered
why they made no more active signs of battle, but afterward
learned that they were awaiting the return of their chief,
who was some distance away engaged in warfare with his
deadly enemies, the Portuguese.

Livingstone was now undecided whether to go on and
risk cutting his way through this warlike tribe, or to stay
and await events. When he remembered that he was at
their mercy about getting over the river, he decided to stay
where he was until the chief's return, although it might be
the most dangerous thing he could do. In a few days the
chief returned. He at once dispatched messengers to Livingstone, asking him his object in coming into his country.
Livingstone sent a politely worded request for a personal
interview. This Mpende very haughtily refused to grant.

Later he dispatched in his place his head man and another one of his chief men. Livingstone found them very sensible old men, though they plainly shared Mpende's hatred of the whites. As they approached they asked Livingstone the question: "Who are you?" "I am a Lekoa, an Englishman," he replied. They shook their heads, as if greatly mystified, while one of them said: "We do not know that tribe. Is it a very good tribe?" "It is a very good tribe indeed," returned Livingstone proudly. "Well, we are glad to hear that. We thought you of the Mozunga [Portuguese], with whom we have been fighting. Our chief hates the Mozunga, and so do we. We did not know there were any other whites but them." "I will prove to you that I am whiter than they, and therefore not of their tribe," said Livingstone, uncovering his bosom and arms. "Did you ever see skin so white as that?" "No, we never did." "Nor hair like this?" "Truly we have not. The Mozunga, though they are white, have neither that hair nor that skin. O now we have it! You are of that tribe of whom we have sometimes heard but never yet seen—the tribe that live over the big water, and who are said to love the black man." "I am of that tribe," returned Livingstone; "and if you will let me I will prove to you that I mean you and your people only good, and that I am bound now on a journey in your interest."

The two men went back to their chief, filled with wonder and delight at what they had seen and heard. Mpende was greatly impressed, and after a long consultation with his councilors was induced to believe Livingstone's story, and to permit him to go on undisturbed; and not only this, but to agree to furnish the party with canoes in which to cross the river.

" To thee, O God, we look! " had been the burden of that humble, fervent, impassioned prayer, and how graciously had it been heard and answered! Well and fittingly has one of the biographers of this truly great man remarked: " In the entire records of Christian heroism there are few more remarkable occasions of the triumph of the spirit of holy trust than the one here recorded."

CHAPTER XX.

GRADUALLY INCREASING SIGNS OF CIVILIZATION — SAND-FILLED
RIVERS—AT MONINA'S VILLAGE—DEATH OF POOR MONAHIN—
WORN DOWN WITH FATIGUE — A CIVILIZED BREAKFAST—AT
TETE—GENEROSITY AND HOSPITALITY OF MAJOR SICARD—ILL-
NESS—ARRIVAL AT KILIMANE—GREETED WITH SAD INTELLI-
GENCE—INSANITY AND DEATH OF SEKWEBU—THE DEPARTURE
FOR HOME—ARRIVAL IN ENGLAND—ENTHUSIASTIC RECEPTION
—LIVINGSTONE'S EXTREME MODESTY—THE QUIET SOJOURN AT
NEWSTEAD ABBEY—LITERARY LABORS.

EARLY in February, Livingstone and his followers,
making their way down the Zambesi, under many
difficulties and dangers, began to observe increasing signs
of civilization. Meeting a party of traders, Livingstone
bartered two elephant tusks for some calico marked " Law-
rence Mills, Lowell, Mass." His men had been reduced to
a state of complete nudity, and he was now enabled to make
them more presentable. The progress of the expedition
was both difficult and slow, owing to the many sand-filled
streams they had to ford. The sand had been washed
down into these streams by the heavy rains, and formed
into great beds. Underneath these, however, there was a
firm stratum of clay. Livingstone says that often during
the dry season the water would all disappear, when these
vast sand deposits would remain like miniature mountain-
heaps glittering in the sun's rays. But, strange to say, if
one would take the trouble to dig a few feet beneath them
he would there find tiny streams of water " percolating over

the clayey bottom." This, Livingstone says, " is the phenomenon which is dignified by the name of ' rivers flowing under-ground.'" He gives this account of his difficulties in trying to ford one of these rivers, the Zingesi: "I felt thousands of particles of coarse sand striking my legs, and the slight disturbance of our footsteps caused deep holes to be made in the bed. The water dug out the sand beneath our feet in a second or two, and we were all sinking by that means so deep that we were glad to relinquish the attempt to ford it before we got half way over. The man who preceded me was only thigh-deep, but the disturbance caused by his feet made it breast-deep for me. The shower of particles and gravel which struck against my legs gave me the idea that the amount of matter removed by every freshet must be very great."

At the village of a chief by the name of Monina the people were much displeased because Livingstone had not brought them a great many presents. He was utterly unable to give them even a handful of beads or a yard of cloth, as his store was thoroughly exhausted. At first they were disposed to act very ugly about it, as they thought he was " putting on." A great war-dance was gotten up, in order to frighten the travelers into giving presents. " They beat their drums furiously," says Livingstone, " and occasionally fired a gun. As this sort of dance is never gotten up unless there is an intention to attack, my men expected an assault. We sat and looked at them for some time, and then, as it became dark, we lay down, all ready to give them a warm reception. But an hour or two after dark, the dance ceased, and as we saw no one approaching us, we went to sleep."

At this place Livingstone had the misfortune to lose one

of his men, the second he had lost since entering upon this journey—the first having died of fever and been buried by the way. This last was one of his chief men, and the circumstances of his death were alike sad and peculiar. During the night, just after the din of the horrid war-dance had ceased, Monahin, who had been complaining of his head for several days, was seen to get up and look toward the village. He did not seem to be more than half awake. "Do you not hear what those people are saying?" he asked hurriedly of the man who was sleeping next to him, and who had been awakened by his movements. "Go and listen." He then walked off in an opposite direction, and was never seen again, although diligent search was made for him for three days. It is probable that a sudden fit of insanity seized the poor fellow, during which he walked off into the woods, and was devoured by lions, as that region was full of them. Monahin's death grieved Livingstone deeply, and he could scarcely leave the place, although further search seemed useless.

Livingstone here describes some of the customs and peculiarities of the tribes along the Zambesi: "At the village of Nyakoba the person appointed to be our guide came and bargained that his services should be rewarded by a hoe. I had no objection to give it, and showed him the article. He was delighted with it, and went off to show it to his wife. He soon afterward returned, and said that though he was perfectly willing to go his wife would not let him. I said, 'Then bring back the hoe;' but he replied, 'I want it.' 'Well, go with us, and you shall have it.' 'But my wife won't let me.' I remarked to my men, 'Did you ever hear such a fool?' They answered: 'O that is the custom of these parts; the wives are the masters.' When a young man takes a liking for a girl of another village, and the parents have no objection to the match, he is obliged to come and live at their village. He has to perform certain services for the mother-in-law, such as keeping her well supplied with fire-wood; and when he comes into her presence he is obliged to sit with his knees in a bent position, as putting out his feet toward the old lady would give her great offense. If he becomes tired of living in this state of vassalage, and wishes to return to his own family, he is obliged to leave all his children behind; they belong to the wife."

On the evening of March 2d Livingstone found himself within eight miles of the Portuguese settlement of Tete. But he was so fatigued, so utterly worn down by the trying experiences of the last days of his journey, that he could not proceed a mile farther. Indeed, he had at this point literally dropped into the arms of his men, and there the camp for the night had to be made, even though it was in a most inconvenient and uninviting spot. He, however, sent forward to the commandant of the post some recommendatory letters he had received while at Loanda. These letters were altogether unnecessary, as news of his coming had reached the east coast months before. Besides, the whole civilized world had by this time heard of the great missionary and his almost phenomenal work in the heart of Africa. Further than this, the Portuguese authorities along the route had all been notified of Livingstone's proposed march to the east coast through a no less distinguished source than official dispatches from England.

It is no wonder, then, that the commandant at Tete, Major Sicard, should have been much exercised over the receipt of the letter by the hand of Livingstone's special messenger, together with the information that the now famous

Dr. Livingstone was within two hours' journey of his post and awaiting his courtesy. Preparations were at once entered upon for a reception befitting so distinguished a personage, while steps were taken to send immediate relief to the courageous explorer who had been reduced to such desperate straits during the last few days. As early as two o'clock the next morning two officers and a company of soldiers, detailed by Major Sicard, appeared at the camp with a supply of provisions. As Livingstone and his men had been for many days past subsisting entirely upon roots and honey, we may easily imagine the joy with which the half-starved men once more partook of a civilized meal. Livingstone says of it: "The pleasure experienced in partaking of that breakfast was only equaled by the enjoyment of Mr. Gabriel's bed when I arrived at Loanda." In fact, so refreshing did Livingstone find it that after eating he walked the eight miles to Tete without "the least signs of weariness," as he himself tells us; although the way was so rough that one of the officers remarked, "This is enough to tear a man's life out." At Tete Livingstone was warmly received by the hospitable and generous Major Sicard. He reclothed Livingstone and his men in the best the place could afford, and secured for them every attention.

Livingstone's principal point of destination, as we know, was Quilimane, on the east coast and at the mouth of the Zambesi. When he arrived at Tete he learned that it was the unhealthy season at Quilimane. He was therefore persuaded by Major Sicard to remain at Tete as his guest for a month, by which time it would doubtless be safe for him to continue his journey. Livingstone accepted this kind offer, which also included his men who had been provided with comfortable huts by the Major's direction.

Having waited the month at Tete, Livingstone was about to start down the river, when he was seized with fever. This was on the 4th of April. By the 22d he had so far recovered as to undertake the journey again. Selecting sixteen of his best men, he set off in canoes provided by the commandant. The rest of his Makololos he left with Major Sicard, who generously offered to give each one of them a piece of land on which he could raise something for himself. He also granted them permission to hunt elephants, the money obtained from the sale of the tusks and dried meat to be spent for articles of use and ornament for Sekeletu and their people. Livingstone's principal reason for leaving so many of his men behind was that a most distressing famine was prevailing at Quilimane. Thousands, chiefly slaves, had perished within the last few weeks. It was certainly a great reproach to the Portuguese government—or rather to its African administrators—that so many helpless creatures should have perished at this place for want of food, when there was an abundance of it at the other stations up the river and it only being necessary to float it down the river.

Major Sicard sent one of his best officers, Lieutenant Murandi, to escort Livingstone and his party to the coast, so that they were relieved of many of the difficulties of the route. Their only unpleasant experience was in having to walk fifteen miles under the blazing sun along a portion of the delta of the Zambesi that was not navigable. From this exposure to the sun, and the fatigue of walking, Livingstone had a second attack of fever, and he suffered greatly on his arrival at Senna a day or two later.

The Zambesi flows into the sea by a number of mouths, which form a considerable delta. The party chose the most

northern of these mouths, which led them direct to Quilimane.   This point they reached May 20th, 1856, just a few
days within four years after the time when Livingstone set
out from Cape Town on his now accomplished journey from
sea to sea.   We have seen by what trials, dangers, and privations that journey was attended to its close.   We know,
too, how fearlessly Livingstone stood at his post under the
most trying circumstances.   Hunger, cold, exhausting heat,
and toil, dangers innumerable, even death itself, he had
been required to face; yet, having a steadfast faith in the
rulings of that mighty Power beneath the shadow of whose
wings he calmly rested, this "man of destiny" valiantly
battled with each in turn.

From Quilimane Livingstone at once communicated with
the Royal Geographical Society regarding his journey to
the east coast.   He had found it every way more promising than his visit to the west coast.   The beauty and richness of some parts of the country he declared could not be
surpassed.   Much of this region was densely populated, too,
especially that along the basin of the Zambesi.   True, a
large portion of the inhabitants were hostile, yet he believed that with due caution and right treatment even this
serious drawback could be overcome.   The antagonistic
spirit of the tribes mostly grew out of the ill-usage they had
received at the hands of the half-caste traders.   As Livingstone had found it elsewhere, so he had found it here—
that wherever the noxious roots of slavery had penetrated
there they had grown and expanded into a moral upas-tree,
tainting all the atmosphere with its infectious poison.   But
what might not the powerful and life-giving presence of
Christian missions do toward the dissipation of this fateful
influence?   How many vigorous strokes toward its utter

annihilation might not *one* determined arm give to the trunk of this deadly tree?

Among the discoveries Livingstone had made on this journey two things that pleased him most were: first, that not a great many miles directly eastward from the country of the Makololo he had found a healthy and elevated belt of land, about "two degrees of longitude broad and of unknown length," which offered most advantageous inducements for the planting of mission stations; and second, that in the Zambesi he had discovered, as he had hoped, an almost unbroken route to the sea. At last he had accomplished his part of this unparalleled undertaking: it now remained for his country and the missionary society he represented to do the rest. But would they do it? He could only communicate with each and await the development of events.

Soon after reaching Quilimane Livingstone had to part with his faithful Makololos. One of the most trying things he had ever been called upon to do was to say good-by to them. He would have liked to put it off a little longer, but the time had come for them to go back to Tete, where they were to await his return from England, he having made all the necessary arrangements with Major Sicard. The grief of the poor fellows when the time of parting had come was most touching. They declared that they could not and would not leave their good father, Livingstone; that wherever he went there were they going too. Again they besought him not to leave them, but to return with them. Livingstone's distress was great, but it was best for their sake as well as his own that he should be firm with them. So he bade them act like men, as Makololo warriors, and as his children and Sekeletu's. This touched the right chord; and on his promising to return soon if God spared his life, and to bring Ma-Robert with him, they bravely turned their faces in the direction of Tete.

But Livingstone did not send all of his men back: he kept Sekwebu, intending to take him on to England. Livingstone's idea was that on his return Sekwebu might be able to tell Sekeletu and his people just what kind of a country England was, thereby increasing the confidence and trust of the Makololo. Perhaps, too, he thought the presence of the black man among his white brothers might be to them a more eloquent plea for the speedy adjustment of the wrongs of his people.

At Quilimane Livingstone learned that the captain, lieutenant, and five men of Her Majesty's ship "Dart" had been drowned off the bar in coming to take him aboard. Of this melancholy event Livingstone says: "I never felt more poignant sorrow. It seemed as if it would have been easier for me to have died for them than that they should all have been cut off from the joys of life, in generously attempting to render me a service." One of his first acts on returning to England was to write a letter to the Admiralty asking a pension for the widow of one of these gallant men. He had never seen her, he said, but he had been "the unconscious cause of her husband's death, and all the joy he felt in crossing the continent was embittered when the news of the sad catastrophe reached him."

Livingstone remained at Quilimane six weeks. At the end of that time Her Majesty's brig "Frolic" was sent to convey him to the island of Mauritius, east from Madagascar, and whence after a sojourn for rest and recreation he was to sail for England. There was a heavy sea rolling as Livingstone and Sekwebu entered the small-boat that had been sent to convey them to where the "Frolic" lay at anchor. This frightened Sekwebu very much. At one moment he seemed on the point of leaping into the water. It was the first time he had seen such a raging sheet of water, and his terror was deep-set. However, when the ship was boarded, and the kind-hearted sailors did all they could to accustom him to the new situation, he became more composed in his mind, though there was still an uneasy look in his eyes. But poor Sekwebu's terror again broke forth—indeed, seemed to reach a climax—when the "Frolic" lay anchored at the entrance to the harbor of Mauritius, and the steam-launch came out to tow the ship in. The moment "the uncouth, panting monster" drew near, with the dense volumes of smoke issuing from her stacks, and puffing and growling like some tormented creature, Sekwebu gave one shriek and jumped from the brig into a small row-boat that lay along-side. When Livingstone followed him and endeavored to persuade him to return, he broke forth: "Go away, good father, and leave me to die alone! It is enough that _I_ alone die. _You_ must not perish. If you do not go, I shall throw myself into the water." Livingstone saw that the poor fellow's terror had culminated in madness, and he scarcely knew what course to pursue. "Remember, Sekwebu," he said persuasively, "that we are going to see Ma-Robert. If you destroy yourself, you will not see her." This had an instant and a most soothing effect upon him. "O yes!" he cried, raising himself suddenly, "to see Ma-Robert! But where is she? and where is Robert [Livingstone's little son]?" In a short time he allowed himself to be taken back to the vessel. In the evening, however, a fresh fit of insanity came on. He tried to spear one of the men, and ran about the vessel foaming like a maddened beast, and before any one could prevent it he leaped into the sea. Here he deliberately dragged himself down, "hand under hand," by means of the chain cable, and was drowned. His body was never recovered.

On the 9th of December, 1856, Livingstone landed in London, and the next morning the *Times* announced that Dr. Livingstone, the "distinguished African missionary and traveler," was once more among his countrymen. Three days later, at a most enthusiastic meeting of the Royal Geographical Society, the president, Sir Roderick Murchison, reminded the members that "they were met together for the purpose of welcoming Dr. Livingstone on his return home from South Africa, after an absence of sixteen years, during which, while endeavoring to spread the blessings of Christianity through lands never before trodden by the foot of any European, he had made geographical discoveries of incalculable importance. In all his various journeys Dr. Livingstone had traveled over no less than eleven thousand miles of African territory; and had come back to England as the pioneer of sound and useful knowledge." A few evenings after, a similarly warm reception was accorded him by his old employers, the London Missionary Society. Indeed, so many honors were now heaped upon him that it would be impossible to record even a small part of them here. He was everywhere treated with the greatest consideration. His zeal, his courage, above all the story of his wonderful achievements in Africa, were the theme of every tongue. Wherever he went people struggled to get a glimpse of him, and the mere announcement that he would be present at a public gathering was sufficient to crowd the building to overflowing. Even the Queen had sent for him to tender her congratulations.

20

All this was surely enough to turn the head of any mortal man; but it had no such effect upon Livingstone. He remained the same modest, unassuming man that we have seen land at Cape Town when his name was scarcely known outside of his own native village. Modesty was one of the most attractive elements of Livingstone's character; it was so thoroughly a part of himself as to be worn at all times unconsciously, which was its potent charm. Some might have said that his modesty was at times too noticeable. Not so. It was painful to Livingstone to be made a hero, to be eulogized for doing no more than he felt it his duty to do. While he put the lowest estimate upon his own achievements, the mere recital of them had quickened into the intensest enthusiasm the heart of the whole civilized world. Once, being extremely anxious to go to church, and yet dreading the notice it would bring upon him, he managed without observation to make his way in by a private entrance to a seat under the top of the gallery, where he would be unseen by the congregation, though seen by the minister. In order to shield himself still more, he held his head down and covered with his hands. But somehow the minister caught sight of him, and most unwisely alluded to him in his last prayer. This gave the people intimation that he was in the building; and the moment the benediction was pronounced they made a rush for him, some climbing over the pews in their anxiety and haste to get to him. A similar scene is said to have taken place in a church at Bath during the meeting of the British Association in 1864.

Another thing to which Livingstone had an extreme aversion was being interviewed for publication. It also greatly annoyed him to have people importuning him for material for a book or a lecture. A well-known gentleman, who was advertised to deliver a lecture the next day, called upon him for the purpose of getting "dots," at the residence of Mr. Frederick Fitch, where Livingstone was then stopping. Mr. Fitch says in allusion to this interview: "The Doctor sat rather quiet, and, without being rude, treated the gentleman to monosyllabic answers. He could do that —could keep people at a distance when they wanted to make capital out of him. When the stranger had left, turning to my mother he said, with one of his gentlest smiles, ' I will tell *you* any thing you like to ask.' "

Livingstone's personal appearance on his first return to England is thus described: "A foreign-looking person, plainly and rather carelessly dressed, of middle height, bony frame, and Gaelic countenance, with short-cropped hair and mustaches, and generally plain exterior. He appears to be about forty years of age. His face is deeply furrowed and pretty well tanned. It indicates a man of quick and keen discernment, strong impulses, inflexible resolution, and habitual self-command. Unanimated, its most characteristic expression is that of severity; when excited, a varied expression of earnest and benevolent feeling, and remarkable enjoyment of the ludicrous in circumstances and character, passes over it."

Livingstone had not more than landed in England when he hastened to join his loved ones. His wife had gone part of the distance to meet him, so that there were now left only his children, mother, brother, and sisters. The meeting with his aged mother was most pathetic; neither had ever hoped to clasp the other in life again. His father's empty place in the family circle affected him deeply. " The first evening," writes one of his sisters, " he asked all about his illness and death. One of us remarking that after he knew

he was dying his spirits seemed to rise, David burst into
tears.   At family worship that evening he said with deep
feeling: 'We bless thee, O Lord, for our parents; we give
thee thanks for the dead who has died in the Lord.'"

Through the hospitality of a noble gentleman—Mr. Webb,
of Newstead Abbey—Livingstone was enabled to enjoy for
several months of his stay in England that rest and recreation of which he stood so much in need.   But he took advantage of this pleasant, holiday-like period to work.   It
was here that he wrote his well-known book, "Missionary
Travels and Researches in South Africa," which, as one of
the most appreciative of his biographers declares, is not
only "a permanent addition to the classic library of English travel, but a noble monument to a man in whose
pages worth shines as much as vigor, and modesty as much
as worth."

CHAPTER XXI.

RETURN TO AFRICA—THE RECEPTION AT CAPE TOWN—THE "MA-ROBERT"—OBJECT OF THE SECOND EXPEDITION—DISCOVERY OF THE TRUE MOUTH OF THE ZAMBESI—THE SAIL UP THE RIVER —ARRIVAL AT TETE—THE KEBRABASA RAPIDS—UNSATISFAC-TORY CONDUCT OF THE "MA-ROBERT"—EXPLORATIONS OF THE SHIRE—DISCOVERY OF LAKES SHIRNA AND NYASSA—STEPS TO-WARD THE ESTABLISHMENT OF A MISSION STATION—UNEX-PECTED NEWS OF THE ARRIVAL OF A LITTLE STRANGER.

ON the 10th day of March, 1858, Dr. Livingstone again left England for Africa. This time he was acompanied by Mrs. Livingstone, their youngest son, Os-well, and the members of an exploring party that had been organized in England for the purpose of aiding him in his further researches. Among the latter were Dr. Kirke, a distinguished scientist, and Livingstone's brother, Charles. The party carried with them the sections of a small steamer, which was to be put together at the mouth of the Zambesi, and by means of which they were expected to overcome many of the difficulties attendant upon their explorations of the river. This little steamer Livingstone had affection-ately christened the "Ma-Robert," the name by which his wife was known among the Makololo and other African tribes.

Recognizing the distinguished services already rendered by Livingstone as calling for a mark of its highest appre-ciation, as well as desiring to invest him with every author-ity in its power while prosecuting his wonderful discoveries, the English Government had appointed him consul for South-eastern Africa. In the meanwhile, through causes which it is unnecessary to state here, Livingstone had severed his connection with the London Missionary Society, though he had by no means abandoned the determination to do mis-sionary work among the natives whenever and wherever he could.

Considering the circumstances that surrounded its organ-ization, as well as the new office that had been bestowed upon Livingstone, this second expedition was looked upon in the light of a national enterprise; and when he sailed from England it was with the eyes of the whole English people upon him. The ever-present object of this expedi-tion is thus set forth in Livingstone's instructions: "To ex-tend the knowledge already attained of the geography and the mineral and agricultural resources of Eastern and Cen-tral Africa; to improve his acquaintance with the inhab-itants, and to encourage them to apply themselves to agri-cultural pursuits and the cultivation of their land, with a view to the production of raw material, which might be ex-ported to England in return for British manufactures."

The party landed at Cape Town. There Livingstone and his wife found Mr. and Mrs. Moffat awaiting them. A few days later Mrs. Livingstone was taken so ill that it was thought advisable for her not to attempt going on with the explorers. She therefore remained at Cape Town until she had partially recovered, when she proceeded to Kuruman with her parents.

Livingstone met with a most enthusiastic reception from his countrymen at Cape Town. He was tendered a grand banquet, at which a magnificent silver box containing eight hundred guineas was presented to him, together with the freedom of the city.   Everywhere he went his consul's uniform, especially the Queen's gold band around his cap, attracted admiring attention.   It would be impossible to enumerate the honors that were heaped upon him.   Livingstone could not help contrasting this visit with one he had made six years before.   Then no one noticed the poor, obscure missionary, who had great difficulty in procuring necessary supplies for the long and hazardous journey since become the joyful theme of nearly every civilized tongue on earth.   Now every one was fawning at his feet.   He would have been less than human had he not bestowed a sarcastic reflection upon the world's ways.

At the mouth of the Zambesi the " Ma-Robert " was put together.   And now we come to the first important incident of Livingstone's exploration of the Zambesi.   It certainly was an auspicious augury that it should have happened before the expedition had fairly begun.   At that day the mouths of the Zambesi were but little known.   Speculation had advanced much in regard to them, while discovery, on the other hand, had proved nothing as yet, doubtless because it had undertaken nothing.   The Portuguese Government, however, was in possession of the secret of the true outlet; but so far, for reasons that will shortly be made known, it had chosen to keep it a secret—further, as a secret well guarded.   The impression left by it upon the outside world was that the Quilimane was the only navigable mouth of the great river.   Their reason for doing this was to facilitate and protect their slave-dealing operations. While the English cruisers, sent to put down the slave traffic, were watching what they believed to be the only navigable mouth of the river, the slaves were quietly slipped through another and a more direct way.   However, to do justice to the local authorities—among them Livingstone's generous friend, Major Sicard—we must state that they knew nothing of these cunning maneuvers on the part of the slave-traders. They were as much in the dark as the outsiders. As proof of their honesty, Livingstone had no sooner discovered the real mouth of the river—the Kongone outlet—than they at once proceeded in a movement to have a station and a fort established at the entrance. Of course it brought them into collision with the Portuguese Government. But upon this feud it is not necessary to dwell.

The most navigable route being now discovered, the "Ma-Robert" went steaming up the Kongone. Everywhere the natives retreated in terror at their approach. This horrid puffing monster, with the dense clouds of black smoke pouring from it, was too much for African nerves. They had never in their lives seen any thing so terrible, or even dreamed of it. Occasionally when the party went on shore they could induce them, after much persuasion, to return to the banks for another look, especially if the panting monster was lying quiet at its moorings; but the moment the whistle blew they all rushed away again in the greatest terror, falling over each other in their mad flight, and shouting at the top of their voices: "Mother! mother! Save us, mother!"

Though there were very few difficulties of navigation to overcome while steaming up the delta of the river, the "Ma-Robert" nevertheless acted very unsatisfactorily, and Livingstone began to fear for a worse exhibition when real obstacles presented themselves, as well as to have an unpleasant presentiment that he had been badly swindled in this purchase. The slowness of their progress, however, had

one advantageous side—it gave Livingstone ample time for
accurate observation.   He was more than pleased with all
he saw.   He found the land of the delta so rich that on it,
he calculated, almost fabulous quantities of cotton and sugar-cane might be raised.   If properly cultivated, he did
not doubt that this delta of the Zambesi could supply the
whole of Europe with sugar.   Nowhere had he seen land
more fertile, or that could be more easily cultivated.   Ten
acres of such land within easy access of some commercial port
would be a little fortune to any man.   The growth of tim-
ber in some places was truly magnificent, many of the trees
towering a hundred and fifty feet high.   In one spot alone
—not more than two or three acres—Livingstone saw ebony and lignum-vitæ enough to have made their possessor a
millionare twice over, had the facilities been offered for their
shipment to England.   Such costly woods as these were
often used as fuel on the " rebellious little steamer."   Knowing their value, the engineer often asserted that it " made
his heart sore to burn wood so valuable."   India-rubber
trees were seen in large quantities, while along the banks
of the river wild indigo grew in the richest profusion.

   The delta also abounded in animal life.   There were
birds innumerable—from the tiny bee-hunter, flitting in and
out among the glossy mangoes, to the tall and stately crane
and flamingo feeding upon the worms and fish along the
edges of the many islands that dotted the stream.   There,
too, were the brown kite, " piping like a boatswain," the
spotted cuckoo, the roller horn-bill, and a host of other
" sma', merry singers," each giving vent to its volume of
delicious sounds, which, combining, made " an African
Christmas seem like an English May."   Animals there
were, too, of every size and variety—from the baby croco-

dile basking in the sun to the monster hippopotamus, the king of the African rivers.

When the explorers started up the delta the prospect was somewhat dreary and uninviting, marked as it was by vast stretches of grassy plains, the only other signs of vegetation being here and there a cluster of stately palms, the " round, green tops of which looked at a distance as though suspended in the air." But the farther they advanced the more charming grew the scenery. The foliage of the trees seemed to vie with each other in their richness and beauty, while in many places the grasses and the ferns shot upward to the height of a tall man's head. From out the clusters of bananas and cocoa-palms peeped the huts of the natives, looking very neat and picturesque, while about them the little patches of garden, in which grew potatoes, pumpkins, cabbages, onions, peas, and many other things, presented a scene of pleasing cultivation. These natives of the Zambesi were evidently thrifty farmers.

At Tete the party was warmly received by the hospitable Major Sicard. As to the Makololos who had been left there to await Livingstone's return from England, they were nearly beside themselves with joy at seeing their father once more. They leaped and danced about him, and were on the point of throwing themselves bodily upon him to embrace him, when one, more observant than the others, suddenly shouted forth: "Look out! look out! you will ruin his new clothes!" For the first time now they all seemed to notice how much improved their father was in the style of his dress. After that they could do nothing but walk around him, and admire the many appointments of his uniform, especially the cap with the gold band. "Why, he is finer even than the Portuguese braves at the forts," they declared enthusiastically. Livingstone's own pleasure on meeting with his faithful men again was considerably dampened by the fact that while he was gone many had died with that dread disease, small-pox; and six of those left, growing tired of work and impatient at Livingstone's long absence, had gone away to dance before some of the neighbor-

ing chiefs.   Among these was a cowardly and cruel chief
by the name of Bonga, who on some slight pretext had
put all the men to death.   The Makololo said: "We do
not grieve for those who died of the small-pox, for they were
taken by Morimo [God]; but our hearts are sore for the
six youths who were murdered by Bonga."   Livingstone
had sad news to impart to them, too.   This was the insanity and death of Sekwebu.   At first they were deeply grieved
by the intelligence, but finally they said: "Well, men must
all die.   They die in one country as well as in another.
Sekwebu too is with Morimo; so we will not mourn for
him, for he is at peace."

On reaching Tete, Livingstone found that the most formidable object that stood in the way of his farther navigation of the Zambesi was the Kebrabasa Rapids.   These
rapids were about twenty-five or thirty miles above Tete.
He had heard of them on his journey down from Linyanti,
though he had not as yet seen them.   He now determined
to go and take a look at them.   He found them fully as
formidable as they had been pictured.   They were formed
by a range of rocky mountains that crossed the Zambesi at
this point.   Here, during the dry season, the bed of the
river narrowed to a channel of not more than sixty yards
in width, through which were strewed masses of rock of every conceivable size and shape.   The rapids themselves extended for fully eight miles.   Livingstone saw that it would
be dangerous to attempt to force a steamer through them
except during a high flood; but he resolved to try the experiment as soon as the stream had become somewhat more
swollen than it was at that time.   On returning to Tete he
learned that these were not the only rapids in the way of navigation; that a few miles farther up there were others almost

as formidable—the Mburuma. In company with Dr. Kirke and four of the Makololo, Livingstone started off in search of these rapids. The party had a frightful experience. Part of the route lay over rocks so hot that the Makololo's feet were burned until they rose into blisters and burst. Leaving the poor fellows by the way to heal their burns, Livingstone and Dr. Kirke pushed on alone. In three hours they made but one mile, while their boots and clothing were completely destroyed. It was evident to Livingstone that had he and the Makololos taken this route in 1856, instead of that through the level Shidina country, all must have perished. It was surely God who had led them aright, and Livingstone devoutly thanked him for his mercy. The Mburuma Rapids were found to be almost as formidable as those of the Kebrabasa, as Livingstone had been told they were. But his faith and courage did not permit him to doubt that engineering skill could in time overcome them. God would certainly open the way.

Waiting at Tete for the rains, Livingstone attempted to stem the Kebrabasa Rapids when the bed of the river had been considerably swollen; but he found it an impossible undertaking with the "Ma-Robert." He now suspected more strongly than ever that he had been swindled by the builder of the vessel. The amount of fuel she consumed was simply enormous. It would have served two steamers double her size, while her furnace had to be lighted hours before sufficient steam could be gotten up to start her off. In addition, she "snorted so horribly" that she well deserved the name the men had in derision bestowed upon her—"The Asthmatic." As to getting up the requisite amount of steam to carry her over the rapids, or any thing like enough even to make the attempt, every effort in that

direction proved a dismal failure. In fact, she was altogether unequal to so much as an ordinary emergency, and
this they soon discovered. Livingstone was both chagrined
and disgusted at this state of affairs. He determined to
communicate with the English Government in regard to
the matter. He did not ask out and out for another steamer of a superior build, but he left it so that they could
offer one if they desired. While waiting for an answer,
however, and knowing that such things were often delayed
to an indefinite time through the want of harmony of some
of the parties concerned, he determined to get another
steamer at his own expense. He was enabled to do this
through the proceeds of the sale of his book. While arrangements were being made for the new steamer, Livingstone decided upon an exploration of the Shire, one of the
most important tributaries of the Zambesi. When his
friends at Tete learned of this determination, they tried to
dissuade him from it. They told him it was a most perilous undertaking, and one out of which he could scarcely
hope to come with his life. Besides the dangers of the
river and the many deadly serpents and ferocious beasts
with which the forest abounded, the natives along the banks
of the Shire were among the most treacherous and blood-
thirsty of all the African tribes. But Livingstone was not
to be deterred from his undertaking even by a knowledge
of such dangers as these. He had faced death too many
times to falter now. So, early in January, 1859, the brave
explorers set forth. They found things fully as bad as
they had been represented. Day after day their lives hung
by a mere thread; but God preserved them.

The Shire, although much narrower than the Zambesi,
was far deeper and easier of navigation. Hence the " Ma-

Robert," though she had behaved so badly at the Kebra-basa Rapids, went along very well now—still, at a snail-like pace.

At the village of chief Tingane a most hostile demonstration awaited the expedition. Fully five hundred men were drawn up in line, facing the river, to receive them. Livingstone boldly went ashore, seeking a personal interview with Tingane. After much delay, during which the aspect of things became more and more threatening, his wish was granted. When Tingane appeared he was seen to be a powerfully built chief, over six feet tall. Livingstone cordially approached and grasped Tingane's hand, frankly stating his object in coming up the river, and politely asking permission to proceed. Tingane was charmed and flattered, and in a little while the permission was unhesitatingly given.

At another village the people acted altogether differently. They seemed overcome with fright, although Livingstone had heard they bore quite a warlike reputation. On the approach of Livingstone and his white companions they fled in terror to their huts, shutting themselves in and refusing to be seen. It was doubtless the "Ma-Robert," more than any thing else, that had frightened them; though the farther Livingstone proceeded the more evidences he saw that he and his friends were the first white men who had ever ascended the Shire. Occasionally on this journey they came upon a village where the inhabitants lived in huts, either built quite at the tops of thick-growing trees or midway of the dense branches. These airy dwelling-places were very ingeniously contrived, were reached by ladders that could be drawn up and let down, and were constructed—as our travelers afterward learned—not only as a protec-

(320)

TREE-DWELLERS IN AFRICA.

tion from wild beasts, but from equally dangerous human enemies.

Livingstone and his companions were favorably impressed with the lower valley of the Shire, which they left the steamer to explore. It was about twenty miles in width, with a deep and fertile soil, shut in by tall, beautiful hills crowned with verdure. Many of these hills rose to an altitude of fully four thousand feet above the level of the sea. The party climbed to the summit of one, called Morambala by the natives. At one side, where it seemed more densely wooded than at any other point, and where the ground was very moist, Dr. Kirke found no less than thirty different species of ferns. In the forests around the base of the Morambala monkeys, antelopes, rhinoceroses, and many of the larger birds, were seen in the greatest abundance. The monkeys were so tame that they often approached near enough to snatch playfully at parts of the travelers' clothing. In the midst of a plain at the northern end they came upon a hot fountain bubbling up to the distance of many feet. It boiled up from the earth in two spouts, one but a few yards from the other. The water of each was perfectly clear, and sparkled like crystal in the sun's rays. Both spouts were boiling hot, and cooked an egg thoroughly done in about the usual time. Penetrating deeper into the forests that grew about the base of this hill, the party discovered two enormous pythons coiled together among the branches of a tree. They were immediately shot and measured. The largest was something over ten feet in length. Some natives, who had followed in the wake of the explorers, besought them for the bodies of the pythons. This being granted, they at once ravenously devoured the reptiles.

The people of this lower valley of the Shire were some-

21

what inclined to be warlike, but they treated the explorers quite hospitably. This was due to Livingstone's manner of approaching them, and his habit of openly avowing the object of his presence among them. They were extensive farmers, raising maize, pumpkins, potatoes, and tobacco in vast quantities.

About two hundred miles up the river the travelers came to a series of cataracts, to which Livingstone gave the name "Murchison Cataracts," in honor of the President of the London Geographical Society. As these cataracts stopped the farther progress of the party, they returned to Tete.

In March, 1859, Livingstone again ascended the Shire. As the natives had received no hurt on his former visit, they now welcomed him cordially. They were convinced that he intended them only good, and as this conviction increased so did their trust in him. On this journey Livingstone formed the acquaintance of Chibisa, a chief whom he describes as " a jolly fellow who laughs easily—which is always a good sign." He reminded Livingstone of Katema, since he had Katema's bombastic tendencies and much of his kind-heartedness. There were two things in which Chibisa believed firmly—one, the "divine right of kings;" the other, that " Chibisa could do no wrong." Though so hospitable toward Livingstone and his friends, he had the reputation of a warrior. This he tried to excuse to Livingstone by declaring that those with whom he fought were always in the wrong, while he was invariably in the right. "I was an ordinary man," he would say to Livingstone, " when my father died, and left me the chieftainship; but directly I succeeded to the high office I was conscious of power passing into my head and down my back. I felt it enter, and I knew that I was a chief clothed with authority, and possessed of wisdom; and people then began to fear and reverence me."

At Chibisa's village Livingstone and his party left the steamer and started overland in search of a large lake of which he had heard during his present and his former visit. On the 18th of April they came upon Lake Shirwa, as it was called by the natives. It was a fine, large sheet of water, and the discoverers felt that it was well worth all the trials and dangers they had passed. Livingstone thought it resembled Lake Ngami, but it was hardly so large. The water, too, unlike that of Ngami, was brackish. Livingstone thus describes the lake: "It was very grand, for we could not see the end of it, though some way up a mountain; and all around it are mountains, much higher than one ever sees in Scotland. One mountain stands in the lake, and people live on it. Another, called Zomba, is more than six thousand feet high, and people live on it too, for we could see their gardens on its top, which is larger than from Glasgow to Hamilton, or about fifteen to eighteen miles. The country is quite a highland region, and many people live in it. Most of them were afraid of us. The women ran into their huts and shut the doors. The children screamed in terror, and even the hens would fly away and leave their chickens." The lake was found to be filled with fish of various kinds; also, with crocodiles and hippopotami in abundance. By a measurement made afterward it was estimated to be fully eighty miles long and nearly twenty in width.

On their way back the valley of the Shire was again examined. Livingstone was still more pleased with it, especially that portion lying between the upper and the lower plains. He found the entire valley to consist of three different levels. First, there was the plain lying immediately along the river banks. This was in many parts close and hot, very much like that of the Nile. Rising above this, in an easterly direction, there was another plain some two thousand feet high and four or five thousand feet wide, with a salubrious and pleasant climate, and rich in vegetation. Lastly, there was a third plain which reached an elevation fully three thousand feet above the second, and was positively cold. To find so many different varieties of climate within so small a radius was both interesting and pleasing to Livingstone. It proved how very wonderful were the resources of this country which he had come to open up. He was more pleased with the central plain than with any other, as we have intimated.

At one point just below this valley the river was exceedingly deep and rapid, "running in some places like a mill-race," says Livingstone, "and with power enough to turn all the mills in England." No danger there from a drought. In addition to the maize, pumpkins, potatoes, and other vegetables already enumerated as growing here in such prodigal abundance, there were sugar-cane, cotton, lemons, and ginger. The cotton excited the admiration of the whole party. It was the most beautiful white cotton they had ever seen. Samples of it afterward sent to Manchester created quite a furor, and were pronounced by the best judges to be of "the finest quality." In his dispatch announcing to the Government his discovery of the lake and this wonderful section of country, Livingstone said: "We have opened a sugar and cotton district of great and unknown extent, and which really seems to afford a reasonable prospect of great commercial benefit to our own country; it presents facilities for commanding a large section of the

slave-market on the coast, and offers a fair hope of its suppression by lawful commerce."

When news of these valuable discoveries reached England, the name of Livingstone shone with increased luster,
if that were possible, while countless tongues were again adding their glowing tributes to the measure of his fame. But
now mark the modest avowal of him who took not one tittle
of the honor to himself, but gave it to that constantly abiding Power which had in every thing guided and upheld him:
"I cannot and will not attribute any of the public attention which has been awakened to my own wisdom or to my
ability. The great Power being my Helper, I shall always
say that my success is all owing to his favor. I have but
been the channel of the Divine Power, and I pray that his
gracious influence may penetrate me so that all may turn
to the advancement of his gracious reign in this fallen
world."

One fruit of Livingstone's discovery of this central valley
of the Shire was the establishment there, not a great while
after, of a mission station, over which Bishop McKenzie,
with some able assistants from the two leading universities
of England—Cambridge and Oxford—was sent to preside.
They found it a most favorable spot indeed, and every
thing promised well until the unfortunate Bishop, through
a rash and indiscreet step, fell into a fatal error which in
the end cost him his life. Unlike Livingstone, who at all
times pursued a conservative course—never, under any
provocation, espousing the cause of one tribe against another—the Bishop, in a moment of righteous indignation,
became the adjuster of the wrongs of a weak tribe that was
being intimidated by a stronger. It was a kindly and chiv-
alric impulse that prompted the Bishop to the step he took,

but that it was also a most injudicious and fateful impulse, the sequel, alas! showed only too well. His life paid the forfeit. He now lies buried on one of the most elevated of the plateaus of the central Shire valley, under the shade of a tall monarch of the African forest, and through its sway-ing branches the winds play the requiem of one truly noble and universally regretted.

But while these missions were being established in the Shire valley through Livingstone's influence, we must not think that he had forgotten his old friends Sekeletu and the Makololos, or their pressing needs. His heart had been with them from the moment of his departure from Linyanti to the present time. One of his first steps on ar-riving in England had been to get a missionary, or mission-aries, sent to Linyanti. He was willing to go himself as their missionary—nay, he would gladly have done so—but he felt that other and more pressing duties were calling him in another direction. As soon as he had acquired a reve-nue from the sale of his book, he proceeded to supplement his petition by the offer of five hundred pounds paid down for an outfit, and one hundred and fifty pounds yearly to-ward the salary of the missionary. Soon after this two mis-sionaries, with their assistants, were sent to the country of the Makololo. The readiness with which Livingstone took so snug a sum from his private income—never at any time very large—and the equal readiness with which he pledged himself to pay the additional one hundred and fifty pounds a year, proved more than ever the sincerity of his desires to better the condition of those for whose final enlighten-ment and elevation he had labored so unremittingly for eighteen years.

Money was never to Livingstone the source of any sordid

consideration. He saw in it merely the means of accomplishing the work to which he had given himself. As to his own personal needs and wants—even that provision for the future about which the least mercenary of men are wont to concern themselves so closely as to forget the claims of others—he left these, as he left himself and all that was his (wife, children, every thing) in the hands of Him who had upheld his every step along the course he had made such an honor to himself and such a blessing to others. "My funds could not be better spent than in this cause," said Livingstone when speaking of it to a friend. " You fear that I will impoverish myself. I have no such fear. People who are born rich sometimes become miserable for fear of becoming poor. I have the advantage, you see, in not being afraid to die poor. If I live, I must succeed in what I have undertaken; death alone will put a stop to my efforts."

Early in August Livingstone began his third expedition up the Shire. He was again accompanied by Dr. Kirke, his brother Charles, and thirty-six of the Makololo men. It was on this journey that the magnificent Nyassa lake was discovered by the explorers, after a twenty days' hard march northward through the Shire country. The very first view of it excited their warmest enthusiasm, for it was the grandest sheet of water they had yet seen in Africa— nearly two hundred miles long and fully fifty in breadth. Like all vast bodies of water, it was subject to sudden and violent storms. Our explorers were caught in one of these storms, and came near being shipwrecked.

The discovery of the two lakes, the Shirwa and the Nyassa, proved of more importance than was at first supposed. They were both found to lie parallel to the ocean, and the

whole traffic of the regions beyond must necessarily pass
through them.   Though greatly pleased by this last discovery, and much impressed with the wonderful country;
nevertheless Livingstone grew sick at heart when he found
that it was the center of an immense district that annually
supplied more slaves for the markets of the coast than any
other of its size in the whole Continent.   Here once more
was he face to face with that dread evil which failed not
to blight every thing it touched; here once more did he
stand within an earthly Eden, over every fair flower of
which the serpent had left its poisonous trail.

The country around Lake Nyassa was densely populated,
far exceeding any thing of the kind Livingstone had yet
seen in Africa.   At its southern end there was an almost
unbroken continuation of villages, the majority of them containing not less than a thousand inhabitants each.   Unlike
many of the African tribes, the people of this favored region
seemed imbued with a spirit of industry.   They cultivated
the soil extensively, raised nearly every thing it was prac-
ticable for them to raise, besides working in iron and cotton, and at basket-making.   Almost every village had its
smelting-house, charcoal-burners, and blacksmiths.   The
axes, spears, arrow-heads, needles, bracelets, and anklets they
turned out, while not of the finest workmanship, were fashioned with much skill.   Crockery and pottery of various
kinds were also manufactured, while strong and serviceable
fishing-nets, after the most approved mode, were made from
the fibers of the buaze, which grows in abundance upon the
hills.   In spite of the creditable beginning they seemed to
be making in the direction of civilization, these people had
many strange, even barbarous customs.   Among others was
the habit of wearing the pelele, or lip-ring, which prevailed

principally among women. A small hole was made in the upper lip and gradually widened, the latter process extending over several years. This continued until an aperture from one to two inches, according to the fancy of the wearer, became permanent. Into this aperture a large tin or iron ring was forced until the lip protruded two inches or more beyond the nose. "Thus," says Livingstone, "when an old wearer of a hollow ring smiles, by the action of the muscle of the cheek the ring and lip outside of it are dragged back and thrown over the eyebrows. The nose is seen through the middle of the ring; and the exposed teeth show how carefully they have been chipped to look like those of the crocodile." To Livingstone's oft-repeated question, as to why they followed this custom, they invariably replied, " O because it is in the fashion!" However, on his putting the same query to an old chief, he was greeted with the following reply, not given without some little attempt at a display of humor: " For beauty, to be sure! Men have beards and whiskers; women have none; and what kind of creature would a woman be without whiskers and without the pelele? She would have a mouth like a man, and no beard. Ha! ha! ha!"

Although inclined to be very prying and curious, the people of this region were quite inoffensive; at least, they never showed any signs of molesting the strangers. It is a wonder, too, especially as they took the white members of the exploring party to be some kind of animal of which they had never even heard. "Their worst annoyance," says Livingstone, " was to lift the edge of the tent, peep in, as boys in England do the curtain of a traveling menagerie, and exclaim, 'Chirombo, Chirombo!' which being Anglicized means, 'Wild beasts, fit to be eaten!'" In a little while, however, Livingstone had made such friends with every tribe visited in the Nyassa country that they no longer looked upon him as a curious beast, but as a most superior being. As the Makololo had done, so did they too in time begin to call him father, and to greet him with a show of the greatest reverence and respect wherever he appeared.

Early in November, 1859, Livingstone found himself back at Tete. Here most unexpected but pleasing intelligence of a domestic nature greeted him. A letter from Mrs. Livingstone stated, among other things, that a little daughter had been born to them on the 16th of November, 1858. "The Lord bless her, and make her his own child in heart and in life!" was Livingstone's fervent prayer when he read these lines. To think she had been almost a year in the world before he had heard of her existence!

CHAPTER XXII.

GOING HOME WITH THE MAKOLOLO — A SECOND LOOK AT THE
VICTORIA FALLS—PAINFUL NEWS—ARRIVAL AT SESHEKE—SE-
KELETU'S TERRIBLE CONDITION—LIVINGSTONE EFFECTS A CURE
—PAINFUL FOREBODINGS IN REGARD TO THE MAKOLOLO—THE
RETURN TO TETE — DEVOTION OF LIVINGSTONE'S MEN — DR.
KIRKE MEETS WITH A LOSS—THE NEW STEAMER "PIONEER"
—ARRIVAL OF BISHOP M'KENZIE AND ASSISTANTS—TO THE
MOUTH OF THE ROVUMA—UP THE SHIRE—AT CHIBISA'S TOWN
—LIBERATION OF THE SLAVES—AN ERRAND OF PEACE TURNED
INTO ONE OF WAR—THE NEW MISSION—ARRIVAL OF MRS. LIV-
INGSTONE, MISS M'KENZIE, AND OTHERS—DISASTROUS ENDING
OF THE LITTLE MISSION—ILLNESS AND DEATH OF MRS. LIV-
INGSTONE—SECOND EXPLORATION OF THE ROVUMA—AGAIN UP
THE SHIRE—AN APPALLING STATE OF AFFAIRS—THE CURSE
OF THE SLAVE-TRADE.

FOR a long while Livingstone had cherished the desire
to return to his old friends, Sekeletu and the Makololo. He therefore departed from Tete for Linyanti on the
15th of May, 1860. Before leaving he employed himself
in putting together and operating a sugar-mill that had
been sent to Sekeletu by a noble lady in England. He
would have liked to carry it to the chief on this expedition,
but it was impossible to do so until he had stemmed the
rapids with the new steamer.

The party left Tete in the best of spirits, especially the
Makololo, whose joy was great when they found themselves
once more homeward-bound. The white men were Dr. Livingstone, his brother Charles, and Dr. Kirke. The Mako-

lolo were very attentive to each of them, but it could be
plainly seen that no one would ever supplant Livingstone
in their affections.   They took it turn about to cut grass
for the Englishmen's beds, and always secured a plentiful
supply, though sometimes at a great discomfort to themselves.   On these beds, with their thick rugs drawn over
them, the three white men slept very comfortably, while
the Makololo tended the fires all through the night, in
watches of from four to five each.   The beds of the Makololo were most ingeniously contrived, consisting of palm-
leaves sewed together around three sides of the square, the
one side being left open so as to enable the man to crawl
into it.

On the 9th of August, 1860, the party reached the great
Victoria Falls, the smoke of which they had seen fully
twenty miles away.   The awe of Dr. Kirke and Charles
Livingstone on beholding this immense cataract was fully
as great as Livingstone's had been on a previous occasion.
Charles Livingstone, who had seen Niagara, pronounced
the Victoria far superior to that in every way.   Here
they remained long enough to make as accurate measure-
ments as possible.   This was chiefly at Livingstone's desire.
He was afraid that he had not been altogether accurate in
his first reports.   So unusual were the dimensions of this
gigantic fall of waters, he also feared that many might ac-
cuse him of exaggeration.   Such a tendency as this was as
foreign to Livingstone's nature as was point-blank deception itself—the latter, as we well know, an utter impossi-
bility with him.   He held in supreme contempt, even loathing, the least inclination to the slightest misrepresentation,
especially so when that misrepresentation was for the purpose of gaining the world's ear.   " The truth, the unblem-

ished, unimpeachable truth, at all hazards," was his motto. He was therefore greatly pleased to find that his former estimates had all been right.

When the party reached the confines of Sekeletu's territory they were greeted by very unexpected and crushing news, especially to Livingstone. Both of the missionaries sent through his efforts to Linyanti had died with the fever; and the assistants, becoming frightened and discouraged, had left the place. If they had only taken liberal doses of the quinine which had been sent along with the supplies, Livingstone thought much, if not all, of this misfortune might have been averted. He suspected that in the confusion of moving to the place, and in the midst of the many exciting incidents that had doubtless attended their settling down among the Makololo, the little packets of medicine had either been neglected or entirely overlooked. On reaching Linyanti he found that his surmises were correct.

At Sesheke the travelers came upon Sekeletu, who had recently taken up his residence there. Having been seized by that fearful disease, leprosy, he had withdrawn himself from the sight of his people, and was now lying in a covered wagon surrounded by a high wall of reeds. He would allow no one to approach him save a female doctor of the Manyeti tribe, who professed to have an infallible cure for the dread malady. So far, however, she had made little, if any, headway. Poor Sekeletu was indeed a pitiful-looking object. Tears filled Livingstone's eyes as he gazed upon him. Sekeletu's joy on once more beholding his much-loved father was pathetic to see, especially as he was weighed down by the knowledge that he must not touch him. Livingstone dismissed the female doctor and installed himself as Sekeletu's physician. Under his skillful treatment, combined with that of Dr. Kirke, Sekeletu entirely recovered. But his once proud spirit was broken: he did not appear like the same man. Besides, during Livingstone's absence he had been very imprudent: he had allowed himself to be drawn into war with several of the neighboring chiefs. Having no martial skill like that of his father, he had been defeated every time. Believing his powers on the wane, many of his people had deserted him. Others, he had every reason to believe, were at this time forming a plot against him. Indeed, as Livingstone feared, the glory of the Makololo was fast passing away. It wrung his heart to see thus early the apparent signs of inevitable decay on a people whom he had hoped to redeem and to render one of the most powerful, useful, and prosperous tribes in the whole Continent. These painful forebodings were now realized. In 1864 Sekeletu died; then ensued a fierce struggle for the chieftainship, during which the outside chiefs, seeing how the people were divided against each other, deemed it a decisive moment for striking their own blows. Thus the broad, beautiful, and smiling country which Sebituane had conquered, and in which he had reigned as a king over his kingdom, became almost as a desolate wilderness, while the once proud race was scattered like chaff before the wind.

As soon as the people learned that Livingstone was at Sesheke they flocked in great crowds to hear him. If he had ever doubted their love and loyalty, he had ample proof of it now. He remained among them several weeks, preaching and teaching, and left at last with his heart filled with the grave apprehensions we have noted.

Many striking incidents marked the journey back to Tete,

but we relate only two of them. At the Mburuma Rapids the travelers had an eloquent proof of the bravery and devotion of the Makololo. While going over the most dangerous of the rapids, the two canoes almost simultaneously lurched and filled with water. They were in the greatest danger of being immediately swamped, in which event all the men would surely have perished. But without a moment's hesitation the four Makololos leaped from the canoes into the water, two out of each; and they ordered a Batoka man to do the same, declaring that "the white men must be saved at all hazards." "But I cannot swim," remonstrated the Batoka. "Jump out, then, and hold on to the canoe," again ordered the Makololo. He dared not longer hesitate. Swimming along-side the canoes, the Makololo successfully guided them over the rapids, though at the greatest danger to themselves. Once on the other side, they ran the canoes to the shore, and began to bail them out as coolly and as calmly as though nothing unusual had happened.

Dr. Kirke and Charles Livingstone were struck with intense admiration for this daring act, and were loud in their praise; but the Makololo seemed to value far more than any thing else the warm clasp of the hand and the expressive glance of the eye given them by Livingstone, for whose sake they would gladly have faced death many times over.

In one of the Kebrabasa Rapids the canoe which bore Dr. Kirke, Charles Livingstone, and two of the Makololo men was suddenly swamped. Each had to swim for his life, and it was with the utmost difficulty that they finally reached the shore. Greatly to the Doctor's regret, he found that he had lost by this catastrophe a chronometer, a barometer, and the many drawings and notes made during the journey.

On the 23d of November the explorers found themselves safe at Tete, after an absence of a little over six months. Early in December they again left Tete. This time they were bound for the Kongone entrance, where they expected to meet the " Pioneer," the new steamer sent for their use by the British Government. They took along with them the " Ma-Robert." which they intended to leave at this point until she could be carried away. But alas! the days of " the asthmatic old lady " were numbered. On the 21st of December she grounded on a sand-bank, where she had to be abandoned. It became necessary to make the rest of the journey on foot, and it was in sore straits that the plucky little band arrived at the mouth of the river on the 4th of January, 1861. Twenty-seven days afterward, on the 31st of January, the new steamer " Pioneer " was anchored outside the bar. As the weather was very rough, she did not venture in until February 4th. A few days later two of Her Majesty's cruisers arrived, bringing, among other passengers, Bishop McKenzie and assistants, who were then on their way to organize the long talked-of mission station in the valley of the Shire.

With the " Pioneer " came orders to Livingstone from the Government to proceed at once to the mouth of the Rovuma River, and there begin an exploration of it. Livingstone had long had his eyes upon this river. He believed that through it he might find a more uninterrupted and promising water-route from the coast to Lake Nyassa than that through the Shire and Zambesi. It was upon such intimations made to the Government that they had sent him directions to sail for the mouth of the Rovuma. The Bishop and his assistants accompanied Livingstone on this trip. If they could reach their destination through the Rovuma and Lake Nyassa, so much the better. If they could not, then they could return and take the route by the Zambesi and Shire.

On the 25th day of February the mouth of the Rovuma was reached. The visitors found there a magnificent natural harbor and bay. They steamed up the mouth with very little difficulty, but shortly after entering the stream found the bed so low that they were soon compelled to return, fearing that if they did not do so they would run aground and have to remain there until the rains came.

Returning to the Kongone, they sailed on that tributary up into the Zambesi, and thence to the Shire. Although the latter river was very deep, they nevertheless had great difficulty in getting over some places. Again a mistake had been made—this time in sending a steamer that drew fully five feet of water. This rendered the vessel utterly unfit for the navigation of many of the shallower streams.

On arriving at the town of his old friend Chibisa, Livingstone was distressed to learn that a fierce war was raging in the country of the Manganja, the very people among whom the Bishop and his assistants were going to labor. They learned that this war had grown out of the horrid slave traffic, which had increased to an alarming extent since Livingstone's last visit. Chibisa also informed them that a large slave party would pass through his village the following morning on its way down to the coast. The warm blood of the generous and impetuous McKenzie was fired by this information. "Shall we not interfere?" he asked Livingstone quickly. Livingstone's own heart was bleeding over the woes of these poor oppressed creatures. He felt that he

22

would gladly give his life to right their wrongs.   But if he interfered in this instance, would it have the effect desired? Would it frighten the dread slave-masters into a future abandonment of this section? or would it only precipitate matters, and thus draw him and his friends into hostile collision not only with the traders themselves but with the slave-dealing tribes?   This was a catastrophe that Livingstone had all along dreaded, and of which he had hitherto steered clear.   But in this case the calls of humanity were especially pressing.   Could he stand by inactive and witness such a sight as he would witness on the morrow?   Had not he and his friends the balance of power in their hands, since there was quite a little army of them, whereas the slave-traders were likely to number only two or three, with perhaps a dozen drivers?   Besides, Chibisa's people were bitterly opposed to the traffic, and would only need a word from Livingstone to gain them as allies.   Hitherto, when he had met the long procession of slaves, he had either been in a hostile country or with but little assistance at hand. Now every thing was different.   What should he do? While Livingstone was thus deliberating the band of slaves arrived.   Before he could reach a decision the cowardice of the drivers had thrown every thing into the hands of the explorers, and there was no longer a call for hesitancy.   The scene is thus described:

"A long line of manacled men and women made their appearance.   The black drivers, armed with muskets and bedecked with various articles of finery, marched jauntily in the front, middle, and rear of the line, some of them blowing exulting notes out of long tin horns.   They seemed to feel that they were doing a very noble thing, and might proudly march with an air of triumph.   But the instant the fellows caught a glimpse of the English, they darted off like mad into the forest; so fast, indeed, that we caught but a glimpse of their red caps and of their heels. The chief of the party alone remained; and he, from being in front, had his hand tightly clasped by a Makololo. He proved to be a well-known slave of the late commandant at Tete, and for some time our own attendant while there. On asking him how he obtained these captives, he replied he had bought them; but on our inquiring of the people themselves all save four said they had been captured in war. While this inquiry was going on he bolted too.

"The captives knelt down, and, in the way of expressing thanks, clapped their hands with great energy. They were thus left entirely in our hands, and knives were soon at work cutting women and children loose. It was more difficult to cut the men adrift, as each had his neck in the fork of a stout stick, six or seven feet long, and kept by an iron rod, which was riveted at both ends across the throat. With a saw, luckily in the Bishop's baggage, one by one the men were sawed out into freedom. The women, on being told to take the meal they were carrying and cook breakfast for themselves and the children, seemed to consider the news too good to be true, but after a little coaxing went at it with alacrity, and made a capital fire by which to boil their pots with the slave sticks and bonds—their old acquaintances through many a sad night and weary day.

"Many were mere children, about four years of age and under. One little boy, with the simplicity of childhood, said to our men: 'The others tied and starved us; you cut the ropes, and tell us to eat. What sort of people are you? Where do you come from?' Two of the women had been shot the day before for attempting to untie the thongs. . . .

One woman had her infant's brains knocked out because she could not carry her load and it; and a man was dispatched with an ax because he had broken down with fatigue."

The number of the unhappy creatures thus liberated by Livingstone and his friends was eighty-four. When they were told that they might go where they pleased or remain with the mission about to be started, they quickly chose the latter, no doubt feeling that they would be much safer near those who had proved to be their benefactors.

After a conference with his party, Livingstone decided that it might be advisable to go on a friendly visit to the chief of the Ajana, the powerful and warlike tribe that was then so cruelly oppressing the Manganja. It would certainly be prudent to endeavor to establish peaceful relations between the two tribes before Bishop McKenzie took up his abode with the Manganja. Unfortunately for this movement, Chibisa accompanied the party. As he was known to be the friend and champion of the Manganja, and a warrior of considerable renown, it is not to be wondered at that his presence should have been misconstrued. The road along which their route lay presented a dreadful aspect. Many villages were in ashes, others were still burning, while the wailing of the homeless women and children was heart-rending to hear. Finally they came in sight of the village they were seeking. Just before reaching this point the whole party had engaged in fervent prayer, led by the Bishop. They then bravely advanced, politely requesting a parley. Doubtless this might have been granted them but for an unfortunate diversion that occurred at the moment. Some of the poor captive Manganja, seeing Chibisa, shouted with joy: "Our Chibisa is come! Our Chibisa, our great warrior, is come!" The instant these cries fell upon their ears the Ajana warriors started up, snatched at their weapons, and rushed at the party, crying, " War! war! war!" Following close upon this dreadful cry came a shower of poisoned arrows. Fortunately none of the party were hurt. Livingstone tried to call out to them to command attention, declaring that they were all friends, but it was impossible for his voice to be heard above the din. The party was now compelled to fire upon the Ajana in self-defense. This was the first time in all his African experience that Livingstone had been forced to resort to such measures, and it troubled his mind greatly. Never, in all the perilous encounters with hostile bands, had one shot been fired, either by himself or by his men; never had one life been taken by their hands. Nay, he might go farther still, and say never had one drop of blood been spilled by them. What a record for a man who had twice passed directly through the heart of the most purely savage country on the face of the globe! So little was Livingstone expecting such an emergency that he had failed to arm himself with even a pistol, and one had now to be forced into his hands. Not that he was a coward, and feared to use the weapon—to think of calling this splendid man a coward!—but that he was bitterly averse to shedding human blood even under provocation.

The encounter was hot and serious, but finally the Ajana were driven off. It was with a sad heart that Livingstone returned to Chibisa's village. Many gloomy forebodings filled his mind, and these increased as he took his departure for Tete, leaving the Bishop and his assistants established in their mission. The errand of peace had ended in one of war. What serious consequences might not now result?

(342)

A MISSIONARY STATION IN AFRICA.

The Ajana were dangerous and desperate, and the new-comers had made enemies of them instead of friends—a state of affairs altogether repugnant to one of Livingstone's nature. His last words to the Bishop were of counsel, that he should be careful and take no further part in attempting to adjust the wrongs of the Manganja, but do all he could to establish peaceful relations between the two tribes. Alas that the kindly and impulsive man did not act in accordance with this advice!

On the last day of January, 1862, Livingstone was again at the little station at the mouth of the Kongone, where he had the happiness of greeting his wife, who had just arrived by Her Majesty's ship " Gorgon." With Mrs. Livingstone came Miss McKenzie (the Bishop's sister) and the wives of two of the other missionaries, who had come out to rejoin their dear ones in the valley of the Shire. The " Gorgon " had also brought along the sections of the new brig, the " Lady Nyassa," which was Livingstone's own purchase, and which he designed principally for navigation on the Shire—hence the name.

While Livingstone was superintending the putting to-gether of the " Lady Nyassa," Capt. Wilson of the " Gor-gon," accompanied by Dr. Kirke and several of the ship's crew, went on with the ladies who had come out to join the mission. At Tete they received news of the calamity that had overwhelmed the little mission and culminated in the death of the Bishop and three of his assistants. The ladies were completely overcome. No course was left them now but to return to the country from which they had departed only a few weeks before, filled with hopeful anticipations.

Finding it difficult to put the " Lady Nyassa " together at the mouth of the river, Livingstone determined to tow

the sections up as far as Shupanga by means of the " Pioneer." Soon after reaching this point he too learned of the
sad fate of the mission. The distress and grief that filled
his tender, sympathetic heart may well be imagined. Speaking of his feelings a short time afterward, he says: " This
blow is quite bewildering; but in this, as in every thing else,
we must bow to the will of Him who doeth all things well."
Alas! he little dreamed of the blow that was soon to fall
many times more crushingly upon him.

Through circumstances that it was impossible for him to
control, Livingstone was compelled to remain at Shupanga
much longer than he had expected. While a moderately
healthy spot during some seasons of the year, Shupanga was
also an exceedingly unhealthy place at other seasons. This
was especially the case during the prevalence of the fever
scourge, by which it was regularly visited once a year.

As the fever period began to approach Livingstone grew
more and more apprehensive, chiefly on his wife's account.
Still, he hoped to the last that he would be enabled to get
off before any thing serious occurred. But alas! he did not.
On the 21st of April Mrs. Livingstone was taken ill. The
symptoms were not alarming at first, and, though very uneasy in regard to her, Livingstone believed that it was only
an ordinary sickness. Instead of changing for the better,
however, the symptoms grew more threatening. In six
days from her attack she was delirious and raging with
fever. Livingstone could deceive himself no longer—his
wife's condition was critical. He tried to prepare himself
for what might happen, but it had all come upon him so
suddenly, so unexpectedly, that it completely unmanned
him. In another day he knew that all hope was at an end
—that the blow must fall, that even now the Omnipotent

Arm was raised to strike it. But it was too much even for him, with all his courage and with all his faith. When the end came he who had faced death in so many forms, who had stood unawed before dangers the most terrifying, broke down and wept like a little child. Can we wonder at this when we recall the heart of him who had been thus bereaved—its deep and abiding possibilities of tender and devoted love? "It is the first stroke I have suffered," he says, in pouring the anguish of his stricken soul out upon the senseless pages of his journal, "and quite takes away my strength. I wept over her who well deserves many tears. I loved her when I married her, and the longer I lived with her I loved her the more. God pity the poor children, who were all tenderly attached to her; and I am left alone in the world by one whom I felt to be a part of myself. I hope it may, by divine grace, lead me to realize heaven as my home, and that she has but preceded me in the journey. O my Mary, my Mary! how often we have longed for a quiet home, since you and I were cast adrift at Kolobeng! Surely the removal by a kind Father who knoweth our frame means that he rewarded you by taking you to the best home—the eternal one in heaven." He had lost her, the wife of his youth, the companion of his maturer years, the sharer of his joys and his sorrows. The strongest bond that held him to earth had been severed; the golden links of the chain that had so long bound his heart a willing captive were rent asunder. His Mary was dead— she whose gentle smile had ever greeted him, even amidst the most harassing circumstances; she whose tender lips had never once reproached him for the hardships of the way; she who had ever been his help and comfort, his sweet fortress of refuge in a wilderness of sorrow, his

cheery fellow-traveler through the earthly pilgrimage. Yes,
she was gone, and he was left to tread the weary way
alone. It is no wonder that in the first outburst of grief
he should have exclaimed, "Now for the first time in my
life I am willing to die! Take me too, O God." Under
the large baobab-tree at Shupanga, which has since become
so inseparably associated with memories of her, and which
has been made the theme of more than one poet's verse,
lies all that is mortal of Mary Moffat Livingstone—a missionary's daughter, a missionary's wife.

This mighty tree under which Mrs. Livingstone lies buried
is full sixty feet in circumference. It has been mentioned
in the works of several explorers as being of an unusually
large size even in that country of large trees. There were
several of these baobab-trees around Shupanga, though they
are found more abundantly in those sections just south of
the Sahara. The tree is not so much noted for its height
as for its breadth. It seldom reaches a distance of over
one hundred feet. On account of its great strength and
durability—some of them are said to live more than a
thousand years—the natives often build their huts within
the branches, reaching them by means of a cunningly contrived ladder. The principal object, however, in building
the huts in the tops of these trees is that it gives the occu-
pant security against the deadly attacks of lions, leopards,
and other dangerous wild beasts.

Livingstone could not be idle, even in the midst of this
crushing sorrow. With the last tears shed upon his wife's
grave, when he was in all probability never to look on it
again, he arose reconsecrated to the work before him. In
a week after her death he was again at his post, helping
with his own hands to put the "Lady Nyassa" together.

BAOBAB-TREE AND NATIVE HUT.

Livingstone and his companions now started on another exploration of the Rovuma. This time they succeeded in reaching a point some one hundred and fifty miles from its mouth. Here they were stopped by cataracts. The people in the neighborhood of these cataracts were peaceable and industrious, and, with few exceptions, received the travelers in a friendly manner.   They were called the Makoa, and were known by a cicatrice on the brow in the form of a crescent, with the horns pointing downward.

This voyage up the Rovuma was almost as disappointing as the first had been.   Although Livingstone succeeded in getting more than a hundred miles farther, he had not found that uninterrupted water-route from the sea to Lake Nyassa which he had hoped to find.   Perhaps, after all, it would be better to seek to establish the course by way of the Zambesi and the Shire.   With this object in view, Livingstone steamed back to the Kongone entrance of the Zambesi, and thence to the Shire.   This was in the beginning of 1863. .

On moving up the Shire Livingstone found a most appalling state of affairs.   His recent wonderful discoveries in the valley of the Shire, as communicated by him to the Government, had produced an outside effect which he had not anticipated.   They had served to stimulate the desires and kindle into renewed vigor the activity of the Portuguese slave-traders, who had already begun to flock in great crowds to this beautiful and promising region.   Happy villages had been depopulated; smiling plains had become the scenes of wretchedness and woe; husbands had been torn from wives, wives from husbands, and children from their mothers' arms; while long lines of miserable, heartbroken creatures, fastened together with chain or fork, were daily urged along like cattle before the lash of their cruel drivers.   The chief instigator of all this horrible work was Mariano, the most cruel of all the Portuguese slave-agents.   He not only laid plans for the capture of slaves, and had them seized and carried off by his agents when-

ever and wherever they could get their hands upon them,
but he also stirred up one tribe against another until war
in its most horrible form ensued.   Villages were set on fire,
and the inhabitants, fleeing for their lives, met a fate far
more dreadful than death by falling into the hands of the
traders.   The ruthless torch was applied to the store-house
as well as to the home; and all their provisions being destroyed, famine resulted.   From this cause alone hundreds
of the villagers perished.   The revolting picture that greeted Livingstone's eyes on his ascent into the valley of the
Shire is thus drawn by his own hand: "A little more than
twelve months before the valley of the Shire was populous
with peaceful and contented tribes; now the country was
all but a desert, the very air polluted by the putrid carcasses of the slain, which lay rotting on the plains, and
floated in the waters of the river in such numbers as to
clog the paddles of the steamer.   Once they saw a crocodile make a rush at the carcass of a boy, and shake it as a
terrier-dog shakes a rat, while others rushed to share in the
meal, and quickly devoured it.   The miserable inhabitants
who had managed to avoid being slain or carried off into
captivity were collecting insects, plants, and wild fruits—
any thing, in short, that would stave off starvation—in the
neighborhood of the villages where they had formerly enjoyed peace and plenty.   They were entirely naked, save
for the palm-leaf aprons they wore, as every thing of any
value had been carried off by the slave-stealers.   The sight
of hundreds of putrid dead bodies and bleached skeletons
was not half so painful as the groups of women and children who were seen sitting amidst the ruins of their former
dwellings, with their ghastly, famine-stricken faces, and dull,
dead eyes.   These made up such a tale of woe and misery,

that those who were dead might be deemed fortunate in comparison with the survivors, who instinctively clung to the devastated spot they had once called home, and those who had been led into life-long captivity."

This beast of slavery was indeed a monster of iniquity so terrible, so strong that even Livingstone's determined hands could not reach about its throat to strangle it. But as long as there was breath in his body he would fight the monster —yea, fight it to the death.

After spending several months in and around the Nyassa country, during which he made a note of many interesting points to be used on future explorations, Doctor Livingstone once more returned to England.

CHAPTER XXIII.

LIVINGSTONE AGAIN IN ENGLAND—DEATH OF HIS MOTHER—
"FEAR GOD, AND WORK HARD"—HIS IMPRESSIONS IN REGARD
TO THE NILE SOURCES—THE RETURN TO AFRICA—THE START
FOR THE INTERIOR—BAD CONDUCT OF THE MEN—THE WORLD
LOSES SIGHT OF HIM—REPORTED DEATH—FEARS AND DOUBTS
—MR. YOUNG GOES IN SEARCH OF HIM—NEWS OF HIS SAFETY
—LETTERS—THE DISPATCHES FROM BANGWEOLO—ANOTHER
PERIOD OF SILENCE AND SUSPENSE—STANLEY TO THE RESCUE.

ON the 23d day of July, 1864, Livingstone reached England; but he left it again on the 14th day of August, 1865. One sad event of this sojourn in England was the death of his mother, which ocurred on the 18th of June, 1865. The account below is taken from Livingstone's journal:

"Monday, June 19th.—A telegram came, saying that mother had died the day before. I started at once for Scotland. No change was observed till within an hour and a half of her departure. Seeing the end was near, sister Agnes said, 'The Saviour has come for you, mother. Can you "lippen" yourself to him?' She replied, 'O yes.' Little Anna Mary was held up to her. She gave her the last look, and said, 'Bonnie wee lassie,' gave a few long inspirations, and all was still, with a look of reverence on her countenance. She had wished William Logan, a good Christian man, to lay her head in the grave, if I were not there. When going away in 1858, she said that she would have liked one of her laddies to lay her head in the grave.

(351)

It so happened that I was there to pay the last tribute to a dear, good mother."

She had been a noble mother indeed, a mother in Israel; and most precious was the memory left to her children.

One of the very last things we find Livingstone doing in his own loved Scotland was attending the exercises of a school where his two youngest children were entered as pupils, and seeing them take prizes. He made a little talk to the children of the school, after much persuasion, in which he gave to them, among other things, this precept, begging them to make it the rule of their daily lives: "*Fear God, and work hard.*" How eminently fitted he was to give this counsel—he who had made these same words the grand key-note of his own life!

When Dr. Livingstone arrived in England the recent discoveries of Capt. Speke and Major Grant were the theme of almost every tongue. These were subsequently added to by the achievements of Capt. Baker, so that the people could talk about little else than the finding of the true sources of the Nile—the settling of the question that had perplexed the world for ages. But somehow, while he had the deepest respect for all these gentlemen, and sincerely joined his countrymen in praise of their brave exploits, Livingstone felt that there must be an error somewhere. He did not believe that the head-waters of the Nile were so far north as Speke, Grant, and Baker had placed them, but was of the impression that they lay farther south, probably in one of the many great lakes which, during his last explorations in Africa, he had heard of as lying between the Nyassa and the Victoria Nyanza. Livingstone had been told so much concerning a lake called Tanganyika that his curiosity to see it was great. He could not get the impression out of his mind that about this lake, should he ever succeed in reaching it, he would discover something of interest in regard to the Nile sources. One principal object of his return to Africa, then, was the desire to find this lake, if possible. An additional strong motive was the anxiety to settle the vexed question of the water-shed of that portion of Africa. Upon this depended to a great extent the final clearing up of the Nile mystery; for Livingstone looked upon it as still a mystery in a certain sense, in spite of what Grant, Speke, and Baker had discovered. But doubtless the strongest motive of all—stronger, since it lay closer to his heart than either of the others—was the desire to do further missionary work among the yet unenlightened inhabitants of the Dark Continent. He had never quite forgiven himself for letting the missionary merge so far into the explorer as to almost lose his identity. Still, it had all been done with an eye single to the good of the wretched creatures whose interests were so closely allied to his own. We have seen why he was so anxious to open up this country to commerce, and how he had hoped and believed from the first that this would be the initial step in the advance of Christian missions. This idea had never left him, and was as strong with him now as when first formed in his mind; and this was why he had seemingly given up his mission work to engage in that of an explorer. He now determined, however, to combine both as much as possible.

Livingstone went first to Paris, thence to Bombay, where he remained some little time perfecting arrangements, and then took passage direct to Zanzibar, the principal landing-place of most explorers starting into the interior. At Bombay he was joined by seven Zambesi men whom he had left

23

there on his way to England for the purpose of receiving
instruction at the Government schools; also by two Shire
valley boys, who had been connected with the mission of
the lamented Bishop McKenzie, and who had been in Bombay for some time with the same object of the Zambesi men.
Livingstone was well pleased to find that these two lads had
not only learned to read but also to write, and that they
had conducted themselves well during the entire school
course. They were exceedingly anxious to be baptized into
the English Church before their return to Africa. Feeling
assured of their sincerity, Livingstone saw that the sacred
rite was administered before their departure. Besides these,
Livingstone added to his exploring party twelve Sepoys
from Bombay, several Suahila lads from the Nassick School
at Bombay, nine men from Johanna (one of the Comoro Islands), and seven liberated slaves. The Johanna men were
headed by a man named Musa, of whom we shall hear very
unpleasantly after awhile. The Sepoys were to act principally as guards, and for this purpose had been armed with
Enfield rifles. To aid in the work of transporting the baggage and goods of the party, they had with them six camels, twelve buffaloes and a calf, two mules, and four donkeys. Ten bales of cloth and two bags of beads were also
taken along to serve as currency, while several boxes of instruments, a box of medicines, and many other useful articles, completed the outfit. The question naturally arises,
" What man but Livingstone would have encumbered himself with such baggage and such a menagerie-like array of
animals, and for what conceivable purpose except for the
benefit of Africa?" No other one, certainly. These tame
buffaloes of India were taken that he might try whether or
not, like the wild buffaloes of the African plains, they would

resist the bite of the deadly tsetse fly. For the same reason the camels were carried along. The mules and donkeys would have to take their chances. The latter he had
seen get through very well on a previous occasion.

The two deadliest native foes to the civilization of Africa,
Livingstone knew only too well, were the fever and the tsetse fly. Could he succeed in counteracting their fateful influence, even in a small part, no expense or trouble within
his power would be spared. He had already found in the
African forests a remedy that had more than once proved ef-
fective against the first dread evil. Might he not, therefore,
hope to find in the camels and buffaloes unassailable substi-
tutes for the oxen that so readily succumbed to the fatal tsetse bite? Alas! he was not to know. Before leaving Zanzibar he had the misfortune, from one cause and another, to
lose nine of his buffaloes; and before he had proceeded far
on his journey the remaining buffaloes and the camels had
perished through the cruelty of some of the men who accompanied him.

At Zanzibar Livingstone was joined by two Shupanga
men, Susi and Amoda; also by two Waiyau lads, Wikatani
and Chuma. The Shupanga men had been wood-cutters
for the " Pioneer," the Waiyau lads among the slaves res-
cued in 1861. They were all greatly attached to Livingstone, especially the faithful Susi, whose name from this
time on is closely associated with Livingstone's, and who
by one brave, beautiful deed of devotion has won the praise
and admiration of the whole civilized world.

Livingstone left Zanzibar on the 19th of March for the
mouth of the Rovuma River. He found it very much
changed since his last visit; so much so, in fact, that he
had to make a landing twenty-five miles above, and march

overland to the banks of the river, regaining them at a point some miles from the sea.   Here the expedition took a direct course down the river toward the Nyassa.   It was a most fatiguing and trying march through an unfavorable country.   Livingstone says of it: " The toil was fitted to wear out the strongest of my men."   As to these men, they were no sooner started than they began to prove how trifling and troublesome they really were, especially the Sepoys and Johanna men.   The Sepoys treated the animals with such cruelty that they were soon all dead.   The Johanna men proved to be great thieves.   They not only stole from the bales of goods and the beads, to trade with the natives for such articles as their covetous souls desired, but they also stole the provisions of the little party as soon as they were procured.   Altogether it was the very worst lot of men into whose hands Livingstone had ever fallen. How many times he longed for his loyal and brave Makololo!   Finally, after a four months' trial, Livingstone dismissed some of the worst of the Sepoys and Johanna men, and sent them back to the coast.

While passing through the Waiyau country the Waiyau boys also deserted, under the pretense of having found their relatives.   The little band was now so much reduced that when they reached Lake Nyassa, on the 8th of August, only the Nassick boys, the Shupanga men, two or three of the liberated slaves, and four of the Johanna men were left. Livingstone remained some little time at the lake, writing up his journals, and making both geographical and lunar observations.   On trying to get across the lake to its western boundary, in order to pursue his march in search of lakes Bangweolo and Tanganyika, Livingstone found that he could for no consideration procure a dhow, the kind of boat used on the lake, as they were all owned by the slave-traders, who were determined he should not cross if they could help it. But the intrepid man resolved to make the journey on foot around the southern end of the lake, and thus reach the western border by way of the land. It was a desperate venture, and no one but Livingstone would have undertaken it, with his little band reduced to a mere hand-ful of men, and almost destitute of supplies of any kind. In describing the experiences of the first stages of the journey, in a letter to his son, under date of August 28th, Living-stone says: "Food was not to be had for love or money. Our finest cloths only brought miserable morsels of the common grain. I trudged it the whole way, and having no animal food save what turtle-doves and guinea-fowls we occasionally shot, I became like one of Pharaoh's lean kine."

Reaching the point at the southern end of the lake where the Shire issues from it, Livingstone was overcome by sad and painful reflections. He thought of the many expedi-tions he had made up this river; of the little mission sta-tion so hopefully planted in the central valley; of the death of the lamented McKenzie; and last, but far from being the least, the departure from earth to heaven of his beloved wife, and of her grave so far away under the shadow of the stately baobab-tree. Then came thoughts of the unhappy ending of the mission work at Linyanti. O how discour-aging seemed every thing in connection with the effort to plant mission stations in this heathen land! Had God failed to hear the cries of his people? Were these be-nighted souls to go on living in the pall-like darkness that shut out from their view every glimpse, every hope of the precious truths beyond? Ah, surely not. God had some good, some wise plan in it all. Livingstone would never.

lose faith that such was the case, and would steadfastly believe to the last that in his own time and in his own way God would send the answer to so many earnest, fervent prayers. O could he have lived ten years longer, to see how gloriously this thing came about! If his longing eyes could have looked upon the brave mission once more planted in the valley of the Shire under the control of the noble Bishop Steere! If he could have seen how grandly the work went forward—the work of "training the poor natives in the arts of civilization, rearing Christian households among them, and proclaiming the blessed gospel of the God of love."

Livingstone strenuously aimed at two things on this journey around the southern end of the lake. One was to spread abroad the great truths of Christianity, and the other to awaken in the consciences of this degraded people a horror of the atrocious slave-trade. At every opportunity he stopped to preach and to teach among them.

Early in September they arrived at the town of Marenga, at the south-western corner of the lake. Here Livingstone was deserted by Musa and the remaining Johanna men, who left him with only a half-dozen Nassick boys and the two Shupanga men. Musa pretended to be greatly frightened at the intelligence brought to Marenga's village by an Arab slave-trader, that all the country in the direction in which Livingstone's little party were heading was filled with dangerous and warlike Mazitu, the most bloodthirsty of the tribes in that section. In vain Marenga said to the men that the situation could not be half so bad as pictured, since he and his people had had no intimation of it; in vain Livingstone assured them that he intended giving the Mazitu as wide a berth as possible. They had long wanted an excuse for leaving him and going back to the coast; besides, they were very cowardly, and they did fear an encounter with the Mazitu, though not in the degree they pretended. So in the time of his greatest need of them they left him almost alone, to fight his way as best he could through the inhospitable country beyond. Not only this, but they stole nearly every thing of any value that remained to him, even some of his instruments, the greater part of his stock of medicines, and all the cloth and beads that were left. He was now reduced to most desperate straits, and but for the kindness of some of the tribes would surely have perished.

In the meantime, Musa and the Johanna men, after considerable delay, had succeeded in reaching the coast. And now a most startling report began traversing the whole civilized globe—a report that brought grief and consternation to the hearts of millions of admiring and sympathetic people. Dr. Livingstone, the devoted Christian missionary and fearless explorer, had been murdered by hostile tribes in the very heart of Africa! The news of this startling calamity had been brought to Zanzibar by one Musa and his companions, who had been of Livingstone's party ever since its departure for the interior, and who had also been with the missionary at the time of the reported murder, and therefore eye-witnesses of the deed. The story told by Musa and his companions was substantially as follows: They—the Johanna men—had followed Livingstone faithfully in all his wanderings until the north-western end of Lake Nyassa was reached. They had then started across the country in a south-westerly direction, when suddenly and without a moment's warning they were attacked by a band of the blood-thirsty Mazitu. The little party, thus surprised, made what

defense it could, but they were so outnumbered by the enemy that death for each one of them was only the question
of a few moments.   Seeing the state of affairs, Musa and
what Johanna men were not already slain managed to escape into a thick jungle, where they were successful in se-
creting themselves; but not before they had seen Livingstone's head nearly severed from his body by the ax of a
Mazitu, who dealt him the deadly blow from behind.   From
the jungle the Johanna men, after experiences too fearful
and harrowing to relate, had managed to make their escape
to Zanzibar.

This distressing story, substantiated as it was by Musa's
companions, was credited by all save a few of Livingstone's
most intimate friends.   They could not believe it.   They
thought it impossible for a man of Livingstone's caution
and cool sagacity to have been caught in such a trap as
this.   But outside these few, whose hopes remained unshaken to the last, the story, having now flown in every direction on electrical wings, was universally believed.   What
could be more probable?   Even a man of Dr. Livingstone's
well-known abilities was liable to be caught off his guard
sometimes; and what was equal to the cruelty, the cunning,
the blood-thirsty vindictiveness of the treacherous Zulus?
This intelligence first reached England on March 7th, 1867,
in the form of a dispatch sent by Dr. Kirke—Livingstone's
old friend and fellow-traveler, who was now Her Majesty's
consul at Zanzibar—to the Royal Geographical Society.
In making the announcement to the Society, Sir Roderick
Murchison, the president, said that while he did so with
feelings of the deepest grief, it was nevertheless not without some hope and belief that the story would prove untrue.   A fortnight later Sir Roderick declared, at a second

meeting, that his faith in the improbability of Musa's story had become only the more strengthened with the lapse of time. It was doubtless probable that Livingstone had been attacked by some hostile band, but that he had been slain he could not believe. His conviction was that Livingstone was somewhere in the interior, cut off from communication with his friends, and he hoped and believed a message would reach them after awhile.

This opinion of Sir Roderick was shared by a few others of Livingstone's more personal friends. The rest of them, including the outside world in general, were of the belief that the brave explorer had indeed perished. He was but a man after all, therefore not invulnerable; and where in all Africa could be found a more cruel and blood-thirsty tribe than the Mazitu? He had said so himself in his book on the Zambesi; and he had started from the coast with the intention of crossing their country in search of Lake Tanganyika. All the world knew that. Hence not only England, but the whole civilized globe, was thrown into the sincerest mourning at news of his death—for dead they surely believed him.

The newspapers now began publishing obituary notices, while letters of condolence daily poured in upon the explorer's family. The loss of such a man at such a time, right on the threshold of the glorious work he had inaugurated, was incalculable. All the world felt it, all the world bemoaned it. When *had* a man before accomplished so noble, so grand a work, and in so short a space? Would his like ever be found again? These and many more such questions were asked, while the regret and the sorrow at his untimely end continued.

A strong desire now arose in the hearts of Livingstone's

friends who still believed him alive to go in search of him. Though perhaps not slain by the dreaded Mazitu—as they fervently hoped he was not—he might nevertheless be in some place besieged by them, and cut off from all communication with the outside world. If such was the case, the matter ought to be investigated at once. This feeling was shared and warmly encouraged by Sir Roderick Murchison, who had first presented the matter at a meeting of the Society. This movement resulted in the sending out by the Society of a well-equipped search party under the command of Mr. E. D. Young, who had been with Livingstone in some of his explorations of the Zambesi. The party was furnished with a small vessel built almost entirely of steel, and so constructed that it could be easily taken apart, when each part formed a burden not beyond the average strength and endurance of an ordinarily strong and healthy man. It was owing to this ingenious construction of the boat that the exploring party was enabled to bear it by land around the Murchison Cataracts, and thus proceed on up the Shire to Lake Nyassa.

The expedition left England on the 10th of January, 1867, on board Her Majesty's ship "The Celt," which anchored safely in Table Bay on the 12th of July. Four days later the men were transferred to Her Majesty's ship "Petrel," and by her carried direct to the Kongone mouth of the Zambesi. On the 6th of August the steel vessel, having been put together and launched, started on its journey up the river. Exactly one month later it shot out into Lake Nyassa with flowing sails. Here Mr. Young for the first time received intelligence that left no doubt in his mind as to the untruthfulness of the report concerning Livingstone's death. At this point they met an Arab slave-

trader, who told them that instead of going round the
northern end of the lake, as Musa had reported, Livingstone had made his way down to the southern end. This
man had also recently seen and talked with the chief Marenga, at whose town Livingstone had been staying before
he moved off in the direction of Lake Tanganyika. Marenga had informed the trader of the cowardly desertion of
Livingstone by Musa and his companions, which was in
turn repeated to Mr. Young. A little farther on this story
was confirmed by the party meeting with two of the liberated
slaves, who had been with Livingstone after his desertion
by Musa, and who had helped him carry his baggage some
distance toward Lake Tanganyika. Having thus obtained
the knowledge of Livingstone's safety up to a period much
later than that given by Musa in his story as the date of
the murder, Mr. Young and the expedition returned to England. While he seemed perfectly satisfied with the work
he had done, there were those who thought he had not carried it out as he ought to have done; that he should not
have been satisfied with merely hearing that Livingstone
was still alive, but that he ought to have pushed on until
he came upon Livingstone himself. But doubtless Mr.
Young had good and sufficient reasons for not pursuing
this course, the chief of which was that he was not prepared
for an expedition by land.

Any further doubts that may have existed in regard to
Livingstone's being alive, after the date assigned by Musa
for his murder, were forever set at rest by the arrival in
England, soon after the return of the expedition, of a letter
from the great traveler himself. It was addressed to his
son Thomas, and bore the date of February, 1867—full five
months after he had been said by Musa to have perished by

the battle-ax of the fierce Mazitu. A few days later a letter from Livingstone, dated the same month, was received by Sir Roderick Murchison. Both of these letters spoke of the great explorer as in ordinary health, and as well started on his way in the direction of Lake Tanganyika. He had on the 15th of January crossed the Chimbwe River, and believed himself to be somewhere in the neighborhood of another great lake, of which he had recently heard much—Lake Bangweolo.

Now followed a time of much doubt and anxiety among Livingstone's friends, as well as of speculation and deep concern to the world at large. For full seven months nothing more was heard of him, though all sorts of rumors in regard to him—first of his discovery, and then of his death—came thick and fast. Other expeditions to go in search of him were talked of, but nothing was settled definitely, though from time to time various supplies were sent by his friends to Zanzibar, with the hope that some way might be found to get them into the interior, perhaps to some place where he might come upon them.

Early in the year 1868 another letter from the great explorer arrived in England. It was dated December 14th, 1867, and was addressed to a Mr. Seward. The intelligence conveyed in this letter was that he had somehow missed Bangweolo, and came instead upon a much smaller lake, Moero by name. He also stated that he had reached the edge of another lake, which he had every season to believe was the long looked-for Tanganyika, but which he had been unable to explore on account of sickness and the hostile state of the surrounding country. The letter closed by saying that he was on the point of starting again for the neighborhood of Lake Moero, where, he had strong grounds for believing, he would find something important in regard to the water-shed of that section.

Following upon this letter there was another six months' of weary waiting, when in July, 1868, there came a batch of most interesting dispatches, all of which were dated "near Lake Bangweolo," and minutely and graphically detailed the great traveler's movements up to that time. After this another long silence ensued, a silence that filled the space of ten months, during which time all that was heard of Livingstone's movements was through a short letter to Dr. Kirke at Zanzibar, under date of May 30th, 1869. In July of the same year Dr. Kirke received another communication which stated that Livingstone was then at Ujiji, on the north-eastern borders of Lake Tanganyika, and unable to proceed for the want of supplies. Intelligence of this being at once conveyed to England, it created a profound sensation and a feeling of the most intense sympathy in Livingstone's behalf. One thousand pounds were at once subscribed by the English Government, which was supplemented by a liberal sum from the Geographical Society and from the purses of many private friends. This sum was forwarded from England to Dr. Kirke at Zanzibar in June, 1870, with instructions to fit out an expedition to go at once to Livingstone's relief. But now numerous delays occurred. More than six months passed away after the arrival of the money at Zanzibar, and still no expedition had started out, though Dr. Kirke had from time to time sent supplies into the interior by private parties, principally through traders, hoping that they might chance in some way to reach Livingstone. But the all-important point was to send out not only a supply party but a search party. Livingstone had been so long in the heart of Africa, cut off from every thing

pertaining to civilized life, that his friends were really growing alarmed about him.   Though much was said and much
proposed, nothing was done, or seemed to have been done,
until late in February, 1871, when Dr. Kirke at last had
his party organized and ready to start from Zanzibar.

In the meanwhile, during all these delays, there had been
much talk in England of sending out a party direct from
that point.   This talk, however, resulted in no prompt action.   Every one seemed willing to do, yet no one could
arrive at any thing definite to be done.   It now remained
for America, with her usual pluck and dash, to come to the
rescue, and to reverse the old fable of the hare and the tortoise by sending the hare straight on to the race, while the
slow tortoise was only crawling about and making preparations to start—or, what seemed to be preparations.   Now,
this is not meant as a reflection upon our English cous-
ins.   We know that Livingstone was appreciated in his
own country, much more than it is generally given living
genius to realize; nay, further, that his country loved
and revered him, and that many honest efforts were made
to have a party go in search of him, and to search until it
had found him.   The trouble was, they wasted too much precious time.   It is almost needless to add that the American
hare won, for all the world knows that it was Henry M.
Stanley, the daring correspondent of the *New York Herald*,
who found Livingstone in the heart of Africa when every
other effort to reach him had failed; and that the man who
sent him was James Gordon Bennett, jr., the proprietor of
that newspaper.

In one of the biographies of Dr. Livingstone, written by
a countryman, we find this somewhat candid confession:
"No one appeared to hope for any thing from the expedi-

tion sent out by the *New York Herald,* and gradually its existence came to be overlooked, or forgotten." No wonder, then, that the sleepy tortoise rubbed its eyes in genuine amazement when the news came that it was not the expedition sent out from Zanzibar, nor the one which started later from England, that had found the great explorer in the heart of the Dark Continent, but the hitherto ignored expedition led by the almost unknown correspondent of an American journal.

Mr. Stanley began his long and hazardous journey into the African interior about the beginning of March, 1871. But before giving some of the principal details of this expedition, we will go back and see just what Livingstone was doing all this time, and where he really was.

(368)

CHAPTER XXIV.

SORE STRAITS—LOSS OF THE MEDICINE-CHEST—ACROSS THE CHIMB-
WE AND CHAMBEZE—LAKE TANGAŇYIKA—MOERO—AT CAZEM-
BE'S—ATROCIOUS CRUELTIES—MISSIONARY LABORS—THE START
IN SEARCH OF LAKE BANGWEOLO—DESERTION OF THE MEN—
RETURN FROM THE LAKE—ON THE ROAD TO UJIJI—DISTRESS-
ING ILLNESS—ACROSS LAKE TANGANYIKA—ARRIVAL AT UJIJI
—DISAPPOINTMENTS — ANOTHER WEARISOME TRAMP — UJIJI
AGAIN—LIVINGSTONE IS FOUND BY STANLEY.

———

AFTER being deserted by Musa and the Johanna
men, Livingstone pushed steadily on in the direction in which he believed Lake Tanganyika lay. Though
the story that he had been murdered was not true, the fear
that he was in sore straits proved to be well-founded. He
was not only harassed by savage foes, but he was half-starved
and sick besides. For weeks at a time he had to subsist entirely on maize, which, he tells us, was the most tasteless
and unsatisfying food. This was at the close of the year
1866. Although so reduced in body, and subjected to such
physical tortures and deprivations, we find his patient, hopeful, and courageous spirit still unquenched. That it was
indeed the same old Livingstone—loving, gentle, submis-
sive, full of faith, and steadfast—these words taken from
his diary, and which were written by him during this trying
period, unmistakably show: "We now end 1866. It has
not been so fruitful or useful as I intended. Will try to
do better in 1867, and be better—more gentle and loving;
and may the Almighty, to whom I commit my way, bring

24   (369)

my desires to pass, and prosper me. Let all the sins of '66 be blotted out for Jesus' sake. May he who was full of grace and truth impress his character on mine: grace—eagerness to show favor; truth—truthfulness, sincerity, honor, for his mercy's sake." And here is an extract from a letter to his son Thomas, under date of February, 1867: "The people have nothing to sell but a little millet-porridge and mushrooms. Woe is me! good enough to produce fine dreams of the roast beef of old England, but nothing else. I have become very thin, though I was so before; but now, if you weighed me, you might calculate very easily how much you might get for the bones." Who but Livingstone could have written thus cheerfully—nay, humorously—under such circumstances? At the beginning of this year (1867) an additional calamity befell him—one more serious than any he had yet been called upon to endure. Through the dishonesty of one of his carriers he lost his remaining stock of medicines. As he was at the time suffering severely from an attack of the fever, we may well believe that the loss of the power of treating himself was indeed, as one of his biographers declares, but "the beginning of the end."

Leaving the country of the dangerous and blood-thirsty Mazitu well to the right, Livingstone passed on in a course almost directly due north. On the 15th of January the party crossed the Chimbwe River. Here they had to wade through a marsh a mile wide, exclusive of the river. The water was up to the arm-pits, and the footing was so treacherous that two of the men came near losing their lives. Fifty miles farther north they came upon another fine river, which Livingstone found out was the Chambeze. He did not doubt that both of these rivers fell into the lake of which he had heard so much recently—Lake Bangweolo. He would therefore, he believed, have only to follow the course of these streams to find the lake. But as his search at present was for Lake Tanganyika he passed on over the rivers. In April he reached the southern end of a lake that he felt sure was the Tanganyika, though it was here known by the name of the Liemba. As far as he could see it proved to be a magnificent sheet of water. The scenery in the vicinity was most striking—never had he seen any more picturesque or beautiful, while the little villages clustered here and there had an air of peace and hospitality rarely met with in this savage country. At this place Livingstone suffered from a severe and dangerous illness, which became all the more alarming through his utter inability to treat himself. Not so much as one small vial from his medicine-chest remained. When he had partially recovered he would have gone on up the lake but that he heard there was a very dangerous and hostile chief up that way who was killing every one who dared to cross his country. Livingstone therefore turned in a direction due west from the lake, and made his way to the town of a friendly chief by the name of Chitamba. Here he remained for three months, when, having the opportunity to travel in the company of some very friendly Arab traders, he started off in the direction of Lake Moero, which he discovered on the 8th of November, 1867.

After staying in the neighborhood of this lake two weeks or so, and making many interesting geographical discoveries, Livingstone determined on going to the town of a chief by the name of Cazembe, of whom he had heard repeatedly, but at no time very favorably. Cazembe was represented by every one who had ever seen him as a fierce and cruel chief—

one, too, who seemed to take the greatest delight in seeing just how atrocious he could make his cruelties. He had a way of punishing his people for the most trivial offenses by cutting off their ears, and even their hands and feet. And yet it was also said of him that he had many fine qualities. He was exceedingly just and liberal with such of his people as never offended, and was quite hospitable to strangers. He had long since disregarded the title of chief, and was now known as King Cazembe; and in a most tyrannical way did he exercise his kingly prerogative.

On Livingstone's arrival in Cazembe's town the king accorded him an impressive reception. It was somewhat like that given him years before by the hospitable Shinte, though Cazembe himself bore no resemblance whatever to the generous and warm-hearted Shinte. When Livingstone entered the place of council he found Cazembe upon his throne, and surrounded by all his chief men and body-guard. Livingstone had just taken his seat when one of the head men arose and made a long and flowery speech to the king, in which he gave a detailed account of Living-stone and of his plans. He said in conclusion that he was told that Livingstone had come to look for lakes and riv-ers. He could not understand what the white man wanted with such things; but he thought his object was a good one. After this harangue the king bade his guest approach, and asked him what he proposed to do. Livingstone told him that it was his intention to go farther south, where he had heard there were many lakes and rivers; then on again up into the north, where he had every reason to believe there were still more to be found. Cazembe was greatly puzzled at this, and shaking his head in a dazed kind of way, asked: " What can you want to go there for?

The water is close here.   Plenty of large waters are in this very neighborhood.   Why do you want more?"   Although the king was so greatly perplexed and mystified, and thought at first that Livingstone must surely be mad, he was nevertheless much attracted toward him, and gave orders that he should be well attended to while he remained in the town, and be allowed to go unmolested anywhere about the country he wished.

Despite the many horrible things he saw here, and the atrocious cruelty of Cazembe as practiced toward his offending people, Livingstone had a very restful and interesting stay at this place, and remained for some months.   As his time and physical condition permitted, Livingstone preached to Cazembe's people.   He would have liked above all things to make an impression for good upon the wicked old king, but somehow Cazembe seemed hard to influence; yet when the day came for Livingstone to take his departure he was not without hope that the words he had from time to time spoken had found lodgment within the chief's breast.   Some months after Livingstone left the place he was greatly rejoiced to hear through a trader that Cazembe had almost entirely abandoned his former cruel mode of punishment, and now resorted to it only in extreme cases.   So much for the silent power of noble and steadfast example; for Livingstone's pure, beautifully consistent life had been more of a reproach to Cazembe than any thing else.   There had not been so much in the words he had taught as in the life he had lived.   O how this should encourage us to make our lives pure and clean and sweet!—not so much for the good they will bring to us as for the aspirations they will awaken in the lives of others.   Let this be our daily desire:

May every soul that touches mine,
By the slightest contact, get therefrom some good,
Some little grace; one kindly thought,
One aspiration yet unfelt, one bit of courage
For the darkening sky; one gleam of faith
To brave the thickening ills of life;
One glimpse of brighter skies beyond the gathering mists,
To make this life worth while,
And heaven a surer heritage.

Livingstone had for some time purposed going to Ujiji, on the north-eastern shore of Lake Tanganyika, where he hoped supplies and letters were awaiting him. He was completely worn out by the hardships of the long marches he had made. Besides, his system was all run down for the want of proper nourishment, as well as of medicine. For two years he had scarcely had any thing to eat but the coarse maize of the country, which had so broken his teeth that it was now with the utmost difficulty that he could chew at all. In all this time he had had neither tea, sugar, nor coffee, with the exception of a small supply of the two latter, given him by a friendly Arab trader while he was at Cazembe's town. Livingstone had therefore intended starting direct for Ujiji on leaving Cazembe's; but while there he had heard so much of the great lake, Bangweolo, that he determined to defer his journey to Ujiji until he should first go in search of the lake. This latter decision sorely discouraged his men. Like himself, they were worn down by the constant fatigues and hardships of the many marches about the country in search of lakes and rivers—all of which seemed to them aimless. On the eve of the proposed departure for Bangweolo all except five of these men rebelled, and refused to stir a foot save in the direction of Ujiji. In his

heart Livingstone could not blame them. It was no wonder they were tired of the "everlasting tramping," as he
termed it, for he himself was sick of it. So he said nothing to them, but left them to pursue their own course. He
reaped the reward of his mildness, for on coming back from
the lake they every one eagerly rejoined him.

Undaunted by the refusal of his men to accompany him,
Livingstone set out in search of Lake Bangweolo with the
mere remnant left to him, reënforced by a small detach-
ment of Cazembe's people. On the 18th of July they came
in sight of the great lake. Much to Livingstone's surprise
he found its surface dotted with numerous small islands,
nearly every one of which was inhabited. The people on
these islands were at first terror-stricken at Dr. Livingstone's appearance, taking him for some supernatural being, they never having seen a white man before. However,
he soon reassured them, and then they crowded about him
in wonder and curiosity. And now for many weary months
Livingstone kept up his tramp, tramp, tramp about the
borders of the lake, ever in search of the same all-absorb-
ing object—any stream that might issue therefrom. At
length when he came upon the Chambeze, at the point
whence it flows from the lake under the name of the Luapula, he was confident he had found the southern feeder of
the Nile. But alas! on the very eve of what seemed to
him the unraveling of the great chain of mystery a link
"turned up missing." On he went once more—on, on, in
the ceaseless tramp that it now seemed to his disheartened
men would never have an end. So many times did he ask
the wondering natives the same question, "Where is there
another stream issuing from the lake?" and so many times
did he go over the ground gone over before, that they

really began to think him mad.   No, he was not mad—only resolute and determined.   But even his iron courage gave way at last—rather, the physical man began so to resent the abuses that had been heaped upon it that the mental man was finally forced to succumb.   What, after all, had these tiresome tramps amounted to?   Many, many things; though not the one thing for which he had so ardently hoped —the one thing that was to make the terrors of the way seem as nothing—the one thing that would be a joyful recompense for all the horrors endured.   He had found the southern end of the magnificent Lake Tanganyika, he had discovered the smaller Lake Moero, and now he had come upon the glorious waters of Bangweolo.   From Lake Moero he had found issuing the river Luapula, which flowed to that lake direct from Bangweolo, and he had found besides many larger and smaller streams that crossed and recrossed the country like the threads of an intricate network.   In addition, he had solved many mysteries; he had cleared up errors made by previous explorers; he had added to the geographical knowledge of the country as no other man had done; still the one vexed question was yet unsettled—the mystery of the sources of the Nile: a mystery which Grant, Speke, and Baker believed they had long ago cleared up, but which some few, principally men of science—among them Livingstone—thought was not the case.

Livingstone felt confident that the sources of the Nile were south of all the lakes except Bangweolo.   He believed that through the Luapula River he could dispel the mystery.   He had seen it where, under the name of the Chambeze, it ran into the eastern end of Lake Bangweolo; then whence it issued as the Luapula, flowing north by the town of Cazembe, and twelve miles below that town entering Lake Moero. On leaving Moero it passed on in a north-westerly course forming Lake Nylenge in the country west of Tanganyika. He had seen all this, and believed that he was at last about to solve the problem of ages. If he could but trace the Luapula to its mouth, then would the missing link be connected with the chain of evidence.

While at Cazembe's town Livingstone heard of a wonderful people who lived in a certain section of country called Rua, which lay to the north-west of Lake Moero. These people lived in under-ground villages fashioned by the hands of Nature, some of them being as much as thirty miles in length. Through these cunningly contrived caves flowed beautiful rills of water as clear as crystal. On the walls, which were in some places of solid marble, were ingenious drawings of men, animals, and of many other curious things, said to be thousands of years old. The people themselves were a strange race, and practiced many customs not known in any other part of the country. They were exceedingly well formed and graceful, especially the women; were not so dark as the generality of their dusky brethren, and had large, fine eyes, the outer angles of which slanted inward. Livingstone had a great curiosity to go and see this people, and determined to do so at no distant day, should life be spared to him.

On the 11th of December, 1868, Livingstone started on the journey to Ujiji, where he hoped to fined supplies, and where he also hoped to pass a season of rest and build himself up for what yet lay before him. He was sanguine of doing this, could he but get the proper medicines and diet. A few days after starting on this journey he was stricken by the severest illness he had yet experienced. He was unable to walk, and a litter was constructed by two of the kind-hearted Arab traders in whose company he traveled, and on this he was borne in turn by four of his men. Though they were willing and faithful, and tried to carry him as carefully as possible, yet the way was so rough that every movement caused him excruciating pain. With the sun glaring hotly down upon his pallid face, the recurrent fever torturing his body, and a distressing cough that never left him day nor night, he was still cheerful and uncomplaining, and not once did a murmur escape his lips! He knew that his own spirit would influence that of his men, and he wished above every thing to keep them patient and cheerful. That he succeeded was attested by the happy bursts of song to which they often gave vent, sometimes in the midst of the most troublous conditions of the way. Though often so racked with pain that to speak many words was positive agony, Livingstone tried to say droll things to the men to get them to laugh—for, in his opinion, the man who can laugh never knows the sharp side of trouble.

On the 26th of February, 1869, the southern end of the great Lake Tanganyika was reached. Here Livingstone felt his spirits rise so that he was enabled to sit up in the canoe for much of the distance. It was a glorious journey, extending over more than two-thirds of the entire length of the magnificent sheet of water. The lake proved fully as beautiful as it had been described. The water was of a deep, serene blue that seemed to mirror all the rarer loveliness of the sky that arched above it. Livingstone gives this description of the southern end, known as Lake Liemba: "It lies in a hollow, with precipitous sides, two thousand feet down. It is extremely beautiful; sides, top, and bottom being covered with trees and other vegetation. Elephants, buffaloes, and antelopes feed on the steep slopes, while hippopotami, crocodiles, and fish swarm in the waters. It is as perfect a natural paradise as Xenophon could have desired. On two rocky islands men till the land, rear goats, and catch fish; the villages ashore are embowered in the palm-oil palms of the west shore of Africa. Four considerable streams flow into Liemba; and a number of brooks, from twelve to fifteen feet broad, leap down the steep bright clay schist rocks, and form splendid cascades, that made the dullest of my attendants pause and remark with wonder."

Ujiji was reached on the 14th of March. Here a bitter disappointment awaited Livingstone. All the goods and supplies he had expected—and much of which had really been sent here—had been stolen and scattered by the parties to whom they had been intrusted. But there was a cheering ray amidst all this gloom. Livingstone heard of other supplies at Unyanyembe, thirteen days' journey distant. He resolved to go thither; but no sooner had he formed this resolution than he found it well-nigh impossible to put it into execution. A fierce war was raging, and all the country was so torn up in consequence that an attempt to cross it was almost sure to be fatal. Only after making close inquiries, however, and finding what a dreadful state of affairs really existed, did Livingstone abandon the idea of trying to make his way to Unyanyembe.

Livingstone remained at Ujiji until the 12th of July, 1869, when, in spite of his still weakened condition, he set off to explore the Manyuema country to the north-west of Lake Tanganyika—on the same old mission bent, clearing up the mystery of the head-waters of the Nile. His one great object now was to trace the course of the Luapula

River. At Bambarré, the village of a chief by the name of
Moenekuss, he was detained nearly six months by ulcers on
the feet. His sufferings were intense, but he managed in
that time to preach many sermons to the people, and to sow
much precious seed. While at this village he heard again
of the people of Rua. There was now the additional intelligence of wonderful fountains, near the remarkable caves,
that leaped straight up from the earth with great impetu-
osity to the distance of many feet. Livingstone pondered
much over these fountains, and the more he thought of them
the stronger grew his desire to have a sight of them. Perhaps they might in some way help him in the solution of
the great mystery that had so long perplexed him. He heard
of them again and again the deeper he penetrated into the
Manyuema country, and by putting together first one thing
and then another he at last came to the conclusion that
these wonderful fountains could be no other than the far-
famed fountains of Herodotus that lay between the sources
of the two mighty rivers mentioned in ancient history, the
one as flowing north to Egypt (the Nile), and the other
south to a country that must be Ethiopia (the Congo). It
made Livingstone's blood leap to think of it. Was the mystery of ages about to be solved at last? He would at least
go and see. But first he must attend to the Luapula.

Now began another long and fatiguing tramp through a
country watered by many rivers—so many, in fact, that
often Livingstone was misled by them—and traversed by a
chain of lakes that formed one of the most magnificent water systems on the face of the globe. Hundreds of miles
were gone over in this way; then, just as he believed himself on the point of solving the mystery that had so long
baffled him, his men refused to go a step farther. Threats,

promises, appeals, persuasions, all alike failed. Weary,
disappointed, sick in body and in mind, he was obliged to
turn back and retrace his steps over a distance of more than
five hundred miles. What made this even more dreadful
was that he believed but one-fifth of that distance, perhaps
less, lay between him and the finding of the lost link in the
chain of evidence. O if some intimation could but have
been given him then that it was the Congo sources he was
so industriously following up, and not those of the Nile!
He did not suspect it then, though to do him justice he
did in the final days of his last long and wearisome search.
The question, however, was left for others to prove conclu-
sively—others who had the advantage of all his accurate
and valuable estimates to help them. But no suspicion of
the real truth of the matter had at this time entered his
mind, and it was therefore with the keenest disappointment
and regret that he found himself compelled to turn back.
At one time he felt like going alone; but that would have
been sheer madness, as he soon realized. He would also
have exercised to the last his authority over his men, but
he said to himself: " I have no right to sacrifice these men
if they do not wish to be sacrificed, for the country before
us may be, as they declare, a wilderness of swamps and
bogs—destitute, too, of food of any kind; and they may
indeed all perish. I will therefore go back to Ujiji, as they
urge me to do, and as my better judgment tells me it is best
to do. There, doubtless, supplies have arrived by this time.
I will go there, get my supplies, hire other people, and try
it again." He went back once more to his old stopping-
place, Ujiji, so utterly worn out with all these years of
ceaseless tramping that he was more like a dead man than
a live one. In body he was mere skin and bone; his feet

were covered with sores; he had no clothes to speak of, while his gray beard and hair gave him the appearance of an old, old man, when in reality he was only fifty-seven, in the prime of life. O how tired he was, and how he longed for rest and for some of the comforts of civilized life! How pathetic! All these things were to be again denied him, and ·the disappointments of this return were to be even keener than those of his first arrival. He had not more than laid his weary head down upon the mat in his hut when his men, who had gone out to investigate for themselves, came back to him weeping bitterly. "What is the matter?" he asked in alarm. "The things have been sent here for us," was the reply, "but Shereef [Dr. Livingstone's agent at this place] has made away with them all. He sold them for ivory, and now he has sent the ivory away to the coast. There is nothing left to us for all our hard services." And they began to cry afresh. Livingstone tried to comfort them as best he could. In the meantime he sent for Shereef. He came looking shamefacedly enough, though he tried to put a bold front upon it all. On being asked to give an explanation of his conduct, he declared that he had not acted until first assured of Livingstone's death. Shereef was a Mohammedan. He had sought the Koran for light. It had been told him that Livingstone was dead. He had then sold the goods *to get pay for taking care of them.* Livingstone knew not what to do in a case of this kind. The most distressing part was his own needs and the pitiable condition of his men. Poor fellows! they did feel their loss keenly, he knew. They had served him faithfully and well—barring that one exhibition of obstinacy, for which he could not really blame them—and it did seem very hard that they should have no reward for their services, especially when he had so many times re-vived their flagging spirits with pictures of what was await-ing them at Ujiji. And thus disappointed, hopeless, sick, destitute of even the commonest nourishments, robbed and defied by his agent, with his men clamoring for their pay, Mr. Stanley found him at last, and brought to him hope, joy, even life itself.

To give a detailed account of even a few of the more prominent incidents of Stanley's search for Livingstone would be beyond the compass of our work, especially in its present dimensions. Suffice it to say that nearly every mile of the route fairly bristled with dangers, and that but for the cool-headedness and unflagging bravery of the man who led the expedition it is doubtful if it would ever have been successful. The difficulties were almost as great as the dangers, but each in turn was surmounted. At one or two points Mr. Stanley had literally to fight his way through hostile tribes. Once he was compelled to stop and build regular fortifications, behind which he lay for many days, not daring to stir a foot onward. He did not get out of some of these "tight places" without paying very dear-ly, as we may believe. But his losses—ten men, two horses, and twenty-seven asses in all—were really very light, when we remember what he had to encounter.

Unyanyembe was reached on the 23d of June. We take up the narrative on the 10th of November, fifty-one days out from Unyanyembe, and on the eve of the little expedi-tion's approach to Ujiji. We will let Mr. Stanley relate what followed, in his own breezy and pleasant way:

"November 10th, Friday.—The 236th day from Baga-moyo, and the 51st day from Unyanyembe. General di-rection to Ujiji, west-by-south. Time of march, six hours.

It is a happy, glorious morning. The air is fresh and cool.
The sky lovingly smiles on the earth and her children. The
deep woods are crowned in bright-green leafage; the water
of the Mkuti, rushing under the emerald shade afforded by
the bearded banks, seems to challenge us for the race to
Ujiji with its continuous brawl. We are all outside the
village cane-fence, every man of us, looking as spruce as
neat, and happy as when we embarked on the dhows at
Zanzibar, which seems to us to have been ages ago—we
have witnessed and experienced so much. 'Forward!' 'Ay,
Wallah; ay, Wallah, bana yango' [Yes, with God's help;
yes, with God's help, our master]; and the light-hearted
braves stride away at a rate which must soon bring us
within view of Ujiji. We ascend a hill overgrown with
bamboo, descend into a ravine through which dashes an
impetuous little torrent, ascend another short hill; then,
along a smooth foot-path running across the slope of a long
ridge, we push on as only eager, light-hearted men can do.
In two hours I am warned to prepare for a view of Tanganyika, for, from the top of a steep mountain, the kirangozi says I can see it. I almost vent the feelings of my
heart in cries. But wait; we must behold it first. And
we press forward and up the hill breathlessly, lest the
grand scene hasten away. We are at last on the summit.
Ah! not yet can it be seen. A little farther on—just yon-
der, O! there it is—a silvery gleam. I merely catch sight
of it between the trees, and—but here it is at last! True—
the Tanganyika! and there the blue-black mountains of
Ugoma and Ukaramba. An immense broad sheet, a bur-
nished bed of silver-lucid canopy of blue above lofty mountains, are its valances; palm-forests form its fringes. The
Tanganyika! Hurrah! And the men respond to the ex-

ultant cry of the Anglo-Saxon with the lungs of Stentors,
and the great forests and the hills seem to share in our triumph... We are descending the western slope of the mountain, with the valley of the Liuche before us. Something
like an hour before noon we have gained the thick mantete-
brake which grows on both banks of the river; we wade
through the clear stream, arrive on the other side, emerge
out of the brake, and the gardens of the Wajiji are around
us—a perfect marvel of vegetable wealth. Details escape
my hasty and partial observation. I am almost overpow-
ered with my own emotions. I notice the graceful palms,
neat plats, green with vegetable plants, and small villages
surrounded with frail fences of mantete-cane. We push on
rapidly, lest the news of our coming might reach the people of Bunder Ujiji before we come in sight, and are ready
for them. We halt at a little brook, then ascend the long
slope of a naked ridge, the very last of the myriads we have
crossed. This alone prevents us from seeing the lake in all
its vastness. We arrive at the summit, travel across and
arrive at its western rim, and—pause, reader—the port of
Ujiji is below us, embowered in the palms, only five hundred yards from us! At this grand moment we do not
think of the hundreds of miles we have marched, of the
hundreds of hills we have ascended and descended, of the
many forests we have traversed, of the jungles and thickets
that annoyed us, of the fervid salt-plains that blistered our
feet, of the hot suns that scorched us, nor of the dangers and
difficulties now happily surmounted. At last the sublime
hour has arrived!—our dreams, our hopes and anticipations, are now about to be realized. Our hearts and our
feelings are with our eyes, as we peer into the palms and
try to make out in which hut or house lives the white man

25

with the gray beard we heard about on the Malagarazi.
'Unfurl the flags, and load your guns.' 'Ay, Wallah; ay,
Wallah, bana,' responded the men eagerly. 'One, two,
three—fire!' A volley from nearly fifty guns roars like a
battery of artillery; we shall note its effect presently on the
peaceful-looking village below. 'Now, kirangozi, hold the
white man's flag up high, and let the Zanzibar flag bring
up the rear. And you men keep close together, and keep
firing until we halt in the market-place, or before the white
man's house.' Before we had gone a hundred yards our repeated volleys had the effect desired. We had awakened
Ujiji to the knowledge that a caravan was coming, and
the people were witnessed rushing up in hundreds to meet
us. The mere sight of the flags informed every one immediately that we were a caravan; but the American flag,
borne aloft by gigantic Asmani, whose face was one vast
smile on this day, rather staggered them at first. However,
many of the people who now approached us remembered
the flag. They had seen it float above the American Con-
sulate and from the mast-head of many a ship in the harbor at Zanzibar, and they were soon heard welcoming the
beautiful flag with cries of 'Binder kisungu!'—a white
man's flag; 'Bindera Merikani!'—the American flag.
Then we were surrounded by them: by Wajiji, Wanyam-
wezi, Warundi, Waguhha, Wamanyuema, and Arabs, and
were almost deafened with the shouts of 'Yambo, yambo,
bana! Yambo, bana! Yambo, bana!' To all and each
of my men the welcome was given. We are now about
three hundred yards from the village of Ujiji, and the
crowds are dense about me. Suddenly I hear a voice on
my right say, 'Good-morning, sir.' Startled at hearing
this greeting in the midst of such a crowd of black people,

CHUMAH AND SUSI.   (387)

I turn sharply around in search of the man, and see him at
my side, with the blackest of faces, but animated and joyous—a man dressed in a long white shirt, with a turban of
American sheeting around his woolly head—and I ask, 'Well,
who is this?' 'I am Susi, the servant of Doctor Livingstone,' said he, smiling, and showing a gleaming row of
teeth. 'What! Is Doctor Livingstone here?' 'Yes, sir.'
'In this village?' Yes, sir.' 'Are you sure?' 'Sure, sure,
sir. Why, I leave him just now.' 'Good-morning, sir,'
said another voice. 'Halloo,' said I, 'is this another one?'
'Yes, sir.' 'Well, what is your name?' 'My name is
Chumah, sir.' 'What! are you Chumah, the friend of We-
kotani?' 'Yes, sir.' 'And is the Doctor well?' 'Not
very well, sir.' 'Where has he been so long?' 'In Manyuema.' 'Now you, Susi, run and tell the Doctor I am
coming?' 'Yes, sir.' And off he darted like a madman.
But by this time we were within two hundred yards of the
village, and the multitude was getting denser, and almost
preventing our march. Flags and streamers were out,
Arabs and Wangwana were pushing their way through the
natives in order to greet us, for, according to their account,
we belonged to them. But the great wonder of all was,
'How did you come from Unyanyembe?' Soon Susi came
running back, and asked me my name; he had told the
Doctor I was coming, but the Doctor was too surprised to
believe him, and, when the Doctor asked him my name,
Susi was rather staggered. But during Susi's absence the
news had been conveyed to the Doctor that it was surely a
white man that was coming, whose guns were firing, and
whose flag could be seen; and the great Arab magnates of
Ujiji—Mohammed bin Sali, Sayd bin Majid, Abid bin Sul-
iman, Mohammed bin Gharib, and others—had gathered

together before the Doctor's house, and the Doctor had come out from his veranda to discuss the matter and await my arrival. In the meantime the head of the expedition had halted, and the kirangozi was out of the ranks, holding his flag aloft, and Selim said to me: 'I see the Doctor, sir. O what an old man! He has got a white beard.' And I—what would I not have given for a bit of friendly wilderness where, unseen, I might vent my joy in some mad freak, such as idiotically biting my hand, turning a somersault, or slashing at trees, in order to allay those exciting feelings that were well-nigh uncontrollable? My heart beats fast, but I must not let my face betray my emotions lest it shall detract from the dignity of a white man appearing under such extraordinary circumstances. So I did that which I thought was the most dignified. I pushed back the crowds, and, passing from the rear, walked down a living avenue of people, until I came in front of the semicircle of Arabs, in the front of which stood the white man with the gray beard. As I advanced slowly toward him I noticed he was pale, looked wearied, had a gray beard, wore a bluish cap with a faded gold band around it, had on a red-sleeved waistcoat and a pair of gray tweed trousers. I would have run to him, only I was a coward in the presence of such a mob—would have embraced him, only he being an Englishman, I did not know how he would receive me; so I did what cowardice and false pride suggested was the best thing—walked deliberately to him, took off my hat, and said, ' Doctor Livingstone, I presume?' 'Yes,' said he with a kind smile, lifting his cap; and we both grasp hands, and then I say aloud: ' I thank God, Doctor, I have been permitted to see you.' He answered: ' I feel thankful that I am here to welcome you.' "

STANLEY MEETING LIVINGSTONE.

CHAPTER XXV.

STANLEY'S DESCRIPTION OF LIVINGSTONE—EXAMINATION OF THE
NORTHERN END OF LAKE TANGANYIKA—THE DEPARTURE
FROM UJIJI—THE SEPARATION AT UNYANYEMBE—NEWS OF
THE FINDING OF LIVINGSTONE—LATER REPORTS OF HIS DEATH
—REPORTS CONFIRMED—THE LAST TRAMP—ILLNESS—LAST
HOURS—DEATH.

UPON the events following Stanley's meeting with
Livingstone, and covering Stanley's stay at Ujiji,
we can touch but briefly. There was much to be told,
much to be listened to, many eager questions to be asked
on both sides. To Livingstone—who had been so long cut
off from the knowledge of home, friends, and of all civilized happenings—the coming of Stanley was like the fresh
and invigorating breath of another world; the reviving of
things that had long seemed dead; the recalling of events,
persons, and places which the way-worn traveler had thought
never to hear of again. Over and over he said to Stanley:
"You have brought me new life! You have brought me
new life!" Long they sat and talked, heedless of the passing time; and not until the gray dawn came stealing
through the chinks of the little hut did they think of lying
down to their brief rest.

Stanley's description of Livingstone at this period cannot
fail to be of interest, so we give it here: "Upon my first introduction to him, Livingstone was to me like a huge tome
with a most unpretending binding. Within, the work might
contain much valuable lore and wisdom, but its exterior

(391)

gave no promise of what was within. Thus, outside, Livingstone gave no token—except of being rudely dealt with
by the wilderness—of what elements of power or talent lay
within.   He is a man of unpretending appearance enough,
has quiet, composed features, from which the freshness of
youth has quite departed, but which retain the mobility of
prime age—just enough to show that there lies much endurance and vigor within his frame.   The eyes, which are
hazel, are remarkably bright, not dimmed in the least, though
the whiskers and the mustache are very gray.   The hair,
originally brown, is streaked here and there with gray over
the temples; otherwise it might belong to a man of thirty.
The teeth alone show indications of being worn out: the
hard fare of Louda and Manajenia have made havoc in
their rows.   His form is stoutish—a little over the ordinary height, with slightly bowed shoulders.   When walking
he has the heavy step of an overworked and fatigued man. ·
On his head he wears the naval cap, with a round visor,
with which he has been identified throughout Africa.   His
dress shows that at times he has had to resort to the needle
to repair and replace what travel has worn.   Such is Livingstone externally."

After a season of rest, necessary to recruit their wasted
energies, Stanley and Livingstone determined upon an examination of the northern end of Tanganyika.   The object
of this was to settle definitely, if possible, the question that
had so long perplexed Livingstone, whether or not the lake
had an outlet at this point.   The investigation was carefully and thoroughly made, but to the disappointment of both
—especially so to Livingstone—it was found that the river
Luzizi, instead of flowing out of the lake as Livingstone
had supposed, flowed into it.   This at once put an end to

Livingstone's belief that the lake discharged itself in a
northerly direction, and also to his favorite theory in regard to the Nile sources—at least such portion of it as was
connected with this lake.

Seeing how worn and wasted Livingstone was, and sur-
mising how futile would prove this chase upon which he
was still bent, Stanley tried to persuade him to return home
with him; but in vain. The more the problem baffled Livingstone, the more he determined to solve it. Much as his
heart yearned for his home and friends—more especially
for his dear ones—still unwaveringly did he stand by what
he deemed a principle of duty. He had parted from the
members of the Royal Geographical Society with the fixed
determination and the promise to settle beyond a question
of doubt, if possible, the latter theory—which not only he
but many of them held—in regard to a more southerly situation of the springs of the Nile than that given by Speke
and Baker. They were all expectant—especially Sir Roderick Murchison, for whom Livingstone entertained the
truest esteem—and sore indeed would be their disappointment should he leave the great problem still unsolved, and
that too upon the very eve of what seemed to him certain
discovery. Besides, he had a personal interest in the solution of the question—nay, a deep-laid, a sacred interest.
We have seen how great was Livingstone's reverence
for the Bible, and for all the events and places described
therein. Feeling thus, he deemed it a religious duty to
throw what light he could upon the mystery that had so
long enveloped the majestic river upon whose placid bosom
the infant Moses had floated. With his usual unselfish-
ness and devotion, he took no thought of himself. What to
him were the flooded plains, the treacherous sponges of the

swamps—nay, even the dread fever, or the still more terrible pneumonia, " worse than ten fevers? "   Fortified by the soul-inspiring knowledge that he was but following straight upon the line of duty, neither the thought of sickness nor of death had the power to turn him from his course.   But, knowing Livingstone so well, we may believe that even a higher and nobler purpose than this actuated him.   More and more, the farther he advanced into the country, had he witnessed the dread horrors of the slave-trade.   No wonder he came to designate it the " open sore of the world," and to call down God's richest blessings upon all who would endeavor to heal it—be he "American, English, or Turk." *

His own brave words also give us the key-note to another and higher motive that swayed him: "No one can estimate the amount of God-pleasing good that will be done, if by divine favor this awful slave-trade, into the midst of which I have come, be abolished.   This will be something to have lived for, and the conviction has grown into my mind that it is for this end I have been detained so long."   And again he says, under date of December, 1872: "If the good Lord permits me to put a stop to the enormous evils of the inland slave-trade, I shall not grudge my hunger and toils. I shall bless his name with all my heart.   The Nile sources are valuable to me only as a means of enabling me to open

---

* The expression from which these words are quoted occurs in a letter to Mr. James Gordon Bennett, of the *New York Herald*, under date of May 1st, 1872, and is as follows: "All I can add in my loneliness is, May Heaven's rich blessings come down on every one— American, English, or Turk—who will help to heal the open sore of the world."   The words were afterward rendered memorable by being inscribed upon Dr. Livingstone's monument in Westminster Abbey.

my mouth with power among men.   It is this power I hope
to apply to remedy an enormous evil, and join my poor little helping-hand in the enormous revolution that in his all-
embracing providence he has been carrying on for ages,
and is now actually helping forward." Speaking of the
unwillingness of the natives to believe in the true purpose
of his investigation, he further adds: "They all treat me
with respect, and are very much afraid of being written
against; but they consider the sources of the Nile to be a
sham; the true object of my being sent is to see their odi-
ous system of slaving, and if indeed my disclosures should
lead to the suppression of the East Coast slave-trade, *I would
esteem that as a far greater feat than the discovery of all the
sources together.*   It is awful, but I cannot speak of the
slaving for fear of appearing guilty of exaggeration.   It is
not trading; it is murdering for captives to be made into
slaves."

Now we know why, in spite of his intense longing for
home and loved ones, he turned away from them and pursued the duties that lay before him in benighted Africa.
We have seen him tried in the old days at St. Paul de Loanda, and by this time we know him too well to believe
that he would have thought of returning home, especially
when the fulfillment of his great object seemed so near.
Yet what a good excuse he would have had for leaving
this unfriendly clime.   He was worn down both in mind
and body.   All his vital force seemed exhausted by the
desperate strains that had been put upon them.   He was
but a shadow of his former self.   It gave him absolute pain
to attempt to walk even a mile.   Nevertheless, he staid at
his post, heroically enduring trials sufficient to have dismayed the stoutest heart.

It was finally agreed that Dr. Livingstone should accompany Stanley on his return as far as Unyanyembe. There he was to obtain such supplies as had been sent to that place for him, supplement them with a liberal portion of Mr. Stanley's—which the latter generously insisted that he should take—and remain to perfect further arrangements and until the arrival of the men Stanley was to send him from the coast. Stanley had assured him that these men should be both able and trusty, so that there would be no further danger of his being placed at the mercy of cowards and thieves.

The parting scene between Stanley and the great travel· er was most pathetic. It is best given in Mr. Stanley's own feeling words: " We had a sad breakfast together. I could not eat, my heart was too full; neither did my companion seem to have any appetite. We found something to do which kept us longer together. At eight o'clock I was not gone, and I had thought to be off at 5 A.M. ' Doctor,' said I, ' I will leave these two men with you, who will stop to-day and to-morrow with you, for it may be that you have forgotten something in the hurry of my departure. I will halt a day at Tura, on the frontier of Unyamwezi, for your last words and your last wish; and now we must part— there is no help for it. Good-by.' ' O, I am coming with you a little way. I must see you off on the road.' ' Thank you. Now, my men, Home! Kirangozi, lift the flag, and *march!* ' The house looked desolate—it faded from our view. Old times, and the memories of my aspirations and kindling hopes, came strong on me. The old hills round about, that I once thought tame and uninteresting, had become invested with histories and reminiscences for me. On that burzani I have sat hour after hour, dreaming, and

Loping, and sighing. On that col I stood watching the battle and the destruction of Tabora. Under that roof I have sickened and been delirious, and cried out like a child at the fate that threatened my mission. Under that banian-tree lay my dead comrade, poor Shaw! I would have given a fortune to have had him by my side at this time. From that house I started on my journey to Ujiji; to it I returned as to a friend, with a newer and dearer companion; and now I leave it all. Already it all appears like a strange dream. We walked side by side; the men lifted their voices in a song. I took long looks at Livingstone, to impress his features thoroughly upon my memory. 'The thing is, Doctor, so far as I can understand it, you do not intend to return home until you have satisfied yourself about the "sources of the Nile." When you have satisfied yourself, you will come home and satisfy others. Is it not so?' 'That is it, exactly. When your men come back I shall immediately start for Ufipa; then, crossing the Rungwa River, I shall strike south, and round the extremity of Tanganyika. Then a south-east course will take me to Chicumbi's, on the Luapula. On crossing the Luapula, I shall go direct west to the copper-mines of Katanga. Eight days south of Katanga, the natives declare the fountains to be. When I have found them I shall return by Katanga to the under-ground houses of Rua. From the caverns, ten days north-east will take me to Lake Kamolondo. I shall be able to travel from the lake, in your boat, up the river Lufira to Lake Lincoln. Then, coming down again, I can proceed north by the Lualaba, to the fourth lake—which, I think, will explain the whole problem; and I will probably find that it is either Chowambe [Baker's lake], or Piaggia's Lake.' 'And how long do you think

this little journey will take you?' 'A year and a half, at
the farthest, from the day I leave Unyanyembe.' 'Yes,
that will do excellently well.   Now, dear Doctor, the best
friends must part.   You have come far enough, let me beg
you to turn back.' 'Well, I will say this to you: you have
done what few men could do—far better than some great
travelers I know.   And I am grateful to you for what you
have done for me.   God guide you safe home, and bless
you, my friend.' 'And may God bring you safely back to us
all.   My dear friend, farewell!' 'Farewell!'   We wrung
each other's hands, and I had to tear myself away before I
unmanned myself; but Susi and Chumah and Hamoydah
—the Doctor's faithful fellows—they must all shake and
kiss my hands before I could quite turn away.   I betrayed
myself! 'Good-by, Doctor—dear friend!' 'Good-by!'
'*March!* Why do you stop?   Go on!   Are you not going
home?'   And my people were driven before me.   No more
weakness.   I shall show them such marching as will make
them remember me.   In forty days I shall do what took
me three months to perform before."

The news of Stanley's finding Livingstone in the very
heart of Africa sent a thrill through the whole civilized
world.   It was indeed most joyful and welcome intelligence,
and the manner of its reception, irrespective of persons or
of nations, fully demonstrated the firm hold the great explorer had upon the hearts of the people everywhere.   But
alas! in little more than a year from the time of Stanley's
parting with him at Unyanyembe the world was again
startled by the report of the great traveler's death.   This
time it seemed too well authenticated to admit of doubt,
yet there were those who hoped against hope to the last
that the tidings were untrue.   He had been reported dead

so often, might not this report too be a mistake? In a short while the news of his death was confirmed by a full statement of the manner of it, received through official sources, together with the information that the body was even at that time being borne across the country in the direction of the coast by his faithful attendants.

Of the particulars of Dr. Livingstone's last illness and death we are enabled to give what is generally conceded to be a most accurate account, thanks to the intelligent narratives rendered by his devoted body-servants, Susi and Chumah, and to the clear and concise style of the manuscripts of Jacob Wainwright, who was the scribe of the party.

After Stanley's departure, Livingstone remained at Unyanyembe until the arrival of the promised men on the 9th of August, 1872. On the 25th of August the little expedition began its movement, though Livingstone was in no condition to travel and suffered pain at almost every step. The men sent by Stanley proved in every respect as they had been represented, and were indeed a blessing to Livingstone. Among them were John and Jacob Wainwright, who had been educated at the Nassick School at Bombay, and Manwa Lera, a trusty and capable half Arab and half native, who had charge of the caravan. Out of the abundance of his grateful heart Livingstone thus wrote to Stanley: "I am perpetually reminded that I owe a great deal to you for the men you sent. With one exception the party is working like a machine. I give my orders to Manwa Lera, and never have to repeat them." O if he could but have had such a company before!

On the 8th of October they reached Tanganyika. Livingstone's condition had by this time become exceedingly

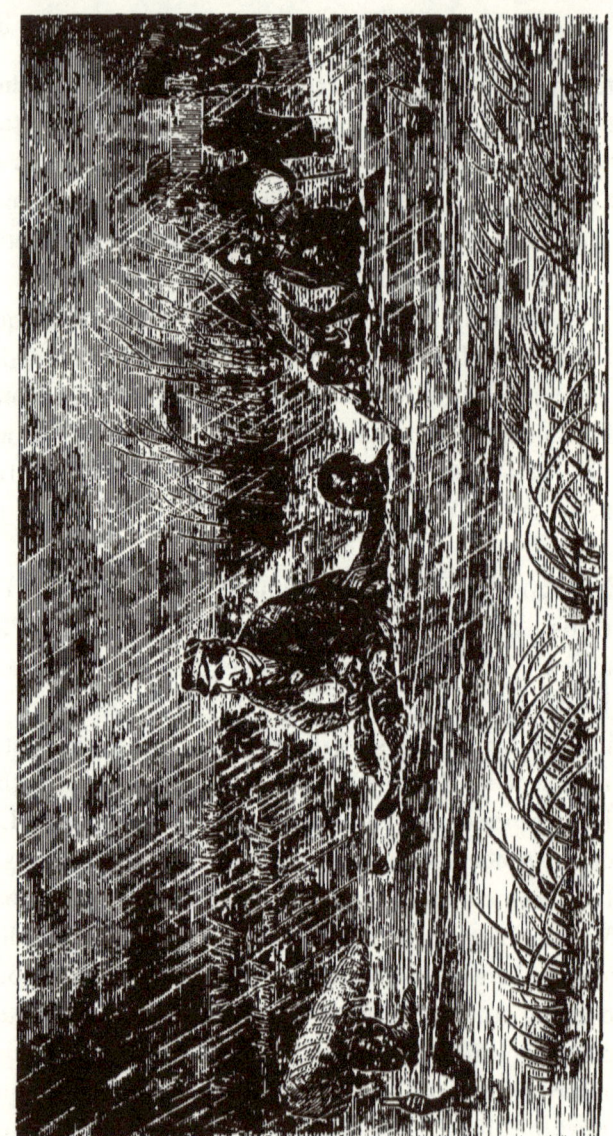

LIVINGSTONE CARRIED THROUGH THE SWAMPS.

distressing, as he now had dysentery in its most aggravated form. But he kept up bravely, daily endearing himself more and more to his men by the sunny cheerfulness of his temper and the constant display of a patience and resignation that seemed to them most remarkable. After a brief rest at Tanganyika, the march was resumed, and went on steadily, though slowly, with but few interruptions and with very little incident. As the fall advanced the rainy season set in; the streams became so swollen that they were often unfordable, and the swamps were in such a condition that crossing them was at the risk of life; but still the daring company pushed on. By the end of the year they had reached and crossed the river Chambeze. Christmas-day, 1872, was spent not far from its banks. Livingstone's entry in his journal on this occasion was characteristic: " I thank the good Lord for the good gift of his Son Jesus Christ our Lord." In the second week of January, 1873, they drew near the south-eastern end of Lake Bangweolo. Here the reign of old winter became more furious. It was unusual for Livingstone to meet in this climate with such cold and piercing winds, such chilling downpours of rain. The streams became more and more treacherous to cross, the water stretching out for miles and miles into the swamps. Often his faithful men were for hours up to their chins in the cold and slimy bogs. They would never suffer him to attempt the passages himself, but carried him over—sometimes upon their shoulders, sometimes upon their heads, according to the depth of the current.

Though suffering greatly, Livingstone had the will to look about him carefully and to note the different phases of the forests through which they passed. Thus he was often rewarded by the sight of many beautiful wild flowers,

26

which here and there peeped from their nooks in spite of
the forbidding weather: " marigolds; a white jonquil-look-
ing flower without any smell; many orchids; white, yellow,
and pink asclepias, with bunches of French-white flowers;
clematis—*Methonica gloriosa*, gladiolus, and blue and deep
purple polygamias; grasses with white, starry seed-vessels,
and spikelets of brownish red and yellow. Besides these
there were beautiful blue flowering bulbs, and new flowers
of pretty, delicate form and but little scent." The weather
grew worse and worse; the inhabitants of the villages
through which the travelers passed not only refused them
food, but purposely misled them as to the route. Hunger
in its sharpest form assailed them. For days they were
literally without any thing to eat. The men were driven
to the verge of despair, while Livingstone's sufferings were
far beyond any previous experience. But for the real no-
bility of character of the men by whom he was now surrounded, and the bond of strong affection by which they
had become united to him, " unexampled in the history of
difficult expeditions," every one of them would surely have
deserted him and fled.

All this hard usage was enough to have worn out a constitution of iron. It is no wonder, then, that Livingstone,
despite his great powers of endurance, succumbed at last,
and that the end of his mortal journey was very near. At
that critical time, however, upheld by his old heroic spirit,
he wrote in his journal: " Nothing earthly will make me
give up my work in despair. I encourage myself in the
Lord my God, and go forward." On the 21st of April a
change so alarming occurred that even he was warned by
it that the work might after all be left unfinished by him.
Still, he gave no hint of this to his companions. On that

same day he wrote in his journal, in a hand so shaky that it was afterward read with much difficulty: "Tried to ride, but was forced to lie down, and they carried me back to the village exhausted." At length, on the 27th day of April, 1873, they came to the banks of the Molilamo River, near to the village of a chief by the name of Kalunganjovu. Here outraged nature seems to have resented with grim determination the many heavy drafts drawn upon her precious store. Livingstone was unable to bear the torture of proceeding farther. The entry in his journal of this date forms the last lines his fingers ever penned: "Knocked up quite, and remain—recover—sent to buy milch-goats. We are on the banks of the R. Molilamo."

From this point we have to rely solely upon the narratives of his men, for the hand that had traced so many brave and thrilling words, that had recorded with such faithfulness every event of his wonderful and checkered life, was now growing pulseless in the cold clasp of death. It was soon evident to his men that he was very, very ill— though they could not believe that he was nearing the end. Kalunganjovu's people were very kind to them, the chief being especially solicitous as to the condition of the man of whom he had heard so much and always so well. He at once sent to Livingstone a present of a kid and three baskets of ground-nuts. The men were rejoiced when they saw these edibles. Having been many days without nourishing food of any kind, the anxious and devoted fellows believed that Livingstone's low condition was in a great part due to this lack of sustenance. They prepared the kid for him after the most tempting manner known to their culinary art, and pounded the ground-nuts and baked them into cakes. But after all their kindly efforts he could not par-

LIVINGSTONE'S LAST JOURNEY.

(404)

take of a morsel of the food. This greatly distressed and
alarmed them, and for the first time they began to entertain
serious apprehensions of his condition.

Livingstone, before he grew so seriously ill, had especially desired to reach the village of a chief by the name of
Chitambo, in Ilala, at the southern extremity of Lake Bangweolo. His men now determined to carry him on to that
point if possible. Livingstone himself was anxious that
this should be done, and after a day or two of rest expressed
his belief that he could stand the journey. Kalunganjovu
readily consented to furnish the canoes. He declared that
every thing in his power should be done for his friend Livingstone. The arrangements were soon perfected, and the
faithful men ready to set out with their precious burden.
On Susi's going to the hut to inform his master that every
thing was in readiness for the start, Livingstone called him
nearer, and told him that he was quite unable to walk to
the door in order to meet the kitanda (the kind of litter on
which they had been carrying him). He further suggested
that the side of the hut be taken out, as the door was too
narrow to admit of the passage of the kitanda. This was
done; he was gently lifted from the bed, placed upon the
kitanda, and borne out of the village. The most difficult
part of the journey now presented itself—that of the passage of the river; for the canoes were not wide enough to
allow the kitanda to be deposited at the bottom of any one
of them. As to sitting up in the canoe, Livingstone was
powerless to do that; and at first there seemed no way of
preparing for him to lie down without danger of upsetting
the canoes. However, a bed was at last arranged in the
bottom of one of them. Then came the painful and difficult task of lifting him from the kitanda to the canoe; but,

thanks to the skill and gentleness of the men, this was accomplished, though many groans had been wrung from the sufferer. The river crossed, then came innumerable swamps and plashes. When they reached any thing like a dry spot, the poor man would beg them piteously to lay him down, if only for a few moments. At last Chitambo's village in Ilala was reached, and here the men were forced to place him under the eaves of a house during a drizzling rain while a hut was being prepared for him. It was evident, from after circumstances, that this exposure helped to hasten his death. Numbers of Chitambo's people approached, and, leaning upon their spears, looked with sorrowful faces upon the pitiable condition of the man whose praises they had heard sounded for so many years. Anon he would open his eyes to behold them, for he was too weak to do more than this or to turn his head feebly from side to side. But the old-time fire of the eyes remained unquenched, although the death-film was creeping on apace. As his gaze rested upon their wondering and pitying faces, every now and then words would escape his lips—words spoken to the glory of that Master whom he had so long and so faithfully served, and from whom he was soon to receive the plaudit, "Well done."

At length the hut was finished, and the dying pilgrim was borne to it and laid upon a bed that was raised from the floor by means of poles and covered with soft, thick grass. A fire was then lighted on the outside, nearly opposite the door, and the boy Majwara, who slept just on the inside of the door, attended to his master's wants at night. During the day Susi, Chumah, Amoda, Matthew, and the two Wainwrights, remained with him in turn, as was their usual custom.

The next day Chitambo came early to pay his respects to Livingstone. After speaking to the chief for a few moments, Livingstone found himself in such pain that he was obliged to send him away, asking him to call again on the morrow, when he hoped to have the strength to talk to him. The men kept watch in detachments beside the fire in front of his door.

About eleven o'clock that night Susi, who had gone to his hut to get a little rest, was summoned to his master by the boy Majwara. At the same time mingled sounds of noisy shouts and cries were heard in the distance. "Are those our men making that noise?" Livingstone asked Susi as soon as he stood beside him. "No, master," Susi replied. "It is Chitambo's people frightening away a buffalo from their dura-fields." A few moments later he said in lower tones, and with his mind evidently wandering, "Is this the Luapula?" "No, master," the faithful Susi again made answer. "It is Chitambo's village, near to the river Molilamo." He once more lapsed into silence, and Susi thought he was sleeping. But again he appeared to arouse himself, and asked, this time in Suaheli: "Sikun' gapi kuenda Luapula?" [How many days is it to the Luapula?] "Na zani zikutatu, Bwana" [I think it is three days, master], replied Susi. He closed his eyes for a few moments, then opened them quickly, and exclaimed as though in great pain, "O dear! O dear!" In a little while he had dozed off again, and fearing to disturb him Susi withdrew. It was an hour or so later that Majwara came again to summon Susi to his master with the words: "Bwana wants you, Susi. There is something wrong with him." On Susi's reaching the side of the bed Livingstone spoke to him in a feeble but quite clear voice. He wished to have some

LIVINGSTONE CARRIED INTO THE HUT TO DIE.

water boiled. Taking the copper kettle, Susi went to the fire on the outside, and soon returned with the vessel steaming. Calling him nearer, Livingstone asked him to bring his medicine-chest, and to hold a candle that was burning some distance away closer to the bed. As Susi did so he noticed that the Doctor could scarcely see, but was groping about in the dark. After much difficulty, even with Susi's help, Livingstone finally selected the calomel he wanted, which he told Susi to place at his side. He then directed him to pour a little water into a cup and to set another empty one beside it. As the faithful servant did as he was requested, Livingstone glanced up at him gratefully for a few moments; then, closing his eyes with a simultaneous expression of the lips that showed he was in deep pain, he said in a voice that the observant Susi remarked was much feebler than when he had first addressed him on his entrance to the hut. "That is all right; you can go now." These were the last words Livingstone was ever heard to speak.

About four o'clock the next morning—given by some as the first of May, by others as the fourth, though now generally conceded to be the latter date—Majwara came running to Susi once more, this time with the frightened entreaty: "Come to Bwana, O do please, Susi! I am afraid! I don't know if he is alive!" The genuine alarm of the lad caused Susi to run to arouse the other head-men—Chumah, Matthew, Chowpere, the two Wainwrights—and all. The men went to the hut at once, fearing the worst. As they entered their eyes beheld what they were not soon to forget. Livingstone was not lying on the bed, as they had expected, but was kneeling beside it, apparently engaged in prayer. For a moment they drew back in rev-

erent silence, fearing to disturb him. They all believed
him alive and engaged in his devotions as usual, and were
on the point of retiring from the hut when Majwara, who
knew better than they, whispered: "There is something
wrong with Bwana, I am sure. Do not go like this until
you have found out what it is. When I lay down he was
just as he is now, and it is because I find that he does not
move that I fear the worst has happened—that he is dead,
the good master is dead!" "How long has he been like
that?" the men questioned, still believing that he was but
kneeling at prayer, so natural was his position. "I do not
know; for a considerable time, I am sure," the lad replied.
Apprehensive that something was indeed wrong, the men
now drew near. The candle that still burned beside the
bed, though feebly because of the accumulated drippings
of tallow and the sputtering wick, yet shed sufficient light
for them to see distinctly every outline of the kneeling figure. He was full upon his knees at the bedside, his body
bent only slightly forward, his hands stretched upward
over the pillow and clasped, his head upon his hands.
Bending down beside him, his attendants listened closely
for a few seconds. He was perfectly motionless; there was
no sign of breathing. Then one of them, Matthew, bent
still nearer and placed his hand upon his master's cheek.
The touch was sufficient, the coldness such as to convey to
him at once the painful realization that the spirit had fled,
and that his good and noble master was indeed no more.
In the still watches of the night, while they slept and took
no heed, the dread messenger had come—but, coming, had
not found him unprepared. With a superhuman effort he
had gathered up the strength that was still left to him,
arisen from bed, and placed himself in that reverential at-

titude which he had so often declared was the only genuine expression of the devout spirit of prayer—upon his knees. And thus had the messenger found him, as he had so longed and prayed it should find him, as a soldier at watch upon the battlements. Yes, death had indeed come to him, and his toil-worn and weary spirit was rejoicing in the beauties of that land

> Where peaceful rivers, soft and low,
> Amid the verdant landscape flow.

Gone forever now, like a harrowing dream that has been and is no more, was the pain, the suffering—the rackings of the dread fever, the awful horrors of the African swamps, the tortures of the blistering African sun. No more weary miles to go over; no more bleeding feet to drag painfully along where sharp stones cut them and cruel thorns pierced them at almost every step; no more icy floods to breast; no more gnawings of hunger, nor maddening thirst. Rest, rest had come to him at last, and he had met it with a smile upon his face—such a smile as we see upon a tired baby's face when its weary head sinks to rest within its mother's arms.

> Death came; but death could not surprise
>   Him who had watched each day with prayer,
> Waiting with longing eyes
>   To show his Lord a faithful servant's care.
> When called the bridegroom and his friends to meet,
>   No oil to buy, no labor to begin;
> With burning lamp, girt loins, and peace-shod feet,
>   Thus hand in hand, through death he entered in,
> And found a bridal garment and a seat.

He had died upon his knees—the last utterances of his pallid lips were words of prayer. For whom or for what had those last agonized entreaties gone up? Surely not for him-

self, since between him and that God whom his eager soul
had hastened so gladly to meet all peace had long, long ago
been made. Were they, then, for his home, his friends, his
dear ones, the loved children his precious wife had left to him?
Did he invoke God's blessings upon the fond faces he was
never more to see on earth, the bright eyes that were never
more to grow glad at his coming, the tender lips whose last
pressure had been laid upon his own? Did he, as in the
old days at Linyanti, when he had prayed the Almighty
Power to have in his keeping the dear ones so far away, to
be "a husband to the widow for Jesus' sake," now entreat
that same sleepless care, that never-relaxing watchfulness
for those so soon to be left fatherless? Ah, surely, surely
this he did! But in the stillness of that midnight hour were
there not other petitions borne upward on the wings of fervent, supplicating prayer? Knowing the object that lay so
near his heart, the presence that had walked with him an
ever-abiding companion since his earliest manhood's years;
the heroic resolution that had set its firm roots into the
very depths of his soul, the steadfast purpose that had never left him day nor night—well may we answer, Yes, yes!
For Africa he lived; for Africa, upheld by the strong faith
in and the love of him who is the God of the oppressed
and the Redeemer of the penitent, had he worked; and
now for Africa, while yet in the vigorous glow of manhood's autumn, had his life been given. Alas, alas, that
he had been called upon to make the sacrifice when the
work was not more than begun! From every shadowed
plain, from out the depths of the darkening forests, from
even the remotest recesses of the dreary mountain heights,
the voices of woe were still calling to him, nor ceased day
nor night. Thousands of perishing souls yet wailed out the

story of their wrongs, while the iron hand of cruelty and
oppression clutched all the more fiendishly about the bleeding hearts of those for the redress of whose wrongs the very
stones seemed to cry out.   O God, was all this to continue?
Was there to be no mitigation?   Were these miserable
creatures to go on perishing, with no hand outstretched to
save?   No, no!   It would all come right in time, and justice be done as only a righteous Avenger could mete it out!
And can we doubt that ere his soul quitted its earthly ten-
ement he failed to wrestle in prayer with God for the speedy
coming of that day?   Well, well do we know that this was
done, and that David Livingstone, with an undying faith
in the righteousness of the cause for which his own life had
been given a pure and willing sacrifice, committed the woes
of stricken Africa into the hands of Him who has said,
"Vengeance is mine; I will repay."

Hastily lifting him to the bed, his stricken servants bent
over him, trying to divine how to restore him, the while
hoping against hope that there might still be some pulse
of life remaining.   But their efforts were all in vain.   Realizing this at last, they straightened his limbs upon the
bed, folded his hands across his breast, placed upon the
body a light covering, and then went out to the fire in
front of the hut to consult together as to what further
should be done.

CHAPTER XXVI.

BEFORE the first flush of the coming dawn had streaked the eastern sky, every man connected with the bereaved little company of explorers knew what had happened during the night. The scene was extremely pathetic, as in the dim, gray light they gathered about the smoldering fire and talked in low, hushed voices. What shall be done? That was the question that presented itself to every disturbed mind. Fully they recognized the complications that surrounded them. The dread superstitions of most of the African tribes concerning the dead were well known to them. Should Chitambo's people become aware of Livingstone's death, it was feared that the body would be immediately seized and subjected to some revolting funeral-rite that would either destroy it entirely or—what would be nearly as bad—place it forever beyond the reach of his men. They could not bear to think of such a fate as this for him, the brave and noble master, even though it was but the mortal part of him that remained, the mere shell of what had been. No, no, it *must not* be! And assembled there about the dying fire, in the struggling light of coming day, those loyal, devoted men took upon themselves a heroic resolution—*come what would, the body must be borne to the coast, and thence shipped to his people*

(414)

in England! It was a perilous and mighty undertaking; but so inflexible was their resolve, so genuine their devotion, that even when all its intricacies and dangers had been fully weighed not a man of them showed the least sign of shrinking from the ordeal.

The first consideration was to keep Livingstone's death a secret from Chitambo's people; but it might have been known that under the circumstances such a thing was well-nigh impossible. The truth soon leaked out, in spite of the efforts made to conceal it. The men were now in actual fear of disastrous results; but they need not have been, as the sequel proved. Chitambo and his people acted not only with reasonableness, but with great generosity. Chitambo declared himself in accord with the men's desire to bear the body of their master back to the coast, and at once set about furthering their plans. He only asked in return that his people be allowed to show all honor to the dead, as it became them to do on the demise in their midst of so great a man as Livingstone, and to engage in their customary forms of mourning. As none of these rites interfered in any way with the repose of the corpse, the men readily gave their consent.

Preparations were now entered into to get the body in such a condition as to admit of its being borne on its long journey to the coast. Under Chitambo's direction a separate hut was built a short distance from the one in which Livingstone had died. It was so constructed that the entire top was open to the air. It was also built of such stout material as would preclude all chance of any wild beast breaking through the walls and thus getting to the body. As soon as the hut was finished the body was borne to it and placed upon a platform that had been erected for the purpose. Here the body was disemboweled, and the heart and other internal organs removed. Jacob Wainwright was then requested to read the burial service, which he proceeded to do amidst the sobs of the men who stood around. A quantity of salt was next placed in the body, and the latter was so arranged as to receive the full glare of the sun. These were the only means taken toward the preservation of the corpse, save putting a small quantity of brandy into the mouth at regular intervals and rubbing some on the hair. Once a day regularly the position of the corpse was changed, and every precaution was taken that it should not be disturbed, the men keeping watch in detachments day and night. No molestation of any kind occurred.

At the end of the fourteenth day from the first exposure of the corpse to the sun, the men began preparations for starting upon their long journey. The corpse was by this time very well dried, and was believed to be in the right state for preservation. Bending the knees inward, so as to render the package shorter, for the convenience of carrying, the men wrapped the body securely about in stout strips of new calico. The next object was to devise safe and convenient means of transportation. As they had neither planks nor tools of any kind, they were at a great loss to know what to do. Finally Susi thought of the bark of the myonga-tree, which could be easily slipped away. One of these trees was then cut, and the bark taken off in the form of a cylinder. In this the body was placed, a piece of coarse sail-cloth being sewed about the whole for further protection. The package thus formed was lashed securely to a stout pole, and so arranged that either four or two men could carry the burden. The heart and other internal organs, together with the viscera, had in the meantime been inclosed in a strong box and buried under a large mvula-tree. Jacob Wainwright was then asked to carve an inscription upon the tree, which he did, as follows: " Dr. Livingstone died on May 4th, 1873." What was more fitting than that his heart should repose in that land over the sin and degradation of which it had cried out again and again, and for the woes of whose stricken people it had well-nigh broken?

Their arrangements completed, the men began their sad homeward march. It is not our purpose to enter into the full details of this trying and hazardous undertaking. The perils and obstacles were such that none but courageous and devoted hearts could ever have overcome them. At more than one place the men had to give up and lie down through sheer exhaustion. Sickness in its most harrowing form overtook them. Some of them died. Fierce enemies attacked them; time and again they were reduced to the expedient of using trickery to get the corpse through. But be it said to the everlasting praise and honor of these noble and trusty spirits—though ignorant and savage ones at best—that they successfully carried through an enterprise which nothing but the high motive-power of love, the incentive of never-failing loyalty, could ever have accomplished. O let us not be stinting in one word of commendation of an act of heroic devotion that must forever stand out luminous against the background of time—that will cease not to be admired so long as the world's heart is attuned to the chords of pure and generous emotions! They were but savage men; they had been little trained in the ways of civilization. But two or three of them could read, one only could write with understanding. They had neither been born nor cradled in the " lap of romance." They

27

knew nothing of those motives that prompt to heroic action for the mere sake of the world's plaudits. Their unfettered spirits had never been bound by the glittering cords of riotous imagination; they had never dreamed away even the smallest span of their lives under the " purple skies of fancy." No, none of these; yet there was that within their hearts, deep within their souls, which bade them lay aside all thoughts of self and follow the promptings of a pure and changeless love. For love they had followed their chosen master through all the terrors of the African swamps; they had with him passed through the horrors of famine and fever; they had kept their faces set in the direction he wished to go when every thing, even outraged Nature itself, was crying out for a return to home and friends · they had attended him as tenderly as women in his last illness; they had chosen to meet the possible fury of a whole savage village; and now, for this same unselfish love alone, they had borne his lifeless body through all that tortuous tramp of more than a thousand miles. What more eloquent plea could be urged for those among whom David Livingstone lived and died, and for whom in his last earthly hour agonized prayer ascended, than the unexampled courage, affection, and devotion of these men—themselves but savages, their home the dark, dark continent?*

The cortege arrived at Bagamoio in February, 1874—nine months from the time of starting out. Here the act-

---

* It will assuredly interest our readers to learn that the faithful Susi is now attached to one of the University Missions around Lake Nyassa. He is a most efficient and earnest worker. On being baptized into full connection with the Church, he took the name of David, in memory of the noble man who first taught him what it was to be a Christian.

ing consul at Zanzibar, Capt. Prideaux, who had previously been notified of Livingstone's death, met the expedition with a cruiser, to which the remains were soon transferred. From Zanzibar the body was shipped to England, accompanied by the faithful Jacob Wainwright. On the morning of the 15th of April, 1874, the "Malwa," bearing all that remained of the brave and devoted Livingstone, steamed slowly into the London harbor, amidst the drooping of flags, the tolling of bells, and the sad booming of guns. Everywhere tokens of profound sorrow, honor, and respect were manifested.

It had been decided, long before the "Malwa" reached English shores, that England would give sepulture to the remains of her greatest missionary and most distinguished explorer nowhere else than in her renowned Westminster Abbey. The body lay in state until the 18th of April, by which time arrangements had been perfected for one of the most imposing public funerals that England has ever seen. The account which follows, taken from one of the leading newspapers of the day, gives a full and feeling description of the obsequies:

"Inside the Abbey, an immense congregation has assembled to wait for the arrival of the illustrious dead. The transepts are crowded with ticket-holders. Notable among the throng are the African travelers, who constitute such a natural guard of honor for this dead man. Foremost among them, in right of gallant special service, and nearest to Livingstone's head, stands Stanley—sun-tanned anew from Ashantee—whose famous march of relief gives America the full right to celebrate at this moment, as we know she is doing, simultaneously with England, the obsequies of the explorer. But for Stanley, Livingstone would

have died long back, without aid or news from us; but near
him are Grant, the discoverer along with Speke* of the
Nyanza; Young, who was with Livingstone in old days,
and who sailed the Nyassa Lake and the Shire River in
quest of him; Oswell, tanned and grizzled with hunting
and exploring under an African sun; and beside them Rig-
by, and Moffat, and Webb, the godfather of Lualaba, and
the faithful friend who buried Mrs. Livingstone in the sad
day of separation of husband and wife; Colonel Shelley, of
Lake Ngami; Waller, of the Zambesi; Galton, Reade—
what a band of Africani! Such a gathering of sunburned
visages and far-traveled men was never seen before; and
indeed the list might be lengthened with the names of a
hundred other famous travelers present, who listen, with
wistful looks, round their great dead chieftain, while Tal-
lis's hymn is being sung, after the lesson read by Canon
Conway. It is a well-known hymn—one which sings of
ultimate rest after wandering, the only rest for all toils and
travels, commencing—

> 'O God of Bethel, by whose hand
>   The people still are fed,
> Who through this weary pilgrimage
>   Hast all our fathers led.'

"After the conclusion of this hymn, in which the congregation joined with much effect, the coffin is borne down the
choir into the center of the nave, where, toward the western end, the grave has been prepared. Here also among

---

* Nearly ten years prior to his death, Livingstone made this entry
in his journal respecting his lamented friend and predecessor Capt.
Speke: "23 Sept., 1864—Went to the funeral of poor Capt. Speke,
who when out shooting on the 15th, the day I arrived at Bath, was
killed by the accidental discharge of his gun."

the dead lying around are ancient far-traveled worthies—companionable ashes for those which are now to be consigned to the same unbroken and majestic rest. The pall is withdrawn, and the polished oak coffin is prepared for lowering into the dark cavity which opens so narrowly and so abruptly in the Abbey pavement, while the choir sings, ' Man that is born of a woman,' to Croft's setting, and then the tender strains of Purcell's ' Thou knowest, Lord.' This is the very last that will be seen of 'this our dear brother;' and now indeed strong men are fain to bend their heads, and sobs, not from women only, mingle with the alternate sighing and rejoicing of the solemn music. The dizzy edges of the clear-story, eighty feet overhead, are crowded with people looking down from that perilous eminence upon the throng around the grave, and shadows are seen at many of the Abbey windows of others peering through at the ' last scene of all.' As the precious burden descends, the inscription on the plate may be seen :

DAVID LIVINGSTONE,
Born at Blantyre, Lanarkshire, Scotland,
19th March, 1813.
Died at Ilala, Central Africa,
4th May, 1873.

" The service draws to its end with the ' Forasmuch ' and the following prayers, read in a clear, sustained voice of the deepest solemnity and feeling by Dean Stanley; and then once more the organ speaks the unspeakable—as music only can—sounding forth ' I heard a voice from heaven.' But the very finest musical passage of all comes last, in the beautiful anthem of Handel, ' His body rests in peace, but his name liveth evermore.'

" Last of all, there rains down upon the lid of Living-

stone's coffin a bright and fragrant shower of wreaths and
farewell flowers from a hundred loving hands; and each of
those present takes a long parting glance at the great traveler's resting-place, and at the oaken coffin, buried in the
spring blossoms and palms and garlands, wherein lies 'as
much as could die' of the good, great-hearted, loving, fearless, and faithful David Livingstone."

The marble slab that now marks Livingstone's resting-
place in the Abbey bears the following inscription:

> Brought by faithful hands
> over land and sea,
> here rests
> DAVID LIVINGSTONE,
> Missionary, Traveler, Philanthropist.
> Born March 19, 1813,
> At Blantyre, Lanarkshire.
> Died May 4, 1873,
> At Chitambo's village, Ilala.
> For thirty years his life was spent in an unwearied effort to evangel-
> ize the native races, to explore the undiscovered secrets,
> and abolish the desolating slave-trade of Central
> Africa, where with his last words he wrote:
> "All I can say in my solitude is, May Heaven's rich blessing
> come down on every one—American, English, or Turk—
> who will help to heal this open sore of the world."

He who works in the field of the world
  Must work with a faith sublime;
For the seed he sows must lie in the earth
  And wait for God's good time.

But nevertheless the harvest is sure,
  Though the sower the sheaves may not see;
For never a word was spoken for Him
  But will ring through eternity.

THE END.